TARK'S TICKS

A WWII NOVEL

CHRIS GLATTE

SEVERN RIVER
PUBLISHING

Severn River Publishing
www.SevernRiverBooks.com

This is a work of fiction. Names, characters, businesses, places, events and incidents are either the products of the author's imagination or used in a fictitious manner. Any resemblance to actual persons, living or dead, or actual events is purely coincidental.

ISBN: 978-1-64875-563-7 (Paperback)

ALSO BY CHRIS GLATTE

Tark's Ticks Series

Tark's Ticks

Valor's Ghost

Gauntlet

Valor Bound

Dark Valley

War Point

A Time to Serve Series

A Time to Serve

The Gathering Storm

The Scars of Battle

164th Regiment Series

The Long Patrol

Bloody Bougainville

Bleeding the Sun

Operation Cakewalk (Novella)

Standalone Novel

Across the Channel

To find out more about Chris Glatte and his books, visit

severnriverbooks.com/authors/chris-glatte

1

Private First Class Clay Tarkington could barely see the outline of his friend, PFC Ethan Henry, even though he was only a few feet away. He whispered, "You see anything out there?"

Private First Class Henry didn't answer right away, but peered over the tipped-over cart and into the street beyond. The darkness was lit with tiny fires from a recent artillery strike. Dust, debris and the smell of sulfur filled the air. He shook his head and ducked back down. In his Southern drawl he said, "Not much...couple bodies."

Tarkington asked, "Ours or theirs?"

Henry shrugged, "Civilians, I think." He spat out a long string of black tobacco juice.

Tarkington got his feet beneath him and peered over, bringing his helmet just above the cover. He could see the crumpled forms, but couldn't tell if they were people, let alone civilians. "Those damned Japs don't care who they kill."

Machine gun fire erupted from a few streets away and Tarkington ducked down and gripped his Springfield. Henry ducked too. "Sounds like the Filipinos are catching it now."

Tarkington heard scuffling and turned to see the assistant squad leader Sergeant Blakesly moving in beside him. "Tark, that you?"

"Yep, me and Henry."

"What's all the racket?"

Tarkington shrugged and answered, "Couple streets over. Sounds like the Filipino section."

"Sun's gonna be up soon. The Lieutenant wants us ready to repulse another attack."

Tarkington nodded. "What else is new? You find us any more food, Sarge?" Before December he wouldn't have dared speak to an NCO that way, but things had changed in the month since the Japanese decided they wanted the Philippines for themselves.

Sergeant Blakesly shook his head. "Nope. Watkins searched through these houses but they've already been ransacked." He reached into his pocket and pulled out a half-eaten chocolate bar. He licked his lips and handed it to Tarkington. "Share this with that crazy Cajun."

Tarkington took it as if it were the most precious and fragile thing he'd ever seen. "Thanks, Sarge."

Blakesly slapped his shoulder. "Keep your eyes peeled and be ready to move back when I tell you. We're almost to the bridge, less than a mile. Just need to slow the Japs and let our boys get across. If you see anything you've got the okay to shoot, but remember our ammo situation."

Tarkington nodded, "We'll be ready." He watched the assistant squad leader disappear into the burned-out building. He opened the chocolate bar and broke it in half, handing half to Henry. Tarkington slid it into his mouth and let it melt on his tongue. He moaned in pleasure. "Mm, that is so good."

Henry put the whole thing in his mouth and chewed. "Terrible stuff, but I ain't complaining." He stopped chewing, swallowed quickly and clutched his rifle. "I saw something."

Tarkington shoved the rest of the bar into his mouth and checked his Springfield rifle, being sure the magazine selector was in the on position and the safety behind the sights was flipped to the ready position. "Where?" he whispered around a mouthful of chocolate.

Henry lifted his chin, "Down at the end of the street."

A loud explosion added to the machine gun fire in the next block and the sky was momentarily lit up with fire and flame. Tarkington ignored it, rested his rifle on top of the cart and flipped up the sight. He kept both eyes open scanning for targets. He didn't see anything, but he'd learned to trust Henry. He'd never steered him wrong and seemed to have a sixth sense. Tarkington and the other men in the twelve-man squad teased that it was his voodoo roots coming through.

Tarkington saw movement from the corner of his eye and he sucked in a quick sip of air and swung his barrel to the right. There was a doorway. He kept his rifle on the darkened opening. The blackness changed and he could see the outline of a soldier peering out. He whispered, "In the doorway on the right, eighty yards." Tarkington felt, rather than saw Henry swing his rifle that direction. At the beginning of this war Tarkington would've fired by now, but their ammunition situation was down to critical levels and he wanted to be sure of each shot. The thought of running out of ammunition frankly terrified him. Henry whispered, "More coming up behind him, two doors down."

Tarkington kept his barrel centered where he thought the Japanese chest would be, and looked beyond. He immediately saw what Henry spotted, but they were further away. He muttered, "I'll stick with the doorway." The shape clarified as the soldier peered further out and Tarkington pulled the rifle stock solidly into his shoulder and touched the trigger. "I'm taking him in three seconds." He felt Henry nod and counted off to himself. When he got to three he stopped breathing and put back pressure on the trigger until the rifle bucked in his hand. Henry fired within a half second, then they both ducked down and worked their bolt actions.

Tarkington blew out a long breath then said, "I'm sure I got the one in the door. You get yours?"

Henry gave him a sideways grin and drawled "Course I did." Fire erupted from down the street and they felt their cover shudder with bullet strikes, but the cart had a thick metal bottom and could withstand the onslaught.

Answering fire from the building to their right rained down on the remaining exposed Japanese soldiers. Tarkington carefully put his head up and saw more mounded bodies. A dark helmet rolled back and forth, slowing with each rocking motion until it finally stopped. He swept his rifle side to side, ready to fire again, but there was no movement.

From the building, Sergeant Blakesly appeared. "You two okay?"

"Fine," answered Tarkington.

"Probably a probe. They know where we are now." The machine gun fire from the next block stopped. There were a few rifle shots exchanged but they soon stopped too. The early morning darkness suddenly seemed unnaturally quiet. Blakesly scanned the street. "I don't like this one bit. I think we're in for a big push." They were joined by PFC Holiday and Roscoe, the grenadiers of the squad. "How many more grenades you got?" asked Sgt. Blakesly.

Roscoe answered without looking, never taking his eyes off the dark road. "Two each." His deep voice always reminded Tarkington of a Hollywood actor.

Blakesly nodded and tapped on Private First Class Holiday's shoulder. "Get your ass over to Sergeant Flynn on the other side of the street. No use both of you being over here."

Holiday nodded and took a look at his buddy then ran across the open road to the one-story building and slithered his way along the wall until he found the flimsy door and disappeared inside.

Blakesly shook his head. "I don't like being split like this any more than you guys do, but our platoon has too much real-estate to cover. Just be ready to move back. You don't wanna be left behind out here."

The unmistakable sound of whistling, incoming mortars broke the silence. Blakesly cursed, "Shit, get inside, get inside."

They scooted into the building and Tarkington shoved himself in a corner and looked at the roof overhead. Half of it was gone, giving them virtually no cover. Henry huddled in next to him, and Tarkington pointed skyward. "If they drop one through there, we're hamburger."

The first shells landed, sending mini-shock waves through the air, along with splinters of shrapnel and wood. The first round was short, but the next was closer. They were walking the shells down the street toward them.

Henry stood and grabbed Tarkington by his filthy shirt and pulled, "Let's get out of this deathtrap." Tarkington got to his feet and cringed as another shell exploded on the street. He followed Henry who led him to a dark stairway leading down to a basement. Henry stopped halfway down and crouched. "This'll do," he drawled.

The Japanese found the range and proceeded to pummel the area with shells. The air was thick with dust and both GIs pulled their shirts over their mouths to keep from sucking it into their lungs. Chunks of plaster and wood fell off the stairway walls, and for a second, Tarkington thought they'd have to move or risk being buried. The entire building seemed to shake and flex.

Finally, the mortar barrage ended. Tarkington pulled the brim of his helmet up and looked up the stairway. There was light filtering through the thick dust and he thought the sun must've come up.

There was yelling, then the unmistakable sound of a Japanese Type-95 machine gun opening up. Without a word they both sprinted up the stairs. The room they'd left was shattered even more than it was before. At least one mortar round had dropped through the open roof and exploded in the center of the room. They didn't see any casualties. The room was full of smoke and smelled of sulfur.

"Sergeant Blakesly!" Tarkington yelled.

A voice from deeper inside the building called back. "We're down here. Stay put, we're coming to you."

Tarkington moved to the doorway and peered into the street. The cart they'd used for cover was gone, blasted to smithereens by a direct hit. He pulled back quickly. "Shit. Japs coming down the street. They've got a tank." Henry spit, "That's just what we need." Bullets ripped into the building and they dropped flat. Bullets lanced through the thin outer walls and smacked into the far wall; making ugly holes, adding to the dust. There was a loud boom followed quickly with an ear shattering explosion. The front of the building crumbled as if built from sand and through the dust cloud Tarkington saw the Japanese light tank rotating it's 37mm gun for another shot.

Japanese infantrymen dashed through the smoke and dust. He brought his rifle up, praying it was still operational. From his prone position he aimed and squeezed the trigger. He worked the bolt quickly and fired at another form, then another, until he'd expended the five-round clip.

Beside him Henry was firing and smoothly working the bolt. Tarkington yelled, "Reloading." He rolled to the side, flipped up the flap on his ammo pouch and pulled another five round stripper-clip. He pushed it into place, filling the magazine. He chambered a round and put the stock against his shoulder.

The tank stopped and pivoted its turret to fire into the building where the rest of the squad cowered. Beside the tank he saw a Japanese soldier holding a sword with one hand and a pistol with the other. *An officer.* He aimed, following his movements and fired. The officer dropped.

He chambered another round and saw another Japanese soldier running through the broken wall with his bayoneted Arisaka rifle leading the way. The soldier saw Sergeant Blakesly and the rest of the squad coming from the next room and shifted his charge toward them. Tarkington fired nearly point blank and the soldier's chest bloomed red as he tripped onto his face. Sergeant Blakesly leveled his rifle and fired into his back, making sure.

Blakesly stepped over him and yelled, "Fall back, fall back." Tarkington and Henry jumped to their feet and followed their assistant squad leader. Blakesly went to the door and was nearly shredded as machine gun fire splintered the wood. He almost fell backwards trying to stop his forward momentum. He turned and ran back the way he'd come. "This way. There's a back door this way."

The room darkened as the tank drove past the doorway. Tarkington could clearly see the blazing red sun painted on the side as it clanked past.

A bullet whizzed by his head and smacked into the wall beside him. He went lower and kept running, weaving his way past piles of debris. More bullets holed the walls.

He saw Blakesly crouched outside the doorway waving him forward. Tarkington sprinted through and yelled, "They're right behind me, Go!" The sergeant waited until Tarkington was safely past then leaned into the doorway and fired.

Tarkington looked back, sure he'd see Blakesly's dead body but instead a mortally wounded Japanese soldier slid through the doorway and ground to a halt at his feet. Blakesly pushed Tarkington, "Move it."

Tarkington ran after the rest of the sprinting squad. They weaved through the little town's broken streets, finally stopping after two blocks. Tarkington slid in beside Henry and Sergeant Blakesly was right behind him. "Spread out. We need to hook up with team one." Tarkington checked his rifle and aimed down the street, using a burnt mound of wood for cover. Blakesly gave them more instructions. "Stay in twos. Stick with your buddy no matter what. This shit will happen quick."

Tarkington was number eleven in his squad, a rifleman and Henry was number twelve, also a rifleman. He looked at Henry, who was on his belly beside him, aiming down the street. Tarkington was glad they were buddied up. They'd been together so long that they knew what the other person was going to do or say before they did. Tarkington whispered, "I'll cover left, you take right."

Henry nodded, "Mmhm," never taking his eye from his trusted Springfield's sights. More firing erupted from their right and the distinct roar from the Japanese tank's 37mm cannon added to the noise. Henry called, "Here they come," and fired.

Tarkington saw Japanese soldiers emerging from around the building corners at the same instant. He adjusted his aim and fired at the nearest man. His shot was off and he hit his shoulder, spinning him around. The wounded man dropped his rifle and scuttled back into cover. Tarkington chambered another round and fired, but only succeeded in splintering the wood of the building.

The rest of the half-squad was firing and three enemy soldiers lay bleeding in the street. The surviving Japanese dove back to cover and Tarkington could hear them calling out to each other. Sergeant Blakesly yelled, "Eleven and Twelve covering fire."

Tarkington and Henry fired as fast as they could, working the bolt action rifles smoothly and sending fire where they'd last seen the enemy soldiers, keeping them under cover while the rest of the GIs moved back.

"Reloading," yelled Henry.

Tarkington fired one more round then leaned over to grab another clip, "Reloading."

"Tark, Henry, move back."

They both pushed themselves to their feet, staying crouched, and sprinted as bullets from their squad-mates whipped past them on either side. They ran straight through, then turned and found cover in an alleyway.

Blakesly yelled, "Find the other half of this squad, Winkleman."

Private First Class Winkleman was one of the two scouts in the squad. He looked at Blakesly, gulped against a dry throat and nodded. He looked to his buddy, PFC Roscoe. "I'm with you Wink, lead the way." Tarkington and Henry stayed in the rear, covering the move. Tarkington kept his rifle trained on the alleyway the Japanese had disappeared behind, but he realized they could pop out anywhere, so he kept both eyes open and swiveled side to side. He jumped when PFC Henry tapped his shoulder, the signal to move out.

They hadn't gone far when the alley they'd just vacated erupted with mortar shell explosions. Tarkington and Henry moved steadily, but kept watching their rear. Once the mortars stopped enemy soldiers would surely follow.

Tarkington was walking backwards with his rifle on his hip. He looked over his shoulder and saw Henry looking back at him, five yards away. Tarkington shook his head, "We need to get out of this damned alley before the Japs turn the corner." Henry nodded.

Finally the half-squad turned south down the next street and left the alleyway behind. Tarkington stopped at the corner, kneeling and aiming his rifle back the way he'd come. *Any second now.* He heard Henry call for him and he was about to comply when he saw movement at the end of the alley. He took a breath and let it out slow. The enemy soldier cautiously came around the corner, his rifle at his shoulder. Tarkington guessed it was seventy yards. He squeezed the trigger and his Springfield bucked against his shoulder. He saw the soldier drop but he had no idea if he'd hit him or just caused him to take cover. He didn't wait around to find out. As he pulled away from the corner the sound of bullets thumping into solid wood made him flinch and hunch his shoulders as he took off after Henry.

The squad crossed the street and entered a two-story building, filling the bottom floor. The inside was stripped - it looked like it might have been some sort of store - but the shelves were bare. Tarkington was relieved to see the rest of the team and breathed a sigh of relief when he counted all six men. He kept his weapon aimed across the street but smiled when PFC Stollman thumped his shoulder and whispered, "Good to see you, Tark."

"You too, Stolly." Despite being covered in grime, PFC Stollman's red hair stuck from beneath his helmet like he was some English king. Before hostilities erupted, he'd been in a constant battle over the length of his hair. By no fault of his own, his hair grew abnormally fast, and unless he shaved it to the skin, the length would be pushing regulations by the second week after a haircut. Now, with near constant combat over the past month, it was a mop.

Staff Sergeant Flynn and Sergeant Blakesly knelt in the middle of the room and spoke in low tones. Henry, Tarkington and Stollman watched the street for trouble. Tarkington wiped his brow. "Sure am glad to have that big thing back beside me," he gestured toward Stollman's Browning Automatic Rifle.

Stollman grinned and caressed the weapon like a long-lost lover, "You keep your grimy thoughts and hands to yourself, Tark. She's a one-man woman and don't you forget it." Henry shook his head and grinned, his dark eyes twinkling, "That hunk of steel's about the only way you'll ever get lucky." He pointed to the end of the barrel, "Looks about the right size for your pecker too," he drawled.

Stollman shook his head. "Damn, with your silky voice, even an insult sounds good, you crazy Cajun."

Staff Sergeant Flynn spoke, "Keep an eye on the road but listen up. We're hooking up with the rest of the platoon back at the bridge. Lieutenant Smoker is dug in on this side of the river and it's our job to hold out while the rest of the company withdraws." Roscoe shook his head and muttered, "Why's it always us that gets the shitty jobs?"

Flynn ignored him and Blakesly gave him a withering look. Flynn smiled, "Roscoe, you and Holiday buddy up and stick with Tarkington and Henry. You're tail-end Charlie." He waited to see if there'd be any more guff. "Alright, move out."

When the others were gone, Holiday elbowed Roscoe in the side. "Dammit, you got me in the shit too, you asshole." Roscoe scowled but didn't speak. Holiday continued, "Just can't keep your fool mouth shut and now look at us; tail-end Charlie with these two..." he noticed Tarkington squaring his broad shoulders waiting for Holiday's next words. "Fine soldiers," he finished with a sheepish grin.

Tarkington and Henry had more time in the regiment, so outranked the other two PFCs. Tarkington pointed across the street. "You two bound over there. We'll cover you, then we'll withdraw by twos, covering each side of the street."

Tarkington kneeled beside the door frame and aimed toward the alley he'd come from, and Henry took the window and leaned out to cover the far end of the street. When Holiday and Roscoe didn't move immediately, Tarkington barked, "Move. You're clear."

Holiday blew out a long breath and Roscoe cursed, but they ran across the street and didn't draw any fire. They took firing positions and Roscoe called out, "Go."

Tarkington and Henry didn't hesitate. Despite the GI's sour grapes, they knew and trusted them to do their jobs. Tarkington sprinted down the hard-packed street to the next alley and slid behind the wall while Henry continued past him and took up position along the opposite wall. Tarkington found the same alley he'd covered before and put his muzzle on it. "Go!" He yelled.

The two GIs across the way ran hunched over, Holiday holding his steel helmet onto his head. Tarkington saw movement at the corner of the alley and squinted over his sights. "Company," he hissed and squeezed the trigger. His bullet whizzed past the corner and entered the wood wall beyond with a hammer like sound.

Henry fired, quickly chambered another round and fired again. "Coming down the street." Enemy rifle shots rang out and bullets whacked into the wood making them flinch.

Tarkington quickly fired again, cringing at the near-misses but wanting to keep the Japanese from having an open shot on the other two GIs. He glanced their way and saw them taking cover across from them in the adjacent alley. Tarkington and Henry pulled out of sight as more bullets tried to perforate them. "Wish we had Stolly's BAR."

Firing from across the street told them it was their turn to dash. Tarkington looked at Henry and mouthed, 'One, two, three.' They both took off like they'd kicked a giant hornet's nest. Roscoe and Holiday banged away keeping the Japanese soldiers off balance. For Tarkington it seemed like the longest run of his life. He was sure he'd feel the heat of a bullet in his back any second, but it didn't happen.

He dove into the next alley and rolled to his feet, breathing hard. He reloaded and chambered another round as Henry crashed around the corner. He tilted his helmet back and wiped the sweaty grime off his forehead. "Could use a cold drink right about now."

Bullets thumped into the wall, sending up a dust cloud which swept over Tarkington like a mini-fog bank. "We've gotta get them across. They'll tag 'em if we try that again."

Henry nodded. "Agreed." He put his back against the wall, inches from the corner. Tarkington got on his belly near Henry's feet and yelled. "Come straight across to us when we start firing. Got it?"

He could hear Roscoe answer, "Got it."

Tarkington looked up to Henry who gave him a slight nod. "One, two, three..." Tarkington rolled once bringing his rifle to his shoulder and fired down the street where he thought he'd seen a muzzle flash. Henry leaned out from the corner and fired. Despite being bolt action, it sounded like semi-automatic fire, as first one fired then the next, in perfect sequence. By the time they'd expended their magazines, Roscoe and Holiday were beside them panting with their hands on their knees.

Tarkington and Henry pulled back as Japanese bullets showered the corner with lead. "Let's get the hell outta here." He pushed the others down the alleyway toward the next street. There was an explosion that was abnormally loud in the confines of the walls. "Jap knee mortar." He didn't think it wise to continue down the alley. "Duck into the building."

Roscoe didn't hesitate, he kicked a flimsy door and the wood shattered. He pushed inside and the others followed. They ran to the back of the building, but there wasn't a back door. The others stopped but Tarkington kept running and barreled into the wall. The light-weight construction crumbled against his weight and he found himself in the adjoining building. Holiday muttered, "Damn wrecking ball," and followed him through.

They heard excited Japanese voices coming from the alley they'd just left and the GIs stopped and held their breath, praying they'd pass by. No such luck. The voices got louder.

Tarkington crept to the edge of the broken wall and knelt, his rifle at his shoulder. A Japanese soldier saw him and his eyes widened as he brought his rifle up, but it was too late. Tarkington fired and at this range, couldn't miss. The soldier's chest exploded in gore and he fell to the ground. A red mist mixed with the dust and slowly settled. Tarkington chambered another round smoothly and waited for the next one, but instead saw two round baseball-sized objects sailing toward him. "Grenades!" He yelled and pulled back into cover.

The others covered their ears and dropped but the dual explosions robbed their lungs of air. A cloud of thick dust cascaded through the hole in the wall. Tarkington coughed and got to his feet, pushing the GIs to move to the back of the building. They found a door, kicked it open and were relieved to see it was the last building. Twenty yards away was jungle.

The four GIs ran out the back and pushed into the jungle. It wasn't thick and they were able to move quickly. There were rifle shots but they couldn't tell if they were aimed at them or not. They kept pushing until Tarkington stopped them a couple of hundred yards in. Breathing hard, they hunkered down and listened for sounds of pursuit.

After two minutes, Tarkington decided they weren't being pursued and got them moving again. "I think the bridge is that way," he said pointing forty-five degrees from their current line. He looked at Henry who had a sixth sense about directions, even in the deepest darkest jungle. He nodded in agreement. "Let's move out." He walked, pushing huge green leaves and cutting grasses to the side.

They walked in single file for ten minutes through mixed jungle and pine forest. Tarkington suddenly held up his fist and went to a knee. Henry came to his side and nodded. "The bridge," he said. Tarkington parted the greenery and saw the jungle had been cleared all the way to the edge of the river canyon and right up to the bridge. He could see foxholes manned by GIs he assumed belonged to Hotel Company. He yelled, "Hey there! Don't shoot, GIs coming out! First platoon, second squad."

There was silence, then a response. "Come on out of there with your weapons over your heads." The four GIs complied and stepped from the jungle. They could see muzzles shift their direction. "Halt!" A soldier stood in his foxhole fifty yards away.

They stopped with their rifles over their heads. Tarkington glanced behind then shouted. "There's Japs behind us and you've got us sitting out here like damned ducks on a pond for Chrissakes."

"I know that whiny asshole voice anywhere. Get your asses over here, Tark."

2

Private First Class Tarkington and Henry were glad to be back with 1st platoon. It had been a week since they'd seen some of the other men. PFC Blaine and Crenshaw from 4th squad had been killed in action. Sergeant Fedderin from 3rd squad had taken a bullet in the leg, but was expected to recover.

Tarkington shook his head when he heard the news. The platoon had been together a long time and he felt each loss deeply. The fact that their company had taken the least amount of casualties in the entire division didn't help to assuage the bitterness.

Now, he sat in the bottom of a foxhole dug into the dirt beside the potholed road leading to the Orani Bridge. Since he'd come out of the jungle, there had been a smattering of GIs from various other companies moving across, as well as a steady stream of civilian refugees.

Henry spit a stream of dark tobacco juice and asked, "Wonder how long we have to stay here?"

Tarkington shrugged, "Till the stream of GIs stops, I guess."

"I haven't seen any GIs in over ten minutes. How we supposed to know if there's more out there? And what about all these civilians?"

"I'm more worried why the Japs haven't attacked. They were right behind us, but it's like they disappeared." Henry spit another long stream.

"You know, that's a nasty habit." Henry was about to respond when they both heard what they'd been dreading - aircraft. Tarkington slugged Henry's leg, "Better get down. Doubt those are ours."

Henry looked up and shook his head, "We even have any?" He pointed to the sky. "Shit, I see 'em. Looks like Jap dive bombers." A couple of seconds later, "Crap, they're coming for us." He dropped into the hole and got as low as possible.

Mobile anti-air guns opened up, sending streams of 20mm tracer fire to meet the threat. Over the sound of the firing, Tarkington could hear the Japanese Ki-30s diving. A long whistle followed as they dropped their bomb loads. The concussive blasts rolled over them.

With each bomb strike the ground shook and their foxholes threatened to collapse. Debris floated in the air and settled onto their uniforms and rifles. Tarkington counted ten bombers, but the bombs were mercifully off-target, mostly hitting the empty open ground to their front.

He brushed the dirt off and looked up from the bottom of the hole to the clear, blue sky. When he didn't see or hear any more dive bombers he got to his feet and peaked over the side. There were smoldering craters, but it didn't appear the attack had resulted in any direct hits on the bridge.

Henry asked from the bottom of the hole, "The bridge still there?"

Tarkington nodded, "Yep. Don't think they were aiming for it though. Think they want it intact."

"Well thank God for small miracles." He brushed dirt off himself and his Springfield and stood. He looked back at the stout bridge. "Hate to think what would happen if they dropped the bridge even by accident."

"Wish they'd let us move to the other side. Haven't seen any GIs for a while now."

There was a whistle and they both spun toward the sound. Suddenly the jungle seemed to come alive with twinkling muzzle flashes. They dropped into cover as bullets whizzed and snapped over their heads. They could hear men yelling, but couldn't tell what was being said. The hammering of the water-cooled Browning filled the air and Tarkington knew it was coming from the bunker on the other side of the road. Over the sound of gunfire, he heard the whistling sound of mortar shells. "Mortars," he murmured matter-of-factly.

Henry was calmly checking over his rifle. He responded, "Yep, smoke rounds."

Tarkington grimaced and peeked over the lip, watching shells landing and spewing smoke. "You're right." He brought his Springfield up and pulled it against his shoulder. "Should be coming soon." The Browning stopped firing as the smoke blanketed the area. Henry sighed and got to his feet, bringing his rifle to his shoulder as though he were working a boring office job.

Staff Sergeant Flynn yelled, "Hold your fire till I give the word."

There was another whistle from the jungle. Tarkington looked at the foxholes to either side and could see his squad member's helmeted heads with rifles at the ready. He took a breath and put his eyes down the sights. He could see shifting shapes coming through the layer of smoke. He tracked a soldier coming straight at him only thirty yards away. He caressed the trigger, waiting for the order. Finally he heard Flynn yell, "Open fire!"

He squeezed the trigger and the charging Japanese lurched but kept coming. Tarkington chambered another round and fired into him again, and this time he dropped and skidded to a halt. The motion of firing, working the bolt and firing again was quick and effortless.

The second water-cooled machine gun opened up and combined with the first, cutting a withering swath of death. Multiple times Tarkington would focus on a soldier, only to have him cut down by the machine guns. He started aiming for soldiers along the edges, away from the main force. He kept firing, being sure of each shot. Finally there were no more targets. He'd shot through three, five round stripper clips as fast as he could pull the trigger. The air smelled of smoke, sulfur and burnt gunpowder.

The firing died away almost as quickly as it had started. He heard Sergeant Flynn calling for a cease fire, but he didn't need to. In front there was a mass of bodies, some still moving but all down.

Tarkington assessed his ammo. "I've only got one more clip after the one I've got loaded. If they do that again, I'll have to throw spitballs at 'em." Henry kept his eyes over his sights, his Springfield barrel still glowing red and the muzzle smoking. "My God, I'm glad I'm not a Jap. What would you do if our guys sent us to the slaughter like that? I mean look at those poor bastards." Tarkington looked over the grisly scene but didn't have an answer.

"Sound off." They heard Sergeant Blakesly holler. Tarkington listened, hoping everyone checked in. He called his own number and sighed in relief that everyone was accounted for. "Call out your ammo situation in order."

Tarkington was shocked to hear how low the entire squad was. Most had one or two clips left, the machine guns each had one more belt. An uneasy silence came over the GIs as each understood what it meant. If the Japanese came at them again they'd run out of ammo and have to fight hand-to-hand.

Staff Sergeant Flynn ordered, "Fix bayonets."

"Oh for Chrissakes. You've gotta be kidding me," complained Roscoe loudly enough for the entire squad to hear.

Tarkington attached the knife to the end of his Springfield. "He's got a point. We should get out while the getting's good."

The smoke slowly drifted away revealing more dead Japanese soldiers. No one dared move from their holes, knowing the jungle still held many more enemies. A shot rang out followed immediately by screaming. From their right, a panicked voice yelled, "Blakesly's hit! Medic!"

Tarkington almost came out of the hole, but Henry held him in place. "Stay down. There's a sniper out there."

A few shots from 2nd platoon answered, but were quickly squelched by the blaring voice of Sergeant Flynn. "Cease fire." After a moment he continued, "Sniper. Stay down. Don't give him a target." Another shot rang out from the jungle, directed at the voice. Flynn hollered back, "Fuck you and your whore mother, Nip!" There was a smattering of laughter from the GIs, but most were too worried about Sergeant Blakesly.

A tense hour passed, the only action being the occasional sniper shot from the jungle. Word passed that Sergeant Blakesly was dead. Every GI felt the loss: he'd been a part of the platoon for over a year, starting as a Private First Class and moving up to a buck Sergeant and assistant squad leader. He was well-liked and his loss felt heavy and deep.

Tarkington heard Roscoe calling from the next foxhole. "This is stupid. No one else is coming. Hell, they'd have to fight their way through the whole Jap Army to get to the bridge now. What the hell we hanging around for?"

Tarkington felt the same way, indeed the entire platoon did, but there was no use griping about it. "Shut your trap, Roscoe," he called back. "Doesn't do anyone any good."

"This is bullshit," he responded.

"You know what's bullshit, Roscoe? Having to listen to your bellyaching all day."

"Fuck you, Tark."

Tarkington shook his head and spoke low, "Course I agree with him a hundred percent." Henry grinned and nodded his agreement.

With the sniper, the GIs weren't able to move around from hole to hole and the isolation was getting to them. Tarkington wondered if they'd even been able to get Blakesly's body out. He wondered who was in the hole with him. It would normally be Holiday, but he was buddied up with Roscoe. *Must be someone from team one... probably Wink.*

A commanding voice disturbed the mid-day stupor. "Listen up men. They've finished wiring the bridge and we've got orders to withdraw." There was a smattering of cheering and Lieutenant Smoker let it die down before continuing. Beside him, Platoon Sergeant McLunty scowled at them. Smoker continued, "We've got smoke coming in ten minutes. We'll withdraw from the outside in. Second and fourth squads will bound behind the line while first and third squads cover. Next will be the machine gun crews, then first, and finally third squad. It's a long way across, so don't dilly-dally. Once across, find cover and be ready to cover the others. There are three Stuart's over there ready to give us more cover."

Tarkington smiled and punched Henry's shoulder. "Best news I've had all day."

Another voice broke through. "Tark, you hear me?" It was the squad leader, Staff Sergeant Flynn.

Tarkington bellowed back, "Yes, Sarge."

"You're my new assistant squad leader." There was a pause as that settled in. "Congratulations, Sergeant."

Tarkington grit his teeth and shook his head, but responded, "Uh, okay, Sergeant."

"When the smoke hits get team two moving. Got it?"

"Yes, Sarge." Another shot rang out and the bullet impacted the back-side of his hole, sending up a geyser of dirt. "That guy's starting to piss me off." He cupped his hand over his mouth and called to the next hole. "Hey Roscoe." He heard a half-hearted reply and continued. "Put your steel pot on the end of your bayonet and draw that sniper's fire."

Roscoe complained, "I like this helmet. It fits me well."

"Dammit, *Private*. Do it."

"Okay, okay, *Sergeant*." A few seconds passed. "Doing it now." There was another shot followed by a bell-sound as it struck the steel helmet. Tarkington peeked over searching for smoke from the muzzle. He ducked back down, took his helmet off and gripped his Springfield. He licked his lips and addressed Henry. "I think he's laying down on this track." He extended his arm to the right slightly. Henry gripped his rifle and nodded. "We go up together right after the shot."

Henry smiled, "Yes Sergeant."

Tarkington grinned back. "Hey Roscoe do it again."

This time he didn't complain. "Ready?" He asked. "I'll count to three."

"Okay."

They waited until the five count before extending over the hole. They timed it perfectly and saw the Japanese sniper's muzzle flash. They adjusted slightly and fired simultaneously then dropped back into the hole.

Roscoe called. "You get him?"

Tarkington and Henry exchanged knowing glances. "Yeah, pretty sure he's no longer a problem."

Roscoe yelled, "Good, cause he messed up my helmet real good."

"Cease fire over there, dammit."

Tarkington yelled back to Sergeant Flynn. "Just taking care of that sniper, Sarge."

There was no answer because the screeching sound of artillery filled the air. Every GI cringed, dreading the sound, but this time it was friendly fire. The popping explosions of smoke canisters sent out thick, white smoke. Tarkington yelled, "Team two, move out!" He hopped from the hole and crouched as Henry jumped out and took off in a low crouch toward the bridge. GIs ran by and Tarkington counted them as they passed then followed, careful to stay behind the staggered line of foxholes. There was a smattering of fire from the rest of the platoon, but no return fire from the jungle.

Tarkington got to the bridge and met up with Sergeant Flynn who was waving men past urging them across the bridge. 4th squad members mixed with 2nd squad and they moved to either side of the span and sprinted across. Tarkington ran along the long straight stretch, hoping he didn't get shot in the back.

He glanced at the dirty brown river far below. He didn't know if there was another crossing point, but getting caught on the wrong side once it was destroyed would be catastrophic. *This'll be where we finally stop them,* he thought.

When he was on the other side, Flynn directed the squad to the right and the GIs used the available cover, pointing their rifles back across the span. Tarkington and the rest were breathing hard. The combination of muggy air and exertion had them soaked with sweat. Rivulets streamed off Tarkington's nose and he wiped it away. He considered himself to be in good shape, but the lack of proper nutrition and constant combat over the past month and a half had affected his stamina. Before the war, he could've sprinted full speed with a full pack across that distance and barely been breathing hard. *This place is gonna kill me one way or another.*

The rest of the platoon was halfway across the bridge span now, having caught up to the struggling machine gun crews with their heavy loads. Tarkington thought they were going to get away with a clean break when he heard the dreaded shrill of a whistle.

Sergeant Flynn stood and started motioning, yelling frantically for the men to hurry. Tarkington perched his rifle on the crook of a tree and sighted across the canyon. The smoke was dissipating but he still couldn't see any targets.

Incoming fire grew in intensity. He could see sparks as ricocheting bullets met the steel of the bridge. There was a boom from this side of the bridge and he saw the plume of white smoke blossoming from the barrel of one of the M3 Stuart tanks. He hadn't seen them until now. He saw the flash of the 37mm shell among the smoke and hoped it shredded the Japanese.

Despite the low visibility, Sergeant Flynn barked, "Covering fire."

Tarkington aimed into the smoke directly across from him and fired. The other two Stuarts fired their main guns and he could see more flashes in the smoke. All at once there were targets everywhere. He spotted a Japanese soldier sprinting, waving a sword and firing a pistol. He took careful aim and squeezed the trigger. The officer's leg buckled and he went sprawling, but he pulled himself up and limped forward. Other GIs saw the officer and before Tarkington could finish him off, he was on the ground with multiple gunshot wounds.

The stuttering of the Stuart's .30 caliber light machine guns entered the fray, sending staggered bursts across the canyon. Charging Japanese faltered and fell as the wall of lead met them, but they kept coming. They were among the abandoned foxholes, some dropping into them and firing. Bullets whizzed by and thumped into the trees, slicing through branches.

Tarkington dropped into a crouch and centered his sights on a soldier in a foxhole. He fired and saw a plume of dirt spout in front of the hole. He adjusted his aim and fired again. He pulled his last stripper clip from his pouch and inserted it into the Springfield's magazine. "Last clip," he said to no one in particular.

He stayed in cover and looked at the men still on the bridge. They were nearly across, running for all they were worth. He could see fallen, unmoving soldiers in the center and he wondered what friends he'd lost.

The Japanese were on the bridge. He aimed carefully, centering his sights on the head of a soldier who was leaning against part of the bridge structure. He fired and the soldier's head snapped back and he dropped out of sight.

He heard Lieutenant Smoker, who'd just made it across urging the rest of the men. "Come on, come on. Get off the bridge. We have to blow it!" He raised his Thompson sub-machine gun and fired a burst, then crouched, desperately waving for the men to hurry.

Tarkington found another Japanese who was moving down the bank trying to get to the bridge's underside. He shouted, "Target the Nips trying to disarm the bombs." He fired and the soldier, who'd been reaching over the canyon to grip a steel pipe dropped into the abyss. Tarkington watched him hit the water and disappear.

The Stuarts kept up a constant barrage of cannon fire and .30 caliber machine gun fire. Finally, the platoon was across.

Despite the heavy volume of fire, the Japanese continued to make progress. Suddenly one of the Stuarts blew up with a rending tear of metal and fire. Tarkington looked across and saw four Japanese Type-95 light tanks going full speed toward the span. There was a plume of smoke from one and a 37mm shell blew up beside the first dead Stuart.

Both remaining Stuarts adjusted their turrets and fired. The lead Japanese tank was bracketed; its right track snapped and it drove off the track and spun to the right, coming to an abrupt halt at the edge of the canyon. It slewed its cannon toward the danger, but the second volley was already on the way and it exploded, lifting the small turret from the main body.

The remaining three tanks spread out and fired, but the Stuarts were already moving and their shells hit empty space.

Lieutenant Smoker yelled, "Blow the bridge, now!"

Sergeant Flynn screamed, "Get down, get down!"

Somewhere behind the Stuarts, a group of Army Engineers pushed the plunger down on the fuse box. The signal traveled along the wire, sparking the fuse. Seconds later there was a crack, like timber snapping and a great plume of smoke rose up from the middle of the bridge.

Tarkington lifted his head and saw the bridge still intact. The Japanese soldiers moving across had thought they were about to die. When the bridge remained intact, they screamed and rose up, charging. A type-95 tank maneuvered to the bridge and started racing across. Tarkington fired his last bullet into the chest of the lead soldier. "I'm out."

The Stuarts fired at the advancing tank, but it was a deflection shot and the shells exploded on the bridge structure. Another 37mm shell hit where the smoke still lingered in the center of the span. Chunks of bridge started breaking away, dropping one hundred feet and disappearing into the dark water below. The type-95 tank hit the middle span and the bridge twisted then broke away. The tank fell through the hole and plunged into the river with a huge splash.

The soldiers stopped, still taking fire from the GIs, then turned and sprinted back the way they'd come. The bridge came apart behind them. Soldiers screamed as there was suddenly nothing left beneath them and they fell to their deaths.

Tarkington watched in fascination, but got back into cover when he felt a near miss buzz past his ear. He looked to Henry who was shaking his head from side-to-side slowly. "Now *that* was something to see."

3

The GIs of Hotel Company were glad to leave the bridge behind. Tarkington was walking beside Staff Sergeant Flynn. "I'll get you set up with chevrons when we get to the rear. Your rank is sergeant and to be clear, you're my assistant squad leader. You're the most senior PFC so you got the job."

Tarkington looked sideways at him as they marched down the hard-packed dirt road. "Shitty way to get promoted."

Flynn nodded and scowled. "Blakesly was a good man." He paused, then continued. "But there's a war on. This platoon's special. Hell the entire 31st Division's special. You've been a part of it, you know what I mean." Tarkington nodded his agreement. "MacArthur's called for I Corps and II Corps to fade back deeper into the Bataan Peninsula to make it harder on the Japs. It's above our pay grade, but it's some old plan called 'Orange' or something and involves consolidating on the peninsula with Corregidor's big guns supporting us from behind. Now that we're across that damned bridge, we're beginning this Orange phase until reinforcements arrive."

"Any word when that'll be?"

He spit onto the dry road. "Course not. They don't tell lowly Staff Sergeants that stuff." He shrugged. "Doesn't matter. The only thing you need to worry about is following my orders and taking care of your men in team two. Did you get more ammo?"

Tarkington nodded, "Yes, Sergeant. We're still low but I got the men resupplied with what we could find."

Flynn slapped him on the back creating a plume of dust, "You'll do fine, Sergeant. Just keep doing what you've been doing. You already know the men and they respect you. Just don't do anything stupid."

"Like volunteer for duty in the Philippines?"

Flynn shook his head, "Hell, I don't blame you for that. Up till the Japs invaded, this was the best posting in the Army."

They walked in silence for a few minutes. Tarkington thought back to just how right Flynn was. Being posted to the Far East was a cherry assignment. The Philippines as a country was under the protectorate of the U.S. government with the promise of independence only five years away.

The Filipino people loved the U.S. and the economy was thriving. The GIs were treated like royalty wherever they went and their paychecks went a long way. Tarkington remembered many nights of frivolity with the local ladies, eating huge steak dinners and dancing the warm nights away for less than the price of a bottle of Coke back home. But that all came crashing to a halt on December 8th, 1941. The Japanese hit targets in Luzon six hours after the attack on Pearl Harbor, and it had been a whirlwind every day since.

The further they marched, the more congested the road became. There was an even mix of soldiers, both Filipino and American, and civilians displaced by the advancing Japanese troops.

Tarkington broke off from Staff Sergeant Flynn and found Henry. His long easy stride was easy to spot among the other soldiers. Henry looked around at all the people, then to the skies. He spit out a long piece of grass. "Mighty tasty target, all of us walking along like this. Hope we don't get any Jap planes or things'll get messy."

Tarkington nodded, "I was thinking the same thing. Don't think command thought about all the civilians tagging along. If the Japs do come it'll be hard to fight back with all these folks."

"Well, at least the river canyon should slow 'em down a bit."

Tarkington shook his head. "Sergeant Flynn told me there's another bridge only a few miles south of the one they blew. We bought ourselves half a day, maybe."

Henry shook his head and drawled, "I was wondering why we abandoned that position."

There were honking vehicles approaching from behind. Tarkington turned as a jeep with a heavy water-cooled Browning machine gun mounted in back, pulled up next to Lieutenant Smoker and Sergeant Flynn on the other side of the road. Tarkington kept walking but slowed, watching the meeting. He slapped Henry's arm, "Maybe we'll be getting a lift."

Henry looked across. "Maybe *you* will, Sergeant."

More vehicles followed the jeep, mostly troop trucks. Tarkington heard Sergeant Flynn yell, "Hey, Tark. Get the men crammed into the trucks."

Tarkington grinned. "Hell yeah. Let's go." He raised his voice to the other men near him. "You heard the man, get into those vehicles." He followed the men, who went to the back of the slowly moving trucks. There were already dirty GIs on the benches but they made room for the new comers. Some of them had to sit on the floor and each pothole bounced them, making them grimace, but it was still better than walking.

An hour later Tarkington wasn't so sure riding in the trucks was such a great idea. Every GI would rather ride than walk, but they were barely making more than walking speed and the trucks bounced and lurched along the unpaved, pothole-filled roads. There was constant jostling and bouncing, forcing them to grip whatever they could find and Tarkington was feeling what little energy he had fading away.

He looked at the men from his platoon; they looked as miserable as he felt. He looked out the back of the canvas-covered truck. There was another truck only a few feet from the rear bumper, the bored looking Filipino driver staring ahead in a trance. *I'm an NCO now. I should get the men out of here. Do them all a favor.* He bit the inside of his lip and shook his head. *That's not what Sergeant Flynn ordered me to do.* He shut his eyes, trying to block out the aches and pains that seemed to emanate from every part of his body.

He knew he had no chance of falling asleep but closing his eyes kept the dust out and allowed his mind to slip away for a moment or two. His eyes snapped open when he heard yelling, followed immediately by machine gun fire.

The truck lurched to the right and tilted as the driver stuffed it into the shallow ditch beneath the thin cover of the jungle. Despite the slow speed, the truck stopped abruptly sending the men sprawling forward. Tarkington yelled, "Out of the truck and spread out!"

He was closest to the back. He leaped out and stepped to the side, directing the GIs toward the jungle. His rifle was slung over his shoulder. A glimmer caught his eye and he looked up. Tall trees bordered the road but he could see the strip of sky directly above and the sight of a shimmering airplane with a blood-red circle on the wing chilled his blood.

The heavy mounted machine gun on the jeep fired short bursts, but the plane kept arcing upward then turned gracefully and picked up speed as it dove back toward them. Tarkington unslung his rifle but didn't bother wasting ammo shooting. He yelled, "Cover, Cover!" and ran into the jungle.

The machine gun kept firing, longer bursts now, and he could hear the streaking sound of the plane slicing through the air, then the jackhammer of the Zero's twin 20mm cannons opening fire. Tarkington threw himself behind a thick palm tree and pulled his helmet tight onto his head. He could feel the impact of the heavy bullets thumping into the ground, metal and flesh. There was a whoosh as something caught fire and exploded, sending shockwaves through the jungle. He felt a slap on his side and thought he might be on fire. He touched his side but felt nothing. He tried to wiggle deeper into the ground.

As quickly as it started, it stopped. The machine gun was silent, replaced with shouts of pain, anger and confusion. Tarkington lifted his head and got slowly to his knees. He looked around the jungle, seeing GI's wide eyes staring back at him. "Anyone hit? Sound off." When no one immediately complied he cursed, "Sound off, dammit." He listened and got confirmation on the men who were in the truck with him. He saw Henry dusting himself off and blowing grit off his rifle.

Henry walked up to him and shook his head, indicating the road. "Looks bad over there."

Tarkington nodded. "Let's get out there and help," he yelled to the shaken men. He walked the few yards back to the road. It looked nothing like the scene before. There was dark smoke spewing from burning vehicles. He noticed the Filipino driver's blank, dead stare from the truck behind his. He didn't look much more than a child. The gaping hole in his head left little doubt how he'd died. He spotted the jeep with the mounted machine gun on its side, facing away. He could see the axle moving as the wheel spun slowly. "Shit, Lieutenant Smoker was in there."

He rushed to the site, having to step over burning debris, with Henry right behind him. He rounded the back of the jeep and saw bodies. The machine gun was bent, still attached to the tripod. The first body was the gunner - dead from any number of wounds.

He went to the next man: it was Lieutenant Smoker. "Lieutenant." He shook his shoulder and felt for a pulse. "He's alive!" He looked for wounds as Henry went to the next man, Sergeant Flynn. Flynn coughed and pushed himself onto his elbows, spit and cursed.

Tarkington slapped the lieutenant's face a few times before Smoker finally opened his eyes and tried to focus on him. He stuttered, "Tark? Wha - what the hell - what the hell happened?" He shook his head and seemed to remember. His eyes widened and he looked frantically at the sky. "Zero! Zero attack!"

Tarkington put a hand on his shoulder and looked him in the eye. "It's over Lieutenant. The Zero's gone. You're okay." He leaned closer. "You *are* okay, right?"

Lt. Smoker looked his body over, doing a personal inventory, and nodded, "Yeah, yeah, I'm okay."

It took hours to clean up the mess left by the Japanese Zero. Destroyed vehicles were pushed to the side and soldier's bodies were stacked into the back of a single troop truck. The truck stayed in the back of the convoy, its contents already putrefying in the hot Luzon sun. The civilian casualties were pushed to the side of the road to be dealt with by the survivors. The soldiers simply didn't have enough room or time to evacuate them.

The attack had been costly, but that was nothing new. Since December 8th, each and every soldier, both Filipino and American, had seen countless tragedies unfold nearly every day. They adjusted, tightened their chinstraps and belts and continued marching.

The trucks finally stopped as the sun was about to set in the west. Tarkington leaned out the back of the stifling truck thinking he'd see more jungle, but instead he saw a bustling hive of activity. Soldiers darted this way and that in the moderate-sized town.

Staff Sergeant Flynn came round to the back of truck. "Here's our new home, at least for the time being. Get the men out and meet me over there." He pointed in the general direction of a landscaped park. "Lieutenant Smoker will address the men, give us all the scoop."

Tarkington nodded and hopped out. "All right men, let's get out of this rust bucket and form up in the park." They were all tired, some stumbling as they had to learn how to use their numb legs again.

The grass was soft and, without being told, the men dropped, luxuriating in the lush greenery. It was the most comfortable they'd been in days. Soon Lt. Smoker joined them and GIs forced themselves to their feet, but Lt. Smoker quickly signaled them to stay put.

He stayed standing and looked them over. There was just enough light to see their tired faces. "Men, as a reward for keeping that bridge open for as long as possible, saving many lives, the CO, Captain Glister lobbied for Hotel Company to get some much needed and deserved R and R." Despite their tiredness, the mention of R and R perked them up and there was a low murmur of approval.

Lt. Smoker held up his hands for quiet. "It's not much, but all we really need is somewhere to rest." He looked around the park. "This park will be our rally point. You're welcome to move around the town, but stay out of trouble. We'll have tents and cots set up and I'll expect every man to sleep here each night for however long this lasts. Understood?" There was a smattering of 'yes sirs. "We're still in a combat zone, just ten miles from the new front line." He put his fists on his hips and continued. "You know how the Nips are though. They could punch through and be among us faster'n you can say 'jackrabbit'." He looked to the sky, "And of course we're not immune from aerial attacks. The NCOs will assign a work party to get started digging slit trenches." He paused then paced a few feet and finished, "You've all earned this. Carry on."

A cheer went up and Tarkington couldn't keep the smile off his face. The thought of staying in one place without someone trying to kill him was intoxicating. He shook his head, not believing his luck.

"Sergeant Tarkington," bellowed Staff Sergeant Flynn. Tarkington got to his feet already dreading having to ask exhausted soldiers to dig slit trenches. "Follow me."

Tarkington looked at Henry who shrugged and didn't rise from the grass. He followed Sergeant Flynn. They entered a single-story building in the center of town. It was officer country. Every officer in the company was there, organizing the building to become a sort of HQ. Tarkington braced beside Sergeant Flynn, who barked, "Staff Sergeant Flynn reporting in with Sergeant Tarkington, sir."

Captain Glister turned to see the two braced Sergeants. He grinned and strode to them. "At ease, *Sergeant* Tarkington. That's got a nice ring to it." He lowered his voice. "I wish this was under happier circumstances. Sergeant Blakesly was a damn fine soldier and an even better man. He was a great leader and a constant help to Sergeant Flynn. I'll expect no less from you. The coming days will be the toughest we've seen and we rely on you NCOs as the backbone of this whole operation."

He paused and Tarkington nodded and said, "Yes sir."

Glister extended his hand and Tarkington shook it. In his other hand he extended the three-chevron insignia of Sergeant. "Find someone to sew this on for you Sergeant. Sorry we can't get you a new uniform, but as you know things are a little slim around here."

He released the captain's hand and nodded. "I know sir. Believe me." He looked the CO of Hotel Company in the eye and saluted, "Thank you sir. I'll do my very best."

Captain Glister returned the salute then held up his finger as if remembering something. "Almost forgot." He barked, "Lieutenant Randall."

A harried-looking lieutenant stopped what he was doing and answered, "Sir?"

"Bring those Thompsons from the back room."

Seconds later Lt. Randall trotted up holding a Thompson sub-machine gun in each hand. Glister took them and handed them to the sergeants. "Found a crate of these as we were bugging out. Must've gotten lost in the shuffle. There's precious few of them, so consider yourselves lucky." They looked over the brand-new weapons, getting the feel of them. "They're crap for long distance, but in this kind of jungle and street fighting they pack a wallop."

Staff Sergeant Flynn nodded. "Thank you, sir. These'll be helpful."

"You can grab ammunition at the depot. We actually have more ammo for those than the Springfields, so don't be shy about stocking up."

4

Once the troops were fed and they had found where they'd sleep, the GIs were anxious to explore the town. It had been a long time since they could wander without the imminent fear of bombardment. The town wasn't far enough back to not be targeted, indeed after the destruction of Clark Airfield in the early hours of the war, the Japanese Air Force could hit any part of Luzon they wanted, but there were far better targets than a quiet town in the middle of nowhere. No one had any illusions about their safety, so every GI had a weapon slung over a shoulder.

Private First Class Stollman walked up to Sergeant Tarkington. He wasn't wearing a helmet and he'd wetted his unwieldy hair in an attempt to tame it but it still stuck up in various directions. "So, *Sergeant*."

Tarkington glared at him. "What is it, *Private* First Class Stollman?"

Stollman's shit-eating grin disappeared and he straightened up and stammered, "Uh, n - nothing Sergeant."

Tarkington grinned, shook his head and laughed. He pointed a finger at Stollman's long, straight nose. "Gotcha." He clasped Stollman's shoulder.

The other nearby GIs relaxed and laughed. Stollman grinned. "Scared me for a minute, Sarge. Some of the boys and I are gonna explore this place." He leaned in close and whispered, "Maybe find some hooch, or some ladies, or both. You wanna come along?"

Tarkington nodded, "Course I do." He caught Staff Sergeant Flynn watching the exchange with a scowl. Tarkington pushed Stollman away, "You go on along. I'll catch up with you." Henry raised an eyebrow. Tarkington addressed him, "I'll see you out there. Just gotta take care of something first." He watched the men stream out of the tent. He hadn't seen them in such high spirits since before December 8th.

He walked over to Staff Sergeant Flynn, who was sitting on his cot cleaning his new Thompson. He stood in front of him until he looked up. "You don't approve?"

Flynn's steely-blue eyes bore into him. "I don't mind the men going looking for trouble. It's why we're here, let 'em blow off some steam."

"I mean you don't approve of me tagging along with them."

Flynn dropped his gaze and inserted the piece he'd just cleaned into its proper place, picked up the next piece and wiped it with an oily rag. "You're an NCO now. I understand that you were a PFC just a day ago and they're your friends. Of course you wanna play grab-ass with 'em, but what happens tomorrow, or the next day, when you have to order one of them to do something that might get them killed?" He raised his eyes and squinted, making the creases deepen along the edges. "You'll hesitate. Maybe send someone who you're not as close to. Skip over PFC Henry for instance, pick Winkleman. The first time that happens, you've lost their respect and you'll have to be shuffled out of the squad and possibly the platoon."

Tarkington broke eye contact and nodded. "I see your point, Sergeant." He looked longingly out the tent flap where the men had disappeared.

Flynn finished putting his Thompson together and shook his head. "Don't look so damn glum, Tark. It doesn't mean you have to be a Puritan or anything. I'm meeting up with the other NCOs at a little bar we know about. You're welcome to join us. In fact, I insist."

Sergeant Tarkington was on his second bottle of what they called 'beer' but tasted like fermented piss. He took a long swig, crinkled his nose, pursed his lips and swallowed. Flynn clapped him on the back. "It's crummy, but it's alcohol."

Tarkington nodded. He could feel the dizzy giddiness coming over him quickly. He'd never been a lush, but he hadn't had a drop of alcohol since the attack and his tolerance was extremely low. He held the bottle out looking for a label, but it was a blank brown bottle. "It's actually not that bad. I think my taste buds are getting numb to it or something."

The leader of the 3rd squad, Staff Sergeant Gideon slammed an empty bottle down and held up three fingers for more beers. The smiling Filipino behind the bar lifted his chin and smiled broadly. He didn't look more than eleven years old. Gideon addressed Tarkington. "You'll be completely numb after a few more of those. They sneak up on you."

The three beers were delivered and the tops popped off too easily. Flynn stood and called for the NCOs' attention. "I'd like to raise a toast to Sergeant Ronald Blakesly." The place went quiet as the NCOs raised their bottles higher. "He was a damn good soldier and, more than that, a good friend. I knew him a long time. We went through boot camp together and came to this island paradise together." He looked around the room and the men met his eyes. He raised his bottle higher and bellowed, "To Sergeant Blakesly, may your tinder always be dry and your aim true." A chorus of "hear, hear" broke out and the men slugged back their beers, draining them to the last drop.

"Another round," Sergeant Gideon proclaimed and the boy shuffled more bottles out to the men faster than Tarkington thought possible.

Once everyone was reloaded, Flynn again called for attention. "I'd like to introduce you to my new assistant squad leader, Buck Sergeant Clay Tarkington." The room erupted and the NCOs clambered around him and started chanting, 'Drink, drink, drink.'

Tarkington grinned and slammed his beer back draining it. He slapped the empty bottle down and another was thrust in front of him and they continued chanting until that was gone too.

They didn't stop until he'd finished his fourth. When he drained it the chanting stopped and they congratulated him, each man introducing himself and shaking his hand. He tried to focus on remembering each person's name - he knew most of them already - but his mind was reeling with the alcohol and he was losing focus.

Someone put on a record and the scratchy sound of someone singing an indecipherable song flowed through the room. The men began dancing and soon Sergeant Tarkington found himself on his feet, arms intertwined with a line of dancing, singing NCOs. They were kicking their legs out as if performing like The Rockettes. Tarkington couldn't keep from giggling. He was thankful for the men on either side, convinced he wouldn't be able to stand otherwise.

Sergeant Clay Tarkington woke to the sounds of whistles, bugles and someone shaking him. He moaned and cracked his eyes, seeing Henry's face only inches away. "Wake up, dammit. Air raid I think."

Tarkington struggled to open his eyes. He sat up and shook his head slightly and felt the worst headache of his life throbbing with every heartbeat. His head spun and he tried to lay back down but Henry was relentless and dragged him to his feet. Tarkington leaned on him and looked around. He stammered, "How? How'd I get here?" Henry took a step, dragging him along. The pain in his head exploded and he saw stars. He tried to get loose, "Just leave me here to die. Oh my God, my head." Henry grit his teeth and pulled him more upright. "You're not gonna die, for Chrissakes you're just hungover. Now move your slow butt before this place comes down around us."

Tarkington nodded. "Lead me. I don't think my head can take the sunlight." The dull thump of an exploding bomb in the distance broke through his stupor. He opened his eyes and stood on his own, willing the pain and bleariness away. He nodded, "I'm okay, but I don't know where the slit trenches are."

Henry made sure he was steady and wasn't going to try to lay down again then waved him to follow. "They're over here, follow me." He trotted out, keeping tabs on his hungover sergeant.

The bombs continued to fall, the thumps getting closer every second. Henry got to the edge of the slit trenches, dug the night before by an unlucky squad from 2nd platoon. There were already bleary-eyed GIs crouching and sitting in the bottom of the trench. Most of them were shirtless and in their underwear, holding rifles.

They slid in and Tarkington was glad for the darkness. He sat on his butt and closed his eyes. Henry nudged him and handed him his Thompson sub-machine gun. Tarkington shook his head and took it from him, embarrassed that he'd left it behind. "Thanks," he muttered.

The bombs fell for two minutes and missed the town, but left carnage and craters on the main road to the east. When the whistles and bugles finally stopped, the GIs got to their feet and brushed themselves off. They all looked tired and the sour alcohol smell seeping from their pores told Tarkington that they'd found their own party.

He pushed himself to his feet and immediately felt queasy. He struggled to keep from vomiting. He swallowed the bitterness, but the man behind him wasn't able to and spewed vomit onto Tarkington's back. The smell was like a trigger being pulled and Tarkington hunched over and released a vile stream of sour beer and whatever else he'd consumed the night before onto the bottom of the trench. The sound and smell triggered more men to lurch forward and soon nearly every GI was spewing. Henry scrambled out of the trench and stood looking down on the wretched scene. He shook his head and drawled, "Damned Yankees can't hold your liquor."

Tarkington finished emptying his stomach and wiped his mouth with the back of his hand. He swayed and looked up at Henry through blood-shot eyes. He handed Henry his Thompson then held his hand out. Henry took it and helped him out of the hole. He'd just got his feet under him when someone barked behind him. "Sergeant Tarkington! What's the meaning of this?"

He recognized the voice of the CO. He turned and braced on wobbly legs. He swayed slightly like a thin palm in a gentle breeze. "No excuse, Captain..." He struggled to come up with his name and was unsuccessful so simply ended with, "sir."

"Christ, Tarkington, the name's Glister, *Captain* Glister." He gestured to the men still getting sick in the bottom of the trench. "I'm the CO of this bunch of drunks."

Tarkington's felt his head would explode at any moment. The pain was making him grimace and he could hardly keep his eyes open. "Captain Glister. Yes, sir I know your name."

Glister looked over his shoulder and addressed Lieutenant Smoker who looked like he wanted to gun them all down. "Get these men squared away with coffee and a greasy breakfast. We're moving to the coast in four hours."

Lieutenant Smoker's jaw rippled as he clenched and unclenched his teeth. He uttered, "Yes, sir. Understood."

Captain Glister wrinkled his nose and added, "Have these men fill the trench back in before we leave. Can't leave this kind of mess for the locals to clean up." He turned and walked away, shaking his head. The men couldn't see his face but he was smiling.

Smoker nodded and barked at his new sergeant. "You heard him, get these men out of the hole, fed and ready to pack up and leave." He stepped close and leaned forward until he was only an inch from Sergeant Tarkington's face. Tarkington tried to keep his eyes open, but the pain was debilitating. He was partially successful. Smoker's brown eyes looked like they could shoot a Howitzer shell. He bellowed at the top of his lungs, "Am I clear, Sergeant?"

Tarkington's eyes snapped wide, and he did his best to match Smoker's voice but came up woefully short, "Crystal clear, sir."

He stepped back from Tarkington's foul breath, "Carry on."

Tarkington relaxed and watched Lt. Smoker catch up to Captain Glister. The encounter had briefly made him forget about his throbbing head, but now it came crashing back with a vengeance and he closed his eyes and rubbed his temples. "I'll never drink again for as long as I live," he uttered. Henry slapped his shoulder, "Sure thing, Tark. Sure thing."

After leaving town, they moved along the main road, skirting abandoned and burned out husks of vehicles of all shapes and sizes. They didn't see bodies, but the smell of rotting corpses was ever-present. The heat, along with the smell and the bouncing of the trucks hitting countless potholes, made the journey south almost unbearable.

Sergeant Tarkington was in a surly mood. His hangover clung to him like a leech. Riding in the back of a troop truck along the dusty, bouncy road wasn't good when he was at the peak of health; with a hangover it was far worse.

He pulled the canteen from his belt and tried to focus on unscrewing the lid. He'd downed four already, knowing it would only get worse if he didn't rehydrate. He finally got the lid off and tilted the canteen to his lips. The tepid, Halazone-laced water tasted terrible and he had to concentrate to keep it from coming back up. He looked at the rest of the men. They all looked just as miserable. "Drink." He growled. "Everyone take a drink, now." The GIs scowled and grumbled but did as he ordered.

Sergeant Flynn rode in the front cab beside the Filipino driver, putting Tarkington in charge of the hungover troopers in back. Upon entering the truck he'd ordered the men not to throw up on the truck floor. If they needed to hurl, they were to push the canvas and throw up outside. Many took this option and the vomit immediately caked with dust and dried into a hard lacquer along the side of the truck. The vomit proved difficult to remove, earning the affected trucks the moniker 'vomit comets.'

Many hours later, through stop-and-go traffic and many false alarm air raids, they arrived in the town of Mariveles on the southern tip of the Bataan Peninsula. The light was fading but Tarkington could make out the waters of the China Sea and the North Channel. He knew somewhere out there was the island fortress of Corregidor, but he couldn't make it out in the fading light. *Those bastards'll never take that,* he thought.

The weary GIs dismounted under Tarkington's burning eyes and took in the sights of Mariveles. There wasn't much to see. The single dirt airfield stretched to the edge of the bay, its point dotted like an elongated letter 't', which was the empty seaplane mooring docks. In makeshift revetments, sat four P-40 Warhawks. He'd heard it was all that remained of twenty-four.

Besides the planes, there were a few tractors and dozers parked along the strip. It looked to Tarkington that they'd been working to widen the strip. *Getting ready for reinforcements,* he mused hopefully. He gazed at the bay. The colors of the evening were deepening to reds and yellows and the water appeared to be on fire. Despite his hangover, he appreciated the beauty.

Staff Sergeant Flynn barked, "Get your gear. Those huts over there." He pointed to rows of small white buildings sitting on platforms a few feet off the ground. "Our new home for the next couple of days." The GIs looked how Tarkington felt, like shit. They dragged themselves to the huts and disappeared inside. The normal banter was absent.

Tarkington was about to follow but Flynn got his attention. "I want those men rested. If they brought any hooch from town confiscate it. No drinking."

The mere thought of drinking again almost made Tarkington lose what little he had left in his belly. "I don't think you have anything to worry about there, sir."

Flynn nodded, "Don't let 'em get too comfy. I'll figure out the grub situation, get 'em fed before they crash." The thought of food almost made him lose it again, but he nodded and followed the squad to the huts.

5

As Hotel Company was settling in for the night, Lieutenant Robert Kelly was watching the sun dip beneath the western horizon from the bridge of the seventy-seven foot long PT-34 of MTB Squadron 3. It was his turn on patrol. The night before PT-32 had had an uneventful evening and Lt. Kelly was hoping for the same.

Since hostilities began, the squadron of four PT boats had been busy. The ever-present danger of Japanese aircraft forced the fast boats to mostly work at night. Despite the lack of enemy contact, each patrol was harrowing. With each passing day, the Japanese got stronger while the defenders lost men and material.

Lt. Kelly had no illusions about the situation. If he got in trouble, he could call on his squadron for help, but once he was on the open ocean there was little chance help would arrive in time. Before hostilities Lt. Kelly was supremely confident in his boat's abilities, however each mission degraded the boat's performance slightly and, without resupply, there was no way to get their crafts back to tip-top condition. The mechanics performed miracles to keep the boats engine's working, but Kelly noticed the slight drops in speed and performance.

Once PT-34 was away from the moorings, he opened the throttles and listened to the engine's hum. It was always thrilling to feel the power of the

1500hp Packard engines propelling them through the glassy waters. To the untrained ear the engine sounded perfect, but Kelly could hear the slight imperfections of an engine in need of an overhaul.

They moved north, slowing and keeping close to shore. They followed the shoreline and entered bays and inlets, ready to engage any enemy they came across, but careful not to attract unwanted attention.

By midnight, they'd gone as far north as they dared. Lt. Kelly ordered the engines cut and the gentle swell of a calm China Sea lapped the sides. They were two hundred yards off the coast, in a small inlet. Even from this distance they could hear the sounds of night animals and the constant racket of insects. The night was warm and the stars seemed close enough to touch. *If there wasn't a war on*, Lt. Kelly thought, *it would be a great place to vacation.*

He was about to order them to turn for home when he heard a faint noise. He leaned forward and Ensign Hayes spoke, "Sir?"

Kelly held up his hand for quiet and closed his eyes, concentrating. He strained and finally heard it again, a dull far-away thrumming of an engine. "Someone's out there," he whispered. "Hear it?"

Hayes hadn't heard anything but had learned to trust his skipper. He concentrated and then he did hear something. His breath caught in his chest and he felt his heart rate increase. He whispered, "I hear it now. Engine or engines."

Kelly didn't wait. "Battle stations, something's out there." In the darkness the men dropped what they were doing and scampered to their assigned battle stations. The engine started and Lt. Kelly cringed at its throaty sound. "Take us to the edge of this point and hold."

PT-34 edged forward until the bow was abreast of the point of land facing out to open ocean. Now the engine noise was louder and all the men could hear it. Kelly felt their tension as they gripped their weapons and readied themselves for action. "Steady," he whispered.

PT-34 idled in place as Kelly tried to pinpoint the sound. He whispered to Hayes, "Sounds like a barge, or something small like that."

Hayes nodded, "Local fishing boat?"

Kelly shook his head, "Not this far north. Gotta be Japs." The idling PT's engine made it difficult to hear the other engine. Suddenly the sound got louder and closer. Each man turned toward a point north and saw the sparkling white wakes of four boats in echelon. Seaman Gordon swung the barrels of his twin .50 caliber machine gun muzzles to the targets and made sure the weapon was primed and ready. Gunner's mates Hodges and Perkins did the same with their mounted Lewis guns.

Lt. Kelly spoke to Ensign Hayes. "We'll attack with surface guns only. Forget the torpedoes."

Hayes nodded and passed the word. Kelly squinted trying to gauge how far away the barges were. "Radio in the contact. Let 'em know we're attacking a force of four Japanese barges near Longo Point. Looks like a landing party."

Hayes nodded and answered with a curt, "Aye."

Kelly glanced behind him and nodded in satisfaction. "They won't see us against the dark backdrop. I want half a knot, let's close the distance." The throbbing idle changed and the PT boat moved from the point like a deadly shark sneaking up on unsuspecting prey.

The barges were still motoring parallel to shore. At their current speed and direction they'd pass the PT boat in a minute or two. PT-34's bow was pointed directly at them. "Turn to starboard ninety-degrees. Maintain this speed." The boat eased into the turn, not making a visible wake and moved north, the opposite direction to the barges. "We'll get behind them, then come up alongside and give 'em all our guns."

Kelly watched the barges closely. If the Japanese saw them, they'd increase speed and break formation, but they maintained course and speed, oblivious to the danger.

When Kelly figured he was five-hundred yards behind, he ordered the 180-degree turn. Once they were heading in the same direction as the barges he ordered, "We attack in one minute. Wait for my order to open fire." He'd raised his voice but figured the Japanese were too far away to hear him. "Give me three knots." The thrust of the boat increased and Kelly could feel the slight vibration beneath his boots change. They were still losing ground to the barges. "Okay, let's open 'em up easy." He held on as the boat surged smoothly onto a plane and the wakes of the barges quickly turned into the shapes of boats.

Seaman Gordon gripped the trigger of the twin fifties. He shifted the muzzles slightly as the PT boat powered toward the targets. He licked his dry lips, suddenly feeling nauseous as the adrenaline coursed through his veins. Finally, Lt. Kelly ordered the spotlight on and yelled, "Open fire! Fire at will!"

Gordon could clearly see the barges now. He concentrated on the rear boat and squeezed the trigger. The sudden muzzle flash from his weapon dazzled his eyes. His first burst slammed into the barge, sending sparks and wood-chunks flying. He squeezed off another burst and saw his tracers lancing into the barge, like something right out of a Buck Rogers comic book. He kept the muzzle steady, letting the movement of the PT boat work the .50 caliber bullets through the length of the target. He kept the trigger depressed. The power at his fingertips was intoxicating.

He stopped firing when the barge dropped from his round reticle, but depressed the trigger again when the second barge filled the space. He adjusted the twin muzzles down slightly and saw his bullets kicking up water spray as they skipped into the hull.

Gunner's mates Hodges and Perkins fired their Lewis machine guns, but their bullets seemed inconsequential alongside the destruction spewing from the twin fifty.

PT-34 continued powering alongside the barges and the guns continued to shred them. Lt. Kelly watched the yellow tracers, knowing each one represented the fifth shot from the twin fifties, but the effect looked like one constant stream of yellow fire. It looked thick enough to walk across. The devastation it wrought on the Japanese barges was obvious. The rear boat was listing heavily, well on its way to sinking. He doubted there could be anyone left alive. The second was taking a brutal beating and looked like it would be joining its twin on the bottom soon.

In the confusion, the two lead barges turned toward shore bringing them closer to the PT boat. There was no danger of a collision, so Kelly maintained course and speed allowing his gunners to concentrate on firing. The smaller caliber Lewis guns were spraying the lead barge while the twin fifty finished sweeping the doomed third barge.

Flickering lights came from the lead barges and for a moment Kelly didn't know what they were, but soon he heard and felt bullets slamming into the hull and he realized his prey still had teeth of their own. For a moment the Lewis guns and the Japanese machine guns dueled, but soon Seaman Gordon's muzzles centered on them and the heavy onslaught swung the advantage to PT-34.

Kelly steered toward shore slightly to put more space between them. The Lewis guns ran out of ammunition at almost the exact same time and the gunners quickly reloaded. The twin fifty continued firing and Kelly leaned over and yelled to Ensign Hayes to remind Seaman Gordon to shorten his bursts. Both barrels glowed red behind the massive muzzle flashes and he worried he'd burn them out. Hayes nodded and moved forward to relay the message.

The second-in-line barge's engine blossomed into flame and the bow lunged deep as it lost power. It was taking on water and slewed to starboard, disappearing out of the spotlight's view. The lead barge suddenly erupted with small-arms fire. Bullets thumped into the wooden sides of the PT boat and ricocheted off the metal bridge and deck. Kelly instinctively ducked but kept the throttle steady.

Seaman Gordon stopped firing and yelled something, but he was faced away and Kelly didn't catch what he said. The lead barge was lit by the spotlight and the Lewis guns opened up, firing short, controlled bursts. The enemy fire slackened as they lost the upper hand and Lieutenant Kelly flashed by them at forty yards. The spotlight stayed on them despite Japanese bullets whizzing close. Kelly yelled, "Light off. Cease fire! Cease fire!"

The light extinguished before the gunners got the word, but once the target was lost in the dark the firing stopped. The steady hum of the engine replaced the sounds of battle. Kelly glanced behind and saw the barges burning in the blackness. He kept his course and speed, heading south and home.

Ensign Hayes was beside him again. "Gordon fried both barrels. They're fused like they've been soldered. Damned fool just couldn't let up."

Kelly grit his teeth at the news. "Dammit. We only have one more set unless we're resupplied soon." Ensign Hayes looked back at the dots of light marking the battle. Kelly nodded, "I think we sank at least two and heavily damaged the others. We don't have enough ammo to finish them off. Report the results to HQ. They'll want to know what the hell they're up to."

Sergeant Tarkington was nudged awake two hours before there was a hint of light in the eastern sky. He instinctively reached under the pillow for his sidearm. "Easy, Sarge. Lieutenant Smoker sent me to wake the NCOs." Tarkington relaxed and sat up. He tried to focus on the luminescent dials of his watch but couldn't make them out. "It's 0345. You're to meet in the mess hall at 0400."

The PFC stood to leave, but Tarkington gripped his arm and croaked, "What's the scoop?" The GI shrugged and went in search of the next NCO. Tarkington rubbed his eyes and yawned. He'd actually been sleeping better than he had in weeks. He slid on his boots, buckled them, then stood and slung his Thompson over his shoulder. It was pitch dark and he fumbled and tripped his way to the front entrance kicking cots and getting curses from the jostled GIs.

He stepped from the building and stopped and listened. The sounds of the nearby jungle filled his senses. He'd gotten good at distinguishing normal night sounds from abnormal and he decided there was no immediate danger.

He entered the mess hall; an abandoned hangar on the far side of the airfield. There was a kerosene lamp burning on a table in the middle of the large space. Around it, he saw all the officers of Hotel Company, looking groggy and half-asleep. Tarkington thought he sensed something else: worry. He'd been one of the last NCOs to be awakened since he chose to sleep with the men rather than the other NCOs. He still wasn't used to not being one of the boys.

He pushed his way into the circle surrounding the table. Beside him Staff Sergeant Flynn grunted and moved over. Tarkington looked around the gathered officers, trying to figure out what the hell was going on.

Captain Glister walked into the room and everyone snapped to attention, but he held up his hand, "At ease, at ease." He laid a yellowed map on the table and Lt. Smoker lifted the kerosene lamp so he could slide it forward. It was a map of the southern tip of Luzon Island, the region of the Bataan Peninsula.

Glister put his finger on a point of land due-west of Mariveles, far behind the Orion-Bagac line of defense I and II Corps held. It wasn't far from their current location. "Last night one of our PT boats encountered a sizable force of Japs on barges trying to land men in this area. The PT boat engaged and sank two of them and badly damaged the other two. It's worrisome and the brass thinks they might be trying an end-around assault on our flanks." He let that sink in. "We're the only line unit back here at the moment. We've been ordered to move and assess if there are any more of these landings. If the Japs get a foot-hold and move inland it could be bad. Roust the men, get 'em fed and resupplied. We leave for Longoskawayan Point in two hours."

The 1st platoon reached the point of land by mid-morning. It was only a few miles west of Mariveles and the half-paved, half-dirt road was well used in this section, making for an easy march. Along the way they picked up men from rear echelon units moving along the road. Every available man, regardless of their position, was ordered to move to the west coast. There was no time to pull more front-line troops from the Orion-Bagac line, and they were already stretched too thin. It was up to Hotel Company - and whoever else they could get their hands on - to contain the suspected landings.

Sergeant Tarkington peered over the edge of a precipitous cliff down to a small strip of beach, shimmering in the morning sun. The green water lapped lazily against the white beach. It looked idyllic, except for a barge, which looked damaged and half-filled with water.

Lieutenant Smoker came up beside Tarkington and took a sharp breath when he noticed the barge. "See any Japs?"

Tarkington shook his head, "No sir."

Smoker saw Staff Sergeant Flynn crouching nearby. He waved him over and, when he got there, put his hand on his shoulder and whispered, "Lets move north. There's only one way up from that beach. We need to get there before the Japs do." Flynn nodded and went to pass the order to the other NCOs.

The GIs attitudes changed as they realized there were enemy troops nearby. The march from Mariveles had been lighthearted. They thought it would be a false alarm and they'd simply spend the day marching in circles, searching for an enemy that wasn't there. Now they braced for imminent combat.

Tarkington felt the familiar surge of adrenaline making his breath suddenly labored. He walked with his Thompson ready, being sure to keep proper spacing. He glanced behind and saw PFC Holiday ten yards back. His rifle with the grenade-launcher attachment, held at port arms.

They had moved a quarter mile before the shooting started. Tarkington passed along the halt signal, holding up his fist. He crouched and tried to decipher what was happening. The shooting was close, but he didn't think it was his 2nd squad firing. They were leading the platoon with Lieutenant Smoker in front. *Who else is out here?* Tarkington wondered.

The sporadic fire changed. Tarkington recognized the hammering of a Japanese Nambu machine gun and he ducked lower. Someone had found the Japanese before them.

The signal to move came down the line and, staying low, he moved forward with his Thompson ready. He swept the muzzle side to side. He wanted to move left and look down on the beach, but it would take him out of view of Holiday. He glanced back looking for Henry, but he was too far back. Tarkington didn't like moving towards combat without him at his side. He'd come to rely on his senses.

The ground sloped downward toward a small creek, which had carved a gash into the cliffs, leading to the beach. The firing slackened, with just an occasional burst from the enemy machine gun but no return fire. Finally they reached the creek and were met with smiling Filipinos holding rifles.

Lieutenant Smoker smiled back and crouched beside them. The rest of the GIs spread out, forming a defensive ring around them. Tarkington moved within earshot and heard Smoker ask. "Where are they?"

An older Filipino, whose face was creased with deep wrinkles, smiled showing cracked and missing teeth. He pointed west and spoke in broken English. "Japs there. We stop."

"How many?"

The Filipino shrugged his shoulders and held up three fingers, one of which had been broken years before and fused into a forty-five-degree angle pointing left. "Kill three," his smile broadened, deepening the creases in his face.

Lieutenant Smoker smiled back and slapped the elder's shoulder. "Good job." He held up a thumb. "How many men do you have?" The Filipino answered by holding up both hands, closing then raising two more fingers. "Twelve men." Smoker nodded and looked to his NCOs. "Spread the men out on either side of this gully. Send a runner to Captain Glister. Tell him we found the Japs."

6

"How many men does one of those barges carry?" Tarkington asked Staff Sergeant Flynn.

Flynn shrugged, "Fifty? Sixty? I don't know." They were dug in halfway up the slope from the creek, giving them a decent view of the glistening beach and the destroyed barge. They had yet to see an enemy soldier, and the machine gun hadn't fired again since they arrived. "Smoker says there could be a lot more than just one barge-load. Figures they only left that one cause it wasn't seaworthy. For all we know there could've been fifty barges."

Tarkington nodded. "Well, as long as they're down there and not up here."

"We have to hold 'em here. There's some Stuart tanks and anti-tank cannons on the way, but they don't expect them until tomorrow morning. We've got a few mortars in support, and about a hundred and fifty guys from rear echelon units in reserve. More Filipinos are coming all the time - not regular Army guys, just civilians - but as you know, they fight like tigers."

Tarkington nodded. "Be nice to know how many Japs are down there."

Flynn shifted in the hole and scratched the back of his scalp. "Whatever they've got, they're in a terrible situation. The cliffs keep 'em penned in. This is the only avenue of attack. We could hold against hundreds."

Tarkington agreed, "It's not like them to plan so poorly. I mean this is about the worst beach they could've picked."

Flynn nodded. "Yeah, maybe they're not where they're supposed to be."

"I hope the brass is keeping tabs on other beaches."

Flynn looked at him through narrowed eyes. "Leave the war planning to the generals, Tark. We concentrate on doing what's right for our squad. Don't worry about that other shit. Clear?"

Tarkington flushed but nodded, "Yeah. I know, just thinking out loud."

Flynn shook his head. "Go check on your team. Make sure they've got ammo and keep 'em hydrated."

Tarkington nodded and hefted himself out of the foxhole. His four grenades clipped to his battle harness swung side-to-side slightly. He looked at the jungle leading down to the beach before moving back to his own foxhole among team two. He nodded at Henry, who spit a stream of tobacco juice onto the dirt and nodded back. The 2nd squad was two foxholes deep and dispersed, so each hole had a distinct area to cover. Flynn had put the BAR man, Stollman, up the slope from Tarkington. Stollman's hole was bigger to accommodate his loader. His ammo carrier, PFC Vick, was five yards back - close enough to toss extra ammunition if he needed to.

Tarkington settled into his hole. He placed two extra magazines on a dirt shelf he'd fashioned with his entrenching tool. The soil was soft and loamy and full of life. Multi-colored worms would poke from the sides of the hole, then pull back upon being exposed to the light. He was thankful for the easy-to-dig ground, but he could've done without all the worms and bugs.

He was abruptly pulled from his thoughts when he heard Henry give a high-pitched whistle. Tarkington froze, knowing his friend would only give a warning if there was something there. Tarkington lowered his head slightly and focused on the jungle in front. He could see halfway to the beach but he didn't see anything out of the ordinary. He gripped his Thompson and kept scanning.

He caught movement in his peripheral vision to the right, towards the creek. He moved his head slowly, while bringing his Thompson above the lip of the foxhole. There it was again, this time more distinct. He brought his Thompson to his shoulder and aimed at the spot. He slowed his breathing, waiting. A flash of movement directly in front caught his attention, but by the time he looked there was nobody there. He saw something small and round arcing through the air and yelled, "Grenade!" while ducking.

There was a series of thumping explosions among the foxholes. There was no way the enemy soldiers were close enough to hurl grenades. "Knee mortars," he yelled. Seven explosions rocked the area and dirt and debris rained down on the cowering GIs.

Tarkington heard yelling from downslope. He lifted his head and saw green-clad enemy soldiers charging up the hill, yelling. He heard Sergeant Flynn, off to his left and higher up the hill, call out, "Here they come!" It was followed immediately with the heavy thumping of Stolly's BAR.

Tarkington rose up and put his Thompson firmly against his shoulder. The enemy soldiers were seventy yards away. He aimed at a green-clad soldier running straight toward him, gripping a long Arisaka rifle with a glinting bayonet. He blew out his breath and fired a burst. It was his first time firing the Thompson.

The soldier kept coming; he realized he'd missed and longed for his trusty Springfield. He fired again and this time saw the soldier stumble and fall onto his face. He shifted aim to the soldier directly behind and sent a burst his way. The soldier lunged to the side and started zigzagging, making a harder target. He tracked him and was about to fire when the soldier suddenly crumpled and Tarkington saw blood spurt out of his back, as though he'd sprung a leak.

The volume of fire increased, pouring into the Japanese soldiers. He heard a Japanese Nambu machine gun open fire somewhere to his right. He saw a muzzle flash just as the ground between him and Henry erupted in fountains of dirt. He ducked and yelled, "Nambu at 2 o'clock."

He waited a fraction, then went up and fired where he'd seen the muzzle flash. More Japanese soldiers were coming up the hill, darting from cover to cover. Tarkington shifted his fire and swept an arc of .45 caliber lead down the hill. His firing pin slammed against an empty chamber and he dropped and called out, "Reloading."

He stuffed the spent magazine into his ammo pouch and smoothly clicked in a new stick magazine full of snub-nosed .45 ACP. He rose up and saw an enemy soldier near a boulder fire his Arisaka then pull back, chamber another round, lean out and fire again.

Tarkington focused his muzzle on the spot and when the Japanese leaned out again, fired. The boulder chipped and a mass of rock dust hovered around the spot. He didn't wait to see if he'd hit him, but swung to another soldier sprinting up the hill. Tarkington held the trigger for a couple seconds then released, cognizant of the Thompson's high rate of fire. His target's headlong sprint stopped when six of the .45 caliber ACP rounds slammed into his belly and chest.

The high rate of fire, along with the cloud of gasses surrounding Tarkington, drew fire. He ducked as the Nambu machine gun fired rounds his way. He curled into the bottom of his hole, while the world a few feet over his head buzzed with death. He took the opportunity to check his magazine. He still had half.

He cringed in the bottom of his hole. Suddenly, a new sound added to the battle, the whistling of mortar rounds. For an instant he thought they were enemy rounds, but was relieved when he heard them exploding downslope, among the enemy. The ground shook slightly and he watched the dirt sides of the foxhole shudder. He wondered where all the worms went.

The Nambu stopped firing and he poked his head over the top and glanced down the hill. He didn't see any more charging soldiers. He brought his Thompson to his shoulder and aimed toward the Nambu and fired the rest of his magazine.

He reloaded and saw an enemy soldier crawling up the hill. He couldn't decide if he was wounded or just trying to stay under cover. He centered his sights on the soldier's helmet and pulled the trigger. The ground erupted in front of the soldier and bullets walked down the length of his body, sending a fine red mist into the air.

Mortar shells exploded near where he'd seen the Nambu. Tarkington looked for more targets but only saw bodies. The rate of fire from his squad tapered and finally ceased. The mortars stopped and suddenly the only noises were the hissing of hot barrels and the crackling of tiny fires. He heard Flynn unnecessarily call for a cease fire.

Tarkington looked behind him and caught Henry's eye. He nodded his way and Henry put his hand to his helmet like he was tipping a cap to a lady on the street. Smoke rose from his rifle barrel.

Flynn called out. "Gimme a count." The GIs of 2nd squad called out their numbers and Tarkington breathed a sigh of relief when they'd all checked in. He could hear other squads checking in too but couldn't tell if anyone had been hit in other sections of 1st platoon. He didn't remember anyone calling out for a medic, which was a good sign.

Tarkington called out, "Ammo check." In order, the GIs called out what they had left. Tarkington was surprised. Despite the seemingly high volume of fire, the men still had well over half. His chest swelled with pride. *These men are pros.*

The rest of the day was quiet. The platoon stayed in their foxholes keeping a close eye downslope, but there'd been no movement since the noon attack. Shadows elongated and the bright midday light faded to softer shades of yellows and oranges. To the north, storm clouds were thrusting into the tropical sky and everyone knew they'd be getting soaked soon. It hadn't rained in days, but that streak was about to end.

He heard someone coming from behind and he turned in time to see the first scout, PFC Winkleman, drop onto his belly and smile at him. "What's the scoop, Wink?"

In a voice that always reminded Tarkington of Mickey Mouse, he said, "Lieutenant Smoker wants the NCOs back there for a briefing."

Tarkington nodded, "Okay. Know what about?"

He shook his head and squeaked, "I just work here, Sarge." He moved off to inform the next NCO. Tarkington watched him go. He moved well through the jungle, having grown up hunting deer in the deep woods of the Pacific Northwest. He was a good choice for the squad's first scout.

Tarkington hefted himself out of the foxhole and staying low, moved past Henry, who gave him a nod. "What's up?"

Tarkington slowed, "You'll know when I know."

He moved up the hill, checking on the men as he passed. Despite the lack of action over the past couple of hours, the GIs were still vigilant and wide awake.

The hill flattened and he stood to his full height when he knew he was over the crest and out of sight of the Japanese. He approached the growing group of NCOs and officers. He looked back the way he'd come. There was no sign there'd ever been a battle.

The NCOs formed one group and the officers the other. When everyone was there, Captain Glister called them together. They formed a circle and listened in the fading light. "I wanna get this done fast and get you back to your men before it's dark, so listen up." All side conversations stopped and he continued. He motioned to three Filipinos crouched beside him, holding rifles that looked too long for them. "These fellas know an alternate way down to the beach. They say it isn't obvious and they doubt the Japs will find it. To be safe, I want them to lead a team down the trail and set up an ambush in case they do find it. It also might be a good vantage point to assess their strength once it's light." He looked around the group. "Who's the best scout?"

Tarkington looked at the officers as they looked at their feet. He knew Winkleman was the best scout in the platoon, but it wasn't his place to speak and he didn't want to volunteer. He focused on Lieutenant Smoker. Tarkington was sure his no-nonsense officer would volunteer them.

Smoker glanced at Flynn and raised his hand, "Private First Class Wink's a good man in the woods, sir. Not sure he's the best, but he's damned good."

"Wink?" Questioned Glister.

"Winkleman. Yes sir."

Captain Glister addressed Lt. Smoker "These men," he gestured to the Filipinos. "This is Eduardo, Nunez and Cesar. They'll guide your team into place." The three Filipinos smiled, showing off crooked teeth. "They're not in the Army, but they're locals and they've been fighting the Japs alongside the regular troops so they know their business."

Smoker looked them up and down. They wore ragged clothing that probably used to be white but was now a dirty yellowish-brown. Each man wore a bandolier across his small chest. Most of the ammo slots were empty. Smoker grinned back at them and nodded. He gestured toward Staff

Sergeant Flynn who looked none too happy. "Sergeant Flynn leads that squad. He'll organize the team."

Flynn nodded toward the smiling Filipinos, then back to Smoker. "Yes sir."

Captain Glister continued. "Better get a move on sergeant." Flynn and Tarkington moved away, but heard Glister continue. "The rest of you be vigilant tonight. You did well staving off that attack, but I think they'll make a push again tonight. Their situation's terrible and they may use the darkness to try to get past us. I want two hour watches every other man." There were nods of understanding around the group. "Be aware of the squad out front and to your left. They'll be mostly out of range, but be aware. I don't want any friendly-fire incidents."

Flynn and Tarkington got to the downslope and went into crouches. Flynn cursed. "Dammit. Can't wait to spend the night on the side of a cliff in the fucking rain."

7

The rain held off until the fifteen-man squad - twelve GIs and three Filipino scouts - were settled in for the night. Getting to the ambush site was a harrowing adventure. They'd followed the sure-footed Filipinos along a knife-edge cliff leading down the left side of the gully.

The Filipinos moved like silent ghosts, making the GIs seem like bumbling buffoons. It was a short distance, but the difficult terrain and the deadly consequences of a fall slowed them down considerably. They finally stopped at a wide section and crammed themselves into whatever cover they could find. An hour later the sky opened up and, despite their over-used ponchos, they were soaked within seconds.

Tarkington was tucked beneath a leaf that was nearly half his size. The rain made the leaf droop until it rested on his back. It did far more to keep him dry than his holed poncho and he was careful not to disturb it too much. Beside him, Henry hunkered as close to a scraggly tree trunk as he could get. In the darkness, Tarkington could see the stark outline of his prominent nose and his mouth moving as he chewed on a blade of grass.

Small rivulets of water ran past his boots, cutting through the dirt, following the path of least resistance. He wondered how high the little creek in the valley, which was no more than a trickle hours before, would get. Perhaps it would become a raging torrent and whisk the remaining Japanese into the sea.

After twenty minutes the rain slackened. Soon it stopped completely, leaving the ground sopping wet and the surrounding jungle dripping. Tarkington felt an uncontrollable shiver course through his body. He gritted his teeth to keep them from chattering. Henry had leaned his rifle against the tree and had his arms wrapped around his knees beneath his poncho. His chin was tucked into the top of the poncho and, in the dark, Tarkington imagined he'd turned into a rock.

After the rain stopped, the jungle night sounds resumed. Tarkington didn't know if he was imagining it or not, but the insects sounded louder than normal, as if the rains had reinvigorated them. The normally pervasive smell of rot was replaced with the smell of soil, rain and grass.

It turned his thoughts to home and for an instant he was back on the farm, bucking hay onto the old flat-bed truck before the unexpected rain storm destroyed their entire hay stock. Beside his little brother, he threw bale after bale to his father, who kicked it into place as quickly as humanly possible. Clay's little brother, Robert, wiped his dirty, sweaty brow and looked over the wide expanse of acreage dotted with countless bales of hay. "Ain't no way we're gonna get all this hay up in time."

Clay hurled another bale and his father guided it into place and exclaimed, "That one's up, now do the next." Robert nodded and got back to work.

Tarkington shook his head, coming back to the Luzon jungle. He smacked Henry's arm. "I'm gonna check on the others."

Henry lifted his head slightly and muttered, "Careful. Gonna be slick as snot."

Tarkington stared into the gloom, but couldn't see more than a few feet. He took a deep breath and reconsidered his decision. He looked up through the thin cover and saw skittering clouds. The dense layer was breaking up and he could see flashes of stars. "Clearing up," he whispered. "I'll wait a few minutes."

The sky cleared more and more until it was nearly filled with stars. Without noticing it happening, he could see much farther down the ridge. He leaned forward, trying to see any movement which might give away the

Japanese on the beach, but there was nothing but jungle and dripping vegetation.

He nearly jumped out of his skin when someone lightly touched his arm. He clutched his Thompson but loosened his grip when he saw the grinning face of one of the Filipino scouts. "Is that you, Eduardo?"

The Filipino's grin filled his entire face and he nodded and whispered, "Come. Sergeant talk to you."

Tarkington nodded and tapped Henry, who had seen and heard the exchange and gave a curt nod, then ducked his head back inside his poncho.

It took all of Tarkington's skill and strength to keep from slipping and sliding off the edge of the ridge, but he finally made it to Staff Sergeant Flynn. Tarkington cuffed Eduardo's shoulder in admiration, the man wasn't even sweating. Eduardo grinned not understanding why the big American was so out of breath.

Sergeant Flynn leaned in and whispered. "Nunez and Cesar saw Jap boats near the beach. Looks like they're reinforcing their position."

Tarkington strained to see, but couldn't see the water, let alone the beach. "I can't see a damned thing."

Flynn shook his head, "Neither can I, but they sure as shit can. They were down the hill during the rainstorm; saw them when it cleared up."

"How many?" Tarkington asked.

Flynn held up four fingers. "That means at least another two hundred soldiers, probably more."

Tarkington had his breathing under control but gulped against a still dry throat. "What's the plan?"

"We've gotta get word back to Captain Glister. Maybe they can shell the beach before they get dug in."

Tarkington exhaled a long breath. "Sure be nice if we still had a Navy out there somewhere. A good pasting from a passing battleship would go a long way."

Flynn nodded. "Maybe Glister can notify those PT boats. At least warn them to keep an eye out." Flynn adjusted his rifle strap and continued. "Send Winkleman back up the hill with Cesar. Relay the message and get back here as quick as they can."

Tarkington frowned. "It's hard enough getting down here when it was dry; the ground's like walking on ice."

Even in the dim light put off by the stars, Tarkington could see Flynn's scowl. "Tough shit. Pass the word, Tark."

Lieutenant Kelly and the crew of PT-34 were busy. Since finding and attacking the Japanese barges the night before, every available boat was on patrol. After the attack the crew had been keyed up and unable to get any sleep. It was difficult to sleep in the stifling tropical heat on a normal day, but after the attack it was nearly impossible. Now the sailors were nearing the end of an uneventful night of patrolling and were exhausted.

They'd weathered the torrential downpour in a sheltered cove but, despite the overhanging foliage they'd tucked beneath, every sailor got soaked. When it finally subsided, they pulled from the cove and motored slowly towards home.

Lt. Kelly was having trouble keeping his eyes open as he gripped the rails. The rain squall came with moderate wind, but now it was as calm as he'd ever seen it. The China Sea's water was perfectly flat and glassy. The only wind came from the gentle three knots from the engine.

The radio crackled to life and Radioman Gutteriez jolted from his near-stupor and reached for the receiver, nearly dropping it. He finally got a handle on it and answered the call.

Lt. Kelly listened intently. The patrol had been tense, but completely uneventful. There was confusion as to where the Japanese force from the night before had gone. He'd heard reports of contact at Longo Point, as well as Anyasan Point further north, but nothing concrete.

Gutteriez, only yards away, signaled the lieutenant to come. Kelly was already moving that way and grabbed the mic and headphones with a questioning look to his radioman, who only shrugged. "This is thirty-four, six. Go ahead."

He listened to the message with growing concern. He finally nodded and signed off. "Understood. Over." He handed the set back to Gutteriez, his eyes worried. "Ensign Hayes."

Hayes was nearby watching his superior officer. "Yes sir."

"The Japs are confirmed at Longo Point. There's been a sighting of four barges offloading more Japs. Apparently, it was done during that rainstorm." He shook his head, "Must've slipped right past us." It was a sobering thought. "Bring the men to battle stations. Longo's another couple of miles south. The barges might still be south of us, but they've most likely already passed. Command wants us to hit the Japs from the sea before they have time to dig in."

Ensign Hayes's voice cracked with barely-contained excitement. "Yes, sir. Battle stations, aye."

Lieutenant Kelly watched his eager ensign do his bidding and shook his head. He'd performed well during the engagement the night before. Back at base Hayes retold every aspect of the attack until Kelly told him to shut his mouth so he could get some sleep.

Hayes hadn't slept a wink in over twenty-four hours. Kelly noticed his eyes drooping during the rainstorm, but now he was like a rejuvenated dynamo and he hoped he didn't trip and fall over the side in his enthusiasm.

Kelly increased the throttles and the sleek PT boat went onto a smooth plane, heading toward Longo Point and combat. His men pulled down their helmets and leaned into their guns, keeping sharp eyes out for enemy barges. Kelly looked at the luminescent dials on his watch. He estimated they'd get to their destination with a couple of hours of darkness left. He was glad for it. He didn't relish engaging a strong enemy force in broad daylight.

Since sending Cesar and Winkleman up the hill three hours before, Tarkington and the GIs of the 2nd squad could hear enemy activity on the beach. Tarkington leaned toward Henry. "Sound like they're getting ready for an assault to you?"

Henry shrugged. He'd pulled his poncho off and sat with his back against the tree trunk, listening. "Whatever they're doing, they don't care who hears it."

Tarkington strained to read his watch-face. "It'll be light in a couple of hours." He looked up the hill, "What's taking Wink so long?" He got as comfortable as he could and pulled his helmet over his eyes. "I'm gonna try for some sleep." Henry mumbled something unintelligible.

What seemed like an instant later, but was actually a full hour, the night exploded in sound and light. Tarkington jolted awake and rolled onto his belly, instinctively pulling his Thompson to his shoulder and aiming down the slope.

Through the trees, he could see beams of light lancing from the sea. The thumping of heavy machine guns filled the thick, muggy air. "What the hell," he stammered trying to make sense of the situation. His fuddled mind finally focused, "Attack from the sea."

Henry was on his belly with his rifle ready. He nodded, "One of them PT boats?" He glanced up, hearing a new sound. "Mortars."

The whistling sound of shells overhead made Tarkington duck his head. For a moment he thought they'd land on their position, until he saw the explosive flashes through the trees. The tracer fire from the sea combined with the mortars from the ridge lit up the night and filled the beach with flying steel. One of the mortar shells erupted high in the sky and burned brightly beneath a small white parachute. The flare turned night to day and cast crazy shadows through the jungle.

Tarkington grinned, "Guess Wink got the word out." The tracer fire from the sea continued and Tarkington could see occasional muzzle flashes through the jungle. "Looks like the PT boat's in the bay. Ballsy skipper getting that close."

The intense fire storm continued for another two minutes then stopped as though someone had hit a switch. The flare drifted lazily to ground and extinguished, bringing the world back to darkness. The fading sound of a powerful engine moving away told Tarkington that the PT boat was retreating. There were a few desperate rifle shots, mixed with yells and screams from the beach. Tarkington blew out a low whistle. "Only lasted a couple minutes, but they took a beating."

Henry nodded, "Hope so."

Light from tiny fires filtered through the jungle. Tarkington glanced at his watch. "Gonna be light soon." He pulled his feet beneath him. "I'm gonna go check in with Flynn." Henry nodded and Tarkington carefully moved up-slope.

When he found Staff Sergeant Flynn he was surprised to see Cesar and Winkleman huddled around him, speaking in hushed tones. Flynn saw Tarkington and waved him close. "You'll want to hear this, Tark."

He crouched beside them and Winkleman gave him a nod and filled him in. "Captain Glister thinks the Japs are gonna attack at first light. After yesterday, he thinks they're gonna try to sneak close rather than attempt the full-frontal, which didn't work out so well for 'em." He gave a quick grin, quickly replaced with a grim scowl. He held up a large handheld radio. "Wants us to sneak close and call in mortar rounds on concentrations." He let that sink in. "Hopes to break up their attack long enough for armor to arrive."

Tarkington scowled. "How close? It's a sheer cliff face to the beach."

Flynn pointed at the three eager Filipinos "They'll lead team two to the beach. You'll be plenty close enough and you'll have good line of sight to the ridge for the radio."

Tarkington's mouth went dry as he digested the assignment which could very well get him killed. Seconds passed as he pictured the scenario. Flynn was about to speak, but Tarkington spoke first. "I'll lead it, but I don't want the entire team. I'll take Cesar, Eduardo and Wink."

Flynn said, "You'll want the team's firepower if you're discovered."

Tarkington shook his head. "If we're discovered we'd need the entire company." He stared at Flynn, who finally nodded. "Besides, we'll have less chance of discovery with just the four of us. Two more guys won't make much of a difference in a firefight."

Flynn nodded. "Take Raker instead of Winkleman. He needs a rest." Winkleman was about to protest but Flynn cut him off. "That's an order."

Tarkington nodded, "Raker's a good scout. I'd like to leave before it gets light."

Flynn took the radio from Winkleman and handed it to Tarkington. "These things are finicky out here, but this one has new batteries and has been tested." Tarkington took it and nodded. "Good luck, Tark and don't do anything stupid."

Tarkington nodded and grinned. "I'm sitting in the dark on a knife-ridge above a beach filled with pissed-off Japs... think that ship's sailed, Sarge."

8

Tarkington felt like a bumbling fool. Compared to the Filipinos and Raker, he was having the most trouble keeping quiet. The Filipinos moved like ghosts and Raker was almost as quiet. Tarkington realized he didn't know much about Raker; just that he was from somewhere in Washington state. He was the boisterous type but always did his job. A solid soldier. Tarkington made a mental note to get to know more about him. *If I'm alive by then.*

They followed a barely-perceptible trail down the slope. The ridge wasn't as wide as where they'd spent most of the night, but it wasn't a knife-edge like the top.

Tarkington moved carefully, making sure of each step. A slip here and he'd tumble all the way to the beach. If he survived the fall - which would take a miracle - the Japanese would certainly put him out of his misery. The strain made him overheat and sweat was dripping off his nose.

Finally he saw the three men crouched and stopped. He carefully came up behind Raker and lightly touched his shoulder, signaling that he was with them. Raker gave a slight nod and continued, concentrating his attention forward.

Tarkington took in the surroundings. They'd descended at least six-hundred feet. He thought he could hear the quiet sound of waves lapping against the shoreline. It was still dark, but the starlight was enough to illuminate the beach off to the right. It still seemed far away, but he knew the darkness could play tricks. He'd have to be even quieter.

The lead Filipino, Eduardo, turned his way and in the dim light. Tarkington saw him give a thumbs-up and a broad smile. Tarkington gave a thumbs-up back. Eduardo suddenly disappeared. At first Tarkington thought he'd laid down, but when he strained to see him, he wasn't there. *What the hell?*

Cesar moved forward, then disappeared in the same spot. Raker turned to Tarkington and whispered, "Tunnel." Suddenly it all made sense. Tarkington realized he'd been holding his breath. He relaxed and stayed close to Raker's back as he moved forward.

After a few feet, Raker stopped and slung his rifle over his shoulder. He sat on his butt and dangled his legs into the black abyss of a gaping hole. He inched forward then spread his hands out and shimmied his way into the earth. He was soon out of sight.

Tarkington shook his head and muttered as he slung his Thompson, "Didn't sign up for this shit." He sat on the edge and tried to see into the hole. It was black and he couldn't see his boots, let alone the bottom.

Every fiber of his being protested, but he forced himself to push forward until he felt his right foot touch a solid piece of ground. He lowered himself, feeling the sides, and found a solid handhold. It was an old root from one of the trees that held stubbornly to the side of the cliff. His left foot found a foothold lower down and his confidence grew.

He could hear Raker's clothing rubbing against the walls, but aside from that, the tunnel was completely silent and utterly black. He wondered if there was a viper curled up down here. He wouldn't know until he felt the bite. He shook his head and scolded himself, *Knock it off Tark.*

He finally got to the bottom. He looked up but the tunnel entrance wasn't visible. There was a light breeze full of sea-smells coming from his right. He reached his hand out and felt the cold dirt of the tunnel only inches away. He skimmed his hand along toward the breeze until he found the opening which would hopefully lead him out. It was low and he had to get on his belly to fit.

He felt his back hit the top and realized there was no way he'd fit with his Thompson on his back. He felt panic welling in his chest, but he took a deep breath, closed his eyes and pushed himself back. He unslung his Thompson and went back on his belly, flattening himself with his arms extended in front. He pushed forward, machine gun first. His back scraped the top, but he felt the hole opening up as he pushed further.

Once his head cleared the initial low ceiling, the tunnel opened up a little. He lifted his helmeted head until it touched the ceiling. He breathed a sigh of relief. The first part seemed to be the lowest section. He slithered forward another twenty feet before he saw the welcome sight of Raker's face peering back at him. Raker smiled and whispered, "This is the end."

Tarkington pulled himself out of the tunnel and into the fresh air. The sound of lapping waves, insects, and the feeling of limitless space around him, was a relief. He looked back at the entrance, it was nearly invisible. Eduardo reached up and pulled a large, leafy branch hanging from above. The entrance disappeared completely and Tarkington doubted he'd be able to find it again without the Filipino's help.

Eduardo and Cesar led the GIs along the edge of the cliff, using rock outcroppings as cover, until they were thirty yards from the tunnel. They wedged themselves in among a group of boulders which looked as though they'd sloughed off the side of the cliff some time in the past millennia.

Tarkington put his back against a mossy boulder and tried to get control of his breathing. The first hint of the coming dawn lightened the sky and the stars faded as though they'd never been there. He gripped his Thompson tighter when he heard the unmistakable sound of Japanese voices.

He looked toward Eduardo, who was peering through the crack made by two boulders leaning against each other. Tarkington scooted his way across the sandy ground and Eduardo pulled back. Tarkington peered through and saw dark shapes moving everywhere. He took in a sharp breath, surprised how close they were.

At first, he didn't understand what they were doing. He watched for a tense minute, then pulled back and saw Raker staring at him. Tarkington whispered, "They're lining up bodies." Raker nodded.

Tarkington carefully pulled off his ruck and pulled out the half-moon-shaped radio. He put his back against the boulder and studied the device. He'd used them before and he'd been given another review before leaving the ambush spot, but the last thing he wanted to do was alert the Japanese with a blast of static. He made sure all the dials were correct then turned it on. He pressed the radio to his face and ear and gently pushed the send button, covering the mouthpiece with his hand. "Six in position. Over."

He pressed it hard to his ear hoping to dampen the response. He heard a slight click then a tinny voice. "One, understand. Six in position. Standing by. Over."

Tarkington's relief was plain on his face. U.S. Army radios didn't always work well in this part of the world due to the humid, tropical conditions and poor design. He hated to think their harrowing journey to this point was all for nothing.

Behind them came an unexpected sound, an engine. They turned toward the bay. Tarkington thought it was the dawn playing tricks on them until he saw the white wake of an approaching boat. The Japanese heard it at the same time and there was a flurry of excited voices. Tarkington went flat on his belly, realizing if it was the PT boat returning, they'd be caught in the crossfire. There were a few boulders behind them, but not enough to stop a full onslaught.

Raker leaned over and whispered, "Jap barge."

Tarkington nodded, seeing the outline for what it was. "They'll walk right past us."

Nobody moved as Japanese infantry from the beach trotted past their position and helped offload another forty soldiers and their gear. More soldiers shuffled by carrying their dead. Tarkington assumed they were victims of the attack earlier in the night. Everyone was flat on their stomachs, pressed as close to the base of the boulders as they could get. Tarkington had his Thompson in his right hand, ready to pull it to his shoulder if they were discovered. The only thing keeping them safe was the quickly-fading darkness. In another fifteen minutes they'd be impossible to miss.

The Japanese worked fast, running up the beach with supplies. The forty fresh soldiers sprinted up the beach and out of sight, their hushed voices fading the further away they got. The barge was still sitting there, parked on the sand with its engine idling. Tarkington willed them to push off and leave before the sun rose. As if in answer, a sailor jumped off the bow and pushed and heaved until the barge moved off the sand. The sailor running the motor increased the throttle and clunked it into gear, but instead of speeding away the engine coughed and died. There was a flurry of Japanese voices. The sailor who'd just jumped into the bow, leaped back out and held the bow. The sailor tried to restart the engine over and over but it only coughed and sputtered.

Tarkington looked at the other's faces. The light was growing every second and he could see their fear. He had to do something or they'd be discovered. He looked around for more cover, but realized any large movements would be noticed immediately and besides, there was no place to go. He pulled the radio to his ear, clicked the button and whispered, "Send HE round now. I'll adjust. Don't respond. Over."

A moment passed and he wondered if they'd left the radio unmonitored, but then he heard the faint click of acknowledgment. The moments slipped past glacially slowly before he finally heard the whistling of a mortar shell. The Japanese heard it too and there was yelling. The four sailors still on the barge looked up at the yelling and leaped into the shallow water to hunker beside the barge.

The high explosive shell landed in the center of the beach, scattering sand and shrapnel in every direction. Tarkington didn't dare turn around. He guessed the range and keyed the mic, "Add two-hundred." He heard the click and hoped he wasn't calling the next round onto his head.

There was a whistling and the next round landed in the water, sixty feet to the right of the barge. "Left seventy." Another click. The others hunkered lower, Raker pulling his helmet tight over his head.

The whistling round exploded to the left of the barge, rocking and sprinkling it with shrapnel and water. A sailor hunkered on that side was thrown into the side of the barge, then disappeared into the shallow water. "Send two more."

The remaining sailors heard the incoming rounds and abandoned their doomed boat, running away from the barge and away from Tarkington's hideout. The two rounds exploded beside it and tore the wood and steel planks from the side. The sailors dove for cover on the far side of the bay, well out of view.

Sea water fell over their position and for an instant it was as though they were caught in another tropical storm. Raker put his hand on Tarkington's shoulder and whispered, "Good thinking, Sarge."

"Let's hope they don't come searching for their man."

Eduardo lifted his head and peered through the crack, then turned and pointed up the beach. "Japs move," he uttered.

Tarkington crawled forward and looked. The Japanese were at the treeline and moving into the ravine. Just like Captain Glister figured, they weren't charging, but sneaking. Tarkington got on the radio. "Japs moving up canyon. Down five-hundred from last shot. Over."

There was another click in response and seconds later the arcing of an 81mm mortar shell. Tarkington watched it explode among the gathering troops. Men were flung sideways, their bodies lit up with the flash. "That's it. Fire for effect." More shells arced over and slammed into the sparse jungle.

Through the carnage, Tarkington saw an officer stand and raise his sword, it glowed in the morning light. He heard him scream an order and there was an immediate surge of Japanese soldiers getting to their feet and sprinting forward. Mortar shells continued to fall, shredding them, but soon the soldiers were beyond the barrage. Raker had his Springfield against his shoulder, the barrel resting in the notch of a boulder. He had the officer in his sights. He caressed the trigger, wanting to fire, but knowing it was a bad idea. He stroked the cool metal trigger, imagining himself pulling the trigger, killing the Jap officer and claiming his Samurai sword for himself. Suddenly the rifle barked and kicked into Raker's shoulder. He was as surprised as the rest of them. The bullet barely missed the officer's left shoulder, it pulped the side of a palm tree only feet in front of him.

Tarkington had just called in another adjustment when he heard the rifle shot. He glared at Raker who looked at him with wide, panicked eyes. He stammered, "I'm sorry. I - I didn't mean to...."

Bullets whizzed over their heads and caromed off the rocks with zinging ricochet sounds. Tarkington didn't know where they were coming from until Cesar pointed toward the sailors across the beach. Tarkington saw the four sailors aiming their burp guns and firing from behind a clump of rocks. Bullets slammed into the ground, spraying them with wet sand. Raker spun his rifle to the threat and fired. Tarkington saw the sailors dive for cover as the bullets showered them with rock fragments.

"We've gotta get outta here, now." He lifted his Thompson to his shoulder, aimed and fired at the cowering sailors. After a five-round burst he yelled, "Go, I'll cover you."

Eduardo and Cesar didn't need to be told twice, but Raker hesitated. "I'll stay, you…"

Tarkington cursed him, "Get the fuck outta here now!" He fired another volley and the rocks seemed to sparkle with the heavy impacts of the .45 caliber bullets. Raker lunged after the Filipinos and Tarkington dropped down, pulled a fresh magazine and swapped. Bullets smacked into the front of the rocks and Tarkington peered through the crack at the main Japanese force. Most of the attackers were out of sight, but there was a small unit of six or seven soldiers sprinting his way along the edge of the cliff, with more men behind providing covering fire. "Shit," he cursed. He poked the barrel through the gap and fired a quick ten-round burst, then got to his feet and took off after Raker.

He ran as hard as he could while remaining crouched, expecting a bullet in the back any second. He saw Raker and the Filipinos firing in both directions. He dove over the rocks they were using for cover, rolled onto his shoulder and slid into another rock which gouged his shoulder and took his breath away. He rolled to his back, gasping for air.

Raker fired through the rest of his five-rounds and reloaded. He saw Tarkington struggling on the ground and he went to his side. "You hit? Where you hit?"

Tarkington shook his head, his eyes bulging and his mouth gasping like a fish on the bottom of a boat. Finally, his breath came back and he was able to speak. "Breath. Lost my wind."

Relief flooded Raker's face and he pulled Tarkington to his knees and shoved him toward the cliff. "The tunnel's right there. Get up there quick, we'll hold 'em off." The thought of the tight tunnel wasn't nearly as scary as it had been before the bullets started flying. Tarkington was about to protest but Raker cut him off, "You're the slowest, you go first."

The words stung, but he knew his scout was right. He nodded and ran to the wall and pulled the heavy shrub aside, exposing the entrance. He didn't hesitate, but thrust into the tunnel and shimmied back and forth with his Thompson in front of him.

After being in the dawn light, the tunnel seemed even darker. He pushed forward, feeling his way, trying to remember the slight turns. He lifted his head to look behind, and his helmet clanged into the rock ceiling. "Shit," he cursed and kept pushing.

He finally pushed his way through the lowest section and when he'd squeezed through, got to his feet. He was breathing hard, filling the silent earth with his bellowing breath. There was shuffling and he felt something hit his boot. He found the first foothold and lunged upward, at the same time asking, "That you Raker?"

Eduardo answered, "Raker on beach, holding back Japs." Despite the firefight, he sounded as though he were out on a relaxing hike.

Tarkington found the handholds and footholds and continued upward steadily, until he finally saw light streaming from above. He pushed himself into the daylight and gave his surroundings a quick look. The sound of battle up the canyon and from the bottom of the cliff made him duck.

He moved to the side of the cliff and looked down. He couldn't see Raker but he could see glimpses of Japanese sailors sprinting across the wet sand with their burp guns blazing. The Japanese infantry was also too close to the cliff for him to see. He raised his Thompson and was about to fire when Eduardo popped up from the tunnel, put his hand on his shoulder and shook his head. "They see us, they kill us." He pointed up the hill and Tarkington nodded.

The cover was sparse. If they were spotted they'd be easy targets against the backdrop of the sky. He clutched where his grenades were usually attached to his harness, forgetting that he'd left them behind to lighten his load. Hurling one down the slope would be too dangerous anyway - he might hit Raker.

Cesar was the next man out of the tunnel, springing out like he'd been shot from a cannon. "Where's Raker?" Tarkington asked.

Cesar nodded and pointed into the blackness, "Close by," he said.

Several nervous seconds later, Raker's helmeted head emerged and he stepped out of the hole and quickly away from the opening. Tarkington leaned over to look but Raker pushed him back and aimed his rifle into the hole and fired. The muzzle flash lit up the hole, and he pulled his head back. "Sumbitch was right on my tail. Think I got him, but there'll be more." He leaned over again and fired the rest of his magazine into the blackness, working the bolt as quickly as his hands would move.

Tarkington pointed at the grenade dangling from Raker's harness. "Send your pineapple down there. That'll stop the hole up and kill anyone following."

Raker's eyes widened and he slung his rifle. "Can't believe I forgot about that. Good idea, Tark. I mean, Sergeant.", he corrected.

Tarkington still wasn't used to being called sergeant so didn't blame him for the slip. Tarkington leaned forward while Raker worked to release the grenade and fired two rounds then pulled back. "Hurry."

Raker finally got the line unwound from the grenade. He'd tied it down so it wouldn't move on his chest and make noise during the mission. He pulled the pin, released the lever and counted to two, then threw it down the hole hard. The GIs stepped back and held their helmets. There was a dull thump followed with the expulsion of dirt, dust and smoke from the hole. It looked like they'd triggered a mini-volcano.

They waited by the side of the hole until the smoke dissipated enough to look in without becoming asphyxiated. Tarkington held his muzzle above the abyss and leaned forward, trying to see what effect the grenade caused. He put his muzzle into the smoking, sulfurous blackness and fired. The momentary muzzle flash lit it up. "Looks at least partially caved in. They ain't getting through there any time soon."

An explosion from the ridge brought their attention back to the battle still raging in the ravine. Cesar clutched Tarkington's arm. "Jap tanks."

Tarkington grinned and shook his head. "Those are ours. The Stuarts we've been hearing about. Japs'll have a tough time getting through those." He motioned forward, "Come on, let's get back to our lines. I'm sick of having my ass hanging in the wind."

9

When they were halfway back to the ambush sight someone in front called out, "Brooklyn."

In the lead, Eduardo dropped into a crouch and Tarkington quickly put his hand to his mouth and finished the challenge phrase, "Dodgers."

Private First-Class Roscoe stepped from behind a tree and grinned. In his deep baritone voice he asked, "What took you so long? Sergeant Flynn sent us to find you, see if you're still alive."

Tarkington smiled and stepped beside him, noticing four other GIs from the 2nd squad crouched in the underbrush. "So nice to be missed." The sound of a Browning machine gun firing into the ravine made them all duck. "We had a close scrape, but no injuries. Where's the rest of the squad?"

"Flynn got orders to return to the main line but he didn't want to leave without knowing your whereabouts. He's probably nearly back by now."

Tarkington grimaced, "Why didn't they just use the radio?"

Roscoe shrugged, "Heard him talking with the messenger they sent, told Flynn they'd lost contact."

Tarkington huffed, "Lost contact...?" He pulled his ruck off and pulled out the radio. It had a clean hole on one side and shredded and torn metal on the other. He held it up and shook it, "Dammit. I don't remember that happening." Raker put his finger through the hole in the canvas ruck. "Another inch or two and we'd be hauling your body out right now."

Tarkington shook his head but pushed the close call from his mind. "Let's get outta here. Eduardo and Cesar will lead the way."

—————

When they were still a couple of hundred yards from the top of the ridge, navigating the knife-ridge section, they could see fighting going on in the ravine below. They were too far away to be in danger, but Tarkington thought it would be a good place to put an artillery observer with a radio. From this far away, the battle seemed neat and clean, but he knew it was anything but.

The Japanese had been fought to a standstill. They'd made more progress than they had the day before, but it was obvious the four Stuart tanks had stopped them dead in their tracks. There were small, smoking craters from the 37mm cannon shots. Every once in a while, one of the Stuarts, which looked like toys from here, would spout flame and smoke from their barrels and another tiny explosion would erupt among the attackers. "Japs are taking a beating," exclaimed Raker.

Tarkington nodded, "Back this far from their lines they don't have air or artillery support. Give 'em back some of what they've been dishing out to us the last coupla months."

The ridge became less sheer and angled back toward the ravine. Eduardo led them off the trail to keep them out of sight of the Japanese. It made the uphill slog slower but safer. Finally they reached the saddle of the ridge and met with friendly forces soon after.

Tarkington sent Raker and the Filipinos off to find food and water while he sought out the rest of his squad along with Roscoe and the others. He saw the back of Staff Sergeant Flynn. He was talking with Lieutenant Smoker. Tarkington came up behind them and snapped, "Sergeant Tarkington and the second squad reporting for duty, sir."

Both Flynn and Smoker turned and grinned. Smoker slapped Tarkington's back. "Good to see you, Tark. What the hell happened? You dropped off the damned world. Thought you guys had bought the farm."

Tarkington shook his head. "Radio took a round but that was the only casualty, sir."

"Sergeant, that was some damned fine work."

Smoker looked around for Raker and the Filipinos. "I sent them to find some chow and refill their water. They'll be along shortly." He shook his head and looked at his muddy boots. "I sure as hell couldn't have done it without them." He looked Smoker in the eye, "They're top notch. When the shit hit the fan, they kept their cool. It's the only way we survived, sir." He pursed his lips, nodded and gestured down the hill. "Well, it paid off. The Japs were delayed long enough to get those Stuarts in place, otherwise we woulda had a hell of a time containing them. Those tanks can put out a hell of a lot of lead. Stopped 'em cold." Tarkington could see the back-end of one of the metal beasts. It was dug into the soft dirt, angled down. White smoke wafted slowly from the barrel and indeed the entire thing seemed to glow with heat and smoke. "Their attack's stalled. I think they're finished."

Sergeant Flynn asked, "Any word on the other landings, sir?"

Smoker saw Tarkington's surprised expression. He pointed north. "They tried the same thing further north in two other spots that we know of so far. This seems to be the biggest concentration though." He shook his head, "Besides that, I haven't heard anything else."

There hadn't been a rifle shot for a while, so they all turned when they heard the bark of a Springfield. Flynn asked, "We staying here?"

Lt. Smoker nodded, "For the time being. The captain wants to clean out this section for good."

Flynn said, "You mean moving to the beach?"

Smoker nodded. "That's the only way to be sure." He slapped Flynn's shoulder, "But not yet. Get some food and rest. Your squad's beat."

Flynn and Tarkington nodded and walked back up the hill away from the festering battlefield. They met up with the rest of 2nd squad relaxing among crates of ammunition that had made the trip from Mariveles with them.

Tarkington saw Henry sitting, chewing a blade of grass and leaning against a crate labeled '81mm.' He slid in beside him and Henry moved over to accommodate him. Henry drawled, "Sounds like you caught hell last night."

Tarkington leaned his head against the crate and closed his eyes. "Yeah. Got pretty hairy."

The silence lingered as images of charging Japanese soldiers filled Tarkington's mind. It seemed like the war had been going on forever, like there'd never been anything before. He desperately wanted to sleep but knew it wouldn't happen. "Tell me about that Grandma of yours."

Henry pulled the blade of grass from his mouth and grinned. "Oma? She's a fireball. She's ninety-five, or thereabouts and can out-drink all of us...well, except Pappy."

"Tell me about that dish she makes. Jumby or Jumbo. What is it again?"

Henry shook his head in disgust, "You damn Yankees. Jam-ba-la-ya. It ain't that difficult." He leaned his head back. "I don't know what to tell you. When she's cooking...well it's like the air isn't something you breathe, but savor. I swear folks from miles away will suddenly be at our doorstep. Folks I haven't seen since the last time she cooked. That's her way though. Pappy always complains that she makes way too much, but she makes it for the whole town. She never turns anyone away, even old Freddy who's an A-1 deadbeat." He shook his head. "There was always something about Freddy and her. He's old as shit too." He gazed into the muggy distance, "When he came around she always scooped from the bottom, where all the good stuff settles, and she always had this little twinkle in her eye when she did it."

Tarkington grinned and looked at Henry with one eye opened. "Think they were doing it?"

Henry's mouth turned down and he punched Tarkington's arm, "Don't talk about my Oma like that." He shook his head, "I don't need that image in my head." He spit between his legs. "Does shit still work at that age? Doubt it."

"Sure, why not?"

Henry shook his head. "I don't wanna talk about that." He lifted his chin. "Tell me about your brother. How's he doing?"

Tarkington's grin faded as he gazed across the torn-up jungle. "Robert's a good kid." He shook his head, "Kid...guess he's not a kid anymore."

"He still at college?"

Tarkington nodded and shrugged. "Haven't heard from him since all this started, but last I heard he was. He's a junior now. He better be, or I'll kick his butt."

"He must be worried about you."

Tarkington looked up at the sky. "Hard being all the way across the world from them. It was bad enough before the Nips attacked, but at least we got mail. Now..." he shrugged, "Now they must be pulling their hair out." A long silence ensued. Tarkington leaned forward, "You think our pay's still making it to them? I mean, half my pay's going to help with his school."

Henry leaned forward and looked his friend over. "Half? You're a damned saint. You coulda saved that and gone to school yourself."

Tarkington shook his head. "Nah, I was never college material. Robert was always smarter. It was never in doubt. I mean when I was done with high school there was never any talk about me going to college. My folks saved up, but it was understood it was for Robert." Henry grunted. Tarkington's mouth turned down. "I wasn't bitter about it; the most natural thing in the world. I only joined up so I wouldn't have to buck another bale of hay... well, at least for a while."

Henry nodded. "Yeah, you ain't too smart."

Tarkington punched his shoulder. "You insubordinate asshole. I should bust you to private."

Henry shook his head slow. "You wouldn't do that. I'd never invite you to try Oma's jambalaya if you did." Henry picked up a stick and started drawing circles in the dirt. "What you think's going on back home? I mean with the war? I've got three younger brothers. Lou's old enough for the service and Willy will be next year."

Tarkington nodded and looked at his mud-caked boots. "We'll take care of these Japs before they get through boot-camp. When the reinforcements come, we'll turn these yellow bastards back and sweep them all the way back to Japan. Make Hirohito eat his damn slippers." Henry nodded, but the silence that lingered was filled with doubt.

There hadn't been a shot fired from either side for two hours. Tarkington had just dozed off when Staff Sergeant Flynn stepped in front of him and kicked his boot. Tarkington jolted, lifted his helmet off his brow and squinted up at him. Flynn went to his haunches. "The captain wants us to sweep the ravine."

Tarkington's eyes opened wider, "You mean attack?"

Flynn shrugged. More men from 2nd squad lifted their helmets and listened in. "Captain thinks there aren't too many left, if any. Wants us to sweep down there and clean out any remnants we find."

Tarkington pushed himself to his feet. "Sounds like an attack."

"Call it whatever you want, Tark, just help me get the men ready. Second squad's leading."

The men moaned but were already rolling to their feet, checking their rifles. "You heard Sergeant Flynn, let's go. Check your ammo, if you're low, get more from supply. Take a final piss or shit and form up."

Flynn pointed, "Meet over there in ten minutes and be ready to go." Ten minutes later 2nd squad, along with the rest of 1st and 2nd platoons, was milling about well back from the edge of the ravine. Lieutenant Smoker said, "Attention," and the men straightened their backs and faced Captain Glister who was sauntering their way.

"At ease." He put his fists on his hips. "Men, there's been another Jap attack along the Orion-Bagac Line. It seems to have been coordinated with this attack and, like this one, it failed. However, there was a small force that did manage to get through a gap in our lines. The gap has since been closed but there's a force of Japs dug into the jungle behind our lines that will need to be dealt with. HQ wants us to finish the Japs here then move north to help eliminate the pockets of enemies that got through. Once done, we'll join the main line of defense." He gestured into the ravine. "We haven't seen or heard any of the enemy for over two hours. The Japs are either all dead, out of ammo, or too tired and injured to be much of a threat, but we have to make sure. The mission's simple. First and second platoons will sweep the ravine all the way to the ocean, killing or capturing whatever enemies you may find." He lifted his chin and looked down his patrician nose. "It's my belief you won't find much resistance, but be careful. They *are*

Japs after all." Lieutenant Govang and Smoker, the two officers snapped to attention. "Get it done."

In unison they said, "Yes sir."

Glister turned and walked back toward the hastily set up tent that was HQ. Lieutenant Smoker barked out orders and 1st platoon split up into squads and spread out. 2nd platoon, led by Lt. Govang spread out behind them.

Tarkington made sure 2nd team had plenty of space between each soldier and when Sergeant Flynn waved his hand forward, he took his first step into the ravine. Two of the Stuart tanks were behind them, but the two forward tanks were still twenty yards ahead. He admired their hulking metal shapes as he walked by, wishing they could roll forward with them. He passed GIs in their foxholes who nodded and grinned and wished them luck in low, hissing voices.

Tarkington made sure his Thompson's safety was off, ready for instant action. He didn't see an enemy body for another twenty yards, then he saw several. The ground sloped downward steeply in sections and there were many downed trees and churned-up ground to maneuver through. He stepped over a downed palm and leveled his sub-machine gun at a group of enemy soldiers tangled together as if they were spaghetti. He couldn't tell where one stopped and the other began. He guessed they were victims of one of the Stuarts 37mm cannon.

He kept his muzzle leveled as he passed them, but it was obvious they weren't playing possum. He stepped into a still-smoking crater and looked to either side. The GIs were keeping pace, their rifles leveled and their eyes open for trouble. More bodies; victims of machine gun fire and mortar shells. The stagnant air was already starting to take on a sour smell and the incessant buzzing of flies filled the air.

He heard a GI from his left call out, "Got a live one over here." It was PFC Stollman, the BAR man. "We helping these guys or putting them out of their misery?"

Tarkington pursed his lips. It was a good question. There'd been plenty of gruesome stories depicting Japanese brutality. Tarkington hadn't seen it personally but an entire squad from 4th platoon had been wiped out and when Hotel Company took back the contested ground the following day, they found the squad hacked and mutilated with their genitals cut off and jammed into their dead mouths. He heard Staff Sergeant Flynn call out, "Medic." *Guess that answers that,* thought Tarkington. "Keep moving forward."

Tarkington looked to his right and saw Henry chewing another blade of grass and sweeping his rifle side to side. He caught Tarkington's look and shook his head.

The unmistakable sound of a screaming Japanese soldier pierced the muggy air. Tarkington looked to his left in time to see the wounded Japanese soldier pull something from behind his back and hold it up. Time stood still as both Staff Sergeant Flynn and Stollman stared in frozen horror. Flynn snapped into action and flung himself into the wounded soldier. His body collided at the same instant the grenade exploded. Flynn's upper body simply liquefied and became one with the Japanese soldier's, leaving two sets of legs and nothing else.

There was a grim silence, then a yell of pain and anguish spewed from Stollman like something from another world. Tarkington yelled, "Stay put, keep watch for Japs." He sprinted to the scene and pulled up short, seeing the grisly results of the grenade. He fought down vomit, forcing himself to swallow the acidic spew. He ran past the carnage and slid in beside Stollman, who was writhing on the ground, clutching his ears and still screaming.

He gripped his shoulder and pinned him to the ground searching for the wound that must be there. "Stolly, Stolly. Where you hit? Where you hit, dammit?" The BAR loader, PFC Vick slid in next to him. "Hold him down."

Vick was much smaller than Stollman, but strong, with wiry, rope-like muscle. He grabbed Stollman's legs and kept them from thrashing. Finally Tarkington got the BAR man's attention by yelling in his face, "Stolly!" Stollman opened his eyes and released the grip on his ears. He looked around like waking from a nightmare. When he saw what was left of Flynn's body, his eyes turned wet and glassy and he reached out for him. He blubbered, "Flynn, Sergeant Flynn. Oh my God, Flynn." Tarkington saw the eyes change from wretched sadness to all consuming rage in a flash. "Cock-sucking-motherfucking-son-of-a-bitch!"

Tarkington held him down as he tried to lunge and attack what was left of the enemy soldier. "Calm down, calm down." He shook him and made him focus on his eyes. "Are you hit?"

Stollman hesitated, taking stock of his body. He shook his head, "Ears are ringing bad." He felt his torso and his groin, "I'm, I'm not hit. S - Sergeant Flynn saved...he saved me. Oh my God."

Tarkington released him and he put his head into his hands and cried. His shoulders shook in convulsions of grief. Vick sat beside him and put his arm around his shoulder, looking up at Tarkington with sad eyes.

Lieutenant Smoker stepped from behind a tree and crouched, taking in the scene. PFC Skinner, a rifleman, was beside him. He took one look at the pair of smoking, bloody legs and lunged forward and lost his lunch. Smoker stepped around him and crouched beside Tarkington. "Flynn?" He asked. Tarkington nodded. Smoker shook his head and cursed. He put his hand to his mouth to maximize his voice. "From now on, no prisoners. Understand? If you come across a wounded Jap, or even one you think might be playing possum, shoot him or stick him. Don't take chances." There was a smattering of acknowledgment. "Vick, take the BAR. I'll have someone take Flynn and Stollman back up the ridge."

Stollman's snapped his head up. He wiped his eyes and his face turned to stone. "Sir, I'm okay. I can fight."

Smoker nodded and pursed his lips, "Okay. Okay." He stood and waved them forward, "Move out."

As they advanced deeper into the ravine, and came across more bodies, shots rang out as GIs made sure. Tarkington could feel the difference in the men. He could feel their anger. Their contempt for the Japanese was palpable.

Soon they were at the bottom of the ravine and at the edge of the beach. Lieutenant Smoker held up his hand and the GIs stopped and crouched. The beach was full of mortar craters and boot prints. The barge was still beached, the boat's right side holed from the near miss of the 81mm mortar shells. Tarkington strained to see where he and his men had been and thought he could see the rocks they'd used for cover. He noticed the neatly lined-up bodies, covered with canvas shrouds, that he'd seen in the first rays of dawn. That seemed like a million years ago, but had only been a few hours.

Smoker caught his eye and waved his arm forward, signaling he wanted his squad to advance while the rest of them covered. Tarkington nodded and signaled 2nd squad to advance. He stepped from the jungle and into the wide-open beach. He had his Thompson's safety off and felt completely exposed. The rest of the squad spread out and moved down the beach steadily.

When they were halfway to the water's edge, Tarkington saw movement on the barge. He threw himself onto his stomach at the same time yelling, "Cover! Barge!"

He put the stock of the Thompson to his shoulder and saw three enemy heads poking above the front of the barge, then he saw the smoke and flash of their burp guns. The air snapped with bullets. He fired; walking his heavy slugs into the barge. Vick opened up with the BAR and the rest of the squad unleashed everything they had. The barge splintered and shredded and sparked. The sea water spouted in great geysers, wetting the boat and making it glisten in the midday sun.

Tarkington didn't see any more enemy heads and the enemy fire had stopped. He quickly reloaded and peered over his smoking barrel. "Cease fire. Cease fire!" Most of them had burned through their clips and he could hear them working to reload. "Raker, Winkleman, with me." He got to his feet, "Rest of you cover us."

He took careful steps, his Thompson at his shoulder, still aimed at the shredded barge. Raker was to his right, Winkleman to his left. At first, they walked, but as they closed they trotted. The gentle lapping of the sea was the only sound. They crouched in front of the barge and Tarkington could smell the shredded wood, it reminded him of a sawmill. There was no sound coming from the barge. He held up his right hand with three fingers extended. He counted down. When his hand was in a fist, they all sprang forward and lunged over the gunwales. Tarkington was first over the side. He saw gray uniforms and blood. He fired into the mass, and their bodies shuddered but they were already dead.

He hopped out of the boat, letting the sea clean his bloody boots. He signaled the all-clear and the rest of the squad rose up from the sand. Beyond them the rest of the GIs stepped from the jungle. He addressed Raker, "These were the sailors we tangled with this morning." Raker nodded, "Yep, think so."

Winkleman jumped from the barge holding his rifle in one hand and a burp gun in the other. "This one's still in good shape." He slung it over his shoulder. "Good for close-in stuff."

Tarkington moved off to the left. "Raker, let's check out the tunnel." Raker nodded and followed with Winkleman close behind.

Tarkington wrapped his sling around his forearm and aimed at the boulders they'd used for cover that morning. It looked completely different from this angle and he wondered if he were in the right spot. Raker pointed, "Entrance is over there." He angled right and, sure enough, Tarkington saw the bushy tree branch hiding the entrance. Raker slowed, leveling his rifle.

Tarkington put his Thompson to his shoulder and crouched, covering him. Winkleman did the same with his newfound burp gun. Raker moved to the entrance and pulled back the branch, keeping his rifle leveled with one hand. He crouched and peered forward. Tarkington tensed, ready to fire at the first sign of trouble, but Raker relaxed, stood and turned back to him holding his nose. "Damn smorgasbord gone bad in there." He let the branch fall back into place and stepped away. "Best leave them be. That grenade really did a number on 'em."

10

After clearing the ravine and beach, 1st and 2nd platoons were back on top of the ridge. It had been a successful mission - the Japanese force destroyed to the last man - but it felt hollow. 2nd squad formed a circle around what was left of their squad leader's body. Someone had found his helmet and rifle and laid it on top of the remains to keep the wind from pulling back the shroud.

Lieutenant Smoker approached and stood beside Tarkington. "He was a good man. A good soldier and leader." Tarkington nodded. "He'll be missed." A breeze came up from the ravine bringing with it the smell of decay and rot. The 3rd and 4th platoons were in the process of hauling the dead Japanese to the beach for a mass burial. Smoker put his hand on Tarkington's shoulder. "Need a private word with you, Sergeant."

Tarkington tore his eyes from the poncho, "Yes sir." He left the circle, following Lt. Smoker to a fallen palm tree. Smoker sat and indicated he should too. Smoker pulled out two cigarettes and handed one to Tarkington. He pulled a well-used Zippo lighter from his pants pocket and struck it to flame, holding it out for Tarkington. Tarkington took a long drag and let it seep out his mouth and nose. Smoker did the same feeling the nicotine course through his brain. "With Flynn gone I need someone to take over the role of squad leader. I know you're a freshly-minted sergeant, but I need you to step up and lead the men. Are you up for that?"

Tarkington looked stunned, but nodded. "Yes, sir. I guess I have to be."

"I've watched you, you're ready. The men respect you and will follow you and that's really what matters." He scowled. "It's not like I have a lot of reserve NCOs lying around."

Tarkington nodded, "Yes sir."

"Any ideas on who to pull up to assistant squad leader?"

Tarkington pursed his lips and looked at the passing clouds, then refocused on the ground. He nodded. "Henry's a good man, but I'd rather have him in second position as a scout with Raker, and move Winkleman to assistant squad leader."

Smoker considered and, after a brief pause, nodded. "Hadn't thought about Winkleman. He's the lead scout, but I can see him switching roles. Good choice. Henry'll be good at scout; he can smell trouble coming a mile away."

"Yes, and he moves well too. He's too quiet for a lead position and would probably resent it if he were put there. He'll be a good counter to Raker at the scout position."

Smoker stood, "Done." Tarkington stood and Smoker held out his calloused hand. Tarkington took it and they shook. "We'll be moving up toward the line in an hour or so. Get the men ready, Staff Sergeant."

Tarkington shook his head, not believing the new title. "Shitty way to get promoted, sir." Smoker scowled and walked off.

The main road along the west coast of Luzon was choked with civilians moving south. Hotel Company was moving north, being forced to march along the edges in single file to avoid the various carts and bicycles.

Since MacArthur instigated Operation Orange in January, the fallback to the Bataan Peninsula, there'd been a constant flow of refugees moving with the GIs and Filipino Army units, but the flow had nearly come to a stop after the initial panic of the first month. Now the roads were choked again, as the civilians saw and heard the fighting in the south.

Tarkington didn't care about the reasons, only the fact that the extra people on the road made it harder for his men to move.

Finally, after a frustrating day of marching, Hotel Company moved off the road and settled in for the evening in a meadow. The men were exhausted. Lieutenant Smoker barked at his NCOs, "Get the men settled. We're bivouacking here for the night."

Tarkington was as tired as any of them but, as squad leader, couldn't show it. "All right, this is it for the night. Spread out, dig a hole and get some grub. You know the drill." The GIs of 2nd squad grumbled and moved off to find their little slices of paradise. The newly-minted Buck Sergeant Winkleman stepped up beside him. Tarkington asked, "How's it feel to lead, Sergeant?"

Winkleman took his helmet off, wiped the sweat from his brow and ran his hand through his thinning hair. "Haven't had to do much yet. Just march and keep them from falling over with exhaustion."

"Make sure they drink. It's easy to get dehydrated out here." They watched a GI suddenly break off from the group and dash off into the jungle, struggling to unbutton his pants. "Looks like Crown's got the shits."

Winkleman nodded. "Everyone's got the shits. You telling me you don't?"

Tarkington shook his head, "No. Shit at least three times a day and it's not what I would call quality."

Winkleman smiled, "If you're saying it's runny, that's an understatement. Three times is nothing. I've seen Crown dash off the road at least four times today."

Tarkington turned serious. "Even more reason to keep 'em hydrated." Winkleman nodded and Tarkington continued. "I remember when I first got off the boat over a year ago. I was so excited, I tried all the local exotic food. That first month was miserable. Never left the latrines and I thought my ass would burst into flame sometimes. My body adjusted, as did everyone's, but now it's as if we're new here again. Not sure why."

Winkleman scowled, "Think the Japs poisoned the water down here?"

Tarkington guffawed and shook his head. "They're devious, but I don't think they're *that* devious." He looked at the sky and saw plumes of clouds building. "Looks like we'll be in for another drenching. Have the men be sure to build drainage into their holes. Let's get them hurried up so we're not eating in the rain."

Winkleman nodded and moved off to hurry them up. Tarkington went looking for the command area. At the far end of the field he saw the company vehicles under camouflage netting. He adjusted his Thompson on his shoulder and walked across the field, nodding to GIs digging holes and eating C-rations. They looked exhausted but, after the victory at the ravine, were in good spirits.

His chest swelled with pride. He hadn't been an NCO for more than a week, but he felt like they were *his* men. They'd been battered and beaten over the last few months but they were still upbeat and confident. It was a testament to their training and their grit. *When we finally get reinforced, the Japs'll wish they'd never heard of Luzon.*

At the trucks, he saw the hastily-erected tent which was the company's HQ for the night. He ducked inside and the smell of mold and canvas wasn't unpleasant. There was a cluster of officers and a few other NCOs milling about. He noticed Lieutenant Smoker and strode up to him. Without looking at him, Smoker asked, "How are the men?"

"Getting settled, sir. Looks like it's going to rain on us again tonight."

Smoker nodded, "Yep. Wish we coulda found a place with cover, but the men'll have to make do."

"Yes sir. They're used to that."

"Captain Glister thinks this might be more than just an overnight bivouac. Looks like we'll be staying here at least a full day. The men can use a rest."

Tarkington nodded, "Yes sir. I agree. Any word on those other beach landings?"

Smoker shook his head, "Only that there were some. I do know they haven't broken out anywhere. If they had we'd be called to help since we're the only regular infantry unit in the area." Tarkington nodded. Lieutenant Smoker turned when his name was called. He waved to another officer then turned back to Tarkington. "You be sure to get some rest too. I need you at your best." He looked at Tarkington's sleeve. "You'll have to wait on your stripes."

Tarkington shrugged, "It's not important sir." He turned to the tent flap and strode into the daylight. The day was darkening quickly. Evening was coming, but the fluffy clouds from earlier had grown and taken on a darker, more sinister aspect. He shook his head and hustled back toward 2nd squad hoping to get settled and get some food before the deluge began.

The sun rose and ended what had been the longest night of Tarkington's life. The rain had come in waves and lasted for two hours, then slacked off, stopped completely, then continued for another two hours.

Foxholes quickly filled with water, despite the best efforts to build drainage. The GIs resorted to bailing the water with their helmets, like they were trying to keep a boat with many holes afloat. It was exhausting and even those lucky enough to have gotten their ponchos secured over their holes had to stay awake and make sure it stayed in place.

Tarkington shared a hole with Henry. While he'd been talking with Lt. Smoker the evening before, Henry had dug a wide hole and staked ponchos out with rope. It worked well to keep the water from flooding them directly but the rivulets of water running over the ground were impossible to keep out and soon they had six inches of standing water, making it impossible to lay down and sleep. Tarkington thought he might have fallen asleep on his feet for a couple of minutes, but he wasn't even sure about that. He just knew he felt like shit. He hadn't slept much the night before either - none of the men had.

PFC Holiday poked his head beneath the poncho. "You in here Sarge?"

Tarkington nodded and growled, "Yeah. What is it Holiday?" Holiday smiled and thrust a coffee pot in his face. "Holy shit, you're a saint." He fumbled in his sopping pack and pulled out a beat-up steel cup. He wiped the grit from the bottom and held it out. Holiday carefully filled his cup and it steamed, warming Tarkington's face. He savored his first sip. It tasted like nectar from the gods. Henry went for his pack, but Holiday shook his head, "Have to share. Not enough for everybody."

Tarkington passed the steaming cup to Henry who smelled it and sipped. He shook his head and handed it back. "You're a magician Holiday."

"Don't you mean a voodoo doctor or something, Cajun?" He pulled back taking the coffee pot with him. "More mouths to feed."

Tarkington took another sip and handed it to Henry. "I've gotta check on the men. Hold this for me while I try to get out of this cesspool." He poked his head out, "It finally stopped raining."

"Course it has. Had to clear up to allow the heat of the day to cook us."

Tarkington noted the edge in Henry's voice. He'd been with him a long time and he knew it took a lot to affect his mood negatively. He was the most even-keeled person he'd ever met. If he was losing it, God only knew how the other men were faring. He crawled from the hole and got to his feet. His boots sank in the mud as he stretched his back. Henry poked his head out and tried to hand him the coffee cup. Tarkington shook his head, "Finish it."

The meadow had become a quagmire during the night. None of his squad had been slated for guard duty, but he doubted anyone had got any sleep. "Jesus, what a mess," he muttered.

Rather than disturb the men, he made his way back to the HQ tent. Every step, his boots sank into the ground and accumulated piles of sticky mud. Soon it felt as though he was carrying ten extra pounds of muck. By the time he got to the tent, he was out of breath and sweating. *What a lovely place.*

Entering the tent was like entering a different world; a dry one. Cots had been put out and the officers of Hotel Company were just rousting themselves, looking wholly rested. He looked down at his uniform, it was dripping wet, his boots leaving great clods of mud. He stopped, thinking he shouldn't muddy the place up. He felt like he'd entered the farmhouse back home that his mother worked so hard to keep clean.

Lieutenant Govang saw him in the doorway. "Jesus, Sergeant. You fall in a mud-hole or something?"

Tarkington's first impulse was to leave and not dirty anything else, like he was being scolded by his mother. That quickly passed as anger flushed his face bright red. His jaw rippled as he ground his teeth together. His men had suffered all night while they'd slept warm and dry on cots. He was beyond sleep-deprived and his fuse was short. "No, sir." He barked, too loudly. "The entire field's a mud-hole. We've been standing in it all goddamned night...sir."

The outburst brought every officer's eyes up. Tarkington opened and closed his fists, trying to get control of the emotions just beneath the surface.

Lieutenant Smoker got to his feet and walked quickly to his newly-minted Staff Sergeant. "Sergeant Tarkington, glad you're here," he said loudly. He put his hand on his shoulder and turned him back toward the door. He could feel Tarkington's tense, corded muscles. He leaned forward and spoke softly so only he could hear. "Take it easy, soldier, before you do something stupid." He went to the tent flap and stepped into the morning light, still guiding Tarkington. As soon as he stepped outside, his boot sank into the mud up to his ankle. He looked down then up at the sodden field. Soaked, miserable GIs dotted the field, moving like zombies. "Jesus," he whispered. "I had no idea it rained that much. We've gotta get the men back to the road, find somewhere to dry out." He slapped Tarkington's shoulder. "Get 'em up. I'll talk to Captain Glister."

Two hours later, they were marching north along the road. The mud and grime had dried and flaked off their faded uniforms like crusty old skin. The column moved slow. Tarkington wanted to find a dry place and lay down. He knew he wasn't alone, but he kept the tired despair he felt inside off his face. He needed to stay upbeat for the men, who were at their wits end, especially the GIs of 2nd squad who hadn't had a good night's sleep since Mariveles. He concentrated on putting one foot in front of the other - that was all he could do.

They walked for an hour before they caught up to their trucks which were pulled to the side of the road. There was still a steady flow of refugees, but they weren't as thick as they'd been the day before. At the trucks, officers were directing the men toward a trail leading west. Most of them didn't notice, just followed the directions given until they found themselves on a pristine beach facing a placid China Sea.

The company spread out, filling the beach and looking around with confused expressions. Tarkington gazed out to sea. *Getting a boat ride?* His fuzzy mind asked. "What the fuck is this?" drawled Henry.

Captain Glister's booming voice answered the question. "I want every soldier stripped naked and bathed along with your clothes. When you're done doing that, the locals cooked up some fine hot chow." He pointed toward the jungle. There was a group of Filipinos waving hello and grinning broadly. They labored over smoking fires and the smell of cooking fish filled the air. "Then find a good spot and rack out. We march again in five hours." There was a roar of approval. The exhaustion fell from their shoulders and they stripped naked in a matter of seconds and trotted into the sea, turning the water muddy.

Tarkington's smile grew until he felt his face would burst. He saw Lieutenant Smoker, twenty yards off, grinning and nodding. All thoughts he'd had of killing the officers in slow, agonizing ways left his mind. He gave Smoker an exaggerated salute, stripped naked and joined the men.

11

With the men's morale restored, the remainder of the march north went smoother and faster. The closer they got to the Orion-Bagac line, the fewer refugees they encountered, making their progress even faster.

The company halted and the officers and NCOs were called forward. Tarkington and Winkleman stood in a small church outbuilding. There was a quiet hum of chatter until Captain Glister entered and someone called out, "Atten-chun!" The chatter instantly stopped and the men braced and straightened their ranks.

Captain Glister looked concerned. "Stand at ease." He cleared his throat and looked them over, then nodded. "Here's the situation. The Jap landings on the beaches south were a disaster for them. The few prisoners we captured told us the landings didn't go as planned. They were poorly coordinated and most hit the wrong beaches. You can thank the PT boats for most of that. However, the thrust at the Orion-Bagac Line, which happened at the same time, was partially successful. At least one regiment of Japanese broke through at a weak point on the western portion of I corps and pushed into the Tuol River Valley. It appears they split into two different forces. The Filipino First Regular Division has surrounded them and essentially cut them off, but they still pose a threat, and take men and material away from the front-line." He paused and looked at the assembled men, who hung on every word. "The Filipinos have asked for help and we've been volunteered."

There was a hum of grumbling. Winkleman leaned toward Tarkington and whispered, "We the only unit left or something?"

Tarkington ignored him as Glister continued. "We'll be in support, just watching the rear, plugging any holes the Japs might try to slip through. Able and Charlie will also be involved, but this'll mostly be a Filipino action. As we've all seen, they're more than capable. We'll stay here tonight, then move out in the morning. That is all. Dismissed."

After a good night's sleep Tarkington woke feeling better than he had in days. There was a hot breakfast of eggs, toast and coffee. There was no talking as the men shoveled food in as if it were their last meal.

As they left the tiny town, the feeling was almost happy. It was 1st platoon's turn to ride the trucks. Tarkington grinned at the bad jokes the men were telling. There was raucous laughter - something he hadn't heard from them since before December 8th. Morale was high. They'd defeated the Japanese thrust at the beaches and doled out real damage. They were moving north instead of retreating south, and even though the newly established Orion-Bagac line was a fallback position, it felt like they were advancing for once. They felt like US Army soldiers again: proud and deadly.

The trucks pulled off the paved road and took a heavily pockmarked dirt road through the jungle. They climbed, taking treacherous hairpin switchbacks that quieted the men. Tarkington was near the tailgate and could see how close the drivers were getting to the sloped edges. It wasn't sheer, but the trucks would definitely tip if they went off the edge. He was ready to bail out at the first hint of trouble.

Finally the road crested the hill and the trucks spread out on a lush plateau and stopped. The men were ordered to dismount. Tarkington didn't like the openness. He immediately searched the sky for enemy planes. The trucks and troops would be an irresistible target for the roving planes of the Imperial Japanese Army Air Force. He felt better when he saw the bristling barrels of multiple 20mm anti-aircraft guns pointing skyward, manned by diligent Filipino troops.

Despite the defenses, he wanted the men out of the field as soon as possible. He saw Lt. Smoker stretching his back. He'd been riding in the second truck's cab. Tarkington ordered, "Assemble the men, I'm gonna talk with Lieutenant Smoker." Winkleman nodded and called 2nd squad to him.

Smoker saw Tarkington coming and waved. He unfolded a map and spread it over the hood of the truck. His brow dripped sweat, splashed onto the paper and immediately evaporated. By the time Tarkington got there, he was folding the map back up. He pointed at the sloping hill a half mile away. It rose up from a ravine full of dense jungle. "That ravine over there's the Tuol river. Far as I can tell the Japs are beyond it, dug into that hill. Looks like they can see every little thing we do." Tarkington nodded and scanned the sky again. Smoker noticed and nodded. "I know. We're exposed. Get your squad to the trees over there, see if it's good ground for the trucks."

Tarkington nodded, careful not to salute for fear of Japanese snipers. He trotted back to 2nd squad. "Let's move to the trees, double time." He trotted off, leading the men the two-hundred yards. It felt good to shake the stiffness from his legs and by the time he got to the cover he was breathing hard and sweating. After sitting for most of the day, it was invigorating.

His senses peaked, searching for some sign of the enemy in the jungle. He waved, getting Henry's attention. He signaled him forward and his new scout nodded and moved. Henry went out of sight but soon reappeared and gave Tarkington a thumbs up.

Tarkington stood. "Move into cover and set up a perimeter." He searched for his other scout. "Raker, run back and tell Lieutenant Smoker to send the trucks. The ground's solid and there's room for the trucks between the trees." Raker nodded and hustled off.

Soon the trucks, along with the rest of 1st platoon, were spread out among the cover of the trees. An hour later, the rest of the company arrived on foot. They didn't look as chipper as they had at breakfast, but they looked far better than they had a day ago. Their perimeter expanded and soon the entire area was filled with tents, foxholes and slit trenches. A mess hall was erected complete with long wooden tables provided by local Filipinos.

Once the men were settled, Tarkington found a shady spot, sat and put his back against a perfect back-shaped Palm tree. He tilted his helmet forward and closed his eyes. A minute later he was jolted awake by someone's presence. He lifted his helmet and peered up seeing three familiar faces. He smiled, "What are you guys doing up here?"

Eduardo's grin went ear to ear, "We followed the caravan. We want to do more."

"Do more? You've already done enough. You're not military. You should be back with your families."

Eduardo, who seemed to be their chosen spokesman shook his head, "We have no one. Our families caught on wrong side. We haven't heard from them since December." He said it as the most matter-of-fact thing in the world.

Tarkington scowled. "I'm really sorry to hear that. I had no idea. I thought you were Mariveles locals this whole time."

Eduardo shrugged. "We grew up there, but settled east, close to Manila. When Japs come we were visiting home." He shook his head, "Family in Manila." He smiled. "We find them when US send help. Take back Luzon."

Tarkington nodded, wondering for the thousandth time when that help would arrive. He got to his feet and looked them over. Their clothing, though torn in places looked clean. Thin shirts hung on their wiry frames as if on hangers in a closet. Each had a Springfield rifle. Though the wooden components were battered, chipped and dark with age and sweat, the metal gleamed without a hint of rust or corrosion. The rifles were nearly as long as they were.

Tarkington decided, "Stay here. I can't guarantee anything, but I'll talk to the Lieutenant, see if I can get you guys attached to my squad."

Nunez, the most diminutive of the three smiled and handed him something dark and shriveled. Tarkington put his hand out palm up and Nunez dropped it into his palm, "Show him this. We kill Japs."

When Tarkington realized it was a shriveled human ear, he nearly dropped it, but instead shook his head and pushed his hand back toward Nunez. "Take it. He already knows you're good soldiers." Nunez shrugged and took the ear back, stuffing it into a pouch which looked to have more ears within.

As the day waned, Hotel Company continued to settle into their new home. The plateau overlooking the Tuol river was a beautiful place. Filipino First Regular Division soldiers manned the anti-aircraft guns dotting the edges of the plateau. There was a full company on the other side of the plateau. Now that Hotel Company was in place and ready in support, the company of Filipinos planned to move against the dug-in Japanese.

It was late in the day and they were formed up facing the river valley when the unmistakable sound of incoming artillery fire made everyone dive and scramble for cover. Tarkington dove into a slit trench. The first few shells landed in the center of the plateau and shook the ground. The second volley landed further north and continued marching toward the Filipino position.

When it was obvious the Filipinos were the target, Tarkington raised his helmeted head and watched as the shells erupted in the jungle. Trees uprooted and flashes of fire winked through the dimness. A secondary explosion rolled over the plateau as a cache of ammo blew up.

Five minutes later the barrage stopped, leaving behind swaying trees and raining dirt and rocks. Winkleman poked his head up beside Tarkington's. "Jesus, that was accurate fire."

Tarkington nodded, "I was thinking the same thing. There must be a spotter nearby. That artillery came from the front lines - no way they could get that lucky."

"Jap radios go that far?"

Tarkington shrugged, "Good question. Seems unlikely they strung commo wire all the way." There was yelling coming from the Filipino position and dark shapes darted back and forth. He pointed, "Glister's sending our medics in to help." He held his breath, hoping the movement wouldn't draw more fire. "Poor bastards took a beating."

They pulled themselves out of the slit trench and Tarkington walked through, checking on the squad. He found Lt. Smoker inside a sweltering tent sipping water and looking over a map. Platoon Sergeant McLunty was beside him chewing his ever-present stogie. McLunty saw Tarkington enter and stood up straight. "How are the men, Tarkington?" Lt. Smoker looked up from the map, a stern look on his face.

"Fine. How are the Filipinos after that pasting?"

Lieutenant Smoker answered. "Actually, their officers took a chance and rushed into the river valley when those first shells landed. They were out of the impact zone. Half the twenty-millimeter stockpile went up in smoke, but there were only a few minor injuries. If the Japs were waiting in the valley, it could've been a massacre, but the gamble paid off."

"That's good news."

Smoker motioned him to join him at the map table. Platoon Sergeant McLunty moved his broad frame to the side, allowing a spot for Tarkington. Smoker placed his finger, "This is our little slice of heaven. The Japs are on this hill, as far as we know. The Filipinos are moving to contact. We'll have a much better idea of exactly where the Nips are soon enough. Our job's support. If the Filipinos get in over their heads we're their reserve. Glister wants two platoons on short standby while the others relax, then they'll rotate the next day." He looked up at Tarkington. "We're on tonight, so have your squad ready to go at a moment's notice. I'll pass the word to Lieutenant Govang."

Tarkington nodded, and stiffened. "Yes sir."

He nodded to McLunty who nodded back, then asked, "How're those Filipino civilians? They seem like good men to you?"

Tarkington could tell McLunty didn't trust them. "They were helpful during the last battle. They kept their heads when the bullets were flying. They saved Raker's ass, and mine."

McLunty grunted. "Keep your eye on 'em. They're not GIs. Keep 'em out of the way."

Tarkington looked at Lt. Smoker who was concentrating on the map. He'd been the one to okay the Filipinos attaching to 2nd squad. McLunty had been against it and Tarkington could feel the tension it had created.

Tarkington nodded and stepped from the tent. He felt he'd stepped from a sauna. It was hot outside, but at least the occasional breeze made it tolerable. He thought about McLunty's comment and decided to ignore it. He'd seen the Filipinos in action and knew he could trust their resolve.

The night was quiet until 2200. Tarkington was sleeping against his favorite palm tree, dreaming of a girl he'd gotten to third base with his senior year in high school. His eyes popped open when the dream girl's face turned to a screaming Japanese soldier. He jolted forward and realized he was hearing distant gunfire. It was coming from the hill across the river. He rubbed the sleep from his crusty eyes and peered into the darkness. He could see flashes a quarter of the way up the hill.

He got to his feet and stretched the stiffness from his back. He moved closer to the edge of the field and crouched. The flashes of battle were much more visible. There was nothing to do but watch and hope the Filipinos could handle whatever they'd gotten into. The last thing he wanted to do was lead his squad into the jungle at night. He moved to the edge of the slit trench and sat on the edge, dangling his feet, watching the light show. There was the soft sound of snoring coming from the darkness.

He knew his night wouldn't involve any more sleeping. He got to his feet and carefully moved behind the line of foxholes manned by two GIs: one awake, one asleep. Normally movement at night in a war zone was a good way to get shot, but this wasn't the front lines. Indeed, most of the GIs were sacked out in hammocks strung from palm trees, not foxholes. Still, he made sure he made enough noise to not be mistaken for a sneaking Japanese soldier.

When he neared one of the furthest foxholes he heard Stollman's challenge: "Babe."

"Ruth," he replied.

"That you Tark?"

Tarkington grinned. Stollman was the only GI who didn't address him as Sergeant. For some reason, it was okay - natural. He never corrected the burly, long haired red-head. "Yeah, it's me Stolly." He sat on the back edge of the hole. Stollman had his bi-pod spread and his BAR aimed across the field toward the flashes of combat. "How's it going over here?" He whispered, trying not to wake the assistant gunner, PFC Vick.

"Sounds like those Filipino boys found the Japs," Stollman whispered back. "Think we'll get called out there to help?"

"I sure hope not. At least not till it's light out." The distant firefight took on another level of intensity. There were more flashes and thumping sounds of mortar fire. "This is sounding more than just a simple skirmish. They're in full contact."

"Our guys got mortars?"

Tarkington shook his head, "Not that I know of. I didn't think those Nips did either."

"Guess you were mistaken." He paused, "Could be those damned knee mortars they're so fond of."

Tarkington nodded but thought they sounded more like regular tube mortars. He stayed on the edge of the hole silently watching the light show. After fifteen minutes the volume of fire decreased, but didn't stop.

The mortars stopped but the chatter of Japanese machine guns continued. Tarkington sighed and shook his head. He got to his feet but stayed crouched. "They're pinned down up there. I'll bet my bottom dollar we'll be moving out in support soon."

Stollman nodded. "Think you're probably right." He patted his BAR. "Not looking forward to humping Bertha up that hill."

Tarkington grinned, "This is what you signed up for, Stolly."

He shook his head, "I signed up for adventure and pussy, not hauling unwieldy machine guns through the jungle."

"Pussy? You thought you'd get laid if you joined the Army? I'm worried about you, need to get you in for a psych eval."

"You ever seen me in my dress uniform? I'm dashingly irresistible."

"Your mother tell you that? I've seen you in your dress uniform..."

"Shit, you're just jealous, Tark. Sign of a weak mind."

Tarkington knew he wasn't going to get the last word in no matter what, so he moved off without replying. He heard another snide remark, but was too far away to understand.

12

At 0400 a runner from Lt. Smoker's staff sought out Staff Sergeant Tarkington. He found him sitting beside PFC Henry and Raker. The two scouts had become good friends over the past few days. Tarkington wondered how - they were polar opposites: Henry, quiet and introspective and Raker, loud and boisterous. Raker talked incessantly and Henry nodded and occasionally interjected. The young runner, PFC Roddy's voice broke as if he were still going through puberty. "Lieutenant Smoker wants to see you, Sergeant."

PFC Raker shook his head, "Jesus, Roddy. Have your balls dropped yet?"

Roddy glared at him and was about to squeak a reply but Tarkington spoke first, "Thanks, Roddy." He slapped him on the shoulder and pushed him away. Roddy trotted away in search of 2nd and 3rd squad's NCOs. "Give the kid a break."

Raker asked, "How the hell'd that kid become a runner? He's so young."

Henry answered in his slow drawl. "He's smart and fast. Two things you're not."

Before Raker could respond, Tarkington stood and said, "Knock it off. Bet this is about relieving the Filipinos, so get your shit together."

He slung his Thompson and trotted towards the command tent. This time of the night was his favorite. Just before dawn the temperature was at its coolest, making it almost tolerable, even pleasant. There were still occasional flashes coming from the hillside. *They've had a long night,* he thought.

He pulled back the flap of the tent and entered the red glow. He saw Platoon Sergeant McLunty, Lieutenant Govang, Lieutenant Smoker and Captain Glister huddled over the map listening as a sweaty and dirty Filipino soldier spoke and gestured. Tarkington immediately straightened up with all the officers nearby. He barked, "Staff Sergeant Tarkington, reporting as ordered."

Captain Glister gave him a half-assed glance, "Come over here Sergeant."

As he found a place around the map, he was alarmed to see the Filipino wasn't only sweating and dirty but wounded as well. His left arm was covered in dried blood and a blood-soaked bandage was wrapped around his bicep. More NCOs filtered in and soon everyone that needed to be there was.

Captain Glister addressed them. He pointed to a circled area on the map. "Charlie Company of the First Regular Division is pinned down by machine gun fire and mortars here. They've been in contact most of the night and are having trouble disengaging. The commander, Major Durante, is worried they'll be flanked and wants us to keep that from happening so he can concentrate on attacking what's in front of him." He paused. "I'm sending second platoon to the right flank, here." He pointed to a spot well down from the original circle and to the right. "And first platoon to the left flank, here."

He looked at Lt. Govang commanding 2nd platoon. "The more obvious flanking risk is from the right. The terrain to the left isn't impossible, but it would be more difficult. If the Japs come I'm thinking it'll be the right flank." Govang looked stern as he studied the map and nodded his understanding. Glister pointed at Lt. Smoker. "I want you ready to send a squad to the right flank if it's more than second platoon can handle. Clear?"

Smoker nodded, "Clear, sir. When do we leave?"

"Now. We'll use what's left of the darkness to get you out of here without drawing any artillery fire. The radios are spotty here, so if you need assistance, use your runners." He looked at the bleeding Filipino. "Get that arm looked at before you go back." The Filipino shook his head, but Glister insisted, "That's an order, son. You'll lead the GIs forward and I don't want you passing out from blood loss." He pushed him toward the waiting 3rd platoon medic, PFC Yap.

Tarkington noticed Yap for the first time. He was short and stocky and his Chinese heritage was obvious. He'd had a rough time since the Japanese invaded. Despite being born and raised in New York City, his looks made everyone suspicious, even long-time friends. When the Filipino saw him he stopped and glared at him, but Yap was used to it. He pulled him to a cot, sat him down and unwrapped his dirty, bloody rag. In his heavy New York accent he said, "Just relax and let old Yap take care of ya." He smiled at the Filipino who looked unconvinced.

Two hours later they were across the Tuol River and moving uphill towards the sounds of fighting. Enzo, the wounded Filipino soldier, was in the lead with scouts from various squads following close behind, including Henry. The morning sun was up and the day promised to be another hot one. In the confines of the jungle, instead of the shade bringing coolness, it simply turned it into a steam bath. The GIs were used to it by now, but it didn't make it any less miserable.

Enzo stopped and held up a fist. The signal was passed back. The scouts went forward, conferred with Enzo, then scooted back to Lt. Smoker and Govang respectively. Henry came back to 2nd squad and knelt next to Tarkington. "This is where we split up."

Sure enough, Lt. Smoker raised his hand and moved 1st platoon to the left and Lt. Govang did the same for 2nd platoon, but to the right.

The higher they went up the hill, the less dense the jungle got. Tarkington was glad for it. Getting through the thickets around the river took far too long and expended far too much energy. The Japanese could've been feet away from him and he'd only see them if he happened to run into them. Up here, he could see about fifteen yards in every direction, which was far better than fifteen inches.

Lieutenant Smoker had split the platoon into two squads and Henry led 2nd squad with Raker close behind. 1st squad was lower on the hill and keeping pace with them. Tarkington had his senses working overtime, listening for anything unusual. The fighting had subsided but not ceased and he assumed Major Durante had pulled back, waiting for the GIs to reinforce his flanks before launching another attack.

He glanced behind him and saw the three Filipinos not far back. They had their eyes open and their rifles ready. They hardly made a sound and he wondered if he should send them forward with Henry but thought better of it, knowing Platoon Sergeant McLunty was lurking somewhere.

Finally they stopped. Henry spoke with Raker, then split off and reported to Lt. Smoker who was a few yards down the hill, with his rifle ready. Raker reported to Tarkington, "This ridge is a good place to set up."

Tarkington nodded, "Show me." Raker nodded and moved off toward Henry, who looked like he'd become a part of the landscape. If Tarkington hadn't known he was there, he'd never have seen him.

He stepped beside him and crouched behind a tree, looking at the terrain. He liked what he saw. They were indeed on a little ridge. If the Japanese came this way, it would be the most direct and obvious route to the Filipino left flank. The GIs were on the high ground with good cover and a ridge they could pull behind if it came to that. It was a good position.

Lieutenant Smoker started directing the men. He put one BAR team up high and the other in the middle. Each had good fields of fire. Tarkington wished, not for the first time, that they had a heavy weapons platoon assigned to them. A couple of heavy machine guns would go a long way out here. The BAR could lay down heavy fire, but was limited by its magazine size of only twenty .30-06 Springfield rounds. As Stollman liked to say, 'Bitch is nasty, but quick.'

The rest of the platoon dug foxholes at ten to fifteen-yard intervals. When it was all said and done, the line stretched for nearly one hundred and fifty yards. Tarkington and his 2nd squad were near the end on the lower side. Lt. Smoker and Platoon Sergeant McLunty were dug in twenty yards back from the main line, in the gap between 1st and 2nd squads. They had a handheld radio, as did the squad leaders. When everyone was settled, McLunty called and Tarkington reported his men were dug in and ready. Now all they had to do was sit and wait.

Just after noon, the firing from up the hill erupted as though someone had flipped a switch. "Filipinos are making their move," Tarkington said to Stollman and Vick.

Stollman nodded and looked over his BAR. He caressed the stock like it was his baby. "Come to papa, my little friends."

Tarkington shook his head. "Crazy bastard. I'd rather the Filipinos take care of 'em."

"And let them have all the fun?" His mouth turned down and his eyes darkened as he sighted down the barrel and moved the muzzle from side-to-side. "Still hafta pay for Staff Sergeant Flynn's death."

Tarkington nodded and swallowed. The vision of Flynn's legs teetering beside those of the Japanese soldier filled his mind. He hadn't thought of it for a while and the realization made him feel guilty. He'd known the man for three years. Flynn had been gone less than a week and he'd barely thought about him. "You're right, Stolly, let 'em come."

The additional sound of mortar fire made everyone duck. It wasn't directed at them, but the instinct was too strong to resist. "Those ain't knee mortars." Stollman nodded his agreement. "Those crafty buggers hauled those tubes along with ammo all the way from the front lines." He shook his head, "Unbelievable." He pointed at the BAR, "Makes your bitching about that little twenty-five pounder sound kinda pathetic." It was meant as a joke, but Stollman gritted his teeth and didn't answer.

They listened to the raging battle and watched their front. After twenty minutes the sounds of battle hadn't diminished. Tarkington shook his head. "If they were making headway it'd be over by now. They must be dug in deeper'n ticks."

Vick cringed at the visual. "I hate ticks. Nastiest things on God's green earth. Had one between my butt cheeks once, bloated to the size of a damned acorn before I finally noticed it. Disgusting."

Stollman was intrigued. He laughed, "What the hell? Bloated? Was it eating your shit or something?"

Vick looked at him like he was stupid and said as much. "You slow or something? They suck your blood, but do it sneaky like. You don't feel their bite cause they use some kind of anes...anes..."

"Anesthetic," Tarkington finished for him.

"Yeah, that's the word. Thanks, professor."

Stollman couldn't keep from grinning. Then he started laughing and had to cover his mouth to keep quiet. "Tark's...," he wiped the tears that formed at the corners of his eyes.

"What the hell's the matter with you, Stolly?" demanded Tarkington.

Stollman got control of his laughter, "Tark's Ticks. That's what we should call ourselves. Tark's Ticks."

"Call ourselves? What are we, some kind of traveling show? No," he said with finality. "We're second squad." Vick nodded and tested it, "Tark's Ticks. I kinda like it." He grinned at Tarkington, "Doesn't mean I want you sucking on my ass though."

Tarkington shook his head, "This isn't up for debate, we're not naming units. Jesus, it's like we're in the glee club in high school or something. Pay attention, I'm going to check on the others."

Without waiting for a response he moved down the line, shaking his head.

———————

Tarkington was laying on the ground beside Sergeant Winkleman's hole, discussing ammunition and water supply, when he noticed Holiday, in the hole with Winkleman, suddenly stiffen. Tarkington stopped talking to Winkleman mid-sentence and focused where he was looking. He whispered, "See something?"

Holiday nodded, "Think so."

The battle still raged up the hill making Tarkington wonder how much more ammunition the Japanese had. He saw movement at the furthest point he could see. He tensed too and noticed Winkleman doing the same. There was definitely something out there. He carefully pushed himself backwards until he was over the ridge and out of sight from the opposite side. He waved and finally got the attention of Eduardo, signaling him to move up.

Tarkington pulled the radio from his pack and called into Lt. Smoker. He heard the gruff voice of Platoon Sergeant McLunty. Tarkington filled him in and soon he saw Lt. Smoker pop up from his hole and locate Tarkington. He waved and signaled him to prepare for contact. Tarkington nodded and moved back beside Winkleman and Holiday's hole, being careful to keep cover between himself and the open slope.

Eduardo and his two compatriots slithered in beside him and were aiming down their well-used Springfield rifles' sights. Tarkington leaned out from the tree trunk and his breath caught when he saw the enemy soldiers coming out of the jungle and trotting toward the ridge-line. He tried to aim his Thompson, but the long magazine wouldn't allow him to, so he put it on the ground sideways. He'd have to join in the shooting once he was able to move forward and drop into the hole with Winkleman and Holiday.

Everyone along the line was now well-aware of the advancing enemy. Unless they were asleep, they couldn't miss them.

Tarkington looked up the hill and saw the long barrel and bi-pod of Stollman's BAR, leveled. He wondered who would shoot first. *Should I? When?* He was about to yell 'Open fire,' when Stollman's BAR barked out vicious five-round bursts. There was a rippling of fire from the others and the exposed Japanese dropped out of sight as puffs of red mist exploded out their fronts and backs.

The Filipinos fired quickly, smoothly worked their bolt actions, and fired again and again. Tarkington pulled himself to his knees and, using the tree for cover, aimed and fired at a soldier limping up the hill with a bloody, dragging leg. The heavy slugs plowed into the soldier's chest and he fell backward, rolled a few feet and came to a stop face-down.

He searched for more targets. There was no one directly in front, so he pivoted further down the hill and fired on three sprinting soldiers. His bullets surrounded them with geysers of dirt and debris and they dove to the ground. Tarkington didn't know if he'd hit them.

He kept his muzzle aimed and was about to pull the trigger when he felt the tree he was leaning against shudder. He was momentarily confused, but soon realized he was leaning out, exposed to the front. He dropped to the ground as more bullets passed close. He cursed to himself, 'Pay attention, dammit.'

He pushed himself backwards and rolled onto his back. He pulled out the half-spent magazine and inserted a fresh one. The firing intensified downslope. He got to his feet and, staying beneath the lip of the ridge, ran down hill. He slid to a stop and crawled to the last foxhole. The GIs were firing as fast as they could work their bolt actions. He tried to picture who was in the hole and finally remembered, *Malaky and Skinner.*

He called out, "Make room, coming into your hole."

One of them, he thought it was Malaky yelled back, "Okay."

Tarkington sprinted forward the few steps and jumped feet first between the two riflemen. He slammed into the front wall and slid down. Skinner looked down at him and smiled. "Welcome, Sarge."

Tarkington got his feet beneath him and steadied himself. "What you got?"

"Japs," responded Skinner before aiming and firing again.

Tarkington popped up with his Thompson leading the way. He saw movement only yards ahead and squeezed the trigger as the shape of a Japanese pith helmet materialized. The face beneath the helmet turned to mush. There was an explosion which sent debris and shrapnel in every direction. Tarkington dropped down and covered his head while bits and pieces of the soldier he'd just shot rained upon them. "Cripes, the guy must've had a grenade!"

"No shit," answered Malaky, who popped up and fired again, then dropped down and worked the bolt as Skinner popped up and fired.

Instead of dropping back down, he stayed up and worked the bolt but didn't fire. He was breathing hard, but managed to say, "Think that might be all of 'em."

Tarkington stood along with Malaky and they searched for targets. Tarkington's Thompson was hard against his shoulder as he searched up the hillside but saw nothing but bodies. He brought the muzzle down and hopped out of the hole from a standstill without even realizing he'd done it. "Stay ready. There may be more. Gonna check on the others." He felt the adrenaline coursing through his veins as he ran back up the hill, stopping at each foxhole, checking the men. The firing stopped and, when he reached the final foxhole, he was relieved to find no one hit.

Lieutenant Smoker was lying on his belly assessing the situation when Tarkington found him. He lay down beside him and saw Platoon Sergeant McLunty on the other side, still chewing on the unlit stogie. Out of breath, Tarkington reported, "Second squad's intact, sir. No casualties."

He nodded, "Good. Think we surprised 'em. They may send a bigger force now they know we're here." The firing from the Filipinos up the hill had tapered off to a trickle.

For a few minutes the only sounds were birds and insects. The relative peace was suddenly shattered with the sound of gunfire coming from behind them. Everyone turned but the fighting was too far away. McLunty spoke around his wet stogie, "That's second platoon, sir."

Lieutenant Smoker nodded, "Sounds like they're getting hit too." The added sounds of mortar strikes alarmed them all. Smoker got on the radio. "This is six of first, do you read me? Over." There was only static. He tried again with the same result. He shook the radio, "Dammit." Tarkington took his out and handed it to Smoker.

This time there was a response although it was broken up. "Large force...Smoker we need..." the sound of guns and bombs came over the radio, then it cut out abruptly. They exchanged worried looks.

Smoker reached out and grabbed a handful of Tarkington's shirt. "Take second squad, find out what's happening." His eyes darted to PFC Roddy crouched nearby. "Roddy, you go with him and report back to me. Can't rely on these damned radios." Roddy's milky-blue eyes were wide and he gulped, his huge Adam's apple rising and falling along his long neck. He stammered, "Yes - yes sir." He gripped his rifle and licked his lips.

Tarkington yelled, "Second squad on me."

GIs' heads popped up and looked around. He was about to yell again when Sergeant Winkleman beat him to it. "You heard him, let's go, let's go." He sprang from his hole and rallied the men from their foxholes.

When they were gathered, Tarkington looked Smoker in the eyes, "Gonna leave you pretty thin if they come at you again."

Platoon Sergeant McLunty stepped forward with fire in his eyes and pushed on Tarkington's chest with his stiff index finger and leaned close.

"You worry about your own sorry ass, *Staff Sergeant.* We can take care of ourselves. Now get gone."

Tarkington grit his teeth but turned away from the surly platoon sergeant and waved his men forward. He pushed PFC Roddy, "Come on, move out," he grumbled. "Scouts out front."

13

The sound of battle got louder the closer they got to 2nd platoon's position. The firing from up the hill intensified too. Hearing gunfire and fighting all around was unnerving and the men's eyes darted in every direction, ready to dive for cover. The mortar fire had stopped, but the steady hammering of a Japanese Nambu machine gun filled the air.

Tarkington thought they should've met up with 2nd platoon by now, but the sounds of fighting were still ahead. As they moved across the hillside they had to work their way through thickets of jungle and re-form on the other side. It was time-consuming and tiring.

Finally, Raker and Henry crouched and held up their fists. The squad crouched and Tarkington moved up to his scouts, staying as low as possible. As he closed, the sound of gunfire was just over a slight rise. The rush to reinforce the platoon didn't mean he wanted to run into the middle of a firefight blindly. That was a good way to get shot by your own men.

He poked his head over the rise and saw muzzle flashes and smoke. There were smoking craters mixed with well-concealed foxholes. He could see helmeted heads rising and falling as they fired then sought cover. He looked beyond them but could only see flashes of movement. He heard the Nambu firing and guessed it was up the hill slightly. Bullets whizzed through the jungle, smacking the ground around and in front of the foxholes.

When the Nambu stopped Tarkington yelled, "Second squad of first platoon coming in! Don't fire on us!"

There wasn't an immediate response but he saw one of the helmeted GIs turn his way and even from this distance he could see fear etched on his face. The GI called out, "Yes, yes, come on! We need help!"

Tarkington evaluated the position. The platoon was on top of a rise, much the same way they'd set up. There was a gully behind the foxholes which would cover them from Japanese bullets, but it would require exposing themselves as they ran down the slight hillside directly in front.

He took a deep breath and addressed the men. "Move fast and get to the gully and spread out. Wait for my orders from there." Roddy looked like he was about to throw up. Tarkington grabbed his shirt and pulled him beside him. "Stay on my butt." He didn't wait for a response, but moved forward with his Thompson ready.

As he crested the lip and moved down the hill he sped up to a run, doing his best to keep cover between him and the Nambu. He leaped over a downed tree and was nearly to the gully when the enemy machine gun opened up. He didn't know if they'd been spotted or the bullets were simply passing through the main line. The effect was the same, bullets buzzed past and smacked into the ground. Behind him, he heard the heavy sound of a bullet hitting meat followed by a grunt.

He dove, curled up and rolled into the base of a thick tree. He winced as he hit it much harder than expected. He grit his teeth and wondered if he'd broken a rib. He looked behind him and saw PFC Roddy's wild eyes staring back at him from only feet away. His skin was even whiter than normal making the stream of blood from his nose seem to glow red. His eyes slowed and lost focus - one went the wrong way, looking to the side - while the other stared directly into Tarkington's soul, then glazed and turned unnaturally milky.

"Roddy!" He yelled, but he knew he was gone. He heard yelling from the others and pulled his eyes from Roddy's, pushing his back against the tree. His side ached, but he grit his teeth and took the pain. He tried to take a deep breath, thought better of it and ran to the gully.

He slid in next to Raker who searched behind him, "Roddy?"

Tarkington shook his head, "Didn't make it." He looked at the assembled squad and counted heads. They were all there, except Roddy. They were all breathing hard. Winkleman shuffled to his side and huffed, "Everyone's here except the runner kid."

Tarkington simply shook his head. "Get them spread out. If the mortars come, we're hamburger." He raised his voice, "Stay in pairs."

"Spread out, spread out Goddammit!" The GIs kept in crouches and moved up and down the gully in pairs.

When Tarkington was satisfied, he moved up the gully to the fighting holes. As he crested, the firing seemed to intensify. He saw a foxhole five yards in front and yelled, "Make a hole," then dove forward, rolled onto his back and slid into the foxhole feet first, landing between two startled GIs.

The GI to his right recovered quickly and smiled, "Glad to see you sergeant. How many men you bring?"

"Second squad. What's the situation?"

"A squad? Where's the rest of ya? We're getting our asses kicked."

Tarkington looked at the soldier's nameplate, "Where's Lieutenant Govang, Private Hyster?"

The PFC shrugged and pointed up the hill. "Last I saw, up there somewhere." Tarkington made a move to leave, but Hyster grabbed his shoulder and held on, "It's murder out there, stay here if you wanna live."

Tarkington looked into his eyes and saw abject fear. He shook his shoulder free and growled, "Pull yourself together soldier." The GI on the other side of the hole was cowering too, making Tarkington's blood boil. "You wanna live? Fire your damned weapons." Neither moved a muscle and Tarkington screamed at the top of his lungs. "Fire now, Goddamn you!" Both soldiers snapped from the fog, lifted their rifles and without aiming, fired. "There you go, now you're helping yourselves." They looked back, more afraid of him than the Japanese.

He stood in the foxhole and put his Thompson to his shoulder. There were darting Japanese everywhere, moving from cover-to-cover under the protection of the Nambu. He fired a short burst and saw his bullets spray dirt into the face of a soldier who quickly dove for cover. He followed the soldier's progress with his muzzle and fired when he saw his legs sticking out. His bullets impacted and he heard a scream over the din of the battle.

His attention was drawn to the winking flashes of the Nambu in the trees. It was too far away, but he aimed and fired a burst anyway. His .45 caliber bullets impacted around the Nambu but it kept firing incessantly. He heard a yell to his right and saw a soldier from 2nd platoon lurch back, then slump to the bottom of his hole. The GI next to him stared then dropped out of sight too. *Machine gun's killing us.* "Cover me!" He yelled and pushed himself out of the back of the hole. He rolled straight back, feeling bullets smacking the ground around him, but he was soon in the safety of the gully and moving up the hill to find Lt. Govang, or someone in charge. He pumped his legs, feeling them burn with exertion.

Winkleman saw him exit the hole. He was laying down beside a boulder. "Where you going, Tark?"

"To find the lieutenant." He saw his grenadier, PFC Roscoe, as he moved uphill. He was on his belly firing his rifle and working the bolt. "Roscoe," he yelled. The private spun around, his eyes wide. "Put a grenade onto that machine gun.

Roscoe's eyes lit up like he'd forgotten about the grenade launcher attachment connected to his barrel. He pushed himself back into cover, reached into his ammo pouch and pulled out a rifle grenade.

Once in place, he risked a glance at the Nambu. He pulled back quickly and looked above him at the tree canopy. He braced the stock of his rifle into the dirt and angled it forward until he thought it was correct and fired. He lifted his head to watch the trajectory, his head suddenly snapped back and Tarkington was sprayed with brains and blood. Roscoe fell backwards, the back of his ruined head landing at Tarkington's feet. There was a neat, puckered hole in the center of his forehead. A thin stream of blood ran up his hairline and disappeared in his thick hair.

Tarkington heard Winkleman's excited yell. "Hell of a shot, Roscoe! That was one in a million." Winkleman pushed his way into the gully. His smile disappeared when he saw Roscoe on the ground. "Shit. Roscoe." He ran the few yards and slid in beside him, but saw the hole and the vacant stare and knew there was nothing he could do. He looked at Tarkington with watery eyes. "Dammit." He shook his head and looked at his shaking hands. "Dammit."

All Tarkington wanted to do was sit down and cry. He felt an exhaustion creep over his body. Before it consumed him, he bit his lip, drawing blood. The sharp pain brought him back to the task at hand.

He closed his eyes and swallowed the pain. His voice was low, "Get back to the men, Sergeant." Winkleman looked up at his squad leader and narrowed his eyes. Tarkington could feel the hatred. "Now," he barked, making Winkleman jump. Winkleman got to his feet, took one last look at Roscoe and moved back to his position.

The intensity of fire continued. Tarkington went twenty yards, pulled himself up and saw more soldier's helmets. He cupped his hand to his mouth. "Where's Lieutenant Govang?"

Off to his right he heard, "Here, who's that?"

Tarkington moved sideways until he was directly behind the lieutenant's foxhole. "There room in there for me?" He yelled.

Govang answered, "Yes. I'll cover you." He popped up and fired his Thompson.

Tarkington lunged forward and jumped feet first into the hole, landing on something soft. He immediately knew it was a body. His ankle folded over painfully but he caught it before it sprained. He sucked in air, "Damn. Who's that, sir?"

Govang fired again and dropped back beneath the lip of the foxhole. He looked down at the body. "It's Sergeant Tillotson." He scowled, "He's dead."

Tarkington couldn't believe his ears. Platoon Sergeant Tillotson was a fixture in the company. He shook his head and muttered, "Thought he was bullet-proof."

Govang shook his head. "I can't move him out of here on my own, so I left him there."

Tarkington could see the hurt in Lt. Govang's eyes. "He'll understand, sir." Bullets snapped overhead and the impacts were loud in the surrounding trees. "Lieutenant Smoker sent second squad to help. He would've sent more, but we got hit too and he expects another thrust. Can you hold?"

Lieutenant Govang shrugged. "Now that the Nambu's gone, we'll have a better chance. Was that your doing?"

"PFC Roscoe, sir."

"Well, let him know it's appreciated." Tarkington nodded, not wanting to add to the lieutenant's obvious pain. He popped up again with his Thompson leading and Tarkington did the same, careful to keep from standing on Sgt. Tillotson's back. Without the Nambu the amount of fire coming from the woods was much less, but still dangerous. Tarkington looked over his barrel searching for targets on the slope in front, but didn't see any.

Lieutenant Govang came off his sights too and searched the area. "I don't like it." He chewed the inside of his cheek. "We knocked a lot of them down, but there's a lot more." He ducked down and pulled Tarkington with him. "Take your squad down the gully and lengthen our line. I think they're trying to flank us from below."

Tarkington nodded, "Yes, sir."

He was about to roll out the back when Govang gripped his shoulder. "Stay low, you won't have any time for foxholes."

Tarkington gave him a curt nod and pushed himself backwards. He rolled as he did last time until he was sure he was concealed in the safety of the gully. He got to his feet and moved down the line until he came to Roscoe's body. In the few minutes since he'd been there, his face had turned gray and the hole in his forehead was filled with dark, congealed blood. He tore his eyes away and yelled, "Second squad, on me."

He continued to move downhill and his squad filtered in one-by-one and two-by-two. "Get me a headcount, Wink."

He immediately barked, "Eleven of us." He'd already counted.

All eyes were on Tarkington and he could tell they knew about Roscoe. "Lieutenant Govang thinks the Japs are moving to his right flank. We're moving down to extend and reinforce."

PFC Holiday, the other grenadier asked, "What about Roscoe? We gonna leave him there to rot?"

Tarkington's face turned crimson and a thick vein popped out on his forehead. "We'll come back for him. Forget about him for now. We gotta win this fight or we'll *all* be left rotting out here." He looked at each man. "Now move."

They had little trouble finding the end of 2nd platoon's line. They were a hundred yards downhill and jumpy, nearly firing on them. Tarkington crawled up to the last foxhole. It was occupied by a PFC Gasteau and Rojas. They were riflemen and informed him they'd hardly fired a shot. Most of the action had been further up the hill.

Tarkington crawled forward to get a better look. There was a slight ridge up the hill, making it difficult to see where the main battle had taken place. The field to his front was covered in tall, thick razor grass. He pushed back and addressed the men. "There's nothing going on at the moment. Spread out and dig holes fifteen yards apart, as quickly as you can. If they come it'll be right out in front and they'll be able to get close before we see 'em." He pointed at Holiday. "How many rifle grenades you got?" He held up four fingers. "I want you to use them wisely, but use 'em. No reason to take ammo home. Now get to it."

Tarkington took out his entrenching tool and started scraping away the loamy top layer of soil and heaping it in front. He dug as quickly as he could. The two riflemen from the 2nd platoon were watching him work and sweat. He wiped his brow then pointed at the nearest man. "Keep an eye out. I want to know the instant you see, or even think you see *anything*." Both soldiers looked away and focused on the overgrown field of razor grass.

Tarkington was halfway done when he heard one of the riflemen speak in a loud whisper. "I think I..."

He was interrupted by the sharp crack of rifles firing. Tarkington dove into the shallow hole. It was twelve inches deep, and not quite the length of his body. He knew it wasn't enough to keep him alive for long, but it would have to do.

There was yelling coming from the grass. He looked to his right and saw the smoking barrels of his two scouts. PFC Henry saw him looking and signaled 'enemy sighted.'

Both riflemen to his left fired, refocusing Tarkington to the front. He aimed the Thompson into the tall grass, not seeing anything but knowing something was there. Movement, a dark shape. He braced and fired a burst. Suddenly there was a piercing yell, the grasses parted and there were Japanese soldiers charging with fixed bayonets on their Arisaka rifles.

Tarkington centered the nearest soldier and fired on full automatic as he swept right, cutting down the first four soldiers before his magazine emptied. "Reloading," he yelled, and rolled onto his side. He found a new magazine and slammed it home. He pulled the bolt until it locked and fired carefully-aimed three-round bursts, moving from target to target until he was empty again.

As he reloaded he heard the hammering of Stollman's BAR. The heavy .30-06 rounds nearly cut soldiers in half, but still they kept coming. *There's too many of them.* He yanked a grenade off his harness, pulled the pin and let it fly. He picked up the Thompson and saw the grenade explode between the feet of a screaming Japanese soldier. The soldier's body simply came apart, sending bits of bone and metal shrapnel into the man beside him, who was pushed sideways by what looked like an invisible hurricane-force wind.

The Japanese were falling, but there were still too many. They'd make it across the twenty yards and be in among the GIs with their slashing bayonets in moments. Tarkington yelled something he'd hoped he'd never have to, "Fix bayonets, fix bayonets."

He got to his knees and fired on full automatic, spraying .45 caliber death into the line of soldiers only feet from the GIs, giving the men time to attach their bayonets. His firing-pin hit an empty chamber and he knew he didn't have time to reload. He lunged to his feet and gripped the barrel of the Thompson. He could feel the distant pain of the red-hot barrel burning his hand, but he ignored it and the scream that erupted from deep within him was primeval.

He braced and swung the butt of the Thompson like a baseball bat. The wooden stock smashed into the nearest Japanese soldier, crushing the side of his face, sending blood spewing from his ears, nose and mouth.

There was another soldier right behind the first, and the bandy-legged soldier lunged his long bayonet at his gut. Tarkington brought the

Thompson back across and parried the rifle to the right. The Japanese continued forward and slammed into Tarkington's chest sending them both to the ground.

He struggled to keep his breath. The enemy's face was inches from his and he could see his flared nostrils and the rage and fury in his eyes. The soldier pushed off, trying to bring his rifle to bear, but it was too long and the bayonet caught in the ground. It was all Tarkington needed. With all his strength he punched the Japanese in the cheek. It was a solid hit and he felt the cheekbone crumple beneath his fist. The Japanese released the rifle and reeled back, momentarily dazed. Tarkington thrust his hips as hard as he could, a move he used to do to get his little brother off him when they were wrestling.

The Japanese was lifted and flung forward onto his bleeding face. Tarkington rolled onto his stomach and shot to his feet. He jumped onto the soldier's back and stomped his head with the heel of his boot, wanting to turn it to pulp. He felt, rather than saw, another soldier bearing down on him. He sprang to the right, into a somersault then onto his feet as another Japanese soldier lunged his bayonet into the space he'd just occupied.

Tarkington threw himself into the soldier's back and tackled him like he was back on the football field in Kansas and the soldier was the opponent's quarterback. Tarkington was much bigger and he heard the soldier grunt as his full weight landed on him. He reached for the knife on his belt and found the hilt. He pulled it and, while the Japanese was still struggling to catch his breath, plunged it into his back over and over, until his hand was dripping with blood.

When there was no more movement, he rolled off and tried to get to his feet. The world spun and he thought he might black out. The blood pounding in his head turned his world red and throbbing. He noticed the soldier he'd been stomping on trying to get up. With dripping knife in hand, he fell onto his victim and jammed the knife into the back of the soldier's neck, stilling his movement and adding to his already bloody hand.

"Sarge, lookout!" He spun and saw his death coming. An officer was standing over him with his curved, flashing sword above his head ready to slash down and separate his head from his shoulders. He couldn't move as he saw the sword coming down. He could hear it slicing the air. Suddenly the sword sparked and deflected off a Springfield rifle. The bayonet slashed into the officer's thigh slicing his leg deeply and he screamed in agony. The officer's eyes came off Tarkington and focused on PFC Henry, who'd thrown the bayoneted rifle like a javelin and was now running toward him, screaming like a banshee.

The officer's eyes blazed as he turned to meet the new threat. Tarkington looked at his bloodied hand and arm making sure he still gripped the knife. As the officer lunged forward to meet Henry, Tarkington plunged the knife into his crotch up to the hilt. The battle cry changed to a guttural whimper and the officer fell to the side trying to pull the slippery blade out.

Henry pulled his own knife and jumped onto the officer's chest, sinking his blade into the space where his neck met his chest. A fountain of blood sprayed up, covering Henry's chest and face with dripping arterial blood.

Both men sat staring at one another as they dripped with blood and gore. Tarkington broke his stare and looked around, as if suddenly remembering where he was. He felt as though he were out of his body and now he was returning. The fighting was over and he could see bodies everywhere, mostly Japanese, but not all.

14

Tarkington had his back against a tree, holding the officer's curved sword. He'd wiped the blade and now it shimmered as it caught the sunlight. Despite the blade striking Henry's Springfield rifle, there wasn't a scratch or even a slight ding. It was light in his hand, well-balanced. He wondered about the Japanese officer he'd taken it from. Was it a family heirloom? Had it been passed down generation after generation, finally ending up in the hands of an American? He ran his thumbnail across the edge and watched thin strands of his nail peel back like butter and float to the ground. It was incredibly sharp. Too sharp to carry.

He pushed himself to his feet and wobbled. The short and violent battle had ended ten minutes ago, but he wasn't back to his normal self. He felt like he was still floating, still reeling. He'd wiped the blood on his pants leg, but there was too much of it. It was caked beneath his fingernails and he doubted he'd ever be free of it.

He looked at his men, who were on their feet going through the Japanese soldier's belongings, pocketing anything good, scattering the rest into the wind. PFC Crown and Malaky were dead. Their bodies were pulled back and lined up side-by-side with PFC Roscoe and PFC Roddy in the gully.

He tore his eyes from them and walked the few feet to the dead

Japanese officer. He straddled him, looking down at the blood congealing on his chest. His mouth was open and he had the same pained look he died with. Tarkington saw what he was looking for. He untied the colored band holding the sword's scabbard and wrapped it around his waist. The sword fit snugly into the sheath, like it belonged there. He turned and walked back to his hole.

Sergeant Winkleman stepped close and pointed, "Here comes Lieutenant Govang."

Tarkington faced him and when he was close, nodded. Govang nodded back and looked at the carnage. He shook his head. "That was some good work, Sergeant. If they'd gotten through, they would've rolled up our whole line." Tarkington didn't respond but looked at the four KIAs. Govang noticed and took his helmet off when he saw them. "Dammit. Who is it?"

Tarkington's voice was scratchy and his throat hurt from yelling. "Roscoe, Crown, Malaky and the runner, Roddy."

Govang pursed his lips. "This fucking war. We'll fashion stretchers from ponchos and get them out of here. You have my word, Tark."

"We leaving, sir?"

Govang nodded. "We got a runner from the Filipinos. They took a beating but were able to push the Japs from their first line of bunkers. They're staying out here, but we're being called back." He pointed, "Another full company of Filipinos are coming to reinforce them."

Tarkington looked where he was pointing and saw Filipino soldiers filtering through the jungle. Some passed nearby and saw the dead Japanese and the bloodied platoon. They gave somber nods as they passed. "Fine with me, sir. I wouldn't want to spend the night out here."

Lieutenant Govang nodded. "Third platoon will take over the quick response responsibilities for the next twenty-four hours. Get your men back to your platoon." He put his hand on Tarkington's shoulder. "You guys saved our bacon, Sergeant." Tarkington looked at the dead GIs. Govang nodded, "We'll get them back, move out."

Tarkington and the rest of 1st and 2nd platoon made it back across the river to the relative safety of the plateau without incident. They were met with concerned stares from the men of Hotel Company that stayed behind and the grateful smiles of the Filipinos still faithfully manning their AA guns.

Captain Glister waited until they were settled then called the officers and NCOs to the command tent. All Tarkington and Winkleman wanted to do was curl up and sleep, but that was not to be.

As Glister entered, the men made a half-assed attempt to get to their feet before Glister demanded they stay seated. "I'll keep this brief, I know you're all exhausted. I wanted you to know how the overall situation is unfolding. The Japs pushed hard and had some success pushing through the Orion-Bagac Line as you already know. We weren't sure how many men they got through, but now it's clear there are two groups, each at least company-sized. This group we just tangled with is well dug-in. The Filipinos wanted to let them wither on the vine and starve to death, but MacArthur wants them out of his rear areas as quickly as possible. He's concerned they'll mount a coordinated attack from two sides. So that's falling on the Filipinos and they're confident they won't be a threat after another few days of fighting."

He nodded and extended his hand to them. "First and second platoons' actions have made that possible and General MacArthur has already heard about your contributions."

The men stared with hollow, tired eyes, barely absorbing any of it. Undeterred, Glister continued. "The threat from the landings south, have also been squashed, thanks in no small part to this company." He smiled, "And there's more good news. A convoy of reinforcements is on its way, spanning a mile long. We just have to hold the line a while longer. Once we're reinforced, I've no doubt the Japs will wish they'd never heard of us."

That brought the men out of their stupor and there were back-slaps, hand-shaking and smiling faces. Winkleman punched Tarkington's arm and Tarkington glared at him. "That's great news, Tark. We haven't been left out here to die."

"I'll believe it when I see it," he growled.

Winkleman pursed his lips and indicated the retreating back of Captain Glister. "He just said it, of course it's true."

Tarkington stood and stared after Captain Glister. "I hope he's right, I really do, but until I see boats offloading, I'd take it with large scoop of salt."

....

Tarkington didn't know what time it was, only that it was pitch dark. Something woke him from a deep sleep. He was about to drift back into the abyss, when he heard the distinct sound of a distant battle. It was like déjà vu from the night before. He was about to roust himself and find out what was happening when he remembered Third platoon had the duty. If the shit hit the fan, they'd send them.

Relieved, he tried to drift back to sleep, but there was a sudden uptick in the volume of fire coming from the hill. He took a deep breath and poked his head from the poncho hammock. A stream of cold water hit the back of his neck and he cursed. *Must've rained.* He wiped the back of his neck and rubbed the cool water over his face. The smell of muggy wetness was thick in his nostrils. He pulled back into his cocoon and stared at the blackness.

He was warm and comfortable. It reminded him of early mornings on the farm, being rousted long before daylight to work the fields and livestock. He always had to literally pull his younger brother, Robert, from the warm comforter until he was kicking, screaming and cussing at him. Their routine was always the same, yet his brother fought it every morning. Tarkington shook his head, *stubborn bastard.*

He felt in the dark for his red-lensed flashlight and turned it on. The soft red glow lit up the inside of the hammock and he rifled through his pack until he found the pocket with the letters. There were five of them, all from his brother. His parents never wrote to him. It didn't bother him, it wasn't something they were inclined to do, it wasn't in their nature. He briefly wondered if they ever wrote Robert at college, but pushed the thought from his mind and opened the last letter he'd received.

He'd received it a week before the Japanese surprise attack on Pearl Harbor. He'd read it so many times he figured he could recite it. It wasn't necessarily gripping reading, just basic goings-on, but it was from a different, more sane part of the world and he liked visiting that world whenever he could.

He carefully refolded it and slid it back into the pocket with the others. He wondered what his brother was doing at that moment. What time of day was it? He wished he could talk about the war with him. He knew Robert would be chomping at the bit to join up and fight the Japanese, if only to help out his older brother. Robert was like that, he'd do anything for you, no matter how out of the way or inconvenient. If it would help, he'd do it no questions asked.

He shook his head, trying to imagine Robert out here fighting. He remembered driving his knife into the Japanese soldiers. He remembered the blood, the agony on their faces. The fear. He remembered the way it felt as their hot life-blood spilled over his hand. He tried to imagine his brother doing that and couldn't. He was as tough as nails, but he didn't have the hardness it took. *He'd be a good officer.* He closed his eyes tight and sent a prayer, "Dear God, protect Robert. Let him serve as an officer on some General's staff away from all this ugliness. Amen." He shut his eyes and tried to ignore the distant sound of battle.

The GIs of 2nd squad were eating a hot breakfast, some kind of oatmeal gruel. It was bland and watered-down, but it was warm and filling and no one complained.

Platoon Sergeant McLunty slurped it into his mouth so fast, he was done before most were halfway through. He leaned back and addressed the NCOs seated with him. "Third platoon went out just before it got light this morning." He looked around at the surprised faces. He nodded, "Filipinos sent a runner. The Nips hit them hard again last night, managed to get close then mounted a banzai charge. It was bad, but those little bastards held."

Staff Sergeant Mulvane from 2nd platoon's 1st squad asked, "We going out too?"

McLunty shrugged, "Depends on how things go today." He paused, listening. "Fighting's tapered off, but who knows what that means. We've been getting radio updates: so far they haven't seen any Japs. They're guarding the Filipinos as they pull out their dead and wounded."

"How bad?" asked Mulvane.

McLunty scowled, "Bad enough." McLunty stood abruptly and adjusted his Thompson sub-machine gun slung over his shoulder. "I wouldn't get too comfy, girls. If the Japs come at third platoon, we'll be called out." They all nodded and he turned and stormed out of the mess hall.

Sergeant Thurston shook his head. "He's in a foul mood."

Sergeant Mulvane's face darkened, "He lost his best friend yesterday. Tillotson and him joined together back in '35. They were like brothers."

The NCOs finished the rest of their breakfast in silence.

By midday the Filipinos, along with the help of 3rd platoon, had removed their dead and wounded from the hillside. The 2nd squad was tasked with helping get them from the riverside up to the plateau and into the makeshift infirmary. Medics, along with an aging civilian surgeon, were kept busy patching up the Filipinos, who were eternally grateful. Despite their obvious pain, they continually thanked them for their efforts.

While Tarkington was dropping off a Filipino soldier with a bullet in his arm, he overheard a conversation between a young Filipino, whose leg was mutilated beyond repair and the surgeon. The doctor explained that he had to take the leg off or he'd die of infection. Instead of bitterness - or even fear - the soldier nodded, forced a smile and apologized for the inconvenience. Tarkington shook his head in wonder. *Where do they find their courage?*

He left as the assisting medic slipped a piece of thick leather between the Filipinos teeth, then tightened the tourniquet as tight as he could get it. The Filipino bit down hard and put his head back, but didn't utter a sound. Tarkington hoped he'd be half as brave, if it were him. The thought was sobering. *Would I even want to live?*

He left the tent and moved aside as another litter bearer brought in a soldier with a bloody bandage wrapped around his head and half his face. "How many more?" he asked.

PFC Holiday's face was a mask of sweat and strain. "This is the last one."

Tarkington wiped the sweat off his forehead and nodded. His stomach rumbled, and he realized it had been six hours since the squad had last eaten. He took a slug of water from his canteen to squelch the hunger and wiped the excess water with the back of his hand. Now that all the wounded were moved, it would be a good time to give the men a break under the trees and have lunch. The mess hall only had enough food for breakfast and dinner, they were on their own for lunch. The C-rations were in short supply too. To extend the rations, they skipped lunch every other day. Today was a lunch day and, despite the grim fare, he was looking forward to it.

The sudden crash of an incoming artillery shell squashed his appetite. He, and every GI in the area, flung themselves flat. The shells erupted on the outskirts of the field and walked through the thin jungle, sending great geysers of dirt and flame into the sky. It lasted less than a minute but in that time ten shells tore up the ground in the Filipino section.

Tarkington got to his feet and brushed the dirt off his front. He looked to the Filipino area and saw one of the AA guns on its side, the barrels twisted. It looked like it took a direct hit. He saw Filipino soldiers running to the spot and pulling prone soldiers from the burning wreckage. Three of the company's four medics ran from the infirmary tent toward the carnage. Tarkington assumed the fourth was still inside assisting the surgeon.

With his hunger forgotten he waved to the men. "Come on, lets lend a hand." He ran across the field with the rest of 2nd squad on his heels. As he got close the unmistakable and now familiar smell of burning flesh assaulted his nose. No matter how many times he smelled it, he never got totally used to it.

The AA gun was blackened with fire and he pulled up short wondering if there was any unexploded ordnance getting ready to cook off. He saw movement at the base of the ruined gun and realized it was a scorched hand reaching out. He didn't hesitate. He ran forward with two others at his side. The Filipino was barely recognizable as a man. He was blackened with bits of pink showing through. The GIs pulled up short, not sure how to proceed. The soldier's blackened hand shook as he continued to reach. Tarkington knew he was doomed; extensive burns were usually fatal.

He reached out and touched the hand, which closed around his. The skin bent and cracked and Tarkington could feel the heat and wetness, but held on. He looked into the man's wide eyes and realized his eyelids were missing. The hand went slack and dropped from his grasp. He let go, seeing the life leave his eyes. He pulled his hand back and stared at his palm.

Burnt flakes of skin were stuck to it. He wiped them vigorously on his pants and backed away.

He bumped into someone and turned to see Eduardo and Nunez looking past him at the charred soldier. Eduardo shook his head and pointed, "Cesar. He wanted to try the big gun." His mouth turned down in sadness, "Bad time."

Tarkington hadn't seen them since returning from the jungle. He looked back at Cesar's remains and was suddenly overcome with rage. "Dammit," he cursed and stormed back across the field.

Sergeant Winkleman found him leaning against a palm tree, idly eating lunch. "You okay, Tark?"

Tarkington looked at him and nodded. "Yeah, just hate sitting here getting whittled down. Those damn Japs are completely surrounded but keep killing us one by one. I wanna get rid of them once and for all."

The hillside suddenly erupted with fire again. They both looked that way, despite having no chance of seeing anything useful. Winkleman stood and adjusted his weapon. He tilted his helmet back and sighed heavily. "May get that chance after all."

15

The sounds of battle on the hill ebbed and flowed like the tides, sometimes loud and continuous, other times muted and sporadic, but never stopped completely.

After 3rd platoon helped extract the Filipino dead and wounded that morning, they were sent back across the river to cover their flanks. It wasn't long before they were probed, but they beat the small force back easily enough without casualties. Unlike the malfunctioning radio 2nd squad had been given the day before, 3rd platoon's worked perfectly and they were able to keep the rest of the company up-to-date with regular reports. Most of the fighting they were hearing was the Filipinos pushing against the dug-in Japanese. It didn't make it any less ominous. The enemy was far too close.

The 2nd squad had just finished their dinner of rice in various forms mixed with chunks of dried meat. Tarkington and the other NCOs of 1st platoon had a meeting with their platoon leader, Lt. Smoker, scheduled for 1700 hours.

He and Winkleman left the men in the mess hall and started towards the command tent. They'd been on the plateau for a few days and little paths were forming in the grass. He glanced down at one that split off and led to the slit trench latrine. Most of the men suffered from diarrhea and Tarkington was no exception. The urge could come on without warning so it was important to know where the nearest latrine was located. Many a meeting had been interrupted by a GI suddenly sprinting away holding his ass. It was so routine, it hardly bore mentioning.

Lieutenant Smoker was already in the command tent, his ever-present Platoon Sergeant McLunty by his side. Smoker read a tattered magazine. Tarkington wondered where he got it and if he could somehow steal it away from him. He hadn't read anything except old letters from his brother, for months and he found that he profoundly missed it. All the paperbacks that normally circulated through the company had been left behind. The few that found their way into soldier's packs had been read so many times they literally came apart in their hands. The pages were eventually used for toilet paper.

McLunty pointed at Tarkington's side and Tarkington immediately realized his mistake. "Where'd you get that, Tarkington?"

He looked at the scabbard holding the Samurai sword swinging from the sash tied around his waist. He'd grown used to the weight of it and had completely forgotten to take it off. He gripped the worn leather handle, "Off a Jap officer that tried to decapitate me with it, Sarge."

Lieutenant Smoker looked up from his magazine and eyeballed the sword. "Can I see it?"

Tarkington nodded, untied the sash and handed the whole thing to Lt. Smoker, who never took his eyes from it. He put out both hands palm up and Tarkington laid it on his hands. He felt foolish, like they were playing at knights of the round table or something.

Smoker hefted the weight and remarked, "It's so light." He clutched the handle and looked at Tarkington for permission. Tarkington reluctantly nodded and Smoker drew the sword from the scabbard slowly, his eyes sparkling at the fine workmanship. Once out, he placed the scabbard on the table alongside the magazine and held the blade straight up and down, studying the fine etchings. "Magnificent," he muttered. "The markings are remarkable; delicate yet profound. This was made by a master." He shook his head. "And a long time ago, I should think."

Other NCOs filtered in until everyone was there and still Lt. Smoker marveled. Tarkington cleared his throat and put out his hand. "Could I get it back, sir?"

Lt. Smoker shook himself from his reverie and looked around the room as if seeing them for the first time. He shook his head and put the sword carefully back into the scabbard. He held it out and Tarkington clutched it and had to yank it from Smoker's hand's as if Smoker couldn't let it go. "I'd like to buy that off you Staff Sergeant."

Tarkington shook his head, "It's not for sale, sir. Reckon I'll keep it, maybe hang it over my fireplace back home someday."

Platoon Sergeant McLunty barked, "You can't keep that, Tarkington. It's against regulations. Looting's a punishable offense." His face was hard and turning deeper shades of red every few seconds.

"Looting? It's a war prize from a vanquished enemy."

McLunty was a simple man from the underside of some backwoods town in Oklahoma. "*Vanquished enemy?*" He mocked. "Well ain't you the fancy one." He thrust his jaw toward Lt. Smoker. "Now give Lieutenant Smoker the pig sticker, before I tear it out of your hands and put you up on charges."

The vein on Tarkington's head throbbed. He considered refusing, after all, what could they possibly do to him? They needed every swinging dick they could get their hands on, particularly NCOs. He looked from McLunty to Smoker who didn't quite return his stare. The only sound was the far-off firefight which had increased in tempo. The other NCOs were in rapt attention, wondering how the mini power struggle would play out. Everyone respected Lt. Smoker, but the surly platoon sergeant was a different story.

Tarkington made up his mind. He extended the sword but when McLunty went to grab it, he pulled it out of reach and shook his head. Before McLunty's head exploded, Tarkington quickly said, "I'll give it to Lieutenant Smoker." He waited until McLunty stepped back before again extending it and adding. "For safe-keeping. Until this shit's over." Lt. Smoker looked him in the eye and put his hand on the sword, but Tarkington held fast. "I'll need your word on that, Glen."

McLunty was about to burst at the seams and tear Tarkington's head from his shoulders. Lieutenant Smoker gave him a sharp look. "It's okay, Sergeant. It's a gentleman's agreement." He looked Tarkington in the eye and nodded. He held out his right hand, "You have my word, Clay."

Tarkington lifted his chin and looked down his nose. He had no choice but to relinquish the sword. He shook Smoker's hand and released his grip on the sword. The exchange was made and the tension in the room evaporated, except from McLunty, who was still shooting daggers from his eyes.

Smoker placed the scabbard and sword onto the table carefully. Tarkington remembered the rough use it had been through on the battlefield. It would take a lot more than dropping it a few inches onto a table to cause it harm.

Lieutenant Smoker turned from the table and addressed the group. "Now, back to business."

Tarkington didn't pay much attention as Smoker talked about shifts and guard rotations and the general day-to-day bullshit it took to run a platoon. He never took his eyes off the sword.

He liked the way it felt at his side, he wanted to wield it in combat, and he was quite sure, despite Lt. Smoker's word, that he'd never get the sword back. He had little faith there were any reinforcements coming from the mainland, which meant his fate was either as a prisoner of war or a dead man. He decided he'd get the sword back if it was the last thing he did.

It was just getting dark when a runner burst into 2nd squad's area. He saw Tarkington whittling a piece of wood and rushed to him. "You're to get second squad ready immediately and prepare to move out, Sergeant."

Tarkington stopped whittling and got to his feet slowly. He towered over the PFC. "What's your name, son?"

He braced, "Private First Class Rabowski. I'm - I'm Lieutenant Smoker's new runner."

Tarkington pointed at his sergeant's stripes. "See these?"

"Yes, they're sergeant's stripes. You're a sergeant."

"I'm actually a *staff* sergeant. You're a PFC, I outrank you." He stepped forward and thrust his finger into the pigeon-chested Rabowski. "I don't take orders from you, son."

"Sorry, Staff Sergeant Tarkington, I was merely relaying the lieutenant's orders. I should've rephrased it."

Tarkington waved his hand like he was shooing a fly, and strode past him toward the command tent. He turned as the men watched him go. "Wink, get the men ready." He spun back around and slunk off to find Lt. Smoker.

PFC Rabowski looked flustered. PFC Stollman hefted his BAR over his shoulder and addressed him. "Don't let it get to you kid. He's had a bad day, and it's about to get worse." Rabowski nodded and suddenly remembered his orders and sprinted off to find more NCOs.

Twenty minutes later Tarkington came back looking worried. "Listen up, second squad." They shuffled closer. "Third platoon is getting hit hard. The Japs have gotten around them somehow and are squeezing them. The platoon's moving up the hill to join the Filipinos before it gets dark. We're to move to the river and make sure the Japs don't cross and make a move on our camp here."

He pointed toward the sound of combat, "Those are our guys up there. The second platoon's staying in reserve. We move out in ten minutes. It'd be nice if we got settled before it gets completely dark, so move your asses."

The men scattered, grabbing packs and any extra ammo they had stashed. Within minutes they were moving to the edge of the plateau, each squad in single file and parallel to one another.

When they got to the edge of the plateau, Lieutenant Smoker stopped them and they crouched. It was still light enough to see the gentle slope leading to the flat floodplain, which extended another hundred yards to the riverbank. The slope was sparse jungle, but got thicker near the river.

Lieutenant Smoker gathered the squad leaders. "Japs might be waiting for us on this side of the river." He pointed at Tarkington, "Send Henry out on point."

They spread out and scrambled down the gentle slope toward the Tuol river. They moved cautiously, but felt exposed on the relatively barren slope. When they got to the flat floodplain, the cover was better.

Tarkington didn't like moving toward the river in the fading light. Despite PFC Henry's skills, if the Japanese had men on this side they wouldn't know it until they opened fire. The fading light, combined with good cover near the river and the GIs exposure, would make for a lethal ambush. Henry moved cautiously.

A tense half hour later they got to the river's edge without incident. Lt.

Smoker directed a few GIs to cover the rest of the platoon as they dug foxholes in the soft ground. Soon there were a series of interwoven foxholes spreading over seventy-five yards up to the river's edge.

Tarkington stepped into his hole, alongside PFC Henry. Despite being squad leader, he'd helped dig and sweat dripped off his nose. He took off his helmet and ran his hands through his dirty hair. He was tempted to sneak to the river and scoop water to douse himself. He decided against it. The evening was hot, but his sweat would cool and he might even get chilled.

Henry took a deep breath and blew it out slow. Tarkington hadn't had as much time with his longtime friend since being promoted to squad leader. "Got any of your Cajun gut feelings?"

Henry pursed his lips and imperceptibly nodded. "I don't like it. Japs had to know we'd come. Why didn't they ambush us?"

Tarkington shrugged, playing the devil's advocate, "Too busy chasing third platoon?"

Henry tilted his head, "Maybe. Seems like they wasted a golden opportunity."

"I've gotta tell ya, I was thinking we'd have contact down here too. Maybe they don't have enough guys. They've been duking it out with the Filipinos for days now, not to mention the men they lost trying to get through us."

Henry nodded and the silence grew, but Tarkington knew what he was going to say before he finally did. "Maybe it's *our* opportunity."

Tarkington whispered, "I was thinking the same thing, but there's no way Smoker will risk it."

"It'd be better with a small force anyway. Call it a recon patrol."

"You really wanna go out there tonight?"

He shrugged and spit, "Better than staying up all night waiting to get knifed or sniped."

"Can't hurt asking, I guess." He pulled himself from the hole, "Be right back." It wasn't fully dark yet, but he moved carefully, making sure the GIs saw or heard him coming. More than one soldier had been killed by friendly fire while moving around at night near the front lines.

He found Lieutenant Smoker's hole. He was dead center of the platoon and a little back from the line. McLunty saw him first and whispered, "What the hell you doing out of your hole, Sergeant?"

Tarkington went to his belly and pulled himself to the edge of the foxhole. "Wanted to pass something by you."

Smoker asked irritably, "Well what is it, Sergeant?"

"I find it strange the Japs didn't have some kind of ambush waiting for us. I mean they must've known we'd send a relief force."

"Well, consider yourself lucky, I guess." He looked at McLunty whose face was blank, then back to Tarkington. "What's there to discuss? It didn't happen."

"It might be a good opportunity for us to probe them. It might be a thin force and we could break them open and be where they don't expect us to be and attack them at first light. We could rout them."

McLunty scowled, "That's a lot of 'mights', Tarkington."

Smoker paused to consider, then shook his head. "It's too risky. Our orders are to hold this line, not attack."

Tarkington nodded, "Yes, sir. No problem, just wanted to run it by you."

McLunty growled, "Get back to your hole, and keep your bullshit ideas to yourself, Sergeant."

Tarkington wanted to reach out and strangle him, but he simply turned and slunk away muttering under his breath.

Private Hisoko cowered in his spiderhole as the enemy force passed over his head, praying no one stepped directly on his cover. He kept still, all his senses tuned to the passing soldiers. He clutched his one grenade, ready to arm and throw it at the first hint of discovery. On his hip, was his only other weapon, his long bayonet knife. He released his breath when he realized he didn't hear any more soldiers and he immediately started counting.

So far, Lieutenant Miro's plan was working perfectly. He'd sent Hisoko and five other soldiers across the river, giving them time before he pressed his own attack up the hill. He gave them two hours to cross the shallow Tuol river and dig their spiderholes, then he attacked.

As Miro predicted, they sent a force from the plateau. That force had just passed over his head and once his count reached five thousand, he and his five comrades would crawl from their holes and attack with knives and grenades. Hisoko knew this would be his last mission. Their intent wasn't to destroy the enemy force, but to drive fear into their hearts, and none of them expected to survive.

Approximately an hour and fifteen minutes later, with his count complete, he slowly pushed the cover back, and slithered from the hole. It was dark, but lighter than the inside of the hole, and he could see surprisingly well with the additional light from the stars. He didn't move as he took in the surroundings. He could hear the gentle flow of the river as it licked the banks. He strained to hear or see any sign of the enemy. He wondered if he'd be killing Americans or Filipinos.

A sound of metal caught his attention and he adjusted his gaze turning toward the sound, but not looking directly at it, relying on his peripheral vision. He was thirty yards from the river. Judging by the sound, the enemy was dug-in right beside the riverbank. He centered himself, taking a deep breath and letting it filter out slowly, exhaling the fear and soreness from his body.

He touched the grenade to make sure it was still there, then slowly pulled the knife and gripped it tightly. He looked to either side, searching for his comrades but knew he wouldn't see them.

He made his first move forward, barely making a sound. He felt his heart rate increase and he struggled to keep his breathing in check. His plan was to move forward until he saw a target, then use the knife and kill silently if possible, without raising the alarm. If he was seen before that, he'd hurl the grenade and follow it with a slashing knife charge. Lt. Miro had been explicit in his instructions, they must use grenades so he'd know if there were, in fact, enemies on the river bank.

Agonizingly slowly, he pulled himself twenty yards then saw what he was looking for: enemy movement. He stilled his body, his breathing and his mind and put his entire focus on the spot. He saw movement again. It looked like a rounded rock at ground level, but knew it was the shape of an enemy helmet. He'd found his victim. He gripped the knife, feeling the handle, willing it to become a part of his body. He moved toward the unsuspecting soldier, only feet away.

Hisoko had his knife in his right hand and used his arms and legs to slowly push forward. He was close enough to smell the soldier's body odor and knew right away it was an American. The edge of the hole was a foot in front of him when the soldier whispered something and it was answered by someone else in the hole. Hisoko froze, his heart wanting to leap from his chest. He felt sure the GI would hear its thumping, but he was focused toward the river, where he thought the danger was.

Hisoko was within striking distance. He pulled his knife-hand to his shoulder, his arm coiled like a snake. The base of the soldier's neck was within easy reach. He took a silent breath, invoked a silent prayer and with all his coiled strength lunged forward in a flash of violence.

He felt the knife pierce the neck and grate against the GI's back bone, before the tip punched out the front and spilled the man's lifeblood. The GI gurgled on his own blood, and fell forward. The knife was stuck, but Hisoko held on and was pulled into the hole with the collapsing GI. The other soldier yelled something he didn't understand.

The dead American crumpled on top of the other GI and his weight, along with Hisoko's, pinned the thrashing, yelling soldier. Hisoko gave one last desperate pull on the knife, but it would not budge. He gave up and reached for the grenade hooked to his back belt. In a practiced, smooth motion he pulled the safety and slammed the primer against his skull, hearing it hiss. He dropped onto the surviving GI, seeing his wild, terrified eyes. There was a flash, then eternal darkness.

16

The screams coming from 3rd squad got everyone's attention. There was real terror in the screams. This wasn't a GI having a nightmare, but something far more serious.

Tarkington and Henry both stared into the darkness. The muffled sound of an explosion made them duck. "Shit, what the fuck's happening over there?" Henry just shrugged. A rifle shot rang out and the muzzle flash looked like a beacon.

More screaming and this time he heard someone yelling, "Japs!"

There was no answering fire, but two more grenade blasts in quick succession. Tarkington wanted to get out of his hole in the worst way and help, but knew it would only make him a target for jumpy GIs.

Henry was on his right. He suddenly looked left, and Tarkington could tell by his reaction that there was someone coming up beside him. Instincts took over. Tarkington simply dropped to the bottom of the hole. The Japanese soldier's knife sliced over his head, missing. Henry lunged forward and grabbed the soldier's extended arm and pulled it straight down, hyper-extending his elbow. The elbow made a 'pop' sound and the soldier screamed in agony.

Tarkington was directly beneath his chest. His Thompson was pointing straight up. He lunged with every ounce of power he could muster and jammed the barrel into his chest. The Japanese soldier was pushed straight up and backwards. He landed on his feet but couldn't recover from the backwards momentum and fell onto his back.

Tarkington didn't hesitate. He put his Thompson to his shoulder, flicked off the safety and fired into the struggling soldier. His muzzle blast lit up the area and Tarkington knew he had solid hits. He stopped firing after expending half his twenty-round magazine.

He kept his smoking muzzle on the unmoving soldier and glanced back at Henry. Through gasping breath, he asked, "Are - are you okay?" Henry put a hand on Tarkington's shoulder and nodded, continuing to scan the area, rifle ready. There was a sudden flurry of firing from the center of the platoon, mixed with more yelling. Tarkington glanced that way but knew better than to put his full concentration in any one direction. "You saved my bacon. I was a second from being skewered."

Henry still didn't respond but kept scanning. Finally, after ten minutes they heard someone yell. "Sound off."

Men started counting off. Tarkington heard Winkleman yell for a 2nd squad head-count. He was relieved to hear his voice. Tarkington realized he was first man, "One," he shouted. Everyone in 2nd squad responded. The 3rd squad had taken the brunt of the attack. They were down three men, KIA. 1st squad had one WIA. PFC Paulson had blocked a Japanese knife with his hand. The blade had gone through his palm. His foxhole mate had killed the Japanese with a bullet to the face.

Tarkington heard Lt. Smoker yell. "Stay vigilant, there might be more."

The rest of the night passed slowly. There were no more attacks. There was still the occasional sound of gunfire up the hill, but nothing too intense. No one slept and everyone was jumpy.

When the night finally relinquished its hold on the hours, the light of day exposed the gruesome scene. One foxhole in 3rd squad held three bodies: two mutilated GIs and a diminutive Japanese. Their blood and guts were mixed, making it difficult to tell where one man stopped and another started. The foxhole looked like a smorgasbord of carnage. When the bodies were finally sorted out, the GIs stood around their fallen comrades. The Japanese body had been thrown into the river. The third KIA was PFC Wilkins. He'd had his head nearly sawed off.

Lieutenant Smoker walked into the circle of men and looked at the casualties. He shook his head. "Dammit. Alright, get them on ponchos and get 'em outta here. PFC Paulson will go with the stretcher detail." Tarkington saw Paulson with a dirty, bloody bandage wrapped over his hand. He had a pained look. He saw Tarkington watching and stared back with bloodshot eyes. He was in pain, but he was alive. Tarkington gave him a slight nod and he nodded back.

As the men pulled out ponchos and fashioned stretchers with their rifles, Lt. Smoker walked past Tarkington and waved for him to follow. He had a cigarette dangling from his lips, unlit. Tarkington followed, taking a quick look across the river. Lt. Smoker went ten feet and crouched behind a tree. Tarkington joined him. "Didn't know you smoked, sir."

He shrugged, "Haven't lit it, but after last night figure why the fuck not." He pointed back toward the plateau. "We found the holes they hid in. Sneaky little fucks." He seethed, then shook his head. "We walked right past 'em." He looked sideways at him, "Where was that Cajun's sixth sense?" Tarkington shrugged, knowing he wasn't upset with his best scout. Smoker sighed, pulled the cigarette from between his lips and smelled the length of it. "They do smell good, but the taste. Can't get used to the taste." He looked at his muddy boots. "Wilkins was a smoker. Never without one. Christ, he's barely eighteen...was barely eighteen."

Tarkington didn't know why he'd pulled him over here. "Listen, sir. There was nothing you coulda done. I mean this kind of shit..."

Lieutenant Smoker looked up quickly and cut him off. "You still wanna go after those yellow bastards? Give 'em some of their own medicine?"

Tarkington's eyes hardened. "I'd like nothing better, sir," he growled in a low, dangerous voice.

Smoker nodded grimly and looked him in the eye. "Captain Glister would never allow it, but he's not down here with us. Our orders are to stay another night before we're relieved. I'd like you to take second squad and dole out some pain."

"What about McLunty? He'll surely be against it and get you in hot water with the captain."

"McLunty's leading the stretcher bearers. I told him to stay at base and fill in the other platoons about the situation down here." He shrugged, "That kind of bullshit. He won't know anything about it."

Tarkington nodded. "I'll inform the men, sir."

Smoker added, "It's not an order, strictly volunteer. Make that clear to your men, Sergeant."

He nodded. "Yes sir, I will."

The remainder of the day, the 2nd squad rested, while the rest of the platoon watched the riverbank.

When Tarkington broached the mission to them that morning, the remaining eight GIs in 2nd squad immediately volunteered. The night before had been terrifying and no one wanted to spend another night out here worrying about another sneak attack.

Now it was evening, the men were awake, eating C-rations. Tarkington was sitting in the bottom of his foxhole licking his spoon clean. PFC Henry was eating slowly, seemingly a thousand miles away. Tarkington stuffed his spoon into his pack. "Won't be needing these tonight." Henry's stare stayed focused. "Hey Henry?" No response. "Hear your mom's a great lay." Still nothing. Tarkington waved his hand in front of his face.

Henry finally, snapped out of it and focused on his squad leader. "What? Huh? What'd you say, Sarge?"

"I said, your mom's a good lay." Confusion and anger crossed Henry's face. "Easy does it. I was trying to get your attention is all. What were you thinking about?"

Henry scowled and shook his head. "Nothing really. Just thinking."

"Come on. Tell old Tark."

"Alright, if you must know." He put his spoon into the tin of red beans. "I was thinking about home. It's February, mid-winter. A nice time of year down there. Temperature's usually in the mid 60s. Rains a bit, but not as much as January. Just wondering what they're doing right now, at this exact moment."

"Probably sleeping, I imagine. It's the middle of the night, isn't it?"

He shook his head, "No they're ahead thirteen hours. They've already lived through the night we're just about to go into. They're hearing the roosters starting to crow."

Tarkington shook his head. "Hate those damned things. Say, you noticed we don't hear too many over here anymore?"

Henry shrugged, "Probably got eaten. In hard times, keep the layers, eat the roosters."

Tarkington looked at him, "You ever have a time you ate the roosters?"

Henry took another spoonful of beans and slowly chewed. Tarkington knew he wasn't ignoring him, but thinking about his answer. He never spoke before first considering his words. He swallowed and put his spoon back in the can, looked at Tarkington and nodded. "Yeah. Right before I joined up and came over here. Pa lost his job at the cannery cause of the depression. We lived off the land a bit, but without the money to buy staples, well, it got pretty tight. I couldn't find a job around town, but the Army was hiring." He looked into his can of beans. "Sure hope our money's still getting to them. I hate not being in contact with 'em. They must be worried sick about us."

"Us? Your family knows about us?"

"Course they do. I talk about all you cusses in my letters. Everyone in the whole division has an open invitation anytime. We ain't got much, but we're happy to share."

"Even the rooster?"

He nodded and grinned, "Especially the damned rooster."

Late in the evening, as the light was fading, the river's surface reflected the sky and turned a soft amber. Tarkington gathered 2nd squad a few yards back from their foxholes. They left everything that would make noise, or slow them down and were left with knives, rifles, grenades and ammo.

Tarkington looked around the circle. They'd been through a lot together and would undoubtedly go through a lot more. Most of them, he'd known for over a year - some attached later - but all of them were good soldiers. They'd all hardened since December, when they'd been well-trained but untested. Now they were survivors. Through sheer grit, skill and just plain luck, they were still alive and on the line.

He kept his voice low, "Tonight is something different. The name of the game is stealth. PFC Henry and Raker, along with Eduardo and Nunes, will lead and switch-off as needed." Eduardo and Nunes both smiled broadly and Tarkington continued. "Our mission is to find and kill the enemy without alerting them to our presence."

He looked around the circle. Men were passing around a blackened piece of burnt cork and rubbing it on their faces and the backs of their hands. With each swipe, they looked more and more deadly. "Unlike the suicide squad from last night, I intend to kill quietly and live to fight another day." Heads nodded. "When we find the enemy, we'll only attack if we're sure we can get away with it." He pointed at Stollman and Vick. "If things go south, I want you ready to deal heavy fire to cover our retreat, then I want you both on our heels. If they're close enough, chuck a grenade to keep their heads down." They both nodded.

"We'll set up a rally point once we're across the river. If you get split up, get to the rally point and wait. We don't want to go looking for someone who's already safely across. I wouldn't recommend coming back across the river until daylight anyway. Lieutenant Smoker knows we're out there and won't fire on anyone unless he's absolutely sure it's Japs, but after last night, everyone's jumpy."

There were nodding heads all around. Henry asked, "Who does the killing?"

Tarkington pursed his lips and pointed at himself. "I'll make the final call when we find the enemy." He looked at each man, "No one does any killing unless it's a life or death situation." The men nodded. "Okay," he looked at the scratched face of his watch. "We'll move upriver and cross at a shallow spot that Raker found. Remember, it's gonna be darker than the inside of a miner's ass, so stay in single file, at arm's length apart." He stood and made sure his magazine was snug in the receiver, checked it was on safe and pulled back the bolt. "Let's go, then."

Eduardo and Nunes sprang up, followed closely by PFC Raker and Henry. The rest of the men filed in behind one another and moved upstream. The air was hot, humid and thick. The late evening chorus of insects and jungle animals was deafening. They passed foxholes and nodded to their comrades. Some looked on longingly, but most were happy to be staying in the relative safety of their foxholes.

PFC Raker led them upstream to the shallows. It wasn't fully dark, but Tarkington nodded and the first five GIs stepped into the river while the other five covered them. Once across, the first group spread out and, after thirty seconds, waved the others across. Tarkington led the second group. The Tuol River only came up to mid-shin here and was easy to walk through.

Once across, he crouched beside Henry and took a deep breath. They'd only moved across the river but it felt like they'd entered enemy territory. He tapped Henry's shoulder and he moved out, followed closely by Eduardo, then Raker and Nunes. Tarkington waited as more soldiers streamed past, then followed when he figured half the squad was past. He heard the rest fall in behind and he concentrated on the surrounding jungle.

Like the opposite bank, the jungle was thickest near the river but quickly thinned out. Soon the walking was easy. They pushed through tall grasses and thickets until the ground started gently sloping uphill. There was a brief flurry of gunfire from up the slope, marking where the Japanese were. The line of GIs stopped, like a squeezing accordion, then adjusted.

Tarkington waited while his scouts listened and evaluated the best way to continue. A minute passed before the line moved again, even slower now. He swept his Thompson side to side, searching for anything which would help him identify an ambush.

The firing stopped and the night took on an unnatural silence. The insects slowly resumed their nocturnal lives, until it was a chorus of chirps, whistles and buzzes again.

Without the firing, they were steering blind. Coming out here seemed like a good idea from the relative safety of the far bank, but now he was out here, he wondered. Doubts flashed in his mind. These were his men, under his command. Sure they'd volunteered, but what choice did they really have? If they refused, they'd become outsiders. He suddenly felt reckless; putting the men's lives at risk for no reason. He felt the doubt rising up, trying to bend his will.

His inner voice reprimanded him, remembering the slaughter the Japanese had wrought since December. They were responsible for the situation. His men were caught up in it. It wasn't fair, but it was the way it was and there was no getting around that. They were fighting a losing battle, but by taking the fight to the enemy they were simply risking an earlier death, postponing what he was convinced would ultimately be a poor outcome.

Even if the rumored, mile-long resupply was on its way, which he doubted, they'd still be hard-pressed to push the Japanese off Luzon. From all accounts the Japanese attack on Pearl Harbor caught the US Navy with their pants down. Even if only half the scuttlebutt he'd heard about losses were true, they'd been dealt a huge blow, perhaps a knockout blow. A resupply would have to come by sea, and without a Navy how would that be possible?

His mind came back to reality when he nearly ran into the back of PFC Skinner's sweat-soaked back. He crouched and fanned his weapon side to side. Skinner tapped his leg and he squinted at him through the darkness. Skinner indicated they wanted him up front.

Tarkington stepped to the side and moved past the line of crouching men. He could see their shining, alert eyes as he passed and he felt pride swell in his chest. These were fine soldiers. *Tark's Ticks,* the name flashed in his mind without warning and he shook his head, but had to admit he liked the sound of it.

When he got close, he noticed his scouts on their bellies. He lay down slowly, careful not to make noise and crawled forward. He tapped someone's boot and the soldier, he thought it was Raker, moved sideways and Tarkington moved into the space. When he was beside Raker, he saw Henry ahead a few more feet and moved to his side. Once there, Henry slowly moved his hand and held up two fingers then pointed. Tarkington could feel the tension which seemed to emanate from his lead scout. That, combined with his slow, careful movements, told him they were very close to the enemy.

Tarkington focused all his senses forward, trying to see, or sense where they were. Finally he noticed a slight movement and he nearly stopped breathing when he realized they were only fifteen feet from two round mounds which could only be the pith helmets of Japanese soldiers. He guessed he was seeing the rear guard of the main Japanese force. He couldn't tell which way they were looking, or if they were even awake, but he froze in place and felt his heart rate increase to what he thought must be unhealthy levels.

At glacial pace, he moved his head until he was looking at Henry who was staring back at him only inches away. Tarkington pushed himself backwards an inch and Henry understood he wanted to withdraw, and he followed suit.

It took nearly ten minutes before they were finally far enough away to move to crouches. Tarkington wiped the sweat and grime from his face, feeling like he'd just run an ultra slow marathon. They moved back another thirty yards before huddling up. In whispered, one-sided conversation he told the others what they'd found. He addressed Eduardo and Nunes. "You think you could check for any more rear guards without being seen?"

They both nodded enthusiastically and Eduardo whispered, "No problem, Tark."

Tarkington saw his huge smile and smiled back. "No heroics, just see if there are any more and get back here as quickly as you can." Each Filipino nodded and moved in opposite directions, melting into the jungle like soundless ghosts. The rest of the squad created a defensive perimeter.

Once the Filipinos were out of sight, Raker whispered, "We can take that rear guard out without alerting anyone."

Tarkington nodded his agreement. He thought so too but wanted to be sure there were no surprises. Fifteen minutes passed before Eduardo suddenly appeared like a ghost from the right. Henry was the first to notice him, but if he'd been an enemy soldier he would've gotten the jump on them easily. Tarkington was once again glad he was on his side.

A minute later Nunes slithered into sight. The perimeter let them in, then collapsed inward, so they could all hear. Eduardo spoke, "One more enemy far that way," he pointed the way he'd gone.

"Far enough away not to see us move on his pals?"

Eduardo nodded emphatically. "Far. No hear us." They all looked at Nunes who simply shook his head. There was no one that way.

Tarkington nodded and took a deep breath. The situation was suddenly stark, real and terrifying. "Okay. We move on the two nearest Japs."

PFC Vick scooted forward and eagerly whispered, "I'll do it."

The corners of Tarkington's mouth turned down. He understood Vick had lost his closest friend, Private First Class Crown, just a few hundred yards up the hill from where they crouched. He shook his head, "You need to stick with Stolly and the BAR. You're our cover if this goes bad." Vick didn't respond, but Tarkington could tell he was bitter.

He looked around the circle. He couldn't clearly see their expressions, but none of them were obviously shrinking from the prospects of killing the Japanese. "Me and Henry will do it, backed up by Eduardo and Nunes." No one spoke. He was in charge and the decision had been made. "We'll move left and come at them from the side. The rest of you, be ready, but know we might be running straight at you if something goes wrong." He paused, making it up as he went along. "We'll yell 'Alamo' if that happens. Clear?" There was nodding all around. He took a deep breath and looked at his watch. He could hardly see the luminescent dials through the scratched surface. "We'll wait an hour. Hopefully they'll get sleepy."

17

Eduardo and Nunes unslung their long rifles and propped them against a tree. Tarkington looked at Henry and shook his head. He couldn't see moving without his trusty Thompson. He slung it crosswise across his back and cinched down the sling until he was satisfied it wouldn't move and make noise. The hour had passed slow as molasses. The night had cooled slightly and despite the clear skies and shining stars, Tarkington thought it was darker than normal.

An uncontrollable shiver coursed through him, not from the slight temperature change, but the coming action. He reached for his knife and drew it in a smooth motion. The heavy blade felt good in his hand. He'd decided he didn't want to wait to draw it in case the snick of the metal leaving the leather sheath alerted his prey. He'd crawl with it drawn and ready to deal death.

He imagined how it would go, thinking back to his training. They'd covered hand-to-hand combat, mostly with bayonets and rifles, but they'd also practiced knife fighting. He remembered the British instructor, a specialist brought in for the occasion, telling them that the best way to win a knife fight was to bring a gun.

They'd practiced with partially-scorched wooden knives. The charcoaled edges marked the opponent, telling them if they'd been stabbed or sliced. He remembered that by the end, they were all covered with black marks and slices. He remembered the Brit holding one of the GI's arms out for inspection after he'd successfully driven his wooden blade in for a kill thrust. The GI's arms were marked with scores of black marks. 'Though he killed the opponent, he'll be out of commission for weeks healing all these cuts and slashes. Moral of the story: no one wins in a knife fight.' He gulped against a suddenly dry throat. *Can't let it come to that. It's all in the sneak.*

He assessed himself. His bladder was empty and his bowels were calm. He looked at the Filipinos and his scouts, who stared back. He nodded and tapped Eduardo, who turned and moved past the loose perimeter and into the darkness with Nunes close behind and to the side. Henry and Tarkington followed, moving side by side.

They moved slowly and silently for what Tarkington thought to be forty yards, before the Filipinos stopped and sat on their haunches. Sweat was pouring off Tarkington's nose and he wished he'd brought a canteen. Despite the weight and noise, it was a mistake not to have brought water. He silently cursed himself and vowed not to make that mistake again. He glanced over at Henry who seemed calm and cool. *Has he ever been flustered?* He was glad to have him by his side.

Eduardo pointed right, indicating the Japanese were that way. Henry looked at Tarkington, who nodded and, both staying in crouches, moved slowly. Tarkington made sure of each step, placing his foot, gradually weighting it, trying to feel for anything beneath his sole that could make noise.

After ten excruciating yards, Henry stopped and lowered himself to his belly and pulled his knife silently from the sheath. Tarkington wished he hadn't pulled his knife early. His hand was sweaty, the grip was wet and he had to concentrate to keep from dropping it. *Another fuck up,* he thought.

He glanced back and was shocked to see Eduardo and Nunes only feet behind him, smiling. Their knives were still sheathed. He wondered if he should change the plan, let them do the killing.

Like Henry, they were used to using their knives. Before the Japanese banzai attack a few days before, he'd never used a knife for anything but skinning deer and other innocuous chores. Henry told him tales of having to stab alligators on the bayou when they were too close for a safe gunshot.

It didn't happen every day, but it happened enough that he'd learned how to handle a knife with skill. Eduardo and Nunes looked like they'd been doing similar things far more often in the jungles of Luzon. *Why the hell'd I volunteer myself for this?* He knew the answer: he wouldn't ask his men to do anything he wouldn't do first. *Tark's Ticks,* he thought.

He slid to his belly and slithered forward until he and Henry were beside each other. Henry's eyes sparkled in the night and Tarkington followed his gaze and saw the dim silhouette of a Japanese helmet and shoulders. He was only twelve feet away, facing down the hill.

He thought they must be on shifts; the other soldier must be sleeping in the bottom of the hole. His sphincter tightened. *What if he's taking a piss and is on his way back right now?* He got control of his pounding heart, pushing the fear down with a concerted effort. He'd deal with whatever hand he was dealt.

Henry moved left and Tarkington followed, wanting to come at them from behind. He felt something large crawl over the sleeve of his right arm. It wasn't the first encounter that night with creepy-crawlies, indeed it was nearly constant, but this was something altogether different. This had weight and he knew immediately it was some kind of snake.

Most of the snakes on Luzon were deadly poisonous. He froze and felt his sweat turn cold and prickly on his forehead. The urge to fling whatever was crossing over his arm was nearly overwhelming. He focused on the snake, trying to see the skin design and color, hoping to God it wasn't a King Cobra.

It moved across his right arm and continued over his left. He suddenly felt the weight of it and he realized his arms were pinned. He decided it had to be a python. They could grow to twenty feet and weigh three hundred pounds. What would he do if it started wrapping itself around his warm body? He'd heard many stories about man-eating pythons. They were a reality here.

He flexed his hand, holding the knife. Could he kill it without making too much noise? No way, he decided, if he stabbed it, the thing would thrash around making it sound like the entire forest was coming down. The thing was huge, and besides, he was pinned.

The snake continued moving over his arms. He could feel the scales as its thousands of bandy muscles flexed and relaxed, propelling it across the jungle floor. He desperately looked for Henry, but he was out of sight.

He couldn't decide what he was more afraid of: the snake or the Japanese soldier only feet away. Would he rather be shot, or crushed and swallowed whole? Neither were at the top of his list.

Finally he felt the weight lessen on his right arm as the end of the snake neared. *The thing must be twenty feet long.* The tail passed over his arm and blood coursed back into his hand, sending painful pins and needles into his numb hand. He gripped the knife handle, barely feeling it. *Shit, how will this work?* He flexed both hands trying to force feeling back into them. He dared a glance back, but Eduardo and Nunes were gone. He suddenly felt very alone. He brought his gaze back to the Japanese soldier, still staring off into the jungle, oblivious to what was transpiring only feet away.

A quick movement caught Tarkington's attention and he saw Henry's silhouette lunge forward like a striking cobra. The Japanese soldier suddenly arched backward as the two shadows came together. There was a sickening gurgling sound as the soldier's throat was cut and his head nearly severed from his shoulders. There was a splash as though a bucket of water had spilled. Another shadow joined the first and there was a yelp which was snuffed out almost as soon as it started.

Tarkington crawled forward, the feeling in his hands finally coming back. He got to the edge of the hole, ready to take on whatever awaited him. He didn't see anything but blackness as he gazed into the hole and, for an instant, thought everyone had simply disappeared, but the iron smell of blood and shit told him there'd been violent death moments before.

Henry suddenly popped up, inches from his face. He looked grim in the dim light of the stars. Eduardo popped up beside him, his teeth white as he smiled. He disappeared back into the hole and Tarkington couldn't see what he was doing but heard the slicing of cartilage and soon he popped up and held up a severed ear, his grin even wider.

Henry ignored him, hopped out of the hole and crouched beside Tarkington. "Couldn't wait for you to finish playing with the snake."

Nunes appeared from their left, grinning and dragging something huge, long and lifeless. Tarkington shook his head and felt the stress of the night fall off his shoulders, like releasing a coat of iron. He had to cover his mouth to keep from laughing like a maniac. It wasn't mirth, but the overwhelming relief of tension. He felt like he'd been blown up to bursting and at the last second before exploding someone hit a pressure valve relieving the stress.

He got control of himself and whispered, "Let's get outta here."

Getting back to the rest of the squad took a lot less time. The four of them still moved carefully, but made sure they weren't too quiet. They didn't want to startle a jumpy GI and get shot by friendly forces.

Once Tarkington was back among the men, he let himself relax slightly. He took a deep breath and blew it out slow, trying to force his muscles to relax. He still felt a bit wound up. The slow sneak, the snake, the kill, it was a lot of stress and they were still a long way from friendly forces.

He sat down and leaned against a tree, silently berating himself again for not bringing water.

Winkleman sat next to him and tilted his helmet back. He handed Tarkington an unfamiliar canteen. He took it gratefully and tilted his head. Winkleman saw his questioning motion and whispered, "Henry took it off the dead Jap. Said you'd probably want a slug."

Tarkington shook his head, "Stupid not to take water out here." He unscrewed the lid, briefly thought about the previous owner and took a gulp. It tasted wondrous as it coated his parched throat. He wanted to knock the whole thing back but forced himself to stop. "How're the men doing? Any trouble?"

Winkleman shook his head, "No problem. They want in on the action." Tarkington nodded but wasn't sure he ever wanted an experience like the one he just had. Winkleman asked, "What now?"

Tarkington looked at his watch. He couldn't believe it was already two AM. "Suppose we should move back to the river. Set up an ambush in case the Japs come looking for us once they find their men."

Winkleman nodded and got to his feet. "I'll inform the men." He was about to move off, but stopped and asked, "What was it like? I mean, using the knife."

Tarkington pushed himself up and faced Winkleman. "I was pinned down by a fucking python. Henry and Eduardo did it." Tarkington couldn't see his facial expression, but the tilt of his head told him he wanted the entire story later.

They were soon moving back down the hill in single file. With each step away from the enemy, Tarkington felt better and better.

They were nearly at the river when gunfire broke out up the hill again. Everyone stopped and crouched but only briefly, before resuming their march.

At the river, Tarkington gathered the men and whispered. "I've been thinking, the Japs might try to pursue us once they find their men. Our path would be easy to follow. Let's move back to the base of the hill, staying off the path we just made. We'll set up an ambush and wait until midmorning." He wanted to apologize for having them leave their water, but an apology would only sow doubt in his leadership skills. "If they don't come by then, we'll get our asses back across the river." The men nodded enthusiastically.

They stayed well off the path and moved parallel to it. When they got to the beginning of the hill, Tarkington directed them to spread out in the shape of an 'L'. Stolly and Vick set up on the bottom part of the 'L', the BAR muzzle pointed up the trail they'd created. If the Japs came, they'd follow the trail and walk right into the ambush. The BAR would begin the killing and the riflemen would finish the job.

The rest of the night passed slowly. Tarkington was on his back looking up at the stars through palm treetops, which swayed gently in a tropical breeze. Before the war, he thought Luzon was paradise. Sure it was hot, and when it rained, it *really* rained, and there were about a hundred different kinds of lethal snakes, but the different shades of green, the clear, warm water, the star-filled nights, made it all worth it. Since the war his views had changed a bit, but it was still undeniably beautiful.

He squinted at his watch. It would be light soon. He took one last look skyward and noticed the black sky wasn't quite as black as it had been. The night was losing its tight grasp, giving way to the coming day. Soon the stars would fade until they disappeared.

He rolled onto his stomach and pointed his Thompson's muzzle up the trail. He wondered who would find the dead soldiers. Would it be the other rear guard, or someone from the main force, coming to relieve them? He wondered how the corpses would look after a few hours simmering in the hole. Had they been ravaged by wild animals? He thought about the python. He shuddered remembering the feel of the snake on his arm. The weight.

He looked for the Filipinos, somewhere to his left, further up the 'L'. Nunes had killed the python and was more excited about it than killing the Japs. He had lugged the two-hundred-pound beast all the way to the river, intent on eating it as soon as he was able to start a fire. Tarkington supposed it would damned near feed the entire platoon. Nunes reluctantly left it beside the river, hoping another predator wouldn't run off with it.

The fighting up the hill suddenly intensified as the sun rose over the horizon and heated the air. Tarkington cursed his water situation for the hundredth time. He was parched and was sure the rest of the men were too, but wouldn't let on. He squinted up the hill and decided that, if the Japs were attacking 3rd platoon, they probably weren't concerned about their rear-guard and weren't heading his way.

He'd made up his mind and was about to pass the word to wrap it up and move out when he heard the distinct sound of metal scraping on metal. He froze, scanning the hillside, but saw nothing. He could feel the tension of the men around him rising and knew he hadn't imagined it. They were coming.

With the continued engagement up the hill, he doubted it was 3rd platoon. It was unlikely they'd broken through and were making a dash to the river. His men knew not to fire until he opened up first, to be quickly followed by the BAR.

He watched the trail, keeping his head down, peering from beneath the rim of his helmet, which he'd decorated with twigs and leaves. The men were similarly camouflaged, virtually invisible.

Finally he saw movement. He forced himself to remain calm, trying to keep his breathing and heart rate in check. He saw the soldier emerge from behind a tree. He took a careful step, stopped and studied the surroundings before taking another step. He followed the trail, kneeling occasionally to study the tracks, then moving again.

He was halfway into the ambush before Tarkington saw the second Japanese soldier. He was moving less cautiously, but careful not to get too close to the lead scout. There were soldiers loosely spread out behind him. They had weeds sticking from their helmets and held long rifles. Tarkington noticed one man held a sub-machine gun and wore a soft hat rather than the pith helmet of the foot soldier. He'd kill him first.

Tarkington didn't dare breathe as the scout passed only feet from where he lay. He had no doubt the scout would be killed in the first volley of bullets from the BAR, so he ignored him.

With the scout past he moved his barrel slightly, aiming in the general direction of the officer. He took a breath and blew it out slow, allowing his fingertip to touch the trigger. He moved the muzzle the rest of the way and pulled the trigger. The Japanese soldier was only yards away and Tarkington saw his chest explode with bright blood as the .45 caliber bullets impacted and blew out his back.

The BAR opened up and it, combined with the rifle shots from the rest of the GIs, was deafening. Tarkington swept his muzzle, firing into bodies until his 20-round magazine emptied. The BAR's bark stopped at almost the same time. Tarkington released the mag and added a new one he had laid out nearby. He put the stock to his shoulder and searched for more targets. Rifles continued to fire as the GIs worked their bolt actions. There were no more obvious targets but Tarkington fired into a nearby soldier trying to crawl away. His bullets walked up his back sending gouts of blood and he stopped moving.

Tarkington swept his smoking muzzle searching but saw nothing living. "Cease fire, cease fire," he yelled and the firing petered out.

GIs got to their feet and were suddenly visible and obvious. Nunes and Eduardo sprang forward, their knives out, ready to collect trophies. Sergeant Winkleman called, "Give me a head count."

Tarkington answered, "One okay," and listened as all eight men answered. He breathed a sigh of relief. No one was hit. He saw Raker move forward near the officer he'd shot. "Raker, see if that Jap officer's got anything useful on him."

Raker nodded and got onto his haunches, balancing his rifle across his legs and went through his pockets. Tarkington walked past the two nearby Japanese riflemen. Both were dead, staring straight up, their grisly wounds seeping blood through their uniforms. By the time he got to Raker, he had a handful of papers and what looked like a crude map. He shrugged and handed it to Tarkington who looked it over briefly and shoved it all into a pocket.

Raker pushed the dead officer onto his belly, exposing the gaping wounds in his back. The .45 caliber bullets left dime sized entry holes but the exit wounds took large chunks of meat and bone. The small backpack was soaked red. Raker opened it and pulled out various items, the last being a tattered American flag. He held it up, "Bastards," he muttered and shoved it into his pocket.

Sergeant Winkleman hustled down the path, stepping over bodies. "I count seven dead. When the firing started there were still at least three that were out of the ambush. We fired on 'em anyway, but they probably made it."

Tarkington nodded, "Alright. Collect their rifles, we'll dump 'em in the river as we cross." He raised his voice, "Move out."

18

When Tarkington was done briefing Lt. Smoker, he smiled. "Well, I'd say that was a successful mission, Tark. Nine Nips KIA and not a scratch on any of ya." He held up the documents and map, "You even managed to bring me something to pass up to Captain Glister."

Tarkington nodded and pointed at the documents. "Since we weren't supposed to be out there, how you gonna explain those?"

"The Captain won't argue with success. I'm the officer in charge down here, he'll defer to my decisions." Winkleman was grinning and shaking his head trying not to laugh. "What's so damned funny, Sergeant?"

Winkleman straightened but couldn't keep the smile from showing. "Sorry, sir. I'm just thinking about our fearless squad leader pinned down by a damned snake a few feet from a Jap." He shook his head and laughed. "I woulda given up a whole year's pay to have seen that."

Tarkington glowered and shook his head, but couldn't keep the smile from coming. "Not good, no doubt about it." He laughed. "I wasn't sure what was gonna happen." He held up a hand, "On the one hand, eaten," he held up the other, "on the other, shot. It wasn't ideal."

Lieutenant Smoker pointed toward the flat ground behind them. "Nunes insisted on a fire, he's cooking snake steaks right now. Promised he could keep it smokeless." He looked that way. "Eduardo and Nunes are good men." He shook his head, "but we can't let 'em keep taking ears for trophies."

Tarkington shrugged, "Better'n scrotums, I guess."

They all laughed then Smoker got serious, "Make 'em curb that shit, Tark. It's not civilized."

Tarkington nodded. "I'll talk to them, sir."

Around noon, 3rd platoon showed up across the river. 1st platoon was ready, having seen movement, but immediately recognized their comrades. They stood in their foxholes and waved and yelled for them to cross.

Lieutenant Smoker shook hands with Lieutenant Grunwald while slapping him on the back. "Damn good to see you, Max." Lt. Grunwald smiled and nodded despite his obvious exhaustion. "How'd you break out? I didn't hear a firefight."

Grunwald shrugged, "We heard a brief but intense battle below us this morning. I sent my scouts to check it out and discovered there weren't any Japs left. They'd bugged out. The Filipinos are pushing forward and think they'll have this pocket dealt with by the end of the day."

Smoker nodded. "You heard second squad's ambush. They were out there last night."

Grunwald nodded, "We came across the bodies. Japs must've been thin and thought another force was coming up behind 'em, I guess."

"Captain Glister's gonna want to debrief you I'm sure, but you and your men look hungry."

Grunwald looked at him hopefully. "Yeah, we've been on half rations."

Smoker slapped his back and guided him toward the rear, "Think your men would enjoy a two-hundred-pound python?"

Grunwald face turned sour, "Aw shit. I thought you meant something good. Snake?"

Smoker grinned, "I haven't tried it yet, but the Filipinos sure are excited about it." The dull thunder of battle rolled down from the hill and Grunwald and Smoker stopped and looked. "Sounds like Major Durante's found the Japs."

Grunwald nodded. "I don't know how those guys have anything left. The Japs kept up constant pressure. Those men, and particularly Durante, haven't slept more than a coupla minutes for days now."

Smoker shrugged, "Guess that goes for the Japs too then."

"Japs too..." His eyes glazed as he thought about the past days, "They're fanatics. Thank God they ran out of mortar shells. They can't have much ammo left. We had to keep a constant watch - they were sneaking around with their damned knives all night." He looked down. "Lost a few men that first night." He looked up and Lt. Smoker could see he was struggling. "We learned to stay awake after that. Slept during the day when we could." The intensity of the firing increased. "Hope they kill every last one of those sons-of-bitches." His tone was dangerous and filled with hatred.

Smoker nodded, "Me too. Me too."

They kept a few men on the line and rotated the watch so everyone got a chance to try the snake. Grunwald's men, once they took a bite, attacked the thick steaks with abandon. Nunes and Eduardo spiced the meat with various plants they found and salt tabs were ground up and sprinkled on the sizzling meat. They'd spread the fire, until there was a long section of coals. They'd fashioned stout limbs and sections of the snake were draped over them. The meat sizzled and dripped juices onto the coals, causing mini-eruptions of flame to lick and darken the meat.

The mood lightened quickly as bellies filled and the GIs of 3rd platoon finally felt safe. The past few days' stress dropped from their shoulders and they joked, burped, farted and ate.

Occasionally, someone would stand abruptly, clutch their ass and bolt into the privacy of the jungle to expel their bowels. Diarrhea was rampant and many men had already been taken off the line with dysentery. It was a problem that could only be fixed by getting out of the jungle, but they all knew that wasn't going to happen. It was a reality they had to live with every day.

―――――――――

The GIs of 1st platoon manned the foxholes along the river bank while the men of 3rd platoon slept. With their bellies filled, and in a relatively safe area, Lt. Grunwald ordered his men to sleep before moving up the hill to report to Captain Glister. Smoker knew Glister must be aching for a report, since 3rd platoon's radio had stopped working the day before, but he understood Grunwald's need to take care of his men first.

They didn't need to be told twice. They simply dropped where they were and the sounds of snoring and deep breathing soon followed. Grunwald himself was propped against a tree with his helmet pulled over his eyes, breathing deep and steady.

Staff Sergeant Tarkington stood beside Lt. Smoker looking the men over. "They've been through hell and back."

"Yeah, and unfortunately there's no end in sight." He lifted his head to the hill listening to the distant sounds of gunfire. It was more sporadic now and further away. "Sounds like this pocket of Japs are through though."

Tarkington followed his gaze. "You think a resupply's coming, sir? A mile-long line of ships?"

The silence stretched and Tarkington thought perhaps he'd overstepped his bounds. Finally he answered, "Doesn't seem possible, but it's the only thing keeping the men's morale up." He looked Tarkington in the eye, "Without hope, this whole thing'll collapse in a week." He adjusted his stance and leaned in, "Don't tell the men anything different. That's an order."

Tarkington stiffened, "Yes, sir. I understand."

"How're your men doing after the long night?"

Tarkington nodded, "Fine, sir. They slept most of the morning and the meal made 'em sleepy again, but they're ready for whatever's next."

Smoker grinned, "Tark's Ticks." He looked for a reaction.

Tarkington ground his teeth, making his jaw flex. "You heard about that?" Smoker gave a slight nod. "It's something the men started when we were on the hill the other day. I'll tell 'em to knock it off."

Smoker shook his head, "No need. Gives the second squad an identity; something to be proud of."

"Ticks, sir? You ever seen a tick? Disgusting."

Smoker smiled and nodded, "Course they are, but they're also strong, stealthy and hard to get rid of. One tiny bite from a diseased tick can take a man down." Tarkington continued to gaze up the hill. "I'm going to talk with Captain Glister about your mission last night. Taking the fight to the enemy like that could really put them on edge. Keep 'em wondering, keep 'em scared." He let that sink in and Tarkington turned from the hill and looked at his commanding officer. "You think your men would be up for that?"

Tarkington's 'do not volunteer for anything' alarm was going off loud in his head but he nodded and said, "Yes, sir. Whatever you need."

Smoker shook his head and pursed his lips. "I need more than that. Sure I could make it an order, but something like this will have to be like last night's mission - volunteer only."

"Mind if I run it by the men first?"

"Of course. I'm not even sure the captain will go for it. Go talk to 'em and get back to me."

"Yes, sir."

Tarkington joined 2nd squad at the foxholes facing the river. He slid in beside Sergeant Winkleman, who made room and asked, "What's the scoop, Tark?"

"Gather the men, the lieutenant wants me to ask 'em something."

Winkleman noticed the worry and nodded, "Sure thing, Sarge."

Minutes later the men were back from the line a few yards sitting in a circle with their weapons resting on their shoulders. Tarkington looked around the circle. He'd known these men a long time, been through a lot with them and he realized he felt a deep connection to each of them. He didn't see Eduardo and Nunes. "Wink, Eduardo and Nunes too." He nodded and sent a man to retrieve the Filipinos, who were snoozing their lunch away.

When they arrived they sat and Tarkington began. "Lieutenant Smoker wanted me to tell you how impressed he is with last night's mission." He paused and looked around the circle. These were combat veterans, men who'd gone to hell and back. "Look, I'm not gonna sugar-coat it. Smoker wants us to do more of it. He wants us to go out and harass the enemy in their own backyards, keep 'em off-balance and scared of the dark." No one spoke, their expressions giving him nothing. "He wants us to do commando type stuff. It's not an order. It's volunteer only, but before you say anything you need to know the score. There's no support out there. If we get into trouble we have to fight our way out. We can't call in the cavalry. We'll be out there with our asses hanging in the wind."

The silence stretched as each man considered. Tarkington half-hoped they'd refuse. He'd lead the squad and be proud of them, no matter what. They'd already lost men and would no doubt lose more as this nightmare continued.

PFC Stollman was the first to break the silence. He looked around the circle, "Well, I for one am in. Sounds like a good way to kill more Japs. I still owe them for Roscoe, Blakesly, Crown," he paused, his voice catching on emotion, "Flynn." He shook his head and wiped the moisture filling his eyes. "I'm in, that's all."

Beside him PFC Vick squeezed his shoulder and nodded. "Yeah, I'm definitely in. Sons-of-bitches have a lot to answer for."

The next man in the circle, Holiday, nodded, "In," as did each man after him.

PFC Henry was beside Tarkington. When it was his turn, he was silent. Tarkington and all the rest watched him intently. For a moment Tarkington thought his friend would decline, he wasn't one to hop on the bandwagon. He had a mind of his own and wouldn't do something out of peer-pressure. The thought of going into the jungle without his steady, trusted first scout didn't sit well with him. Henry pulled out a deck of tattered playing cards. "We'll leave these on the Japs we kill."

He handed the deck to Tarkington who turned the first card over. He shook his head and passed it along to the next man. Scrawled on the white space was the phrase 'Tark's Ticks' and a drawn death's head. Henry grinned, "Been working on that all morning."

Tarkington laughed, "You crafty son-of-a-bitch."

An hour later, 3rd platoon was roused and they readied themselves to march back to the plateau. Lieutenant Grunwald found Tarkington. Tarkington saw him coming and stepped out of his foxhole. Grunwald stuck his hand out and they shook. "I hear you led second squad last night." Tarkington nodded. "I think your action had a lot to do with the Japs leaving our flank.

I just want to tell you good job, and thank you." He looked around at the other GIs. "Be sure to tell your men."

They released hands and Tarkington nodded, "Yes, sir. I'll do that. See you back at HQ."

Grunwald nodded and walked back to his platoon. Tarkington thought he looked sickly. He remembered him as a strapping athlete. Before the war, he'd insisted on leading his platoon in calisthenics and there were damned few soldiers that could keep up with him. He'd been a college athlete, track and field, and Tarkington had heard he held records in the high hurdles. Seeing how his tattered uniform hung from his thin frame made him shake his head. *This war's killing him.*

Sergeant Winkleman walked up beside him. "Heard he lost some men out there."

Tarkington nodded, "Yeah, Zachary and Hammond."

"Seems like he's withering on the vine."

Tarkington turned toward him. "Yeah, I was thinking the same thing. Looks like he's lost half his body weight. Smoker says he has trouble eating. Just doesn't have an appetite. Guilt's eating him up, I think."

PFC Rabowski, Lt. Smoker's runner loped up and stopped in front of him. "Lieutenant Smoker just got the word, we've been called back to HQ. Wants to be out of here in half an hour, Staff Sergeant."

Tarkington nodded, "Thanks Private. Carry on." He ran off to find the other NCOs, but the word was already passing from man to man. Tarkington looked across the lazy waters of the Tuol River to the far bank. The greenery shimmered through the hazy air. Being close to the water made the day's heat almost tolerable. Moving back to the plateau would be like moving back into a furnace. He raised his voice. "Second squad, we're moving out. Top off your canteens and police the area. We leave in twenty minutes."

The GIs grumbled and pulled themselves from their holes, keeping wary eyes on the far bank. There'd been no sign of enemy activity all day, but they'd learned you live longer if you kept your guard up.

For the next two days they stayed on the plateau. In the evening of the second day, Major Duerte and his Filipino company descended from the hill, victorious. They claimed the near total destruction of the Japanese pocket of resistance. They'd pushed them off the hill and forced them into the waiting fire of Able Company of the First Filipino Division. The victory was complete, they'd taken no prisoners.

The 1st platoon re-occupied their old positions among the trees. On the second day back, Tarkington was sitting in his hammock. He thought about the Japanese sword and his anger flared. An idea came to him and he went searching for Sergeant Winkleman. He found him sitting on his hammock reading a faded letter. He saw him coming, "What's up Tark?"

Tarkington stood in front of him with his Thompson slung over his shoulder. "There's a meeting this evening at 1800 to go over plans and company bullshit." He leaned closer and lowered his voice. "When that happens I'll need you to cover for me. I'll be late. Tell 'em I'm shitting."

Winkleman nodded and the edges of his mouth turned down. "Okay. What will you actually be doing?"

"It's best you don't know. As far as you know, I'm suffering from a bout of diarrhea."

Winkleman nodded and asked, "This have anything to do with an antique Japanese sword?"

Tarkington stepped away, surprised. "How'd you guess that?"

Winkleman shrugged. "You can't just waltz in there and steal it. He'll notice it's gone right away."

"It's not stealing, it's mine. It's war booty."

He nodded, "Yeah, but that's neither here nor there. We've gotta make him think he's still got it, otherwise he'll sic McLunty on you. He's been chomping at the bit to make trouble for you and that would be just the thing. Stealing from a superior officer would land you in the brig quick."

Tarkington's surprise was evident on his face. "Seems like you've been thinking about this. Why?"

Winkleman looked past him and yelled, "Hey Skinny, come over here."

PFC Skinner stopped cleaning his sidearm, a Japanese Nambu pistol he'd found somewhere along the line, and trotted over. "What's up, Wink?" He glanced at Tarkington, "Tark," he acknowledged.

"The staff sergeant wants his sword back. Tell him about our plan."

"Your plan? Who else is in on this?" asked Tarkington.

Winkleman grinned, "The whole squad's in on it. What they did is horseshit. We can't let 'em get away with it. That sword's rightfully yours."

PFC Skinner grinned at Tarkington's stunned silence. He turned and motioned them to follow. As they went, the other GIs noticed and pulled in behind, until there was a line of GIs. Skinner led them deeper into the jungle until he got to a stack of boulders. He stepped behind them and pulled back a thicket of branches.

Tarkington realized the thicket was actually woven together, making a sort of camouflage door. Skinner placed the door on the ground. He crouched and stepped into a little room formed by the boulders on one side, and a thick palm on the other. More thatched walls connected the space, making it nearly invisible to anyone that didn't know it was there. "What the hell's this?"

Skinner poked his head back out and motioned him to follow. Tarkington looked to Winkleman, who grinned and motioned him to enter. He crouched and followed Skinner. The room was small, too short to stand in. Once inside, he noticed Japanese war trophies. Against one wall were stacks of Japanese bayonets, neatly folded Jap flags, and five more Nambu pistols, along with Japanese ammo, but the most prominent piece was a Japanese sword, propped up on the wall in its scabbard.

"Where'd you get all this stuff, Skinny?"

Skinner's smile showed off crooked and broken teeth. "Collecting and selling's in my blood, Sarge. Pop owns a trade shop back home, been working with him since I was knee-high to a grasshopper." He winked, "Acquisitions is my specialty." He moved his hand like a car salesman showing off the newest Ford. "Figure this stuff'll be worth a fortune back home."

"Home? How the hell you plan on getting it home?"

He shrugged, "I'm not. Just saying, wish I could. Stuff's worth a lot here too though. When we were in Mariveles I made a fortune selling to the rear echelon guys. They're itching for war booty."

Tarkington reached out and gripped a flag. "Where the hell'd you get so many Jap flags?"

Skinner grinned sheepishly. "Don't look too close, they're not real. I cut up an old silk parachute, been dyeing the red Jap circle onto 'em." Tarkington put his fingers through what looked like a bullet hole. Skinner nodded, "They sell better with a little battle damage. The chumps don't know the difference."

Holiday stuck his head inside, "Unless it rains, then they notice."

Skinner's grin disappeared, "Yeah, the dye's low quality, runs like soup when it rains, but we move around so much it hasn't caught up to me yet." He ran his hand through his greasy hair. "I was glad to get out of Mariveles though. Made a bundle that day."

Sergeant Winkleman pointed. "Show him the sword."

Skinner nodded and handed the scabbard to him. Tarkington took it and looked at the etchings. He gripped the handle, it felt similar to his but not the same. "Suppose you wanna sell this to me?"

Skinner looked offended, "No, it's not for sale. Pull it out."

Tarkington was confused but did as he asked. He pulled slowly in the confined space and when it was halfway out, it ended with a jagged break. Tarkington's shoulders fell, "Hmm, broken."

Skinner nodded, "Yep and I don't have the rest of it. Damned shame."

Tarkington nodded and put the broken blade back into the scabbard. He was about to tell them he appreciated the thought but he didn't want a broken replacement. Winkleman spoke first. "The plan's to swap this one with the one Smoker stole from you."

Tarkington shook his head. "That'll buy a little time, but he'll obviously figure it out when he pulls the broken sword out."

Winkleman shook his head, "He never pulls it. Thinks of it as too precious or something. He barely even picks it up, just stares at it sometimes."

"How the hell d'you know that?"

Silence stretched as he looked from man to man. Skinner shrugged, "We've got a man on the inside, you could say."

Tarkington thought about the men around Lt. Smoker, none of them were in 2nd squad and he knew it couldn't be Platoon Sergeant McLunty. "Who?" he demanded.

Skinner looked to Winkleman, who shrugged and said, "That new runner, Rabowski. He's at Smoker's beck and call round the clock."

Skinner grinned again and added, "And he's about two hundred dollars in debt to me."

Winkleman nodded. "The debt'll be paid when he makes the switch."

Skinner scowled, "We'll see about that. Two hundred bucks is a lot of dough, Sergeant."

"How's it possible I never knew about this stash of yours?"

Skinner shrugged, "I don't advertise. The people that need to know, know and the ones that don't, don't."

"How the hell you move it from place to place?"

Skinner's mouth went flat and he squinted, "Now, now, Sergeant, I'm willing to help get your sword back, but you don't get to know *all* my secrets."

Tarkington put both hands up, "Okay, okay. Probably best I don't know."

19

FEBRUARY 25TH, 1942

With the Japanese incursion past the Orion-Bagac line squashed, Hotel Company moved north to reinforce the line. A trip of only twenty miles took two full days due to refugee-clogged roads. The Japanese had pulled back from the line licking their wounds and, everyone assumed, getting ready for another assault. The locals took advantage of the respite to move south.

When Hotel Company finally arrived, they filled a gap near the center of the line, bridging I and II Corps. Tarkington's 2nd squad still only consisted of eight GIs and two Filipinos. There simply weren't any more men to bring their numbers back up to full strength. Everyone that could be spared from rear positions had already been transferred to line units long before. Cooks, mechanics and drivers were all down to the bare minimum to keep the operation going.

The 1st platoon took the center position between 2nd and 3rd platoons. There were already foxholes and slit trenches but they got to work expanding and making them better. Lt. Smoker ordered a detail to move forward and hack down the incessant foliage which seemed to grow inches in a day. By the time evening came, they'd hacked a kill zone that stretched forward forty yards from their positions.

Captain Glister chose to place one of the rare heavy machine gun units in their midst and 2nd squad got busy, helping to fortify their position with cut palms and anything else they could get their hands on which might stop a bullet, or deflect an artillery shell fragment. There was a hurried frenzy to get the defensive positions done. No one had any illusions that the lull in the fighting would last long.

Tarkington was sleeping in the bottom of his hole, while PFC Henry stayed awake and on guard, when the first mortar rounds whistled overhead. His eyes snapped open and he could see Henry's face light up with each mortar shell impact. The shells weren't close, so Henry didn't duck. In a gravelly, just-woke-up voice, Tarkington asked, "What's going on up there? Any movement?"

Henry didn't look at him but shook his head. "Just more harassment fire to keep us awake." He grinned and looked down at him, "It's working on you anyway. Go back to sleep. I'll wake you in an hour."

Tarkington pulled his feet beneath him and stood up, sighing. "I'm too damned hungry to sleep anyway." Henry kept staring into the night, and Tarkington continued. "Didn't realize how good we had it back south. We didn't eat like kings, but we got more than the guys up here. Last I heard, we're getting damned low on food and ammunition." A shell landed in the freshly-cut field and lit up the area for an instant. "Could really go for a burger right about now." He grinned, "Or even some of that python."

"Doesn't do any good thinking about it. Just makes it worse. Put it out of your mind. Think about sex."

Tarkington looked at him curiously. He'd never heard Henry mention sex in all the time he'd known him. It wasn't odd, just never came up with him. "Sex?" he asked.

"Yeah, when you have to take a piss, or you're hungry, or anytime you're uncomfortable and can't remedy it, think of sex." Tarkington continued to stare and Henry explained. "Humans are geared toward procreation; it trumps everything else. So, if you want to get over being uncomfortable about something, think of sex and you'll forget all about the other thing."

Tarkington shook his head, "So you're walking around with a hard-on all the time?" He couldn't keep from laughing.

Henry shrugged, "Nah, I don't let it get that far, just the notion is enough to curb things."

Tarkington guffawed, "I had no idea you were so dirty-minded."

Henry shook his head, "Human nature."

The shelling stopped. Tarkington's gut cramped and he bent slightly. He tried thinking of sex, forming a picture of a cute Filipino prostitute he'd lain with before the war. The image of her naked, perfectly brown body filled his mind but was suddenly replaced with her holding a plate with a huge rib-eye steak. He shook his head, the gnawing hunger returning. "Doesn't work for me, dammit. It's also human nature to eat regularly."

There was another mortar attack two hours later. Neither had done damage except to their sleep.

Just before the sun came up, Tarkington noticed PFC Rabowski hustling toward him in a crouch. Seeing him reminded him of the sword. There hadn't been an opportunity to make the switch yet. As he got closer, Tarkington wondered if he were coming with news about the operation, but realized the young man wouldn't know he knew of his involvement.

He stopped at the edge of the hole and nervously looked beyond, towards the killing zone, which was getting lighter by the second. He pulled his eyes away and whispered, "Lieutenant Smoker wants to see you and Sergeant Winkleman, Staff Sergeant." Since being reprimanded, he followed protocols when dealing with 2nd squad's leader.

"Thank you, Private." He pointed further down the line, "Winkleman's two holes down." The scrawny kid was about to leave but Tarkington grabbed his arm and Rabowski turned. Tarkington saw a flash of anger, which quickly disappeared. *Kid doesn't like being grabbed.* He released his grip. "How's my sword doing?"

Rabowski's eyes grew to saucers and he sputtered, "S - Sword? What sword, Sarge?"

Tarkington leaned in closer. "When you gonna make the switch?"

Rabowski looked terrified thinking it was some kind of trick. He looked at Henry who ignored him, then searched the other holes, looking for Skinner, no doubt. He was a couple of holes down. Too far to see. He licked his lips and whispered, "Soon." He looked side to side, conspiratorially. "Soon as I can, I will. He just unpacked it and put it on the little stand he made."

Tarkington nodded and pushed him on his way. He grumbled to Henry, "Wonder what he wants now."

He walked on stiff legs back toward officer country. Lt. Smoker was sitting on a rock, shaking dirt from the inside of his boots, when he found him. Tarkington strode up and said, "Reporting as ordered, sir." He pointed over his shoulder, "Sergeant Winkleman's right behind me."

Smoker finished tapping out his boot and slipped it on but didn't buckle it. He motioned when he saw Winkleman. "Come in. I have something I wanna discuss with you." Tarkington nodded and noticed PFC Rabowski watching him. He grinned and followed Smoker. "Have a seat on my cot, gentlemen."

Tarkington and Winkleman removed their helmets and sat. It was all Tarkington could do not to lay down on the comfy cot and drift off to sleep. He noticed the samurai sword spanning between two carved pieces of ornate wood. The scabbard fit perfectly in the carved wood notches. It looked like it was on display in a museum.

Lieutenant Smoker saw him looking. "Found the holder in a local shop while we were moving north. Wondrous how well it fits."

"Looks like you're taking good care of it for me, sir," Tarkington said trying to hide the sarcasm and failing.

"That's not why I brought you two here, though." Both sergeants focused on their commanding officer. It never ceased to amaze Tarkington how well-groomed he always was. It didn't matter if they were marching or fighting, he always seemed to be coiffed and freshly-shaved. Tarkington felt his own scruff and immediately regretted not shaving before coming. "I brought you here to discuss another night mission."

All thoughts of shaving and stealing back the sword disappeared. He glanced at Winkleman, "We're listening."

"Those mortars last night... it happens every night somewhere along the line. Lieutenant Meyer from Able Company told me they've been sticking to the same pattern for the past two weeks. They harass the same section for two nights, then move somewhere else randomly, but they always do two nights in a row." He looked at them expectantly. Both sergeants stared back, waiting for more. "Don't you see? Last night they hit our section. If they stick to routine, they'll do it again tonight. If you guys are out there waiting, you can intercept them."

Tarkington leaned back and considered. "What's the range on those things? I mean, they might be well behind the lines, firing from the middle of a full regiment of Japs for all we know."

"Lieutenant Meyer says they found where they fired from a week ago. Found the trampled grass from the base plates. They were only a couple hundred yards back."

Tarkington nodded, "Sounds reasonable they'd pull the same thing. Think they use the same spot each time?" Smoker shrugged, "If we could find the spot they used last night we could stake it out and wait for them to come back." He grinned, "Be like taking candy from a baby."

The GIs of 2nd squad moved beyond the lines an hour before dark in the hopes of finding where the Japanese mortar crew fired from the night before. Tarkington had little hope they'd be able to find the spot before darkness, but figured the risk of moving in daylight outweighed the chance.

They carried only what they needed: weapons, ammo and this time, water. They'd been given all the ammo they wanted and Tarkington made sure each man had two grenades. They were in short supply but since they were putting their asses out there it was warranted.

He'd briefed the men on how he wanted the operation to work. They'd move beyond the line and search for the firing position. If they found it they'd set up an ambush and wait. If they didn't find it they'd hunker down and wait until the fireworks started, then move to contact. He made it clear he wanted to use grenades to keep any nearby Japanese from honing in on their rifle shots. It was to be a quick strike and a quick retreat, and only happen if everything looked good; in other words, if it looked like they could pull it off.

They moved slowly, following the Filipinos and scouts. Besides the mortar attacks, there'd been no enemy contact since the pockets were annihilated. Tarkington hoped this wouldn't be the night the Japs decided to move into their forward positions and attack.

Once they were beyond the cleared killing-field and into the jungle, the remaining daylight seemed to dim by half. They moved in an arrowhead shape with PFC Henry at the tip and Tarkington in the middle.

Tarkington saw PFC Stollman hold up a closed fist and crouch. He did the same, signaling the men behind. They'd only moved fifty-yards into the jungle. If Henry was stopping this soon, he'd spotted something.

Staying in a crouch, Tarkington moved forward, touching Stollman's shoulder as he passed. His face was painted dark with streaks of grease. He hefted the BAR like it weighed nothing. The next man was Nunes, who grinned at him as he passed. He still had the necklace of Japanese ears hanging around his neck.

Raker saw him coming and pointed forward, never taking his finger off the trigger guard of his rifle. Tarkington slowed as he passed him, seeing Eduardo's back and, beyond him, PFC Henry. Henry was immobile, all his concentration forward. Tarkington pulled up beside him and looked at the area he was so focused on. He didn't notice anything.

Long seconds passed and Henry still hadn't moved. Tarkington could feel the tension which seemed to emanate from his lead scout's body, like heat from a stove. Tarkington leaned in and touched his shoulder lightly. Henry didn't look at him, but murmured, "Something's out there. I can feel it."

Tarkington didn't answer but nodded and concentrated on the surrounding jungle. The normal evening jungle sounds of monkeys, insects and life were undisturbed, but he knew better than to doubt Henry's combat radar.

There was sudden movement from the treetops. Tarkington glanced up and put his finger on the trigger. There it was again, but this time he saw monkeys moving through the treetops. He leaned into Henry, "Monkeys."

Henry still didn't move. The monkeys started yammering incessantly. He'd seen it happen before when humans entered their area. He'd even seen them hurl shit and piss onto passing GIs, but this monkey troupe wasn't focused on them. If they were, they'd be directly overhead. These monkeys were upset at something else, something in the treetops.

The tops of the trees still had a tiny sliver of evening sun touching them. The monkeys were screeching, surrounding a huge tree with thick branches. Henry whispered, "Sniper," and slowly brought his rifle to his shoulder. Tarkington did too, aiming in the general area but not seeing anything out of the ordinary except the crazy monkeys. Tarkington heard Henry take a shallow breath and slowly let it out, then the Springfield barked once, making the monkeys screech even louder and jump around in a frantic frenzy of displeasure. Henry quickly worked the bolt and fired again.

This time, Tarkington saw something besides monkeys. A bigger form dropped from the large tree, fell a few yards then snapped to a halt and swung, crazily spinning. "Holy shit, I see him now. Nice shot."

Henry kept his smoking muzzle trained on the dangling sniper, but it was obvious he was dead, hanging by his foot which was tethered to the tree by a six-foot rope. The monkeys leaped to the tree and inspected the dead sniper, hurling insults and feces.

Tarkington looked behind him and signaled Raker to stay put. Raker nodded and passed the signal to the others. He whispered, "See any more?"

Henry shook his head but kept his rifle aimed toward the trees. "Think there's more?" Tarkington asked.

Henry finally relaxed, brought his rifle off his shoulder and said, "I think that was it. Nice to have help from the monkeys for once."

Tarkington nodded but had a decision to make. The shots might've attracted attention. If the Japs were close they might send a squad to investigate, or they might not have heard anything, or they might assume the shots were from their sniper.

The light was fading fast. He made his decision. He tapped Henry and pointed right, "Take us a hundred fifty yards that way. Find a good spot to hunker down."

Henry nodded. Tarkington took one last look at the dangling sniper surrounded by excited monkeys. He figured he'd be visible for another twenty minutes, then it would be too dark. If the Japs investigated and found their man dead, they'd know there was a group of enemies out here and make a concerted effort to find them.

He saw Eduardo smiling at him and he waved him forward. He pointed at the sniper's body. "Can you climb up there and get rid of him? Would the monkeys be a problem?"

Eduardo spotted the body and slapped Henry's shoulder in admiration, then nodded, "I climb, unggoys know me. No problem." He saw Tarkington's confusion and explained, "Unggoy is monkey."

"They know you?" Eduardo's grin grew and Tarkington shook his head. "Get up there and get back here quick. We'll cover you."

Eduardo looked back and caught Nunes' eye. He gave him a slight nod and moved toward the big tree, keeping low but moving fast. He held his rifle in his right hand, low to the ground. He snaked through the sparse jungle, his senses on high alert.

He reached the base of the tree and looked up at the dangling body, still swaying slightly. He heard dripping and noticed a small pool of blood. The monkeys were gazing down at him. Despite what he told Sergeant Tarkington, the monkeys didn't know him and would not like him climbing what looked like their favorite tree. The Japanese sniper must've climbed the tree when the monkeys were away, he thought. Picking this tree had cost him his life.

He slung his rifle and looked back the way he came. He saw PFC Henry leading the squad forward to better cover him. He smiled but resisted waving. He leaped, grabbed the first branch and pulled himself up from branch to branch until he was forty feet off the ground. The monkeys started yammering again, watching his approach with extreme interest. Eduardo gave them a reassuring smile and lowered his eyes. He'd killed many Macaque monkeys for meat and he supposed they sensed this, so he kept his eyes down, being as innocuous as possible.

He was at the same level as the dangling Japanese. He saw two bullet holes: one in his neck, one in his chest. He marveled at Henry's shooting skills. He was the only American whose jungle skills were even close to his own. He moved like a native, silent and deadly.

He reached for the next branch and pulled himself up. The monkeys were squawking and making quick dashes at him, which he simply ignored. He knew they wouldn't attack him unless he were obviously injured or they were protecting young. He continued to keep his eyes down, and did his best to ignore them. He pulled out his knife and, holding the tree trunk, leaned out over space and touched the taut rope. The instant his razor-sharp blade made contact, the rope snapped and the Japanese soldier dropped, bouncing from limb to limb all the way to the ground.

Eduardo glanced up at the monkeys just in time to see one hurling feces. He saw it coming but fought the instinct to move out of the way. The shit hit him in the chest and splattered. He moved down the branches without looking back. Sometimes allowing the beasts a victory was the best way to not rile them more. There was renewed squawking. He was descending, obviously leaving, so something else must have got their attention.

He froze and looked out over the sparse jungle to the north. It was nearly dark, but he could clearly see men moving toward his tree. *Japs*, he thought. He moved to the other side of the tree trunk, shielding himself from the approaching enemy squad and waved to get the attention of the GIs. He saw PFC Raker at the base of the tree, checking the sniper, paying no attention to him. He finally saw Tarkington looking at him.

Eduardo signaled as best as he could that there were Japs coming. Tark seemed to understand and he passed it along to the others. Raker was out of reach though and still going through the sniper's pockets. He had to get his attention quick or he'd be seen.

Eduardo scraped the shit from the front of his shirt and worked it into a ball. He threw it hard and watched it hit Raker's shoulder and splatter his face. Raker looked up - annoyance and disgust on his face - but he saw Eduardo frantically motioning and knew he was in trouble.

20

There was no time for Eduardo to get out of the tree before the Japanese would be upon him, so he made himself as small a target as he could and slowly pulled his trusted rifle off his back, resting the barrel in the notch of a branch coming off the tree trunk.

Even in the dim light he could see multiple targets. He counted at least ten soldiers. He took his eyes from his sights and looked down at the base of the tree. PFC Raker was on his belly using the dead sniper's body for cover. Eduardo could see his rifle resting across the man's bloody chest.

He looked toward the rest of the squad and saw them moving to the right, out of the way of the advancing enemy and toward a thicker part of the jungle. He hoped they weren't seen in the next few minutes or they'd be sitting ducks.

He brought his eye back to his sights and found what looked like either an officer or an NCO. He was dressed like the others, but he held a pistol rather than a rifle, setting him apart and earning Eduardo's interest. He didn't know if he should shoot, or wait until his squad did. His instincts told him he should shoot, but perhaps Tark was trying for a surprise ambush-style attack, and shooting too early would ruin it.

The lead enemy soldier was close, only a few yards from the base of the tree. The monkeys had stopped squawking, perhaps feeling the tension of the coming battle. The lead enemy scout stopped suddenly and held up a hand. Eduardo could barely see him against the green and brown foliage, but something had spooked him. Did he see the dead sniper and Private Raker only yards away? Or did he notice the movement of the men further back.

The officer crouched and held up a hand and the rest of the enemy squad stopped and crouched. Eduardo made his decision. If he didn't shoot now, he'd lose sight of the officer in the darkness. The officer was close. He couldn't miss. He adjusted his sights slightly and pulled the trigger. The rifle bucked and he saw the officer's head snap back and his body crumpled to the ground in a heap. He smoothly worked the bolt, chambering another round before the Japanese reacted. He shot the man directly behind the officer and saw his chest blossom red as he dropped his rifle and fell like a sack of rice.

Before he could chamber a third round, the rest of the Japanese reacted. The muzzle flash was easy to spot and they unloaded a volley of fire. Eduardo pulled behind the thick trunk and felt the tree vibrate with bullet impacts. Branches and leaves broke off and the air was alive with bullets. Despite the danger, Eduardo couldn't help but smile. He'd killed another two of them. Two more that would never return to their hated homeland.

While the air around him buzzed, he looked down and saw Raker fire his first shot. He didn't dare expose himself to see if he hit anyone, but continued watching the second scout working the bolt action and firing over and over. The enemy fire directed at him shifted to Raker and Eduardo took the opportunity to lean out the other side of the tree.

He saw a muzzle flash and quickly aimed and fired behind it slightly where he hoped the Japanese soldier would be. He quickly chambered another round and fired again before pulling back. Once again, the tree shook and splintered, but absorbed the bullets. Eduardo muttered a low apology to the tree.

A quick motion beneath him caught his attention and he saw Raker just finishing throwing a grenade. Eduardo had forgotten he had two grenades himself.

Since it was the first time Nunes and Eduardo had had them, Sergeant

Winkleman had spent a good portion of the day teaching them with a deactivated grenade. It was the same weight, just lacked the explosives.

He'd shown them how to arm and throw them. He'd even set up barrels and they tried to put the grenade into them from various distances. He and Nunes had enjoyed it very much, making it a competition. By the time they went on patrol, they were experts.

Raker's grenade exploded lighting up the early darkness for an instant and sending shockwaves and shrapnel in all directions. Eduardo slung his rifle and pulled one of his two grenades off his belt. He made sure of his footing on the thick branch, making sure he wouldn't fall. He found the pin, pulled it and leaned out while holding the tree trunk with his left hand and threw it as far as he could with his right. He was forty feet above the ground. The grenade traveled over the Japanese and exploded ten feet above their heads, sending chunks of metal in a wide arc.

Eduardo was thrilled to hear screams of agony. Charged with success, he pulled the second grenade and leaned out again, but before he could throw it, he felt something hot and extremely painful drill into his hip. His right leg gave out and he dropped the grenade as he fell back into the crook of the tree.

The grenade bounced off limbs and finally exploded ten feet from the ground. The explosion took Eduardo's breath away for an instant and, despite the pain in his hip and leg, he looked down towards Raker with fear in his heart.

He saw him writhing back and forth on his back with his hands over his ears in agony. *No, no, no.* He yelled "Raker!" But he knew his ears would be ringing the same way his were and that he couldn't possibly hear him.

Through his screams and ringing ears, Eduardo heard a new sound and knew the rest of the squad was in position and pouring fire into the remaining Japanese.

He heard more grenades. He ground his teeth against the pain and leaned out to see explosions lighting up the area. He saw enemy soldiers lit up in freeze-frame flashes of blood and gore.

He gripped his rifle and aimed as best he could. He saw a dark figure running away. He tried to hold steady. He pulled the trigger but the soldier continued sprinting away unscathed. A second later the waves of pain rolled over him like an ocean swell and he slipped into complete darkness.

Tarkington watched Eduardo scamper up the tree and whispered to Henry. "No wonder the monkeys know him - he must've taught them to climb."

Henry nodded, "He's impressive."

Tarkington touched his arm, "Move forward so we can cover him better." Henry nodded and moved forward. When he was a few yards ahead, Tarkington and the rest of the squad followed.

Raker came up next to him and whispered, "I'll move forward and check the body once he cuts it down." He held up a playing card with the words 'Tark's Ticks' and the death's head skull, and grinned.

Tarkington didn't know how he felt about that but didn't object. Anything that messed with the enemy was a good thing, he thought and the fact that it seemed to boost the squad's morale was also a good thing.

In the dying light, he saw Eduardo reach out and cut the rope, sending the sniper's body crashing through the branches. He thought he heard bones snapping and he cringed inwardly, but knew the soldier was beyond pain. Raker looked back and Tarkington nodded and crouched as Raker bounded past Henry and slid in beside the body at the base of the tree.

The rest of the men spread out, forming a loose perimeter. The jungle was sparse and he felt exposed, but knew they wouldn't be there much longer and the quickly approaching darkness would help conceal them.

He scanned side to side forming a plan in case they were attacked. The area to his right was much thicker, he'd find better cover there if he needed to. He noticed Raker laying on his stomach with his rifle across the corpse. He scowled then caught movement up the tree and saw Eduardo still halfway up the tree, gesturing like a wild man. When he saw he had Tarkington's attention he signaled there were Japs coming.

Shit, He thought, *we're exposed.* He looked beyond Raker but couldn't see the enemy. The way Raker held his rifle steady told him they were close. Tarkington had to get the men to cover where they could attack whatever was coming from a better position.

He got the squad's attention. Henry and Nunes were in front but they'd also seen Eduardo and were low and waiting for orders. Tarkington pointed toward the cover thirty yards away. They'd have to travel over an even more exposed area, but it was the quickest route, and he could tell by Eduardo's frantic motions that the enemy was just over the slight rise.

Staying as low as possible and still moving fast, he went right and entered the open space. He glanced left, where the enemy would be and thought he saw the green uniform of a Japanese soldier. He was about to halt the men - they'd be caught in the open - when there was a rifle shot followed quickly by another. He knew it was Eduardo. There was an instant of silence, then the gates of Hell opened and the return fire shredded the tree. Tarkington could see Eduardo grinning as he cowered behind the tree trunk. *Crazy bastard.*

He saw his opportunity. He waved the men forward while the enemy was preoccupied with Eduardo. During a lull, he heard Raker fire and the volume of Japanese fire increased again and he assumed they were firing on the new threat. He ran hard and could hear the thumping boots of the others right on his heels. If the Japs saw him, he'd know about it in a second. He heard a grenade explode and kept moving.

He lunged into the heavy cover, pushing brambles aside, forcing his way in. He pushed for a couple yards, hearing the others doing the same. He finally came out the other side, ignoring the cuts and scrapes from thorns and vines. There was another explosion followed by men screaming. "Come on, we can flank 'em." He sprinted, whacking vines out of his way. Another grenade explosion. *They've only got one more between 'em. Have to act fast.*

As he moved, he glanced through the foliage and caught glimpses of muzzle flashes. It was nearly dark, the last vestiges of daylight giving him just enough light to move confidently. The muzzle flashes increased and he stopped the men and pointed. The men readied themselves. Tarkington pointed to the ground and got onto his belly, crawling forward until he was at the edge of the open space. The Japanese were only yards away. He could see their green uniforms every time a muzzle flash lit them up. Tarkington whispered, "Grenades," as he pulled one off his belt.

He pulled the pin, reared back and hurled it into the night, then ducked down along with everyone else. He kept his head down as the pops and blasts of multiple grenades exploded. More screams of agony came from the Japanese position. Tarkington fired his Thompson, picking out dots of green, until his magazine ran out. He quickly reloaded while the rest of the squad continued firing.

He saw a lone Japanese soldier sprinting away. He heard a rifle crack from his left, *Eduardo,* but the fleeing soldier kept running. Tarkington aimed and fired just as the soldier passed a tree, and Tarkington's slugs shredded bark, but left the lucky soldier unscathed. The soldier disappeared into the night.

"Move forward, be careful. Remember what they did to Flynn." Tarkington got to his feet and kept his muzzle toward the enemy as he made his way to the tree. It was fully dark now and he called out, "Raker, Eduardo. Where are you?"

There was no immediate answer and he wondered if he'd acted too late. As he neared the base of the tree, he heard moaning and someone writhing around. He saw the bullet riddled body of the Japanese and for an instant thought it was Raker, but then he saw the private holding his ears, rocking side to side. He propped his Thompson against the tree and kneeled down at the same time calling, "Vick, get over here, Raker's hit."

PFC Vick, though not a real medic, had more in his medical kit than the others and so became the squad's de facto medic. He stumbled from the darkness, stopped at the Jap and froze. "Not him - Raker."

Tarkington pointed and relief flooded Vick's face. "Oh shit, I thought that was him." He hopped over the sniper's body and unsnapped the pouch hooked to his belt. He gripped Raker's shoulders trying to hold him still. "Where you hit, buddy? Where you hit?"

Raker shook his head and released his ears. "I - I'm not hit, Japs threw a grenade, burst in front of the tree. Might've burst my eardrums." He looked up in a panic. "Where's Eduardo? He was up the tree."

A form darted past them and leaped, grabbing the lowest limb and swinging like a trapeze artist upward. He disappeared into the darkness, moving up the tree as though gravity had no effect. Seconds later they heard Nunes call, "Help. Help me! Eduardo hit!"

Raker had gauze stuffed in his ears. Vick didn't think his eardrums were burst - there was no blood - but the gauze made him feel like he was doing something for him. Eduardo, on the other hand had a jagged bullet wound in his right hip. He was unconscious when they first lowered him from the tree and Vick thought he was dead, but upon closer inspection, he was breathing.

Now Eduardo was draped over Vick's shoulder and he could feel the wetness as the wound bled down his side and the back of his pant leg. He'd done his best to cover and bind the wound, but the constant jolting as he trotted back to their lines caused more bleeding. Eduardo was awake and, despite the agony he must be feeling, never made a sound.

Tarkington's only focus was to get them back to their lines and get Eduardo proper medical care before he lost too much blood. The darkness made it difficult but he moved fast, not worried about stealth. If a Japanese force had gotten between them and their lines, they'd be dead by now.

They finally broke out of the jungle and into the buffer area. He couldn't see any signs of Hotel Company but knew they were only forty yards away in the darkness. He halted the men and they bumped into each other before finally stopping and crouching. He could hear them breathing hard. He put his hand to his mouth and called, "Second squad coming in with wounded. Don't shoot."

He waited for a response and finally got one. "Babe."

"Ruth," he answered. He got to his feet and waved the men forward, "Come on."

He saw soldiers standing in foxholes with their rifles ready. When they saw Vick carrying Eduardo they moved forward to help. He was placed on a stretcher and carried toward the rear. Raker was standing nearby and Tarkington told him, "You too Raker. Get your ears checked out." Raker didn't move. "Someone tap his shoulder and get him moving." He waited until it was done. "Wink, with me, the rest of you resupply and get some rest."

The men moved off, glancing back the way Eduardo'd been taken. Tarkington and Winkleman walked side by side to find Lt. Smoker. Winkleman asked, "Think he'll make it? Eduardo?"

Tarkington nodded, "Think so, he's a tough old cuss, but I'm no doctor."

They found Lieutenant Smoker standing outside his tent waiting for them, his hands on his hips. "Heard the firefight, I put the men on alert."

Tarkington nodded, "Yes sir. But I don't think the Japs are coming in force. We tangled with a sniper and figure the force we encountered was coming to check on their man."

Lieutenant Smoker nodded in the darkness but held up his hand. "Captain Glister will want to hear this. Save it for him."

They followed Lieutenant Smoker further back, weaving past snoring GIs.

Captain Gima listened to the near hysterical private tell him how his entire squad was wiped out. When he was finished, Gima nodded and with a wave sent him away. The private saluted and left the tent.

Captain Gima addressed Lieutenant Eto. "That one ran away from the fight. I can see it in his eyes. He's a coward."

Lt. Eto nodded, "Yes, sir. What would you have me do?"

The captain considered, "Nothing for now, but keep an eye on him. If he runs away again, we'll have to punish him." Lt. Eto bowed slightly. Captain Gima stood, put his officer's cap on and adjusted the strap. "Assemble your squad, bring stretcher bearers. I will accompany you to the site of the battle." Lieutenant Eto clicked his heels, saluted and left the tent.

Captain Gima grabbed the sub-machine gun leaning nearby and checked it was loaded. Since being ordered to pull his company back from the line days before, he was itching to get back into the fight. He felt the Filipinos and Americans were close to breaking and wanted his company to be at the front of the attack when they did.

He didn't agree with General Homma's assessment, that they needed to soften up the line with more artillery and air attacks, but it was not his place to question orders. Someday he'd be in command of the Division and he'd be more aggressive, but for now they were pulled back awaiting the arrival of hundreds more artillery pieces.

He wrapped his belt around his waist, making sure he had two magazines for the Type-100 sub-machine gun. He hoped they encountered the enemy. He wasn't a commander that stayed in the background. He led from the front - which didn't always sit well with the other company commanders - but he craved battle, like his ancestors before him. To him, it was like air. It sustained him and kept him alive.

He ducked, walked out of the front of his tent and adjusted his uniform. There were lamps around camp, putting off low light. It was poor light-discipline, but he allowed it since the Americans and Filipinos had lost all their aircraft. He saw Lt. Eto standing with his hands behind his back, watching his twelve-man squad form in front of him. They had their backs to Captain Gima.

Gima waited until they were assembled then walked to the front. Lieutenant Eto barked, "Attention," and the men snapped to attention.

Gima took his place beside Lt. Eto and looked the men over. They were fine, victorious and honorable soldiers. He was proud to lead them to the enemy. He noticed more than half the men had long stretchers resting on their shoulders beside their slung rifles. He nodded and murmured to Lt. Eto, "Carry on, Lieutenant. We leave immediately." He looked around and asked, "Where is the private? He needs to lead us to the spot."

Lieutenant Eto's lips turned white as he pressed them firmly together. He pointed, "He comes now, sir. He was getting his wounds checked."

Captain Gima saw the skinny private scampering towards him with his head down. He noticed a white bandage wrapped around his upper arm. When the private was close, he stopped and snapped his heels together and gave the officers a quick salute and a bow. Gima addressed him. "I didn't realize you were wounded, Private. Can you lead us back to the battleground?"

"Hai, sir," he instantly answered.

Gima nodded. Perhaps this boy wasn't a coward after all. "What is your name, Private?"

"Private Hano, sir."

Gima indicated the direction of the front line, "Carry on, Private Hano."

Captain Gima watched him move toward the darkness at the edge of camp and Lt. Eto and the rest of the squad followed. He found his place near the center, being sure Lt. Eto was a few soldiers away. He held his sub-machine gun at the ready, his trigger-finger resting on the trigger guard. He doubted the enemy would still be lingering, but it was better to be safe.

They moved slowly for an hour before the procession finally stopped. He squinted into the darkness but couldn't see more than a few men. After half a minute he moved forward and found Lt. Eto.

Eto pointed and, again, Gima strained but couldn't see anything. He did, however, sense something. He didn't know if it was a premonition or some faint smell, but he knew a battle had been waged nearby. He put his hand on Lt. Eto's shoulder and pushed him gently forward. Eto nodded and signaled for the men to advance.

Soon they were among bodies. The smell of dead men's bowels and the early phases of decomposition filled his senses and he did his best to ignore it. He breathed through his mouth and watched the squad spread out to the perimeter while the men with the stretchers started hefting bodies.

Captain Gima walked until he came across a soldier on his belly. In the faint light from the stars he could see the soldier's shirt was glistening, as if it were wet. He crouched down and put his fingers on the man's neck. It was cold and he knew immediately he was dead.

He was about to move on to the next man when a slight breeze moved something on the man's back. He squinted and reached for it, pulling away what looked like a playing card. He held it up, shifting it back and forth, trying to see it better. He thought it was the five of hearts, but he couldn't be sure. He scowled and looked closer, there was something more but he couldn't make it out.

He crouched, set his machine gun down and brought his flashlight out. He signaled the closest soldier and whispered, "Give me your tunic and helmet. The soldier did so immediately and without question and Gima put the helmet on and draped the shirt over his head. He turned the flashlight on and shone it onto the card for three seconds then shut it off and handed the helmet and tunic back to the soldier.

Minutes later, Lieutenant Eto approached him. "Sir, there are no survivors. The first group of stretcher bearers are loaded and ready to move out."

Captain Gima nodded. "I will lead them back to headquarters myself.

Stay vigilant, there may be enemy nearby." Lt. Eto nodded and Gima asked, "Have you found playing cards?"

Lieutenant Eto nodded and pursed his lips. "Hai. On every soldier, sir."

Gima murmured, "Tark's Ticks." The lieutenant looked at him quizzically. "Collect all you find and bring them back with you."

"Yes, sir."

21

Staff Sergeant Tarkington worried that the success of their mission would lead to more such raids. But for the rest of the month they stayed on the line and didn't venture forward. He was glad 1st platoon, and particularly 2nd squad, was allowed to act as line soldiers. It gave the men time to settle into the line and get used to things.

On the evening of March 1st, he commandeered a jeep and visited the field hospital where Eduardo was being treated. He knew he'd had surgery to remove the bullet and was recovering, but he hadn't had the chance to visit yet.

He finally found him in a stuffy ward filled with other Filipino and American soldiers. Eduardo waved when he saw him and his smile reached ear-to-ear. Tarkington stood beside him and looked him over. He was shirtless and had a clean bandage covering his right side. "How you doing, soldier?"

Eduardo nodded and gave him a thumbs-up, something he'd picked up from his American counterparts. "I good as new, Sergeant Tark." He looked around like he didn't want others to hear, then said, "Doctor won't let me go back."

Tarkington grinned and shook his head. "Rest awhile. You got shot for Chrissakes."

Eduardo nodded. "Yes, shot here." He pointed at the bandages then his head, "Not here. I'm good as new."

"It's only been a few days. It must hurt like hell. Can you even walk?"

Eduardo took it as a request and started to move to the side of the bed, but a nurse ran up and scowled at Tarkington. "What's wrong with you, Sergeant? You can't expect him to walk yet!"

Tarkington was taken completely off-guard and held up his hands, "I didn't ask him to... just asked if he could."

She scolded him again. "Course not, he was shot just a few days ago. You know how long a gunshot wound takes to heal? It's like losing a limb almost." She shook her head like he was an idiot. "Shame on you."

Tarkington didn't have a response and was afraid saying more would only make it worse. Eduardo shook his head. "I not lose leg. I good as new."

The nurse looked at him as though he were a cute puppy and rubbed his shoulder. "Of course you won't lose your leg. The surgery was successful. Don't let Staff Sergeant..." she looked at his faded, stenciled name, "Tarkington put that idea in your head."

Tarkington held up his hands. "You're the one that said it, not me. Criminy sakes, it's like a damned nuthouse in here." He looked at her name. "Sergeant Lundy."

She looked at him and smiled. She wasn't the most attractive female he'd seen, but she was the first non-native woman he'd seen in a while and the newness was intriguing. "I'm only funning with you, Staff Sergeant Tarkington."

He blushed and nodded. "Well I guess I fell into that one." He lowered his voice and moved her away from the bed slightly. "How's he doing, really?"

The corners of her mouth turned up slightly. "He's doing fine, really. The doctor pulled the bullet out cleanly and there's been no sign of infection. He's expected to heal quickly."

"How quickly? I mean, what's your best guess?"

She moved closer to Eduardo who was straining to hear. "He needs at least a month for the tissue to heal properly, but he's determined to get out sooner than that. If he rests and does the exercises," she pointed at him as though scolding him, "he could be walking around in another week and a half."

Tarkington smiled. "You hear that? Another ten days," he held up his fingers, "and you'll be out of here."

Eduardo shook his head. "Ten days second squad be gone. Don't want to fight with new unit. Like second squad. Tark's Ticks," he said proudly.

Nurse Lundy scrunched her nose and Tarkington thought it made her look cute, like a young girl. "Tark's Ticks?" she asked. "Tark?" She pointed at him, "Short for Tarkington?"

He looked at the floor. "It's - well, it's something the guys came up with, you know, for a squad name."

She scowled, "Didn't know we were naming squads. Is this like some kind of football game to you?"

He shook his head and she turned and walked away, shaking her head. He watched her go, admiring her rather wide, but alluring backside, then turned back to Eduardo. "You made me look like an idiot in front of her."

Eduardo looked at Nurse Lundy then back to Tarkington. "You like her?"

Tarkington shook his head and his mouth turned down. "No, and she definitely doesn't like me." He saw her greeting another patient. She bent over to better hear him, showing her backside. "Nice ass though," he muttered and Eduardo started chuckling until tears streamed down his cheeks. "Keep it quiet, dammit. She'll hear you."

Eduardo shook his head, finally getting control of his laughter. "Ass, funny word for woman." He wiped the streaks of tears away and turned serious. "I be back to second squad soon, Sergeant Tark."

Tarkington drove the six miles back to the forward area and parked the Jeep in the same spot he'd found it. It was nearly dark, but he kept the headlights off to keep from attracting the attention of Japanese zeros. He shut off the engine and scooted away fast, pretending he'd been authorized to use it all along.

"Hey you," he heard someone yell. He kept walking, keeping his pace, forcing himself not to look back. "You there, I know you can hear me."

The owner of the voice was close, so he turned and saw an irate Platoon Sergeant McLunty charging at him. When McLunty recognized him his anger turned to a devilish grin. "Well, well, well, if it isn't Staff Sergeant Tarkington."

Tarkington faced him and puffed out his chest, "Hello Platoon Sergeant McLunty. What can I do for you?"

"Cut the bullshit, Tarkington. You stole that jeep. Even you won't be able to get out of a theft charge, you lout."

Tarkington shook his head, wondering how much McLunty saw. Did he actually see him drive up and park? He doubted it or he would've approached him sooner. "What jeep?"

McLunty scowled and shook his head like a disappointed father. "Lying only makes it worse. I'm putting you up on charges. What do you think about that?"

Tarkington glared at him. "I don't know what you're talking about, Sarge."

The vein on McLunty's forehead popped out and his face turned red and he barked, "You will address me as Platoon Sergeant McLunty. Understood?"

Tarkington braced, looked straight ahead and repeated, "I don't know what you're talking about, Platoon Sergeant McLunty."

"Why you little pissant, sack of..."

His tirade was interrupted with the distinct whistling of incoming artillery. McLunty looked up but Tarkington grabbed his shoulder and pushed him forward. "Incoming, there's a slit trench that way!"

McLunty slapped his hand away, "Get off me, you little..."

The noise grew in intensity. Tarkington couldn't wait any longer. He dove sideways at the same instant the ground heaved and he felt the heat and shock wave of a nearby explosion. He was lifted off the ground and hurled ten feet closer to the slit trench. More explosions erupted all around him.

He lay as flat as possible, feeling the ground shaking beneath him. chunks of trees and clods of dirt rained down on his back. He looked to where McLunty had been but there was nothing there. "McLunty!" He yelled but there was no answer, only more explosions.

His instincts took over. He didn't remember crawling, but he covered the thirty yards to the slit trench in record time and slid in face first. He stayed on the bottom holding his helmet close to his head. He curled his legs into his body making himself as small as possible. The ground vibrated beneath his body and he thought sure the walls of the trench would cave in on him and he'd suffocate.

He had no concept how long the barrage blasted the area, but it seemed like a long time later that the bombs finally moved to a new section. He slowly became aware of the relative calm and opened his eyes.

It was pitch dark inside the trench. He looked up but immediately regretted it when his eyes were pelted with dust and debris and he quickly looked down and rubbed the dirt from his face. He tried to spit but his mouth was dry as cotton. He gagged and thought he might throw up, but held it down. His ears were ringing and his head pounded. *McLunty.*

He forced himself to his feet and swayed. He lifted his chin to see over the lip. He could see the bright flashes up the line of more artillery. This wasn't harassment fire, this was the real deal. In the darkness and confusion, he had no idea if he was looking toward the rear or the front. Then he saw fire consuming the jeep he'd borrowed. It was burning brightly, as though it had taken a direct hit. "McLunty!" He yelled again, but his throat was dry and through his ringing ears he wasn't sure he'd made more than a slight squawk.

He hefted himself out of the trench with a force of will and a grunt and stood swaying on the lip. He finally got his feet stable and leaned forward, hoping his legs would catch him. They did and he staggered forward, weaving like a drunk. "Sergeant," he squawked again. He got to the approximate spot he thought he'd been speaking with McLunty but there was no sign of him.

He took another step toward the jeep and nearly tripped on something. He backed up and squinted. The light from the jeep fire lit up the ground in front and he could see two smoking boots. He fell to his knees and vomited over what was left of Platoon Sergeant McLunty's remains.

The barrage lasted most of the night, sweeping back and forth over the entire Orion-Bagac line. Tarkington stayed in the slit trench until it finally stopped then staggered his way through the carnage and found 1st platoon.

The area was clobbered. None of the tents survived and many vehicles burned brightly in the early morning light. He helped a few dazed GIs who were walking aimlessly, find their buddies and cover. He instructed them to stay in their holes until further orders.

He saw many GIs still hunkered in their holes, some still clutching their helmets tight to their heads as though the barrage was still happening. He also saw bloody rags of clothing and parts of men scattered here and there. He saw a smoldering tree with what looked like a shredded arm near the top branches.

He saw the foxhole occupied by PFC Henry. He was covered in dirt and his hole was partially covered with tree branches. He had his rifle pointed toward where the enemy would be and flinched when Tarkington slid in beside him. "You alright?"

Henry nodded and spit. "That was bad. Really bad. Worst I've ever seen by a long shot."

Tarkington nodded, "Any movement?"

Henry shook his head. "Quiet as a church out there."

"Where's Lieutenant Smoker?"

Henry pointed, "He's over there, came through here not long ago making sure we were okay and ready in case the Japs come."

"McLunty bought it." Henry looked at him, "I tried to push him to cover but he was too busy chewing me out. Not much left of him."

Henry shook his head. "Doubt he's the only one. No one from second squad got hit, but there's definitely casualties from other squads."

Tarkington looked grim. "Yeah, I saw body parts and lots of blood but have no idea who or how many."

"Lord have mercy," Henry muttered.

Tarkington slapped Henry on the shoulder, "Glad you're okay buddy. I'm gonna go see Smoker."

Henry just nodded and kept his vigil forward. Morning light streamed through the trees and smoke and dust gave it an orange tint, adding to the hellish feel of the landscape.

He encouraged the men he passed, stopping and telling them to keep a close eye and be sure their weapons were clear of debris. Despite the shellacking they'd taken, they were still ready to fight and Tarkington was proud of every one of them.

He finally found Lt. Smoker trying to get through to someone on the radio. He wasn't having any luck. When he saw Tarkington his eyes lit up momentarily. "Glad to see you made it, Tark." He looked down at his boots, "Unfortunately that sword of yours didn't. My tent took a direct hit, things in a million pieces."

Tarkington grimaced wondering if Rabowski had made the switch yet. He entered the large foxhole and nodded at the radio operator who was ducked down, looking sheepish. He nodded back and looked at the sky as if it were filled with more enemy shells. "Seems trivial at the moment, sir." replied Tarkington.

Smoker nodded slowly, "I thought there'd be a follow-on attack by now, but nothing's happened. I haven't heard any fighting since the barrage stopped. Doesn't make sense."

Tarkington nodded and looked out over the killing field. He looked Smoker in the eye, "McLunty didn't make it, sir."

Smoker's eyes widened for an instant and Tarkington saw true sadness flicker before they turned hard again. "Dammit. Where - where is he?"

Tarkington didn't want to tell him what he found. "He's back there a couple hundred yards. There's - well there's not much left of him."

Smoker's lips pursed and he shook his head. "He was a good man. I know you and him didn't get on well, but..." he stopped and tilted his head to a new sound. Tarkington heard it too and they looked up. "Shit," he cupped his hands around his mouth and yelled as loud as he could, "Air-raid, air-raid, take cover!"

Tarkington threw himself into the bottom of the hole beside the quivering radioman and listened as the buzz of engines grew louder. Soon the air was alive with droning aircraft followed immediately by whistling bombs.

Once again, the ground shook as the bombs marched along the ground in parallel lines of destruction. The devastation was mostly east of their position. Tarkington risked a glance over the lip of the foxhole, making sure Japanese infantrymen weren't moving forward while they had their heads down. Instead of soldiers he saw the flashing silver of Japanese zeros diving toward their position. "Strafing run!" He yelled. He brought his Thompson to his shoulder and lined up on the closest fighter. They were diving hard and fast and he figured they'd be very low when they finished their runs.

It seemed like the lead fighter was coming straight at him, targeting him alone. He knew there was no way the pilot could pick out individual men, but it felt personal somehow. He ground his teeth together and kept his muzzle aimed and his trigger finger poised. He saw the winking flashes of the planes machine guns, followed immediately by great geysers erupting in the empty killing zone and marching straight at him. He squeezed the trigger and held it down, then rolled and watched the fighter flash over the trees with scant inches to spare.

Lt. Smoker gripped his shirt. "You crazy bastard! You'll get yourself killed doing that."

Tarkington couldn't seem to catch his breath, as adrenaline surged through his body. He stayed down as wave after wave of fighters swept the area with deadly fire. "Where the hell's the anti-air for Chrissakes?"

Smoker yelled over the din of hammering machine guns and nearby aircraft engines. "Wiped out by artillery. We're getting our butts kicked."

Finally, the strafing stopped. Lt. Smoker pushed Tarkington, "Get to your squad and prepare for an attack. I've no idea if anyone else is alive, but by God we'll give 'em a fight."

Tarkington nodded and ran back to his men, checking as he passed. No one was hit, but everyone was mad as hell. PFC Holiday was cursing a streak that even Tarkington found impressive. "Be ready, and wait for the word before opening fire."

They eagerly waited for the attack but after a few hours it was evident it wasn't happening. Tarkington felt his eyes growing heavy as he tried to stay vigilant. No one had slept a wink and now that the adrenaline had worn off, they were struggling to stay awake. Tarkington passed the word for every other man to sleep and soon he heard the soft sounds of snoring. He shook his head trying to keep his eyes open. Henry tapped his shoulder, "I've got it. You need sleep, Tark."

"You sure?" He nodded and Tarkington drifted to the bottom of the hole and was asleep in seconds.

22

MARCH 12TH, 1942

The twice-a-day artillery barrages made the GIs of Hotel Company dig their foxholes deeper and with more fortifications, until they resembled mini-bunkers. Interconnected trenches were built from foxhole to foxhole to eliminate the chance of being caught in an exposed position.

The GIs felt much safer, although there were still the occasional casualties from direct hits, or simply being unlucky. Tarkington didn't know why the Japanese hadn't attacked yet, but he felt the new fortifications would make it much tougher on them when they did.

Without the constant pressure of attack, they were able to position what was left of the heavy machine guns and anti-tank guns making Tarkington feel even better about their chances. They'd even managed to place Howitzers atop Mt. Samat, a mile and a half behind the main line of defense, despite the harassment of enemy aircraft. There'd been no fire missions and Tarkington supposed they were saving every precious shell for the inevitable push.

Tarkington was in his fortified bunker, staring at the Samurai sword. He'd dug out a secret compartment in the far corner of the foxhole and concealed the opening with a lid from a wooden ammunition box. Henry and Holiday were with him, keeping an eye out for Lt. Smoker.

True to his word, PFC Rabowski had sneaked into Lt. Smoker's tent, only a day before the first big artillery barrage, and swapped the intact sword with the broken one. It was a seamless operation, made all the better by the obliteration of Lt. Smoker's tent the next day. Even if he'd found the blade, which he hadn't, he would've assumed it was broken by the shelling. The only problem was, Tarkington had to keep it hidden. He wanted it strapped to his waist when the Japanese attacked, but couldn't risk it.

Henry whispered, "Smoker's coming."

Tarkington quickly sheathed it hearing it slide perfectly into place with a satisfying metallic scrape. He stowed it, placed the crate lid over the hole and moved to the front of the hole to stand looking out over the killing ground.

Lt. Smoker and Lt. Govang came around the corner and the GIs snapped to attention. "At ease," said Smoker.

Tarkington could tell something was wrong. Both platoon leaders looked almost ill. "What's happened? What's wrong, sirs?"

Smoker guffawed, "That obvious, huh?"

Tarkington shrugged, "Let's just say, you should stay away from poker, sir."

Lt. Smoker sighed heavily. "Mac left the island last night. Apparently Roosevelt ordered him off the island a couple weeks ago, but he kept postponing it. He and his family finally evacuated last night."

No one spoke for a long minute. Finally Tarkington nodded. "Well, it's what I thought all along. There's no reinforcements coming."

Lt. Govang took his steel pot off and wiped the sweat from his forehead. "Looks that way. They wouldn't be pulling him out unless there was no hope left."

Holiday asked, "So what's that mean for us? We getting out of here too?"

Lt. Smoker looked at Govang who avoided his eyes. Smoker shook his head, "Nah, our orders are the same: hold the line as long as possible."

Holiday looked grim but nodded. "Battle to the death then. Just wish they'd come and get this shit over with." He looked out over the sun-drenched field and the dark jungle beyond.

"Who's in command?" Tarkington asked.

"General King's taking over command. He's a good man. Not as flamboyant as MacArthur but, as far as I know, a good solid commander."

"Think the Japs know? I mean they might use it as an opportunity to attack," Tarkington mused.

Lt. Smoker shrugged, "Who knows? We can assume they do and I'd expect them to attack sometime this week. They've brought in massive amounts of artillery as you know and their damned bombers are constantly overhead. We've got nothing left to throw at them."

Tarkington's lips pursed and he flicked a bug off his cheek. "We've got a strong position here. I think we can hold a long time."

Smoker dithered his head back and forth. "Maybe, if we had enough ammo. There are some new orders though." The men looked at him in anticipation. "We're to be ready to fall back at the first hint of our lines breaking. If there's a breach we're not to move men to fill it but to pull back to Mt. Samat and defend the high ground. That's our rally point."

"Mt. Samat? What happens if the Japs surround it while we're on it? We'll be cut off."

Smoker answered his staff sergeant. "If that happens, we'll continue to pull back. Understand?" Tarkington nodded. "Command took a chance letting this get out. Captain Glister said they considered keeping Mac's departure a secret, afraid it might affect the men's morale, but decided they had a right to know the situation." He looked the men over. "Nothing's changed. Not really. Now we know there's no relief and no chance of rescue. I expect the men to perform in the same brilliant manner they've been performing."

Tarkington nodded, "Yes, sir. They'll do their duty."

When the officers moved out of earshot, Henry drawled. "We are well and truly fucked."

Tarkington scowled at him but completely agreed with the Cajun's assessment.

That night the intensity of the barrage was noticeably increased and lasted longer. Much of the fire was concentrated on Mt. Samat. Tarkington was thankful it wasn't all falling on Hotel Company but he was concerned if any of the Howitzers would survive.

At dawn the ground shook once again with mid-level Japanese bombers dropping their deadly eggs over the lines. He was curled up, watching through the slats of the heavy wood trunks which formed the roof of his hole. There'd be a flash, followed immediately with a deafening clap of sound and the earth would shake.

He remembered counting the seconds between lightning strikes and thunder back on the farm, each second equated to one mile, his father told him. Here, he couldn't distinguish one from another. It was a constant din of sound and flashes. The ground shook as if it were made of jelly.

Finally the bombs stopped. He unwound his body and shook the thick layer of dirt and debris off his shoulders and helmet. Any vestiges of the night were gone. The earth didn't care about the bombing, the sun had risen and lit up the land like it normally did, not heeding the sickening punishment the humans heaped upon one another. It didn't seem fair somehow. How could this bombing, which made him whimper in fear like a child, mean so little in the grand scheme of time?

He stood and moved to the front of the hole and peered through the thick smoke and dust. Chunks of tree and great clods of dirt still rained down. The cleared area gradually came into focus. There were great smoking craters where a line of five-hundred-pound bombs had impacted. He shook his head. If there'd been a wind, or if the bombers had been slightly more to the right, those craters would've been all that was left of 1st platoon of Hotel Company.

There was a zipping sound, followed with a thunking impact against the wooden barrier in front of his hole. As the fog from the punishing bombing cleared from his head, he realized he was hearing bullets.

He squinted and saw forms rushing across the open ground. It had been so long since he'd seen an enemy soldier, he almost didn't believe his eyes. Finally he yelled at the top of his voice, "Japs! We're under attack! Get ready!" Holiday came forward and Tarkington slapped his shoulder, "Make sure Winkleman's awake and Stolly's ready with the BAR." Holiday nodded and ran off, dirt streaming from his helmet.

PFC Henry pushed his rifle through the front of the hole a couple of yards from Tarkington and licked his lips. "Looks like the wait's finally over."

"We'll know soon enough if our machine guns are still operational."

Henry cursed, "Shit, tanks."

Tarkington saw the hulking shapes of Japanese light tanks speeding from cover. The staccato firing from multiple machine guns on either side of his hole opened up and he saw Japanese infantrymen fold and fall out of sight. He had his Thompson slung on his back and a Springfield at his shoulder. He heard Henry's rifle bark. He put his sights on a running soldier and fired. The buck against his shoulder felt good and the burnt powder smell filled his nostrils and made his eyes burn. His target kept coming and he worked the bolt-action, adjusted and fired again. This time his target seemed to trip and dropped out of sight.

He found another darting shape and fired. The soldier spun and fell. The machine guns were firing in short bursts, wreaking havoc on the enemy. The Japanese tanks surged forward, their main guns silent but their front machine guns spewing fire. Tarkington saw soldiers using the tanks for cover. He fired, dropping one he had an angle on.

The tank stopped, rocking on its chassis, and the hand-cranked 37mm cannon moved slightly and fired. There was an explosion to Tarkington's right and he figured it was directed at the nearest machine gun nest, but he could only see to his front. The machine gun paused, but soon continued firing.

A blast from a dug-in anti-tank gun turned the stopped tank into an inferno. The soldiers behind it scattered but were swept by withering machine-gun fire.

Tarkington saw a group run past the burning tank and he moved his barrel, tracking them and fired at the lead man, but nothing happened. He worked the bolt-action and fired again. The soldier went down screaming and clutching his bleeding belly. A trailing comrade kneeled and dragged the wounded man toward a bomb crater. Tarkington aimed carefully and fired. The soldier dropped.

The enemy was halfway across the clearing, making use of the craters from the aerial bombardment. A tank weaved around the burning hulk and Tarkington heard another roar and watched the second tank take a direct hit but the shell glanced off. It lurched to a halt and the turret slowly turned and elevated. The dull, brown metal sparked as the machine gun nest swept it with .30 caliber bullets. A soldier behind, dropped sideways.

The 37mm cannon fired. There was another shot from the anti-tank gun. This time it penetrated, leaving a gaping hole in the front glacis. Soon fire erupted from the hole and the tank's hatches sprang open spewing tankers. Machine-gun fire swept the tank and cut down them down.

More tanks charged forward weaving around the fresh bomb craters. Tarkington carefully aimed each shot, making sure he didn't waste any ammo. He heard Henry's steady firing to his left, and Stollman's BAR.

Tarkington could see five more tanks churning across the field. Another anti-tank shell slammed the lead tank's tread and it spun to the left, suddenly losing traction. The following tank slammed into the stalled tank and the sound momentarily dwarfed the din of battle.

Another shot from the anti-tank battery and the lead tank erupted in flame. A second later, it exploded, sending hot metal and flames in every direction. Flame engulfed the other tank and soon it was burning fiercely too.

Tarkington saw nearby soldiers suddenly become human torches. They ran in every direction, desperate to escape the scalding heat. He ignored the doomed men and concentrated on the soldiers still running headlong toward him.

The three remaining tanks fired their cannons, sending shells toward the anti-tank gun. The machine guns sticking from the front, spewed fire. Tarkington ducked as his hole was swept. Bullets thunked into the wood and he felt the impacts through the dirt wall.

He checked his ammo, he'd already gone through more than half of his stripper clips for the Springfield. He had two grenades on his harness and four magazines for his Thompson.

He stood and looked out the slit. The tanks were maneuvering and he thought they must've silenced the anti-tank gun. The machine guns to either side continued chattering, spewing death.

He aimed and fired at a soldier's helmet poking up from a bomb crater. The helmet flew into the air. He saw another soldier beside the first looking back at the man he'd just shot. Tarkington fired and the soldier spun backwards and disappeared into the crater.

The tanks halted their advance and fired their cannons, targeting the machine gun nests. The metal sparked as the machine guns tried to stop them. There was an explosion to Tarkington's left and the machine gun nest stopped firing.

Tarkington fired his last bullet and ducked down. He reloaded and leaned the rifle against the wall and unslung his Thompson. He pulled the charging handle and staying low moved toward the machine gun nest. As he passed Henry he yelled, "I'm checking on the machine gun crew, be right back!" Henry didn't take his eyes from his sights, but nodded and kept methodically firing.

Tarkington moved into the light of the trench system. His bunker was covered, keeping it cool and relatively dark. The trenches were open to the sky and the sudden light and heat made him feel exposed. He stayed crouched and moved past 2nd squad soldiers busily firing and reloading.

He came to another bunker entrance and stepped through. Stollman was firing controlled bursts from the BAR. Vick was close, firing his Springfield. Tarkington tapped Stollman's leg, "You doing okay on ammo?"

Stollman looked back and shrugged. "I've got enough for a bit, but could use more." Bullets smacked the wooden roof, sending splinters onto their helmets.

"I'm checking the machine gun crew."

Stollman shook his head, "They've had it. Fucking tanks got it. Vick already checked, says the gun's blown to shit along with the crew."

Vick fired, worked the bolt and looked over at Tarkington and nodded. "Not much left of 'em, Sarge."

A new sound made them all pause. Stollman hunkered lower, "Shit, artillery."

Tarkington heard the same thing but shook his head. "That's ours. Hallelujah, I didn't think I'd ever hear friendly artillery again." He moved beside Stollman and peered from the firing slit. Great geysers of dirt and flame erupted in the center of the field. The three remaining tanks jolted forward trying to close the gap but the artillery was accurate and bracketed them. Japanese infantrymen were flung into the air like rag dolls and Tarkington couldn't help but cheer. "Yeah!" He pumped his fist, "give 'em hell."

It was a brief barrage, less than a minute but the effect was devastating.

Tarkington left the bunker, heading back the way he'd come. He heard Stollman's BAR bark a short burst. He stopped in the trench and poked his head over the lip. He could see much better from this vantage point. The three tanks were burning, turning black. There were still infantrymen, but they were hunkered, no longer charging forward.

He ran along the trench encouraging the men. "Be sure of each shot. We've stopped the bastards cold."

He entered his bunker and Sergeant Winkleman was there with wide eyes. "There you are. We're moving back. Smoker says the line folded east of us. The Japs pushed through and we're to skedaddle back to Mt. Samat."

"Dammit," Tarkington seethed. "We'll never have a better defensive line than we've got right now." He shook his head bitterly, "We could hold 'em here forever if we just had enough ammo."

Winkleman stared at him, then shrugged, "Neither here nor there. We gotta move back now or we'll be cut off."

Tarkington slammed his fist into the dirt wall. "Dammit. Okay, pass it along, we're moving out. Have the men meet right here. We leave in five minutes." He tapped Henry's shoulder and he moved down the trench-line to inform the rest of 2nd squad.

The firing from the field increased in tempo. Tarkington heard more engine noises and went to the firing slit. "Shit, more tanks coming." He saw an enemy soldier stand and look back, waving the tanks and his men forward. Tarkington found his rifle and centered the officer's chest in his sights and fired. The officer staggered and looked down at his chest. Tarkington fired again, and the officer went to his knees momentarily then toppled over.

He fired the rest of the magazine and turned in time to see the rest of 2nd squad breathing hard, watching him. "Alright use the trenches and move quick, stick together. If you get separated, get to Mt. Samat." He looked to each man. They were energized and their eyes blazed with life. "Let's go!"

The GIs filtered out of the bunker and into the trench. Tarkington watched the last man leave, then went to where his sword was hidden. He took it out and wrapped the belt around his waist. The solid weight felt good. He gripped his Thompson and followed 2nd squad into the trench.

He followed them around the ninety-degree turn leading toward the latrines and the rear. He could hear firing coming from the field and heard the buzz of bullets slicing through the air above his head. There was no way they could see him, they were simply firing as they advanced. Over the din of fire, he could hear the grinding churn of the enemy tanks.

They had to get out of the area before the tanks made it past the bunkers or they'd be mowed down once they left the relative safety of the trench. He caught up to the last man, Sergeant Winkleman. They were running, but not fast enough for Tarkington's liking. "Move, move, move," he yelled and the line surged forward as the GIs straightened up and sprinted.

Soon they broke out of the back of the escape trench and leaped over the festering, fly-infested latrine. The line spread out as men darted in and out of trees and boulders. Bullets whizzed past, thudded into trees and zinged off rocks.

The 2nd squad mixed with the rest of 1st platoon. A GI to the side of Tarkington grunted and went down in a heap. Tarkington stopped to help, and saw the first tank's underbelly as it churned over a bunker then flopped down once over the obstacle. It was seventy yards back. He lunged for the fallen GI at the same instant the front machine gun turret's muzzle winked and flashed.

Bullets swept inches over his head as he dove and landed beside the GI. He was helmet to helmet with him. He pulled the helmet trying to get the soldier's attention. It slid off and Tarkington felt bile rising in his throat as the GI's brains sloshed into the helmet.

He got to his feet and took off running, trying to put as many trees as he could between himself and the tanks. He leaped over more bodies, glancing at their faces, trying to gauge if they were still alive. He could feel fear in his belly, rising through his throat, telling him he'd be shot in the back any second. He ran until his legs finally seized and he fell to the ground, out of breath, petrified and completely alone.

23

Tarkington was on his back for a full two minutes trying to catch his breath. He closed his eyes, desperately trying to suppress the fear that had gripped his heart like a vice during his headlong run. Anger flooded his body and he turned onto his stomach, the word 'coward' flashing in his head like a beacon.

He looked from side to side, trying to get his bearings but there was nothing but sparse jungle, dotted with pines. He heard firing and a brief firefight off to the left, which ended with the crash of an explosion.

He pushed himself to his feet and felt his body shaking from exertion and lack of food and water. Suddenly his thirst gripped him and he clutched at his side, feeling the sword but not his canteen. He looked desperately around for it, but decided he must've lost it sometime during his shameful run.

He closed his parched mouth and tried to think about anything but his thirst. He grit his teeth and shook his head but couldn't get his mind to shift to anything but getting water. He thought of home, but the image of cool well-water cascading from the spigot made his thirst even worse. He held out his hand, it shook the way he'd seen old-timer's hands shake while sipping lemonade on the porch. *Lemonade!*

He forced himself to stand, his legs still shaky. He knew Mt. Samat was due south. He glanced north and didn't see anyone coming. He briefly thought about retracing his steps but knew it was a stupid idea. He shook his head. *Pull yourself together, Tark. You find first platoon, you find water.* The thought energized him and he moved shakily south, his Thompson over his sweat-soaked shoulder.

The sound of fighting was like background music. It droned from all sides, sometimes building to a crescendo, then dropping to a shot here and there, but never quite stopping. He heard aircraft overhead and wondered briefly if they were friendlies but quickly put the ridiculous notion from his mind.

The plane's sounds changed and he recognized the high-pitched whistling wings of diving aircraft. They were off to his left. The whistling was quickly replaced with the impact of bombs.

He kept walking, wondering what they were attacking. The sounds continued, over and over. He got to a clearing and looked up, seeing the bright metallic Zeros slicing through the air, attacking a raised bit of land. A thought kept trying to rise to the surface of his thirst-addled brain. Finally he shook the cobwebs out and realized it had to be Mt. Samat. The Japs were attacking Mt. Samat. It suddenly made perfect sense to him and he wondered what the hell was wrong with him.

The thought brought his thirst raging to the surface again. The need to find water suddenly consumed every part of his being. His mind crystallized for an instant. *I'll bet there's water coming off that mountain.* He veered toward the mountain, ignoring the blossoming explosions.

Sergeant Winkleman stopped running and kneeled beside a thick tree, trying to count men as they passed. Stray bullets still whizzed through the trees occasionally but he couldn't see any Japanese and figured they couldn't see him either. His breath came in hard gasps, making his chest hurt. Sweat poured off his face and he wiped his eyebrows trying to keep his eyes clear.

2nd squad was all accounted for. He needed to tell Staff Sergeant Tarkington. That's when he realized he hadn't seen Tarkington. He turned and followed 2nd squad toward Mt. Samat.

The GIs stopped when they came to a dirt road. Sergeant Winkleman panted up next to them and looked around, "Has anyone seen Tarkington?" The GIs looked around. There were GIs from other squads mixed in and they shook their heads along with everyone else. "Shit," he muttered.

PFC Henry pointed back the way they'd come and drawled, "I saw him stop to help someone. I haven't seen him since though." He stood, "I'll head back there and get him."

Sergeant Winkleman shook his head, "Negative. The Japs are coming hard. Our orders are to get to Mt. Samat. He's probably mixed in with another squad, just like these guys."

The GIs of 2nd squad looked doubtful, and Henry looked ready to disobey the order. "What if he ain't?" asked Raker. "Henry and I will either find him or figure out what happened."

He moved to go but Winkleman put his hand on his chest, stopping him. "You lead the men to Mt. Samat. Tell the lieutenant what's happening. Henry and I'll see about Tark."

Raker was about to protest but Winkleman didn't give him a chance, simply turned and moved off. Henry glanced at Raker and winked. "Meet you at the mountain."

Sergeant Winkleman knew it was a bad idea, but the men wouldn't allow them to leave Tarkington behind. They revered their squad leader. Indeed he'd taken on Godlike status throughout the entire platoon. Winkleman wondered if the men would be so adamant if he were the one missing. He shook his head, anger flashing with the selfishness of the thought. He wasn't Tarkington, but he was trusted by him and that was good enough for him.

He crouched when he heard a rifle crack. Henry came up beside him like a ghost. He leaned close to his ear, "He was another hundred yards or so."

Winkleman nodded and pushed him forward, knowing Henry was much better at seeing trouble before it found him. He gripped his Thompson and glanced back, but the squad was out of sight. He waited until Henry was ten yards ahead and followed, trying to stay quiet.

Henry moved from tree to tree with the grace of a ballet dancer. Winkleman did his best, but had to work just to keep him in sight. They'd moved nearly a hundred yards and he was just about to move to the next tree when he saw Henry hold a fist up. Winkleman froze and moved his eyes side to side, looking for movement. He didn't see anything, but knew if Henry saw or even sensed something, it should be taken seriously.

Without looking back, Henry's hand went from a fist to flat and he lowered it slowly. Winkleman glacially moved to his stomach, careful to keep the muzzle of his Thompson clear and pointed in the correct direction.

He lay on the jungle floor, his eyes searching but he still didn't see anything. Then he heard it, the faint sound of talking. It was so faint, he wondered if he were imagining it at first.

He watched Henry, who was low and utterly still, his rifle aimed forward. The sound increased, as though the speech had been carried on a slight breeze. Then he saw movement. Two soldiers were moving forward with their long rifles aimed at a rock. They approached the rock carefully, keeping their rifles ready as though it would spring to life at any moment. Winkleman realized, it wasn't a rock but a body. He recognized the dull, faded green of a GI's uniform and he swallowed hard. *Is it Tark?*

The soldiers were twenty yards away. Winkleman didn't dare raise his Thompson to his shoulder. He looked beyond the soldiers. He couldn't see any others. He wondered where the tanks were and realized the trees would be too tightly spaced. They'd probably moved to the road along with the rest of the infantry. Now they'd broken through, they'd want to move fast to make the most of the headlong retreat.

Winkleman watched in horror as the nearest Japanese soldier kicked the inert form and he heard a grunt of pain. His mouth went dry, the GI was alive. The soldiers started yelling. The furthest soldier put his rifle to his shoulder and took a tentative step back, while the first advanced and kicked again. Winkleman could hear the solid thunk of boot hitting flesh and he felt anger building.

The nearest Japanese talked quickly, a staccato stream of foreign words which sounded like gibberish to Winkleman's Western ears. The soldier aiming the rifle nodded and pulled something from his hip, and attaching it to the end of his rifle with an audible 'click'. Winkleman knew what was about to happen and knew he couldn't sit idly by and watch.

The anger flooded his senses and, without making a conscious decision, he got to his feet and ran straight at the pair with his Thompson leveled from the hip.

The Japanese looked up in astonishment. The nearest soldier, who had stripes on his shoulders, reacted fast and turned towards him, bringing his rifle up at the same time. Winkleman realized he might hit the wounded GI if he fired. He stopped and brought the Thompson to his shoulder, but knew the Jap had him beat. Suddenly the enemy soldier's chest erupted with blood and he dropped to his knees. Winkleman aimed and fired three more rounds into his chest and he toppled backwards.

The second man was frozen in place, his mouth open, seeing his death coming. Winkleman strode toward him, his Thompson's muzzle aimed at his chest. He didn't want to fire over the wounded GI. He wanted to be sure he only hit the Japanese. Anger coursed through his veins and he stopped when he was mere feet from the soldier, who continued to stare.

The Japanese still held his rifle, the long bayonet scraping the dirt. Winkleman's finger touched the trigger, but he didn't fire. The soldier looked young and terrified and, despite the rifle, helpless.

The anger subsided, replaced with pity. His eyes locked with the enemy. The soldier's eyes suddenly flashed with anger and, with tears streaking down his cheeks, he raised his rifle. Winkleman yelled, "Stop!" but the rifle continued to rise. He had no choice. He pulled the trigger and the soldier's diminutive chest exploded, taking the full brunt of three .45 caliber bullets. His eyes never left Winkleman's but the anger did, replaced with emptiness. He fell backwards into a heap which suddenly no longer looked human.

Henry ran up, slung his rifle and bent down to help the wounded GI. He grunted and strained to get him up and finally had to yell, "Dammit Wink, snap out of it. I need your help here. We gotta get outta here before those shots bring others."

Winkleman tore his eyes away and shook his head. The image of the dead soldier's eyes sank deep into his soul, promising to come out late at night and torture his sleep for the rest of his days.

He slung his Thompson, feeling the heat coming off the muzzle. In a daze he moved to the other side of the wounded GI, whose head lolled to the side, caked with blood and dirt. Henry was struggling to get him hitched to his side and upright. Winkleman went to the other side and wrapped his beefy arms around the soldier's back, forcing him upright.

The soldier moaned, clearing Winkleman's head. With his free hand, he lifted the GI's face, seeing if he recognized him and, at the same time, checking for a wound. The GI's helmet was missing and his dark hair was caked with blood, suggesting a head wound. "That you, Pullman? Hey, Pullman, wake up soldier, we got you now. We got you." The soldier's head flopped forward and he muttered something incoherent. "I think it's Pullman from third squad."

Henry nodded, "Uh huh, well he's a heavy son-of-a-bitch. Let's get moving."

"What about Tarkington? He might be further back."

They started forward, half-carrying, half-dragging Private Pullman. Henry shook his head. "If he is, those Japs probably already ran him through." He shook his head, "I can't explain it, but somehow I don't think he's back there. He's okay."

"That Cajun sixth sense of yours?"

"Something like that," he murmured back through strained breathing.

They struggled, moving back towards the road. There was still the occasional shot, but nothing directed their way... at least they didn't think so. Winkleman doubted he'd be able to hear an advancing tank column over his heavy, labored breathing and his pounding heart.

Pullman dropped into unconsciousness. He hadn't made a sound in a long time, but they couldn't stop to find and treat his wounds. They'd get him back but they didn't know if he'd still be alive.

They finally got to the road and found no one waiting for them. Winkleman ordered them to move to the mountain, but he thought perhaps someone would hang back, just in case.

They stopped and Winkleman looked left and Henry looked right. "Clear to the right," Henry gasped.

Winkleman looked up at the sudden roar of enemy planes flying overhead. They were in a line and as he watched, he saw winking flames firing from their wings. Dark objects detached from their underbellies and soared gracefully toward the side of Mt. Samat. There was a shuddering explosive thump and Winkleman saw flames erupting up the side of the hill. "Hope to God nobody's beneath that," but he knew there undoubtedly was, and probably his own men.

Henry's voice was laced with unease, "How's it look left, Wink? Can we cross?"

Winkleman tore his eyes from the macabre air-show and looked down the dirt road. It turned out of sight twenty yards away, but he couldn't see anything coming, no dust clouds or clanking tank tracks. "It's clear, let's go."

They leaned forward, dragging the top of Pullman's boots across the road, leaving train-track-like divots. If they were being followed, it'd be an easy task.

They got to the other side and had to maneuver across a ditch. Winkleman's foot caught and he tripped, pulling Pullman and Henry down with him. He released Pullman's inert body and laid on his back, his chest heaving for air. "Rest," he gasped. "Need a quick rest." Henry stopped trying to lift Pullman, nodded and laid back too.

Five minutes passed before Winkleman got his breathing under control and felt somewhat normal. He leaned over Pullman and put two fingers deep into his neck, searching for a heartbeat. He adjusted and pushed again then laid back. "He's gone."

Henry sat up and looked Pullman over. "Must've bled out."

"Dammit. I should've stopped back there and stopped his bleeding."

Henry shook his head and pointed at a gaping hole just beneath Pullman's shirt collar. It was filled with dark, thick blood and was the size of a baseball. "There was no way we coulda helped that."

Winkleman stared at the gore then shook his head. "Damn them. Damn this war."

Henry suddenly tensed and leaned forward, looking down the road. His voice turned icy. "Something's coming."

Winkleman got to his feet, "Need to get away from the road. We're too close."

"Too late," Henry whispered and rolled himself and Pullman's body into the ditch. Winkleman rolled too and his boots smacked Henry's head. He scooted forward until he cleared the lead scouts head and pulled as much brush and cover as he could grasp over the top of himself.

The first vehicle passed only feet away. Winkleman was on his side facing the road, tucked as deeply into the ditch as he could push himself. The driver of the first troop transport was only feet away and Winkleman could see his Asian features clearly as he slowly crept along the road. The rear of the truck was full of soldiers, their sweat soaked backs to him. There was a mounted Nambu machine gun on the roof pointing the way they were driving. It was manned by a soldier who used the gun's handles for balance.

More trucks followed, some towing small anti-tank cannons and artillery pieces. Six light tanks passed and Winkleman could clearly see the drivers and tank commanders poking their goggled faces through the open hatches. Dust was thick and he wondered how they were able to breathe. More trucks and then a flurry of small jeeps with mounted machine guns brought up the rear.

Winkleman and Henry stayed put until the dust settled. "Think that's all of 'em," whispered Winkleman.

Henry poked his head out and looked each way. "Think you're right. Japs are definitely behind us now."

Winkleman took his meaning. "I know, but we have to link up with first platoon and they're up this hill."

"Think that column's gonna pass, or take one of them mountain roads up the hill?"

Winkleman shrugged and adjusted his Thompson on his back. "I don't know, but we better get a move on unless we wanna fight our way through 'em."

Henry suddenly clutched Winkleman's arm and put his finger to his mouth. He pointed up the hill and whispered, "Someone's coming." He slid his knife from the scabbard and hunkered down.

Winkleman slipped into the ditch. He couldn't hear anything except buzzing insects and the far-off drone of enemy planes. Then he did hear something, or more accurately, somebody. The unmistakable footsteps of an approaching human. Winkleman cursed himself for not having his own knife out. If they were seen, Henry would have to act, or Winkleman would be forced to fire the Thompson.

The footsteps were nearly on top of him, but suddenly stopped. Winkleman's mouth went bone-dry. He didn't dare move but peered beneath his helmet, trying to glimpse whoever it was only feet away. Sweat ran down his forehead and pooled into the side of his eye, stinging, but he didn't wipe it away. Was he about to be bayoneted?

A gruff, whispered voice, "You fellas ready to come outta there yet? Think it's clear."

Winkleman recognized Staff Sergeant Tarkington's voice and lifted his head from the ditch. "Tark? That you?" He got to his knees, debris cascading off his back and helmet.

Tarkington was there, kneeling, holding his Thompson by the barrel, his sheathed sword sticking out behind him. He was grinning. From behind him, Henry emerged like a wraith, seemingly appearing from thin air. Tarkington looked at him with surprise and Henry sheathed his knife and grinned, "Getting sloppy, Tark."

Winkleman thought Henry was in the ditch and was just as surprised as Tarkington. "How the hell'd you do that?"

Henry looked at him, confused. "Do what?"

Winkleman didn't prod but shook his head. "Glad you're on our side, Henry." He refocused on Tarkington. "What the hell happened to you? We've been looking for you."

Tarkington shrugged, "Tried to help a fallen GI, but he was already gone. By the time I was able to get up and run, everyone was gone and the Japs were right on my tail. Fired an arsenal at me, but I somehow managed to get away. When I stopped running, I had no idea where I was, but I saw those Jap Zeros hitting the hill and knew it had to be Mt. Samat, so I veered back this way. I saw you three when you crossed the road, but then that convoy came." He looked around, "Where's the third man?"

Winkleman pointed into the ditch, pulled back the foliage and shook his head. "It's Pullman from third squad. He's gone."

Tarkington reached down and took Pullman's dog tags, then stood, looking grim. "Anyone got any water?" He asked hopefully.

Henry pulled his canteen and handed it to him. Tarkington's hands shook so badly he had trouble unscrewing the cap. He finally got it open and took a long pull, forcing himself not to drink it all. He wiped his mouth with the back of his hand, relishing the coolness. "Thanks," he handed it back. "Well, time to get back into the war, gentlemen. Take us up the hill, Henry." Henry nodded without a word and moved up the hill with his Springfield ready.

24

It took most of the day to find Hotel Company and 1st platoon. Mt. Samat had been bombed mercilessly and they had to skirt bare areas and spots where the forest still burned, making their route circuitous and slow. They had to cross the mountain road multiple times, as it wound up the mountain in a series of hairpin switchbacks.

When they were near the top, they were challenged by a ragtag group of GIs from an artillery battery. Tarkington didn't recognize any of them. They looked skeletal and sickly.

Once they worked out that they weren't Japs, they led them past a minefield on the road. Tarkington asked, "How many Howitzers you got left?"

The nearest man guffawed, "None. Between the Jap artillery and airstrikes, there's just nothing left."

Tarkington leaned toward Winkleman and grumbled, "Then why the hell we up here? There's nothing left to defend."

They followed the human skeletons a couple of hundred yards up the hill until one pointed. "There's your H Company."

Tarkington saw a group of GIs milling about, sifting through what looked like the remains of buildings. "Thanks," he murmured as he passed. "What're your orders now you don't have guns to man?"

The soldier tilted his head. "Lieutenant told us to watch for Japs coming up the road." Tarkington nodded.

They watched the two soldiers walk back the way they'd come. Their rifles looked huge next to their thin frames. Winkleman shook his head, "They look spent and near starved."

"Yeah, food's in short supply. We've been lucky."

"Half rations are lucky?"

"More'n those two are getting by the look of it," Tarkington replied. He pointed forward, "Let's find someone knows what the score is up here." He strode with purpose and Henry and Winkleman followed.

As they approached, men started recognizing and greeting them. Tarkington saw Lt. Govang. He had his back to him and was leaning over a map laid out on a flat piece of charred wood.

Tarkington shifted his sword to his back. "Sir, Staff Sergeant Tarkington reporting."

Lt. Govang spun and smiled as he looked him up and down. He extended his hand and they shook. "Glad to see you in one piece, Sergeant. That was a hell of a fight back there."

Tarkington nodded, "Good to see you too, sir. Any idea where first platoon is?"

Govang nodded and waved his hand, "Somewhere on the north slope." He looked at Henry and Winkleman and nodded. "This all you got with you?"

"I got split during the retreat and these two went looking for me. The rest of second squad made it, far as I know." He dug into his pocket and pulled out Private Pullman's dog tags and held them out. Govang held out his hand and Tarkington dropped them in his palm. "Pullman didn't make it."

Govang studied the etched writing and rubbed his thumb over the dried blood. "He wasn't the only man we lost today. Not by a long shot." He stuffed the tags into his pocket and turned back to his map.

Tarkington asked, "Any idea what we're doing up here, sir?" Govang looked back over his shoulder with a questioning look and Tarkington pressed, "What I mean is, the big guns are destroyed and the Japs are rolling past us on the main road. There's nothing left up here to defend and if we don't leave soon, we'll be cut off."

Govang pursed his lips. "You should leave the strategizing to Captain Glister, Staff Sergeant."

Tarkington nodded and adjusted his Thompson. "Yes, sir."

He took a step to leave and Govang added, "We're up here to give the rest of the division a chance to escape. If the Japs take this hill, they'll have a commanding view of the entire peninsula. They'll load this mountain with artillery and shoot us like ducks on a pond."

Tarkington looked at the ground then back up at Lt. Govang. "Well, at least that makes some sense. Thank you, sir." Govang gave him an annoyed wave and went back to his map.

When he was ten paces away, Lt. Govang called to him, "Oh, one more thing Staff Sergeant."

Tarkington stopped and looked back. "Sir?"

"If Lieutenant Smoker sees that sword, he'll have a shit-fit. We've got enough problems, take it off and stow it somewhere."

Tarkington gave him a sideways smile and gripped the hilt, "Yes, sir. I'll do that."

He saw someone limping up from behind Lt. Govang. Tarkington stopped and stared. It wasn't a GI, and the limp told him everything. He grinned and called, "Eduardo? Is that you?"

Lt. Govang looked up at the wounded Filipino then back at Tarkington. "Take him with you, he's been driving me nuts wanting to go find you."

"How'd you get out of the hospital? You're still wounded." Tarkington said as he stepped back and saw the bandage still wrapped around Eduardo's hip.

Eduardo could barely speak around his smile. "I left when bombs and planes come. Attack coming, so I left at night. Had to find second squad, but only made it here before attack. Now second squad come to me."

Tarkington pointed at his hip. "Does it hurt?"

Eduardo shook his head emphatically, "No hurt. I can fight. No problem."

Tarkington looked at Henry and Winkleman who grinned back.

Winkleman said, "You're one tough son-of-a-bitch, Eduardo."

Eduardo's smile grew even more and he pointed, "I take you to second squad."

They moved over the top of the hill, exchanging greetings and some handshakes with GIs from 3rd and 2nd platoons. There were a lot of other men milling about they didn't recognize and Tarkington figured they were more cannon-cockers.

There wasn't much left on top of Mt. Samat besides smoking craters, charred tree stumps and broken and twisted artillery pieces. As they moved down the north slope, they came across a line of blackened Stuart tanks. Every hatch was open, as if the men inside had been forced to leave in a hurry. Tarkington hoped they all made it out and wondered if any of the tanks had been involved with the beach attacks in February. That seemed like a million years ago, but it had only been a few weeks, back when they thought they still had a chance at winning.

They finally found 1st platoon a couple hundred yards below the crest of the mountain. They were dug into a burned-out barren section and faced downhill. About two hundred yards below them was part of the mountain road. Tarkington looked the position over. It would be a good spot to ambush whatever came up the road and had a good open killing ground if the Japanese tried to come straight at them. The flanks, however, would be difficult to defend without more men.

"That you Tarkington?" It was Stollman.

Vick, right beside him turned, pushed his helmet back and put his hand on his hip. "Well, well, look what the Wink dragged in."

Tarkington grinned and walked to the edge of their hole and sat down. Winkleman did the same but Henry crouched and looked around the area, evaluating the defenses. Tarkington asked, "Miss me?"

Stollman shook his head and grinned, "Not a bit. Thought maybe the Nips did you in back there."

Vick shook his head, "I never doubted old Wink and Henry would find ya. Them two together? They might find you dead, but they'd find ya."

"Any action up here?"

Stollman shook his head. "Only been here a coupla hours. These holes were already dug. We cleaned out some of the shit, but we didn't have to do much." He pointed at the road, long late-afternoon shadows crossed it. "Saw a Jap jeep, but he got a look at us and beat feet outta there. We got a few shots off but didn't hit anything. Probably made him shit his pants though."

"Reconnaissance you think?"

Stollman nodded, "Probably. But who knows with the way everything's messed up. We've also seen GIs passing by down there. It's like we're all mixed together. No one knows exactly where the other is."

"Well, sounds like they know where first platoon is anyway," said Winkleman with a sigh. Henry got to his feet and waved back at a soldier forty yards away. "I'm gonna go join Raker, unless you have something else for me, Tark."

"Nah, go on. I'll track down Smoker, see what the scoop is." He pulled himself to his feet and untied the sword belt. He wrapped the scabbard in it and handed it to Stollman. "Can you keep this safe for me? Don't wanna cause a stir with the lieutenant."

Stollman took it reverently and leaned it against the dirt wall. "I'll guard it with my life."

Tarkington shook his head, "Nah, just make sure it doesn't get stolen or seen by the wrong person." He looked around, "What direction's he in anyway?" Vick answered, "He's on the right flank. Maybe a hundred yards that way," he pointed.

Tarkington nodded and slapped Sergeant Winkleman's back. "Let's go find out what's going on, Wink."

They found Lieutenant Smoker in the bottom of a foxhole, smoking a ragged and bent cigarette. They crouched on the edge of his hole and Tarkington said, "Haven't seen one of those in at least a month," he indicated the cigarette.

Smoker took a long drag and blew it out slow. "It's my last one. Been saving it, for what, I don't know. It's good to see you two made it."

"Yes sir, you too," answered Tarkington. Lt. Smoker kept smoking and the silence lingered. "So, uh, what's the plan, sir?"

Smoker took one last drag, nearly burning his lips. He held the tiny bit of smoking tobacco up and studied it before grinding it into the side of his hole. He blew out the smoke and it filled the hole. "Plan?"

"Yes, sir. For holding this hill. I ran into Lieutenant Govang, he said we're to defend this hill until the rest of the division's safely away."

Lt. Smoker adjusted his position so he could see over the top of the hole. He nodded and pointed toward the road. "If and when the Japs come up the road, we're supposed to stop them." He shrugged, "But we don't have enough men. They'll be able to flank us pretty quick. They won't be stupid enough to attack up the open space. When that happens, we'll have to move back up the mountain."

Tarkington glanced at Winkleman, and scowled. Lt. Smoker didn't seem himself. "Is something wrong, sir?"

Smoker looked at him and winced. "Wrong?" He looked at his boots and shook his head. "I don't know anything that's right, Tark. I lost a lot of men this morning. Good men. Men with parents, girlfriends, wives, kids." He pointed at the road. "And when they come up that road, I'll lose more. We don't have enough ammunition to last more'n a couple minutes in a fight. No support. Hell, even our vaunted leader saw the writing on the wall and left us out here to die. We've been abandoned. Our government, Roosevelt and all the rest. We're already dead to them. A lost cause. A fucking footnote in a history book, Tark." A long silence followed. Smoker folded his arms on the lip of the hole, rested his chin on his hands and sighed. "Leave me alone. I need to be alone for a bit."

Tarkington didn't reply but left him brooding in his hole. Winkleman followed and when they were far enough away said, "He's lost his nerve."

Tarkington shook his head. "I don't think so. He's a good man who had a bad day. He'll be alright. Once the bullets start flying, he'll be back to his old self."

They found an empty hole near Stollman and Vick. Stollman gave him a mock salute and grinned. Tarkington grinned back and flipped him the finger. He yelled, "How much ammo you got for the BAR?"

Vick reached into his belt and pulled out two magazines. "These and the one loaded. Three mags."

Tarkington nodded and whispered to Winkleman. "Jesus, Smoker's right. They'll burn through that in minutes. Find out how much ammo second squad's got. I need an accurate count before it gets dark." Winkleman nodded and labored out of the hole, "Oh and Wink?" Winkleman stood over him waiting for another order. "Thanks for coming back to get me. Means a lot."

Winkleman nodded, "You'd do the same for me."

The sunset turned the sky brilliant with reds and yellows. The air was hot and humid but there was a slight breeze, making it almost pleasant. Winkleman returned with grim news. 2nd squad along with the rest of Hotel Company, had fled the battle with just what they had in their ammo belts. After they split up the remaining ammunition, each man had three stripper clips for their Springfields and one grenade each. Winkleman and Tarkington each had four magazines for their Thompsons and, once they ran out, they'd have little chance of finding more ammo.

Two hours passed and the sounds of battle seemed louder in the darkness. There were distant flashes in every direction, making Tarkington feel surrounded. An artillery strike lit up the horizon to the south and he suspected some unfortunate convoy, trying to move under the safety of darkness, was being pasted. *How long until the Japs come up to finish us off?*

As if in answer, he heard the sounds of struggling engines. He peered over the edge of the hole at the road below. It looked pale, nearly white, in the light from the half moon. He put his Thompson against the dirt wall. He slapped Winkleman who jolted awake instantly. Tarkington whispered, "Something's coming. Alert the men." He glanced at Eduardo to his right, who was already up and alert.

Before Winkleman could follow the order there was someone behind their hole moving quickly in a crouch. Tarkington recognized PFC Rabowski's high-pitched voice. "Lieutenant says to get ready for contact. Wait for first squad, conserve ammo and be ready to pull back. Rally point on top of the hill." He kept moving, repeating the same order again at each hole.

Tarkington nodded, "Told you Smoker'd get his shit together."

Winkleman shrugged and aimed his Thompson down the hill. "He's awful quick to retreat," he grumbled.

"Hell, we shoulda never come up here. They'll brush us aside like we're not even here. We won't slow 'em down enough to make a difference. The sooner we're off this hill the better, and if it means firing a few shots and running, well, fine with me."

"Never like running away. Getting damned used to it by now though."

Tarkington pointed, "There. See the lights?"

Through the trees, around the corner from the part of the road they could see, was a line of yellow headlights moving up the hill. "They're not even worried about their lights. Coming up here like they're going to the damn market for eggs."

"They'll be in range of first squad pretty soon." Tarkington pointed right, "You can just make 'em out."

Winkleman nodded, "I see 'em. Hope they're able to get back up the hill before they're mowed down."

"Hopefully they got the mines placed in time. Once they go off and we see their grenades, that's the signal to cover fire."

Winkleman acted annoyed. "I know the plan, Tark."

"I know - just helps me to say it out loud." He suddenly felt the familiar weakness and faint nausea which came before every firefight. He'd felt it so many times in the last few months, he wondered why it still surprised him.

The line of vehicles continued to grind up the hill, making the tight switchbacks, until they were on the section of road directly below them. Tarkington licked his lips and brought his Thompson to his shoulder. He squinted over the sights, keeping pace with their slow progress.

There was a sudden, blinding flash which lit up the first truck. The concussive sound rolled up the hill like something alive and Tarkington ducked his head instinctively. The truck lifted off the ground, tilting downslope slowly as flames and shrapnel swept through the cabin, instantly killing anyone in the cab and flinging the soldiers in the back in every direction.

Tarkington cursed himself for watching. He'd ruined his night vision. The 1st squad was up and hurling grenades toward the following vehicles and troops. Tarkington aimed, making sure his safety was off. Compared to the massive mine explosion, the grenades looked like firecrackers going off, but the brief flashes lit up other vehicles and he could see Japanese soldiers darting like moths around a porch light.

There were a few shots from other sections but 2nd squad held their fire. Tarkington had both eyes open scanning. It was a long shot for his Thompson and he didn't want to shoot over the heads of 1st squad, who were running as fast as they could back up the hill. For the time being, at least, there was no pursuit.

He felt like he was watching a football game, cheering for the men retreating up the hill. He muttered to himself, "Come on you bastards, move it."

Beside him Winkleman commented, "They're gonna make it."

They'd just made it past the halfway point when the Japanese finally reacted and muzzle flashes from the road erupted, and soon tracer fire from a Nambu machine gun sliced through the night.

Tarkington aimed at the muzzle flash, which looked to be mounted on the back of a truck. He fired a short burst, adjusted and fired again. He was acutely aware of his ammo situation. Eduardo's rifle barked and he smoothly worked the bolt and fired again.

The fire from the road subsided, allowing 1st squad to continue trudging up the hill. Bullets started whizzing and snapping past Tarkington's ears as the Japanese saw their muzzle flashes and adjusted their fire. The Nambu's tracer shifted towards him and it seemed like it was shooting tennis-ball-sized bullets directly at him. He ducked down, pulling Eduardo with him. He felt the impacts through the dirt wall as bullets slammed into the ground all around their hole.

Eduardo popped up, aimed and fired, then quickly ducked again. Tarkington went up, found a muzzle flash and fired two more rounds, then ducked. He yelled to Winkleman. "Gotta keep 'em concentrated on us. First squad's almost clear." He saw Winkleman nod and stand up with his Thompson at his shoulder. He fired and the flash lit up his half-bearded face. He dropped back down, pulled the magazine and checked it, then slammed it back into place.

Tarkington lifted his head, trying to see 1st squad's progress. In the dim moonlight, he could just make them out as flitting shapes. He saw they were near the top. Most of the enemy fire had shifted his way, but he could tell by their low crouches and quick dashes to cover, that they were still taking fire.

Up and down the line of foxholes 1st platoon's muzzle flashes lit up the night. Tarkington watched as a GI from 1st squad bolted from cover, took a few steps then dropped. Even over the din of battle he heard the soldier's agonized scream. *Dammit.* He aimed and fired until his magazine ran dry, then dropped into his hole and swapped it out for a fresh mag. *Two left.*

He fired single shots, aiming carefully, trying to make every shot count, but he was firing at muzzle flashes, his only intention to keep the enemies' heads down.

He saw GIs from the retreating squad finally making it to the line of foxholes and disappearing into the safety of the holes. Tarkington stopped firing, watching to see what the Japanese would do next. He yelled, "Hey Stolly!"

"Sarge?" He answered.

"You still got the sword?"

"Of course. I'll send Vick."

Moments later Vick was sliding into the hole beside him. He handed over the sword and scabbard, still wrapped in the cloth belt. "Here you go, Sarge. Think we'll be leaving here soon?" he asked nervously, glancing down the hill.

Tarkington nodded, "Hopefully. How much ammo'd Stolly go through?"

"Not much, less than a mag. He was careful."

"Good. Get back to your hole and be ready to move. Rendezvous on the ridge." Vick nodded and ran off in a crouch, covering the twenty yards to his hole in seconds.

Tarkington wrapped the belt and tied it securely around his waist, then moved the scabbard to his right side and gripped the leather handle. It felt good in his hand, natural.

Winkleman was watching him. "If you have to use that thing, we'll be in deep shit."

Tarkington nodded and looked down the hill. "See anything?" The only light coming from the road was from the burning lead truck. He could still make out the outlines of more trucks and see the occasional muzzle flash, but the headlights had been extinguished. "Looks like the road's blocked for now."

Winkleman agreed, "Yep, and first squad made it to cover."

Suddenly there was a flurry of muzzle flashes from the forest to the right of their position, followed with answering flashes from 1st platoon's right flank. "Shit, they're trying to flank us, just like the lieutenant said." The Nambu opened up from the road, sweeping the defensive line in front of them. Tarkington dove down as bullets sent geysers of dirt into the night air. He yelled, "Watch our front, they may be making a move." He watched Eduardo poke his head up then quickly back down. "See anything?"

Eduardo shook his head, "Just the big gun."

The Nambu's fire shifted right and Tarkington took the opportunity to take a look. He saw forms darting in front of the flaming truck, moving from the road to the open slope. He ducked down, "A few coming our way, but can't tell if they're gonna attack, or just finding cover." The firing from the right intensified. "We don't have enough ammo to hold them off for long."

He aimed downslope, holding his muzzle on the last spot he saw the Japanese soldiers. A muzzle flash pinpointed their position and Tarkington fired just behind the muzzle flash. He was rewarded with return fire. He dropped below the surface and leaned his back against the hole. He saw Winkleman looking at him. "At least they don't have mortars or artillery."

"Not yet at least."

Stollman opened up with the BAR, sending a stream of heavy slugs downslope, then paused, "Japs coming up."

Tarkington took a look. He saw shapes in the dim light moving erratically up the hill. He steadied his muzzle and fired twice. His target dropped but from this range he doubted he'd hit him. He moved to the next target and fired a five-round burst. He saw the soldier spin away and fall out of sight. The Nambu shifted fire, concentrating on the BAR. As one, 2nd squad dropped deep into their holes, letting the bullets sweep over them harmlessly, but allowing the soldiers to move forward. "We gotta get outta here, dammit."

Finally came the words he was waiting to hear, "Retreat to the ridge. Retreat!"

25

Tarkington was the last man to leave the defensive line, making sure his squad was well away before following. He took one last glance down the hill and fired a short burst blindly, left to right, then jumped out of the hole and sprinted after his men. He heard someone right beside him and saw Eduardo. "Dammit, I told you to retreat with the others."

"Retreat, yes. With you." Despite his recent wound, he was easily keeping up. Tarkington looked past him, seeing the flank trying to disengage with the force of Japanese in the forest. He hoped Lt. Smoker was dealing with the situation. He thought perhaps he should veer that way and help them out, but orders were orders and he continued chugging toward the ridge. A bullet snapped close and he instinctively dodged right and went lower.

He saw the back of Stollman who was being slowed down by the heavy BAR. Vick was with him keeping his gunner close. Vick glanced back at the duo and relaxed when he recognized them. "Jesus, Tark. Thought you were Japs."

He gasped, "I'm not that ugly, Vick." He came up beside Stollman. "Come on, move your ass." He gripped his shoulder and pushed him forward. More bullets snapped and whizzed past.

Stollman redoubled his efforts and lunged forward. Finally, they saw a line of soldiers taking cover and aiming rifles their way. Tarkington raised his hands and waved, yelling, "Don't shoot. Don't shoot." They ran past the line of soldiers and kept running until they recognized 2nd squad, hunched in the dim moonlight, breathing hard. They slid in beside them and Tarkington directed them. "Spread out and find cover, but be ready to move. Wink, report."

"Second squad accounted for. We're low on ammo, but we're all here."

A flurry of movement from the left got Tarkington's attention. He saw Captain Glister striding to him with purpose and he stood to greet him. Glister asked, "Where's the rest of first platoon, Sergeant?"

Tarkington pointed right, "Coming up the hill, we were the left flank. The Japs hit the right flank. They were trying to disengage. Lieutenant Smoker ordered us back here."

There were still muzzle flashes from the forest. Captain Glister assessed their position and finally nodded. "Move your squad behind this line and see if you can lend a hand. I need everyone together up here."

Tarkington nodded and felt a surge of adrenaline helping his tired muscles. "Yes, sir." He barked, "Second squad, break's over. Henry," he saw Henry glance at him, "You and Raker lead us to the right flank."

Henry nodded and slapped Raker's leg as he passed and they trotted toward the firefight. The rest of 2nd squad followed in a loose line.

A minute later they were on the sloped ground leading down to the forest. Tarkington took in the situation. He saw GIs firing and moving up the hill, but the intensity of enemy fire forced them to take cover, making their progress slow. He squinted, trying to find Lt. Smoker, but there wasn't quite enough light and he only saw darting shapes and muzzle flashes. It was easy to see the enemy position. They were firing from cover with the intensity of troops not concerned about ammunition.

Tarkington crouched beside PFC Henry and Raker, while the rest of the squad set up a loose perimeter. Winkleman joined them. "What's the plan?"

Tarkington pointed at the Japanese position. "We're above them. They're fully engaged." He licked his lips taking in the whole situation. He pointed right and raised his voice enough for everyone to hear. "Lets move above them and take them from the flank. We'll start with grenades and give 'em everything we've got, then break away." He looked around and saw

Stollman and Vick, "Stolly, you and Vick find cover and when we're busting our tails back up the hill, cover us with the BAR. Don't fire until then. Got it?"

Stollman nodded, "Got it, Sarge."

Tarkington looked around at the dimly-lit faces. "Stay low and quiet. Lead on scouts." Henry and Raker nodded and moved out but not as fast as before, being careful not to run into any Japanese that might be waiting for such an attack. Eduardo stayed beside Tarkington.

The firing from the GIs trying to escape up the hill had fallen off considerably. Tarkington hoped it was due to lack of ammo, rather than lack of life. There was a sudden uptick in the firing from the area where Captain Glister was and Tarkington realized that the enemy had finally made it up the slope and were engaging. They'd have to make this quick, then get the hell out of there, or they'd surely be cut-off.

They made it to the left flank of the Japanese in the forest without being seen. Despite the lack of return fire, the Japanese were still firing with abandon. Tarkington was grateful for the muzzle flashes marking their positions. Henry stopped and went onto his belly. Raker did the same. Tarkington watched Henry signal: the enemy was within grenade-throwing distance. Tarkington signaled the rest to move forward and spread out.

He watched the GIs slowly move closer with their rifles ready until they were abreast of Henry, then they went onto their bellies. Tarkington moved up until he was near Henry and Raker. He went to his belly and pulled his one remaining grenade off his battle harness. He set it in front of him, put his Thompson beside it and slowly got to his knees. The rest of the squad mimicked him. He looked side to side, seeing their dark silhouettes poised, like snakes ready to strike.

When he was sure everyone was ready, he pulled the pin. It made a slight metallic sound which was drowned out by the Japanese rifles barking continuously. He flicked the lever, reared back and flung the two-pound lump of explosive death toward the muzzle flashes.

He continued to his belly, clutching his Thompson and bringing it to his shoulder. He kept his eyes closed and his head down. A second later his grenade, along with seven others, exploded amid the Japanese. Agonized screams followed. Tarkington pushed himself onto one knee and aimed. He saw movement, adjusted his aim and fired three quick rounds. The rest of his men joined in and the din of fire was overwhelming. He yelled as loud as he could, hoping Smoker, if he were still alive, would understand what was happening. "Get outta there, first platoon. Now!"

He didn't wait for a response but leveled his muzzle and fired into shapes, silhouettes and muzzle flashes until his magazine ran dry. He swapped out his last mag and got to his feet. He fired twice then yelled, "Second squad, fall back!"

Out of the corner of his eye, he saw Henry and Raker stand and run back the way they'd come. He could sense Eduardo still beside him, not willing to leave until he did so. Tarkington saw a Japanese soldier dart from cover only yards from him. The closeness startled him, but he quickly adjusted, aimed and filled his chest with three rounds. The Japanese staggered and dropped.

Tarkington spun, slapped Eduardo, who was working the bolt of his rifle. "Come on," he ordered and took off after the rest of the squad. Seconds later he heard the heavy, controlled bursts of the BAR and saw the long flame from the muzzle, off to his left.

He pumped his legs and felt his lungs burning for air, but he kept charging up the hill. Beside him, Eduardo barely made a sound and Tarkington was sure Eduardo could've outdistanced him easily even with his wound, but didn't want to leave him.

They reached the staging area moments later, at the same time as the BAR fired its last shot. Through gasping breaths, Tarkington yelled, "Cover Stolly and Vick with whatever you've got left." He aimed into the now-dark forest and fired quick, two-round bursts until his magazine emptied.

He saw two dark shapes approach and recognized Stollman and Vick. He glanced at the main slope, where 1st platoon's right flank had been. He didn't see any movement and hoped it was because they were already up the hill and away. He couldn't stick around to find out. "Move out. Back to the top," he yelled.

Despite burning lungs and legs, the GIs turned and trotted back the way they'd come. They caught up to a group of GIs struggling along, helping wounded men. 2nd squad swarmed around them, helping with the wounded. Tarkington searched the faces, recognizing all of them. He knew there were quite a few missing. Relief flooded him when he saw Lt. Smoker helping a limping soldier.

Tarkington went to the other side of the injured man and put his arm around his waist to take some of the burden off the lieutenant. Smoker glanced his way. Tarkington was shocked. He seemed to have gone through an entire lifetime since he last saw him only hours before. He looked old and tired and barely hanging on. He ignored it, "Good to see you, sir."

Smoker grunted his reply, "You too, Tark. Was that you back there on the flank?"

Tarkington nodded, "Yes, sir. Captain Glister's idea. He's just ahead."

Lieutenant Smoker nodded and they struggled ahead, having to nearly drag the GI. "I - I lost a lot of men..."

He was going to say more, but Tarkington interrupted. "You did all you could. Let Eduardo take your place. We'll get him the rest of the way. Glister's waiting for you." It wasn't true but he figured it would take Smoker's mind off his losses and refocus him on the task at hand. The 1st platoon needed competent commanders if they hoped to survive the next few hours.

Eduardo slipped in between Smoker and the wounded GI, pushing him out of the way. Smoker looked at the diminutive Filipino as though he were from another planet. Eduardo gave him a broad grin. "I good. You go."

Lt. Smoker took another look at Tarkington and nodded, but still seemed in a fog. Tarkington yelled, "Raker, take the lieutenant to Captain Glister."

Raker appeared beside him and pulled his arm, "Come on, sir. He's right up here." Smoker nodded and allowed the scout to lead him.

The Japanese coming up the bare slope were repulsed, but it took most of Hotel Company's ammunition. Once all the platoons checked in and gave Captain Glister reports on their condition and remaining ammunition, he had no choice. It was midnight, the moon was low on the horizon and the darkness was reclaiming whatever light it gave off. "We've got no choice. We have to retreat off this hill while we still have a chance." The three remaining platoon leaders and various NCOs nodded their agreement. Glister continued. "Pull the men off the line as quietly as you can. I don't want the Nips hearing us pulling out. Meet back here in ten minutes or you'll be left behind." He looked at each man. "Once assembled we'll move out right away, with the scouts leading."

Eight minutes later what remained of Hotel Company was assembled loosely around the top of Mt. Samat. They were shuffled into platoons and soon moved out down the southeast slope in single file. As soon as they entered the south side, the darkness intensified and it was difficult to see the man in front.

Henry, Raker and Eduardo were in line with the other scouts a hundred yards ahead of the main body. Captain Glister briefed them before heading out, telling them he had no real idea if they'd run into trouble. If they did, the plan was to wait until the rest of the company caught up, then charge through any resistance with what little ammo they had and fixed bayonets.

To Henry it was a suicidal plan. If they ran into a large enemy force they'd be cut to pieces as they tried to push through, but he was a lowly private and kept his opinions to himself.

Henry could only see Raker to his right and Eduardo to his left. The other scouts were out there, he could hear them, but he couldn't see them. He thought they were making far too much noise. They were exhausted and getting sloppy at the exact moment they needed to be at their sharpest.

So far it hadn't mattered. He figured they were more than halfway down the mountain and they hadn't seen any sign of Japanese. Captain Glister's choice of moving down the less populated but thicker southeast slope was paying off.

They'd traversed some difficult terrain, having to bypass a cliff area at one point and skidding down a steep slope alongside a waterfall, which was probably beautiful during the day but terrifying at night. Now they were traveling through thin jungle and the ground was noticeably flatter. Henry figured they were nearly at the base of the mountain, which didn't make him feel any better. The easier terrain would make it more likely to run into trouble.

He crouched and stopped when he came to a break in the jungle. There was a well-used game trail just in front of him. He didn't want to cross it before he knew it was safe. He listened to the night sounds but was interrupted when he heard a scout pushing through the jungle as though on a Sunday stroll off to his left, beyond Eduardo. It was obvious the GI wasn't going to stop and inspect the trail. Sure enough, he continued forward. Henry couldn't see him, but could hear him perfectly and he cursed under his breath at the man's carelessness. *Gonna get us all killed.*

The sound stopped briefly and Henry thought it must be because he'd crossed the smooth, dirt trail. Perhaps he'd wander down it, hoping it would lead to friendly troops. The noise started again, however, when the scout pushed through the jungle on the other side of the trail and resumed his southeasterly march.

There was a sudden scream, followed immediately with multiple rifle shots and Henry saw muzzle flashes in the jungle to his left about where he guessed the scout would be. Henry dropped instantly to his stomach and noticed Eduardo and Raker doing the same. He had his rifle at his shoulder, his last clip in place. Against orders, he hadn't attached his bayonet. He felt it threw off his aim, and he wouldn't need it until he was truly out of ammo anyway, at least he hoped not.

There were no more shots and no more screams. The night was unnaturally quiet. The night animals and insects briefly paused with the sudden crashing fire. Henry focused his entire being on listening, smelling and seeing what was beyond in the darkness, but there was nothing. He felt Raker move slightly and he pulled his hand off his rifle and held his palm up hoping to keep him quiet for a few more seconds. Raker stopped moving, though he doubted he could see his signal.

A GI called out from the left, his voice faint and faraway. Henry shook his head slightly, wondering what the scout could possibly be thinking that would make him give away his position like that. There was movement in front and to the left and Henry figured it was the shooters reacting to the voice. He could hear the dull murmur of whispering then the relatively loud sound of humans moving through jungle. It sounded like a lot of soldiers and gave Henry goosebumps, despite the warm night. They weren't getting out of here without a fight, apparently.

He waved his hand, and got Eduardo's attention. The Filipino slithered close, his normally smiling face looked worried. Henry whispered in his ear. "Go back and bring second squad here." Eduardo nodded and disappeared the way they'd come without a sound. Raker nearly made it to Henry's side before Henry heard him. He looked right and motioned him closer. He whispered, "We'll hang tight. I sent Eduardo back to get Tark and the others. We'll have a better chance of getting through these guys with second squad." Raker nodded, moved away a couple of feet and nudged up against a thick tree trunk.

Long minutes passed before Eduardo finally returned with the rest of 2nd squad. Tarkington slithered forward on his belly, following Eduardo's every move until he was beside his lead scout. "What you got?"

"Japs. Lots of 'em, moving east toward that idiot that yelled. I think the shooting was a careless scout dying."

The callousness of the statement would've surprised, and even angered, Tarkington even a month ago, but now it was normal. They were in survival mode, pure and simple. "The rest of the company's bottled-up, wondering what the hell's going on. They're moving forward to contact. Once they do, the fireworks'll start."

Henry seethed, "We need to stop 'em. We might be able to get around them by swinging west."

Tarkington nodded. "They're about to burst at the seams and once they do, they'll be no stopping them."

Gunfire suddenly erupted to the left and Tarkington instinctively ducked. There were flashes and zipping tracers lancing into the night. There was a smattering of return fire, which was immediately answered with a throaty and heavy onslaught. It looked as though you could walk across the tracer fire. "There's at least two, probably three Nambus out there," yelled Tarkington. For an instant he was frozen in indecision. The 2nd squad was relatively safe here, with no obvious enemy to their front, but the rest of the company was in deep shit. He pushed himself to his knees and ordered, "We'll move forward and hit their flank."

Sergeant Winkleman asked, "With what? Half of us don't have any more ammo."

Tarkington growled, "That's what the pig-stickers are for." He indicated Raker's bayonet. His Thompson didn't take the bayonet attachment. He'd found two spare rounds of ACP and loaded them into an empty mag and that was all the ammo he had left. Once gone, he'd use it as a club.

Silence greeted him as the thought of charging well-armed Japanese soldiers, at night, with only bayonets, filled their minds. Henry sighed and attached his bayonet with a click that seemed to seal their fate.

Tarkington felt his legs would give out as the nerves of pre-combat adrenaline made him suddenly weak. He had to swallow the bile threatening to come up and the bitter taste almost made him gag. He pushed past it, knowing he'd feel better once he started moving. He got to his feet and the others did too. He put his hand on Henry's shoulder and pushed him towards the dark trail.

He'd just stepped onto it when there was a brief respite in the Japanese fire. A sudden and crazed scream rose from the jungle. More and more GI voices joined and soon the night air was filled with screaming GIs. Tarkington knew at once what it meant. Hotel Company was charging the Japanese, hoping to push right over the top of them with sheer force of will. "Ah, shit!" He yelled, "Come on." He ran as fast as the darkness would allow, toward the Japanese muzzle flashes.

Branches and thorns whipped his face and arms as he pushed through, but he kept charging. He nearly bowled over the first Japanese soldier he came to. He wasn't firing so Tarkington didn't see him until he'd nearly run him over. The surprised soldier had on thin wire glasses. Tarkington slapped the stock of his Thompson across the soldier's face and he heard bone crack as the shattered glasses flew off his face. He ground the heel of his boot into his neck and put all his weight on it as he used him as a step. He felt the sickening crunch of his larynx being crushed, but didn't look back.

Another soldier appeared, as if from nowhere, with his rifle raised. Tarkington didn't have time to attack, so sprang to his right and crashed into the base of a thick tree. He felt pain arc through his shoulder and down his arm. He rolled to a knee and tried to bring up his muzzle but his arm was tingling and didn't seem to work anymore. The Japanese rifle fired and the bullet thunked into the tree trunk an inch from his head. He rolled to his back and tried to get as close to the tree as possible. He could hear the Japanese chambering another round.

Tarkington held the Thompson like a pistol with his left hand, and leaned out the other side of the tree trunk. The barrel swung side to side unsteadily and he pulled the trigger, firing a single shot into the ground. The Thompson bucked and he rolled to his right making the pain in his shoulder worse. He heard a guttural scream of agony and looked up to see Sergeant Winkleman with his bayonet buried in the Jap's guts, twisting. He pulled it out and, even in the darkness, Tarkington could see the stream of blood that followed the blade.

Tarkington got to his feet unsteadily and Winkleman turned toward him with fire and hatred in his eyes. Tarkington raised his hands and Winkleman recognized him and the man he knew returned as though a mask had been removed. "You okay?"

Tarkington shook his right arm and felt the numbness leaving, replaced with hot pins and needles. "Yeah, thanks to you."

The firing intensified as the GIs of Hotel Company crashed into the Japanese force blocking their retreat. Tarkington saw the withering fire from one of the Nambus only yards away. He put his Thompson to his shoulder and felt the trigger. *Think I have one left.* Though his fingers still tingled, he could feel the coolness. He aimed carefully and fired his last round. The soldier manning the Nambu toppled over, but was soon replaced with another. Henry appeared and carefully aimed and fired twice, dropping the shooter.

Sudden movement from the left caught their attention. Tarkington dropped his spent Thompson and unsheathed the sword. A crazed GI burst into them with his bayonet swinging and jabbing. They jumped aside and the GI continued running past them disappearing into the night, still screaming like a crazy man.

PFC Stollman joined them, still clutching his BAR. Tarkington asked, "You still got ammo for that thing?"

Stollman gave him a quick shake of his head, his eyes continually scanning for threats. "Couldn't bring myself to leave her behind." Two screaming Japanese soldiers charged, lunging from the darkness with fixed bayonets.

Stollman jumped back, half a second before being skewered. He swung the heavy BAR into the back of the first soldier's head as he overextended. The stock struck the back of his head and instantly caved it in, sending blood and brains out his ears. He dropped without a sound. The second soldier lunged toward Stollman's back and he knew he'd die in another instant. Suddenly there was a slashing flash as Tarkington took him midsection. The sword sliced through bone and muscle, as though through water, and the soldier simply fell into two pieces.

"Christ almighty." Stollman exclaimed.

Tarkington leaned forward and pulled the rifle from beneath the first soldier. As he searched for ammo, Henry fired and dropped another enemy soldier running past. Tarkington found an ammo pouch. He wiped the sword on the dead man's shirt and sheathed it. He loaded the Arisaka and chambered a round. Everyone stared at the severed body in stunned silence.

The firing tapered off, but the crazed screaming had not. The GI's panicked run through the Japanese force seemed to have worked. Tarkington wondered how many men were lying dead and wounded in the darkness. "We've done all we can do. Let's get the fuck outta here." He took another glance behind him and stepped to the south. "Watch behind us. Move out second squad, double time."

They couldn't run without slamming into trees and brambles, so they took on a consistent lope which ate up ground until they felt relatively safe. The sounds of battle and screaming had ceased, replaced with the occasional crack of a rifle and the calling of monkeys. By the time they stopped running, there was a hint of morning light on the eastern horizon.

26

By mid-morning, 2nd squad had reformed with the remnants of 1st platoon and Hotel Company, and was streaming south along the main road along with the rest of the division and I Corps.

The men were exhausted. They hadn't slept for over twenty-four hours and had been fighting most of the time. Tarkington watched a man sway and drop. He remained face-down and Tarkington thought he might be dead. "Check that man," he pointed and the nearest GI went to him, kneeled and shook his shoulder.

The soldier lifted his head and was helped to his feet. Tarkington shook his head, they needed to rest and eat. The road was choked with GIs moving south side by side with refugees doing the same thing. Eventually they'd run out of peninsula. *Then we'll have to move to Corregidor.* He looked at the haggard refugees, still pulling carts and bikes piled high with their possessions. *What will happen to these people? Command won't take them to Corregidor.*

He'd seen how the Japanese treated prisoners of war. They considered any surrender a great dishonor and treated soldiers as less than human if they surrendered while they still had breath in their lungs. He doubted they'd have any more mercy for civilians. He figured they'd consider them a burden. Something to get rid of as soon as possible.

He looked at Eduardo, whose family was in Manila when the Japanese attacked. How must it be for him? Tarkington thought about his own family back in the States. They must be pulling their hair out with worry.

Eduardo's limp was more severe than normal, probably because he was as worn out as everyone else, perhaps more. His wound wasn't healed and must hurt like hell all the time. He shook his head and once again thanked God that the Filipinos were on their side.

We've let them down. The big US of A has let them down. Eduardo saw him watching and instantly straightened up and gave him a smile. Tarkington could see the strain just beneath the surface and it tore at his heart. He thought about Nunes, who hadn't been seen since the attack. He hoped he was killed outright. If he were captured it wouldn't go well for him. The Japanese would view a fighting civilian as a spy and he doubted their executions would be quick and painless.

Finally, they came to a point in the road that passed a decent-sized village. Hotel Company was steered into it by an MP. As Tarkington passed the MP, he wondered if he had any idea what company, or even what division he was directing. Had someone directed this move, or was he simply directing the most haggard-looking men into the village? He decided he didn't care, as long as his men got to stop marching and could drink and eat something.

They streamed into the open space and saw a water spigot. It was in the center of the open space, and Tarkington guessed it was the center of the village.

The ground around the spigot was muddy and tracked with countless boot prints. They'd been able to fill their canteens from the occasional streams coursing off Mt. Samat, but they were down to the dregs and needed refills. The well-water would be cold, pure and refreshing.

Men queued up, handing their canteens off to GIs, who took it upon themselves to pump and fill. The rest of the men simply sat down and started rifling through their packs for whatever food rations they could find.

They were low on food. They hadn't been resupplied for days. Some had left the front line so fast, they didn't have time to grab their packs and were without food completely. Those men didn't starve though. Everyone was in this together; ammo, water and food was shared, in that order. It meant no one was left starving, but everyone was hungry.

The town was deserted and completely devoid of food. It had been picked clean by countless groups of hungry GIs. Tarkington saw PFC Yap applying a bandage he'd fashioned from a dirty uniform over the arm of PFC Rabowski, Lt. Smoker's runner, and local grifter. After getting his canteen filled, Tarkington walked up to the pair. Yap looked up, "Hey Sarge. What's the scoop?"

Tarkington shrugged, "Don't know really. Just followed the rest of the company in here." He took a long swig from his canteen, his Adam's apple rising and falling.

He'd lost a lot of weight since December and his features were just as skeletal as everyone else's. He wiped his mouth with the back of his hand. He still had dried blood on his face from the soldier he'd cut in half. He noticed the back of his hand coming away bloody and poured the rest of the canteen over his head, scrubbing his face. He tilted his chin toward Rabowski. "Hey, Ski, you got any food tucked away somewhere?"

Rabowski looked at him with a hurt expression. "I wouldn't keep anything from the guys." Tarkington gave him a sideways look and Rabowski added, "Well, I've got some candy but there's not much to 'em and they're good bargaining chips for better stuff. I've had guys trade me actual food for bits of candy with hardly any nutritional value. They're almost better'n cigarettes."

"What'd you do to your arm?"

Rabowski shrugged, "Jap bayonet sliced me." Yap grinned and shook his head. "I've seen a lot of bayonet wounds today. This looks more like a thorn bush, Ski."

Rabowski shook his head emphatically. "It's a bayonet. Last night when we ran through 'em." He held up two fingers, "Scout's honor."

Tarkington's grin turned serious. "If I find out you're holding out on me, it won't go over well with the men. If you've got food, you better not hoard it. Understood?"

Rabowski looked hurt again. "Of course Staff Sergeant. I'm on your side." He pointed at the sword hanging from the embroidered belt. "See you got the sword. Looks good on you."

Tarkington gripped the handle. "If you think I owe you one, think again, Private. You paid your debt to Skinner."

Rabowski grinned and nodded. "Yep, that was a good deal, I'd say."

The heat of midday washed over them as they rested in the abandoned village. After filling canteens and eating what they could find, most GIs lay down and slept. Tarkington had his head resting on his pack beneath the shade cast from a dilapidated hut's deck. He didn't know how long he'd been asleep when the sound of far-off engines pulled him awake.

He opened his eyes and concentrated. Had he actually heard something, or was it a dream? He was about to shut his eyes again when the noise increased and there was no doubt. He sat up and scooted from beneath the deck, put his hand over his eyes to shield them from the glaring sun and searched the sky. Since they were in a clearing, he could see a good portion of the clear, blue sky. The sound seemed to come from everywhere at once. He couldn't pinpoint it but there was no doubt it was getting louder.

Other GIs were stirring and looking skyward. Suddenly there was the unmistakable hammering noise of a Japanese machine gun. "Cover," he yelled, but the GIs were already moving. The only cover was the buildings, and the GIs scrambled beneath them and hugged the ground.

Tarkington saw a flash over the road and spotted a Zero only feet above the trees. He could see the flashing guns strafing the road. GIs and refugees ran from the road, many coming into the village seeking cover.

He put the Arisaka rifle to his shoulder and tried to follow the plane as it arced upward, but he knew it would be a waste of ammo. Indeed, there was very little firing. None of the men were willing to burn through ammo with such a low chance of hitting anything.

Another Zero zipped past, firing. The road erupted in dust, geysers of dirt and blood. Some of the refugees, unwilling to leave their possessions, were cut down as they tried to pull their carts off the road.

A third Zero made a run, slewing the wings side to side, spraying death into the gully alongside the road. Tarkington couldn't help himself, he had to fight back. He gave the speeding Zero a good lead and fired. The kick against his shoulder felt good. He knew it would be a miracle to cause any damage, but he felt better. He watched the plane arc up, unscathed. It made a graceful turn, joining its comrades as they moved off, seeking out other targets.

With the threat passed, the GIs filtered out from beneath the houses and stood around wondering if they should go back to sleep or get ready to march. The dust was thick over the road and there were cries of pain. Tarkington was almost immune to the sound by now.

He spotted Lt. Smoker walking his way. He looked better than the last time he'd seen him. He stopped in the center of the village and barked, "We're staying here until dark, so find a good place to rack out. We'll form up at 1800 hours right here."

There was a smattering of relieved comments as the GIs moved to find shady spots to spend the next few hours.

At 1700 hours, 1st platoon's officers and NCOs were called to meet at the impromptu HQ, which had been set up in the biggest building in the village. Tarkington was sure to leave his sword with Henry for safekeeping. He walked alongside Sergeant Winkleman, who asked, "What's this all about?"

Tarkington shook his head and spat. "I don't know, but I doubt it's good news. It's never good when one platoon is pulled from the rest." Winkleman nodded his agreement.

Tarkington entered the building and, when his eyes adjusted to the low light, saw Captain Glister, Lt. Govang, Lt. Smoker and a Major he didn't recognize. The Major was short and balding and looked like he should be in an accounting office crunching numbers, rather than on the front lines in Luzon.

There was nowhere to sit, so they stood and looked expectantly at the officers. Captain Glister stepped forward. "Hotel Company will be marching out of here in an hour. We'll march most of the night, getting as far south as possible. Hopefully all the way to Mariveles." He indicated the Major, "This is Major Grinton. He's with G2 intelligence."

The major looked completely unprepared to be standing before them. He fidgeted and sweated more than the temperature warranted. He looked tired and overworked, just like everyone else, but he also had a nervousness to him, which labeled him as a pencil-pusher rather than a combat soldier.

He stammered, "Men," he dropped the pencil he was holding and bent over to pick it up. He stuffed it behind his ear cleared his throat and started again. "The situation's not good. The Japs are pushing hard after the break-through. We're spread all over, but the main Allied Force is still intact, for the most part. With the constant harassment from the air, we need to move at night, but the Japanese are only a couple of miles behind us. They've slowed, probably to move onto Mt. Samat with artillery. Once in place, they'll be able to shell us nearly all the way to Mariveles. That, combined with the air attacks makes movement during daylight impossible." He paused and wiped his brow. Tarkington thought he might pass out any moment. "Which brings me to why you're here."

"Here it comes," Tarkington whispered from the side of his mouth.

"We need a blocking force behind us. We need to slow the Jap advance so we can establish another line of resistance." He licked his lips and looked around the room. "First platoon has been chosen for the task."

There was a smattering of angry voices which were silenced by Captain Glister. "All right, can it."

Staff Sergeant Mahoney from 1st squad raised his hand and Captain Glister pointed at him. "Sir, we don't have much ammo. What're we supposed to slow 'em down *with?*"

Captain Glister took over the briefing. "I was getting to that. We've consolidated enough ammo for you to get the job done. Along with Spring-field ammo, we also have crates of grenades and mines. You'll have a squad from the heavy weapons platoon attached to you with two .30 caliber Brownings and two mortar tubes." There was a smattering of conversation and nods of approval. "You're job isn't to stop the Japs, but to slow them down. Hit them quick, inflict damage and retreat. Don't get into anything protracted. You'll be completely on your own, we can't send help." He looked around the room, "Any more questions?"

Tarkington stepped forward, "We getting more rations, sir?"

Glister nodded, "Yes, you'll be fully resupplied before going out." More nods of approval. Glister put his hands behind his back and leaned forward. "Listen men, I don't want any heroics. It's thirty miles to Mariveles give or take. We should only need two nights to get there. I'll leave it up to the lieutenants on how you want to go about attacking, but I wouldn't expect you to need to hit them more than twice. If you cause enough chaos, it'll slow them down considerably."

Tarkington felt odd watching the rest of Hotel Company moving south without them. The GIs of 1st platoon were almost giddy as they filled their pockets and packs with ammunition and C-rations. The heavy weapons squad looked none too happy to be joining them and stood off by themselves giving furtive glances to the receding backs of the rest of the company.

Lieutenant Smoker was back in charge, his stupor from the Mt. Samat battle, gone. Tarkington was glad to see him taking charge and looking confident. Once H Company was out of sight, he addressed the platoon. "I'm sending second squad up the road a mile, along with all the scouts and these Filipinos." He indicated a group of fifteen Filipino men holding saws and axes. He looked directly at Tarkington. "You'll provide security while half the Filipinos cut trees for a blockade. You'll also bury mines on the road beyond the blockade. Before you leave, do what you can to set booby-traps on the blockade itself. We'll be a half mile behind you and should be done with another blockade by the time you're back. When they get to our blockade, we'll hit them with mortars and small arms." He held up his index finger for emphasis. "Don't get pinned down. Throw a grenade, fire a few well-aimed shots and get the hell outta there. Got it?" There were nods all around. "This is the rally point. If you get split up, come here as quick as you can." More nods. "Okay, move out second squad."

Tarkington barked, "Scouts out." PFC Raker, Henry and Eduardo trotted up the road, followed by the rest of 2nd squad and seven of the Filipinos.

Winkleman leaned in and whispered to Tarkington, "Why we always picked for this kind of shit?"

Tarkington shrugged, "Could have something to do with this," he touched his sword hilt. "I'm sure he noticed it, but I wasn't about to go into combat without it. It's my good luck charm now."

Winkleman grinned, "Tark's Ticks out in front again."

"Yep."

27

When Tarkington figured they'd gone a mile, he stopped them and they moved to the ditch on the right side and hunkered down. They listened for anything out of the ordinary. The strip of road was lighter than the surrounding jungle, which was pitch black. The constant hum of insects and the yammering of night animals was loud and constant.

Eduardo moved to Tarkington's side and gave him a thumbs-up. Tarkington gave a curt nod back. If Eduardo thought it was safe, it was safe.

Tarkington signaled the men to move forward and spread out. Staying in crouches, they moved into the surrounding jungle, finding cover and kneeling. The Filipinos were given the go ahead and they scampered into the jungle, looking for likely trees to cut down.

Soon sawing and chopping sounds filled the night. Tarkington shook his head, not liking the noise, but they had no other choice.

There was no traffic. The stream of refugees had ceased, which was good, but also ominous. Anything coming down the road now would be the enemy. He strained to hear over the din of wood-work, but realized if a Japanese convoy came, he wouldn't hear their engines until it was too late. He silently willed the workers to hurry.

PFC Stollman and Vick were in front of him. If the Japanese made an early appearance, the BAR crew would be their best chance of getting out alive. He touched the grenades hanging from his harness and felt the weight of the Springfield ammo on his belt. They'd be able to put out a good amount of firepower, hopefully enough to break away.

A half hour later, he heard the first tree falling with a prolonged moan, then a mighty crash. He looked behind and saw a large tree settling across the road. It looked stout and immovable. The smell of sawdust and dirt reminded him of the sawmill back home where they bought their fencing materials. The memory seemed like something from another lifetime, like someone else's memory.

He called out, "Get the mines set out. Hurry."

"Yep," called out PFC Skinner. Tarkington saw Skinner and Holiday moving around the tree. Each soldier had a bulky mine tied to their backs. Like all good infantrymen, they'd bitched and complained about the extra weight, not to mention the increased chance of being vaporized.

Tarkington returned his attention forward. He saw his lead scout, Henry, frantically signaling. Tarkington's breath caught in his throat, something was coming.

He focused forward, trying to see or hear what Henry had. Henry was the furthest man forward, crouched in the ditch beside the road. He could hardly see him and had only seen his waving because of the lighter background of the road. He doubted Henry could see him any better.

Tarkington got into a crouch and, as quietly as possible, moved forward. He passed Vick and Stollman and whispered, "Be ready to move back." He continued, having to move around and through brambles, keeping off the road. Finally he was beside Henry. He noticed Raker there too. He heard the faint sound of engines. He tapped Henry and whispered, "Move back. Now." Henry and Raker silently moved along the ditch staying low.

Tarkington stood and signaled the only remaining man across the road, Winkleman. He hoped he saw his frantic signals. He strained to see if he were moving but couldn't tell one way or the other. The engine sounds grew louder and he saw a flash of dimmed headlights through the trees. Staying in a crouch, he hustled to Vick and Stollman, who were already moving back with the scouts. Tarkington stopped and again signaled the invisible Winkleman. If he didn't retreat soon, it would be too late.

He moved around the massive tree trunk and ran to the road along with his scouts and BAR team. Skinner and Holiday were placing the mines in the holes the Filipinos had dug. They quickly covered them, patting them down as best they could. Branches were placed carefully on top and leaves and brambles added too.

Tarkington hoped to see Winkleman, but he wasn't there. "Henry, go get Wink, quick. Raker, cover him."

They moved off to the left side of the road. Raker crouched behind the tree, resting his rifle on top as Henry vaulted over it like a monkey. The sound of engines was close, just around the corner. Once the headlights illuminated the blockade, the convoy would stop and deploy troops to investigate. Once that happened, it would be hard for Winkleman to move without being seen.

He watched them finish camouflaging the mines. He hoped it would be enough, but doubted it would stand up to concerted scrutiny. His orders were not to engage, so the next blockade would be treated with less scrutiny, but if the Japanese saw Winkleman, he'd have no choice. He wasn't here to sacrifice men.

Headlights suddenly lit up the area, the light streaming through gaps between the road and fallen tree, making them freeze. Brakes squeaked as the convoy came to a stop. Tarkington pushed Stollman to the right and signaled the others to the left. If the shooting started, he wanted the advantage of a crossfire. He glanced back at the BAR crew, but followed the men left.

He heard yelling in Japanese and figured troops would be streaming through the area in moments. He pulled up beside Raker and placed his rifle on the tree, aiming at the front windshield of the lead truck. He pulled his eyes from his sights and searched for Henry and Winkleman, but the glaring lights ruined his night vision and he couldn't see either of them.

He saw shapes moving in front of the lights. Japanese were cautiously moving forward with their rifles ready. Tarkington figured it was thirty yards to the lead truck. He released his grip on the trigger and carefully pulled a grenade off his harness. He carefully let his rifle lean on the tree. Skinner and Holiday followed suit.

He'd try to throw the grenade beneath the lead truck. It was a long throw but he had a good arm, at least that's what his high school baseball coach once told him. More soldiers stepped in front of the headlights. He figured there were many more he couldn't see moving into the cover of the jungle.

The nearest soldier stopped ten yards from the blockade and turned back to the truck and yelled something. It was now or never. Tarkington pulled the pin, reared back and hurled his grenade as far as he could. His arm still hurt from the night before and hurling the two-pound grenade didn't help. He cursed under his breath.

The Japanese whirled back around catching the quick throwing movements of Skinner and Holiday. He called a warning, which was interrupted with the blast of a grenade going off beside the truck on the driver's side and peppering the cab with shrapnel.

The nearest soldier writhed as bullets scythed through his body until he finally dropped. The other two grenades went off among the soldiers in front of the truck sending them to the ground with fragmentation wounds. Tarkington hoped Henry and Winkleman hadn't caught any fragments.

He picked up his rifle and fired twice into the truck's grill, hoping it was out of commission. He fired at a soldier on the ground, lit up by the still-shining headlights. He caught movement in the shadows to his left. Two men he figured must be Henry and Winkleman. "Fall back!" he yelled.

Suddenly there was a ripping sound and the air came alive with snapping bullets. There was a Nambu machine gun mounted on the back of the truck. Bullets stitched the tree trunk and Tarkington could feel it vibrating. The BAR opened up from the right. The truck pulsed with impacts. Windows shattered, the wood siding splintered and the Nambu stopped firing. "Pull back, Now!"

The men took off, staying to the side of the road as best they could, but ended up on the main road so they could run flat-out. The initial surprise of the attack wore off and the Japanese sent volleys of fire down the road, but the GIs were around the slight bend in the road and relatively safe. They kept running though, finally stopping with their hands on their knees, breathing hard.

Tarkington did a quick headcount, everyone was there. He found Winkleman gasping for air with his head leaned back as though gazing at the stars. Through heavy breaths he asked, "Wh - where were you?"

Winkleman shook his head and grimaced in pain before answering. "I - there was a snake. Big fucking snake. Couldn't move."

Tarkington shook his head, "Snake? You get bit?"

Winkleman pointed at Henry who was grinning. He drawled, "I killed it for him. One of those caped sons-of-bitches."

Winkleman nodded, "By that time it was too late to move."

Tarkington shook his head in disbelief. "Let's keep moving. Come on, double-time. It won't take long for those bastards to blow through that tree."

Captain Gima wasn't happy. The huge tree blocking the road meant more delays. Every delay meant the Americans and their puppet Filipinos would have time to dig in and more of his men would die as a result.

For the hundredth time he cursed this backwards island and its people. What kind of country only had one usable road? Once they defeated the colonialists, the Empire of Japan would build roads and pull these backwards people into the modern world.

He gnashed his teeth as he watched another stretcher with a wounded soldier pass by. The cowardly Americans were resorting to guerrilla-style attacks. It was a sign they were on their last legs but it was also effective at slowing their advance.

He had orders to push forward and crush any resistance, trapping the Allies near Mariveles and killing them before they could escape to the island fortress of Corregidor.

He'd been incensed when ordered to halt while two companies assaulted Mt. Samat. They'd met resistance but soon overwhelmed the forces there. However, instead of immediately resuming his attack, they were ordered to wait while artillery batteries were hauled up and placed.

His men were tasked with building the revetments the guns were placed in. He didn't mind hard work, but his men were combat soldiers - not engineers - and while they wasted an entire day digging holes, the Allies moved further away.

He was brought from his thoughts by a loud explosion that rocked a nearby truck and fluttered his uniform. That would be his demolitions team trying, for the second time, to blow a hole in the massive tree. The first explosive had damaged it, but not enough to split it. The team was reprimanded by Lieutenant Eto. From the sounds of it, they'd used plenty of explosive this time.

He strode from behind the cover of the truck and saw the results. The tree was in half, indeed most of it was shredded, nearly all the way to the edge of the road. Bits of wood splinters, dirt and dust filtered down all around him, plinking off his shoulders and hat. Lt. Eto warned, "Better take cover, sir. There's bound to be bigger pieces."

Captain Gima glared at his cowering lieutenant. "Move forward and see if it's passable, Lieutenant."

Lieutenant Eto immediately moved, keeping a wary eye toward the night sky. Gima watched his silhouette against the burning wood. From here it looked like a successful breach. Moments later Lt. Eto returned and nodded, "It's open, sir. There's a crater, but it's passable."

"Did your men find any more mines?" A segment of the engineers, along with an infantry escort, had moved around the tree checking for traps and mines. They'd immediately found two anti-tank mines buried haphazardly in the road. They had removed them and searched further down the road.

"They're still out there, sir. But if they'd found more they would've sent word."

"Good. Mount up and move out, we'll pick them up on the way." He slid into his jeep and spoke to the driver. "There's a crater but it's passable." The driver nodded his understanding.

The first troop truck ground forward, the gears grinding harshly before finally slipping into place. The second truck was close behind. The jeep was third in the long line of trucks. Many were filled with soldiers but most contained ammunition and supplies for the spearheading company.

They passed a burned-out truck, a casualty of the ambush. He glanced at the burned Nambu machine gun tilted toward the stars and wondered what became of the soldier who'd manned it.

The lead truck slowed as it bounced into the shallow crater and churned up the other side. Captain Gima stood in the passenger side and watched the second truck maneuver through it without difficulty. He was thankful it wasn't raining. If it were muddy, they'd be forced to fill it in, creating yet another delay.

After a few minutes of driving, he had his driver pull to the side, allowing more trucks to pass. He walked to the side of the road undid his pants and took a leak. His driver had his pistol out and scanned the area. "Relax, Haru. It would be very unlucky and unlikely that I chose to piss near an enemy."

"Yes, sir," he replied but did not stop scanning the jungle for threats.

Gima hopped back into the jeep. They'd just got back into the lineup when the truck in front of them jolted to a stop. Gima stood and watched the truck behind them barely stop in time. He glared at the Private clutching the wheel. He looked like he would die of fright. "Now what?" Gima raged.

He hopped from the jeep and moved to the left, walking past troops, who watched him curiously. He strode with purpose, his sub-machine gun snug against his chest. Lieutenant Eto was running towards him. When he saw Gima, he stopped and pointed, "Another roadblock, sir."

Gima barked, "Dismount," at the same time he heard the whistling of incoming mortars. "Cover," he yelled and dove into the ditch on the side of road. He was joined immediately by his driver, who had his pistol out. Gima pulled his head down, "Get down, you fool."

The mortars fell in pairs and walked up the line of trucks. There was a loud clang of metal and he glanced up in time to see the fourth truck in line take a direct hit. The hood was flung into the air and there was a brief secondary explosion as the gasoline in the engine burned. The second round hit the bed of the truck sending wood splinters and metal shrapnel in every direction. He didn't see any soldiers in the truck, thank the gods, but the truck was turned into a useless inferno.

As quickly as the mortars started, they stopped. There was a brief second of relative silence, then the popping of more explosives, followed immediately with withering fire from machine guns and rifles. He strained to see muzzle flashes, but buried his head in the ditch when the ground to his right erupted in geysers and ricochets.

He rolled to his back and extended his Type-100 sub-machine gun in the general direction of the incoming fire and squeezed the trigger. He knew he had little chance of hitting anything, but he might keep their heads down. He went back to his belly and crawled forward, staying low in the ditch. If he could make it twenty more meters he might have a better shot.

He heard the hammering of machine gun bullets slamming into the metal sides of trucks. He lifted his head and saw one of his men lean out with his rifle extended. He fired then crumpled and fell as though he were a used-up toy.

Gima felt rage building. His men were being slaughtered. He crawled the rest of the way and popped to his knees with his sub-machine gun ready. He saw a muzzle flash only fifteen meters away. He fired, spraying the area back and forth until his magazine ran dry. He dropped down as the air above his head came alive with zipping bullets. He struggled to find another magazine and when he did released the empty and slammed in the new.

In the time it took to reload, the shooting stopped. He got to his knees and aimed, searching for muzzle flashes. His men were firing now. He squeezed the trigger and fired controlled bursts where the enemy was moments ago. He realized they were trying to break contact, a hit-and-run guerrilla tactic. It enraged him. He wouldn't allow it to happen. He yelled, "Attack!" and ran straight at the spot he'd seen the muzzle flashes.

His men, seeing their company commander charging the enemy alone, roared into action, screaming, running and firing. Soon they caught up to their commander and passed him. "Don't let them get away. Kill them all."

He followed and noticed a body. It was the GI he'd shot earlier. He fired twice into the inert body making sure, and stepped past.

He moved around the downed timber and stepped onto the road beyond. He could see his men running down the road, sometimes stopping to fire, but he couldn't see the enemy and there was no return fire. "Dammit," he seethed.

There was an explosion down the road that lit up the night, followed by a scream that cut to his soul. He yelled at Lieutenant Eto who'd come around the log with his sub-machine gun ready. "Call them back. Get them back here. The road's mined."

Lt. Eto took off as fast as his legs would carry him, calling for the men to halt. Captain Gima seethed, feeling anger - fueled by helplessness - course through his body. He hated these cowardly GIs and their vile Filipino puppets. He vowed, then and there, he'd show them no mercy. He'd make sure they died like the cowards they were.

Minutes later the soldiers were trotting back up the road, led by Lt. Eto. Gima watched soldiers carefully lay two ragged bodies on the ground near the roadblock. Lt. Eto saw him looking. "Mine. Probably an anti-tank mine, killed them both." He held out a burnt playing card and Captain Gima took it and studied it. In the glow from the burning trucks he could see it was the king of spades. He could also see the etched writing, 'Tark's Ticks.' "They must've placed the entire deck of cards on the mine. They were scattered everywhere, floating down like confetti."

Gima stuffed the card into his front pocket. "They will pay for this butchery."

28

The 1st platoon didn't stop running until they were back at the turn-off to the village where they'd started their mission hours before. They figured the Japanese had stopped pursuit and would be working to open the road back up. They'd heard at least one of the big anti-tank mines detonate.

Tarkington put his hands on his knees and bent over, trying to catch his breath. Lieutenant Smoker ordered between gasps, "Set up security while we catch our breath." Tarkington looked to Winkleman, who nodded and tapped Holiday, who staggered to the edge of the road with his rifle ready.

Tarkington asked, "We need to set up another roadblock tonight?"

Smoker considered, then shook his head. "Took them awhile to get through the first one and the second tree's even bigger. That, along with the mines, should be enough." He pointed into the darkness towards the village. "Captain Glister said he'd leave us a few trucks." He found 1st squad's leader kneeling in the dark. "Mahoney, bring the trucks out. They're in the village somewhere."

He gave him an animated salute and said, "Yes, sir," with a happy lilt to his voice. "Mighty kind of the captain."

"Indeed. Get me a head count Staff Sergeant," he ordered Tarkington. "Yes sir."

Minutes later the trucks, with slits for headlights, trundled out of the village. There were three of them. Tarkington leaned toward Smoker's ear. "Second squad's still got eight GIs plus Eduardo. Third's got eight too. The heavy weapons squad lost two guys back there. They're down to seven and first squad didn't lose anyone. They've still got six." He scowled, "That's thirty soldiers, sir."

Smoker nodded, "Miracle we didn't lose more. Well, let's load up and get outta here. We might have to cram a bit."

Suddenly there was a yell from Holiday, which was cut short with the sound of many guns opening fire at once. Tarkington dropped to his belly instinctively. He heard Lt. Smoker grunt and fall awkwardly on his side. The air snapped with bullets. The hammering sounds of bullets tearing holes in metal as the idling trucks were swept, was deafening.

Tarkington saw Staff Sergeant Mahoney, who'd been leaning out the driver's side window of the lead truck, disappear as his head snapped back with multiple impacts.

The distinct sound of a heavy Nambu machine gun filled the air and he could see the thick stream of tracer fire slamming into the trucks and the men inside. The second truck's fuel tank ignited sending up a concussive wave of heat, which swept over the cowering GIs. The blast engulfed the third truck and he watched in horror as GIs scrambled from the inferno, their clothes on fire.

He aimed and fired at the source of the tracer fire, working the bolt as quickly as he could make his hands move. Eduardo was beside him, doing the same. Tarkington looked toward Smoker and saw him on his back. He was staring straight up, his mouth gaping open and closed like a fish out of water. He was holding his stomach, which glistened with wetness.

Tarkington moved to him and pulled himself half onto his body and yelled into his face, "Stay with me Smoke, stay with me! Medic!" he called but he knew it was too late.

From the darkness, Yap came running. Bullets whizzed and snapped, seeming to fill every square inch, but still he came and slid in beside Lt. Smoker, like he'd just stolen second base. He went straight to work, applying pressure to the wound. "I got you, I got you, I got you," he repeated like a mantra.

Smoker lifted his head and grabbed Tarkington's shirt with his fist and through bloodied teeth, ordered, "Get 'em outta here, Tark. Get to the jungle. Fight another day." Tarkington ignored him and hurled his last grenade toward the muzzle flashes.

He heard the heavy throb of PFC Stollman's BAR come to life. His grenade exploded with a crash and he took the opportunity to get into a crouch. Yap was still holding pressure, trying to wrap a makeshift bandage around Smoker's midsection.

Tarkington leaned over and put his head under Smoker's armpit and lifted. He got halfway up when he felt impacts shudder through the lieutenant's body. He could feel the life leaving him and he dropped the sudden dead-weight. He went down with him and they were face-to-face. Smoker's normally vibrant eyes were dead. He simply wasn't there anymore.

Tarkington tore his eyes away and the world was in slow motion. Yap had tears streaking down his cheeks as he cussed and screamed at the Japanese. A hole suddenly appeared in his forehead and he dropped backwards as though being pulled by an invisible force.

To his right, he saw Henry and Eduardo firing continuously from their bellies, working the bolts like well-oiled machines. Raker hurled a grenade which tumbled end-over-end and seemed to sizzle as it cooked, then bounced into the forest and exploded. There was no sound, just slow motion. His mind reeled trying to piece it all together but there was too much.

Suddenly the world came flooding back, like a slap in the face from a sumo wrestler. The sound was deafening, the pace impossibly fast. His cheek suddenly burned like fire and he fell backwards. Eduardo saw, or heard it, and was instantly on him. Tarkington's vision was filled with the worried Filipino's kindly face. He pushed him off, shaking his head clearing the sudden cobwebs.

He moved to a crouch and saw the Browning .30 caliber machine gun laying on its side next to a GI whose face was caved in and smoking.

"Raker, on me!" He yelled and lunged for the weapon. He didn't remember moving the twenty feet, but he was beside the machine gun, lifting it and suddenly Raker was with him, holding the tripod steady while he dropped it into place.

Bullets smacked a dead GI in front and the body pulsed and quivered with each impact. Tarkington lifted the breech and Raker fed the belted ammunition into place from a nearby ammo can. Tarkington pulled the bolt back and, sitting behind it, squeezed the trigger unleashing hell.

The flame shooting out the barrel singed the dead soldier, setting his ragged uniform on fire. Tarkington kept firing, sweeping the muzzle side to side, watching every fifth round ignite and steady his aim with tracer.

For an instant, the Nambu and Browning were evenly matched, spewing death, but the Nambu ran out of ammunition and went silent. Tarkington continued squeezing the trigger until the muzzle glowed white-hot. Finally a bullet overheated, exploded and rendered the Browning useless.

Raker got to his feet and pulled Tarkington with him. "Come on!" he yelled, and pulled him backwards toward the abandoned village.

Tarkington shook him loose and yelled. His ears rang so bad, his voice sounded distant in his own ears, "Fall back to the village. Fall back!" He realized he'd left his rifle on the ground, so he pulled the only weapon he had left, his sword. He stood defiant as GIs streamed past him and bullets sliced the air all around. He counted far too few soldiers before Eduardo nearly tackled him, pushing him back behind the burning truck.

Once behind the trucks the intensity of fire subsided. They ran straight back and kept running until they were well away from the light of the fire and had pushed into the jungle beyond the village. They didn't stop running until the sound of burning trucks and exploding ammunition was only a memory.

Tarkington sheathed his sword and hissed, "Stop here." The sound of his own voice sounded foreign to him, as though he'd been transformed into something he didn't recognize.

He shut his eyes as he caught his breath, reliving scenes of bodies shredded by bullets, terrified, pained eyes beseeching him to help, and being completely unable to do so. Lieutenant Smoker's eyes suddenly turning from alive and vibrant to cold and dead in an instant, as though he'd never been.

He opened his eyes and stared straight back the way they'd come. He saw Eduardo, Henry, Raker, Skinner, Stollman, Vick and Winkleman standing beside him, catching their breath. "Is this it? Is this all?" He asked.

After a long pause, Winkleman answered, "Eight. There's eight of us left." He shook his head, "It was a damned massacre," he uttered, trying to keep his voice from breaking. Minutes passed before he asked, "What - What're we gonna do now?"

Eduardo answered, "Come with me. My people will help."

Tarkington looked at him curiously and Eduardo pointed to PFC Vick. For the first time, Tarkington noticed he was injured and leaning on his gunner, Stollman, for support. "You're hit," he said matter-of-factly and moved to him.

Vick pulled his bloodied hand away from his side showing the grisly wound. "It hurts real bad."

"Anyone else hit?" he asked, looking from man to man.

They all shook their heads. Henry pointed at Tarkington's cheek, "You're hit too, Tark."

Tarkington touched his cheek and winced as he felt the deep gash. He'd forgotten about the heat he'd felt slapping him during the battle but now his own salty sweat dripping into the wound made him slightly dizzy with pain. He silently cursed himself, knowing his pain was minor compared with Vick's. "It can wait. We need to get Vick cared for."

Eduardo pointed. "I know this area. I know a place. I take you there."

<hr />

They fashioned a stretcher, tying their shirts and pants across two rifles and after doing what they could to stop his bleeding, laid Vick onto it carefully.

They followed Eduardo deeper into the jungle. He urged them forward, afraid the Japanese would pick up their trail, but the thicker the jungle became, the harder it was to maneuver the stretcher and the slower they went.

Finally, after climbing a slight incline for five-hundred feet, they descended, and the downslope was much more open.

At the bottom of the slope, they stopped at a small creek bouncing happily through the valley. They were exhausted and thirsty. They waded in and dunked their heads. Tarkington thought it was the best tasting water he'd ever experienced and he drank deeply.

Raker floated on his back, letting himself be pulled to the end of the pool where he bumped up against a rock. He opened his eyes and nearly shit himself when he saw a looming figure staring down at him with a rifle barrel only inches from his nose.

"Drop it," Henry said, stepping from the night with his rifle aimed at the side of the man's head. The man only grinned and Henry froze when another rifle barrel appeared near his temple. Henry took his finger off the trigger and raised his right hand, still holding his rifle with his left.

Eduardo said something in rapid-fire Tagalog and the rifle barrels went down, although only slightly. He spoke to Tarkington, who was clutching the hilt of his sword. "These men help us. These men from village. Good men. We can trust these men."

The GIs were taken to the village, which was far from any road. The only access was along jungle trails which were well hidden and only the locals seemed able to find.

Eduardo explained that one of his sisters-in-law was from the village. His oldest brother had met her when she'd been in Manila to see the big city for the first time along with other teenagers from her village.

He'd immediately become infatuated with her during her week-long stay and insisted they keep in contact. She'd explained that her village was far too remote and he should forget about her, but he'd persisted, finally marrying her in the village a few months later.

The wedding was a huge event for the villagers and Eduardo's family was almost considered royalty. The couple had settled in Manila a year before the Japanese invasion. Now, he didn't know either of their fates.

Vick's wound was thoroughly cleaned and an herb poultice applied to stymie infection. He'd passed out the night they arrived and didn't wake until the fourth morning.

At first the GIs were skittish, keeping their weapons ready in case the Japanese suddenly appeared to wipe them out. They took turns on guard duty, despite the village elder assuring them his men would know of any approaching Japanese in plenty of time to either hide or, if the group was small enough, ambush them.

A week into their stay, they'd relaxed a bit. The war seemed to have passed them by. They still heard and saw the occasional Japanese aircraft but the village's isolation deep in the inaccessible valley, kept the war out.

For the first time in a long time, they were well fed. Tarkington, who'd given up on ever having a normal bowel movement again, was pleasantly surprised to actually have some substance. Despite the recent loss of nearly the entire platoon, they couldn't help but be in good spirits.

Another week passed and Tarkington was sitting beside Vick, who was sitting up in bed eating cooked lizard meat. Vick's recovery was remarkable. Two weeks before, he'd been at death's door, now he was smiling, sitting up eating and talking. "How long you figure we'll be here, Tark?"

He shrugged, "Depends on you. Once you're ready to travel, we'll try to link back up with Division."

He shook his head, "In that case, I don't plan on ever getting better."

Tarkington knew he was joking, but there was also some truth there. How could he ask his men to go back to half-rations and getting shot at? "You know as well as I do, we can't stay here forever. Those sons-of-bitches attacked our country. We have to get back in the fight." It sounded hollow even to him. He gave Vick a hard look, "I can't shake the image of Smoker and all the rest dying on that road. I *need* to get back in the fight."

Vick's smile faded and he nodded. "Yeah. I know. Me too." He lifted his shirt and poked around his wound. "Still hurts but nothing like before. I don't know, maybe another week?"

Tarkington nodded. "We'll take as much time as you need. The last order I got from Smoker was to retreat to the jungle and continue the fight."

There was a commotion outside, raised voices both in Tagalog and English. Tarkington put his hand on Vick's shoulder and stood. "Stay put, I'll see what that's all about." He walked to the door of the thatched hut and peered out.

Two villagers with ancient rifles were talking animatedly with their hands and holding out pieces of paper to Eduardo. Eduardo took the paper, read it and looked worriedly back at Tarkington.

Tarkington stepped down the stairs, gripping his sword hilt and strode to the group. More GIs, seeing the commotion converged on them. Tarkington thought they looked nearly as healthy as they had before the Japanese attack in December.

Eduardo handed the sheet of paper to Tarkington. It was a pamphlet with both English and Japanese writing. There was a caricature of a Japanese soldier's boot stepping on the American flag. The short bit of writing said: 'April 9th USAFFE surrenders Bataan to Japan.'

Tarkington's jaw rippled and he handed it to Winkleman, who passed it along. "Think it's true?"

Eduardo said, "These men saw celebrating Japanese on the road, singing and drinking Sake."

Tarkington nodded, "Surprised it took this long, honestly."

Winkleman asked, "So what are we supposed to do? Give ourselves up?"

The GIs fidgeted and murmured amongst themselves. Tarkington shook his head, "No one gave me an order to surrender." He looked at each man. He took a deep breath and let it out slow. "Look, I'm the ranking soldier here, but I'm not going to order anyone to continue the fight. Far as I'm concerned the Japs are still the enemy. I've seen what those sons-of-bitches do to prisoners. I decided long ago, I'd sooner take a bullet from my own weapon than surrender and be at their mercy." He stopped and shook his head, "But that's just my own thoughts. I intend to keep fighting until I'm given a direct order to the contrary, but I'm not gonna force any one of you to join me." He paused and met their stares, then turned and continued, "I'll give you as much time as you need to..."

He was interrupted by Henry's southern lilt, "We already talked about it." Tarkington looked confused. "It was only a matter of time. We saw this coming. We're sticking with you."

Tarkington saw Winkleman smiling and nodding. "We're Tark's Ticks."

VALOR'S GHOST
Tark's Ticks #2

**Allied forces on Luzon surrendered to the Japanese...
Tark's Ticks didn't get the word.**

Staff Sergeant Tarkington and what's left of his squad are holed up deep in the interior, living among friendly villagers. They are ready to take the fight to the enemy, but this will be a different kind of war. Hit them hard and fast, create chaos and make them pay for their brutality, then disappear into the jungle like ghosts.

They fight in terrible conditions, in an unforgiving jungle, taking what they need by force. There are no reinforcements coming, they can only rely on each other.

The Imperial Japanese Army is closing in. If captured they'll be shown no mercy, for Tark's Ticks are being hunted by a relentless foe who has vowed revenge.

**Get your copy today at
severnriverbooks.com/series/tarks-ticks-wwii-novels**

ABOUT THE AUTHOR

Chris Glatte graduated from the University of Oregon with a BA in English Literature and worked as a river guide/kayak instructor for a decade before training as an Echocardiographer. He worked in the medical field for over 20 years, and now writes full time. Chris is the author of multiple historical fiction thriller series, including A Time to Serve and Tark's Ticks, a set of popular WWII novels. He lives in Southern Oregon with his wife, two boys, and ever-present Labrador, Hoover. When he's not writing or reading, Chris can be found playing in the outdoors—usually on a river or mountain.

From Chris:

I respond to all email correspondence.
Drop me a line, I'd love to hear from you!
chrisglatte@severnriverbooks.com

Sign up for Chris Glatte's reader list at
severnriverbooks.com/authors/chris-glatte

Printed in the United States
by Baker & Taylor Publisher Services